ALL THE
DIAMONDS
IN PARIS

ALL THE DIAMONDS IN PARIS

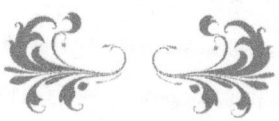

KRISTIN HARMEL

First published in United States in 2025 as
The Stolen Life of Colette Marceau by Gallery Books
An Imprint of Simon & Schuster, Inc.

First published in Great Britain in 2025 by Mountain Leopard Press
An imprint of Headline Publishing Group Limited

1

Cataloguing in Publication Data is available from the British Library

Trade Paperback ISBN 978 1 0354 2639 3

Offset in 12.45/18.02pt Bembo Std by Six Red Marbles UK, Thetford, Norfolk

Printed and bound in Great Britain by Clays Ltd, Elcograf S.p.A.

Headline Publishing Group Limited
An Hachette UK Company
Carmelite House
50 Victoria Embankment
London EC4Y 0DZ

The authorised representative in the EEA is Hachette Ireland,
8 Castlecourt Centre, Dublin 15, D15 XTP3, Ireland (email: info@hbgi.ie)

www.headline.co.uk
www.hachette.co.uk

To my incredible cancer-fighting team at AdventHealth, Florida Cancer Specialists, and Winter Park Concierge Care—especially Dr. Anu Saigal, Dr. Sonalee Shroff, Dr. Afshin Forouzannia, Rochelle Drayton, Tara Thomas, Dr. Clark Rogers, and Dr. Neha Doshi.

To the thousands of readers who sent cards, emails, messages, and gifts to lift me up through some of the darkest days of my breast cancer battle in 2022–23.

And to all those who are overdue for a mammogram, breast exam, or other recommended cancer screening: Please call to schedule yours today. It could save your life.

PROLOGUE

The twin bracelets were born on a Monday in May 1927, conceived by a jeweler in Paris for one of his best clients, Salomon Rosman, whose family had dealt in diamonds for generations.

The jeweler was a man named Max Besner, and his passion was creating pieces he hoped would outlive him by hundreds of years. If one poured his heart and craftmanship into his work, if one used only the finest gemstones and metals, one's creations would be passed from generation to generation for a long time to come.

Besner loved a challenge, and what Salomon Rosman was asking of him made him glow with pride.

"You are the only one in France who can do it, my friend," Rosman said as he handed over a small bag of diamonds. "I want Hélène to know how much I love her, and how much I love our children, too."

"Twins, my friend," Besner replied, beaming. "A blessing."

Rosman's wife had given birth the day before to two healthy babies, a son they named Daniel, and a daughter they named

Ruth. "A blessing indeed," Rosman agreed, his voice thick with emotion. "I want them to inherit the jewels one day. But since there are two of them . . ."

"I must make two pieces," Besner concluded.

"But my wife must be able to wear them as one," Rosman said. "Beautiful on their own, but stronger together."

"Just like your children, who will always be able to rely on each other," Besner said with a smile. He pulled a velvet-lined tray from beneath the counter and raised a brow at Rosman, who nodded his permission. Besner poured Rosman's jewels out, resisting the urge to gasp at the sheer number of them, the dazzling beauty, a constellation of tiny, perfect stars. "There are hundreds," he managed to say. He hoped his eyes were not bulging; what if Rosman saw how impressed he was and decided that he was not the man for the job?

"What good are jewels if they sit in a drawer collecting dust?" Rosman said. "No, they must be brought to life. I've been saving these over the past few years."

With his forceps, Besner picked carefully through the small fortune before him, turning over stones here and there, counting, assessing. As he watched them catch the light, his mind was spinning, imagining the ways he could put them together to make something extraordinary, something the world had never seen before. Already, he was picturing a celestial design, moon and skies and heavens.

"I think I will make—" he began, but before the words were out of his mouth, something strange happened. Through the open window high above his workbench, a butterfly flitted into the room, the first one Besner had seen all spring, and the only one he had ever seen within these walls. His shop was on the rue Choron, quite near the Grande Synagogue de la Victoire, but not particularly close to any of Paris's sprawling parks. The world outside his doors was cement and brick, not a welcoming place for such creatures.

This one didn't seem lost, though. In fact, it seemed to know exactly where it was going. It fluttered casually down and landed gently on the rim of the velvet tray of gems, as if it, too, was waiting to hear what the jeweler had in mind.

But Besner was no longer thinking of night skies. He was staring at the butterfly, a striking creature with snow-white wings with edges that looked like they'd been dipped in ink.

"A *Pieris brassicae*," Rosman noted with a smile. "My wife's favorite. She says they mean good luck and balance in the world."

Besner stared at the butterfly on the table. As if showing off, the creature slowly lifted and lowered its magnificent wings. They caught the light in a way that seemed as magical and improbable as the sparkling of the diamonds spread before the two men, and at once, Besner had his answer. He looked up at Rosman. "Then she shall have bracelets modeled after one."

"Modeled after a butterfly?" Rosman sounded dubious.

The jeweler bent to get a better glimpse of the creature's wings. "Twin bracelets," he said slowly, the diamonds already arranging themselves in his mind, pieces of a puzzle only he could see. "Apart, they will look like lilies of peace. Together, a beautiful butterfly."

Rosman looked first at the gems, then at the butterfly before them. The creature itself seemed to be considering the proposal. And then, as if it knew its job was done, it lifted off. It hung suspended in the air between the two men for a few seconds before it rose and fluttered back toward the window, leaving the way it had come in.

Rosman turned his attention back to Besner. "It's perfect," he said. "Hélène and I will give our children wings, and they will soar."

The jeweler felt a tingle of excitement, the kind that came when he knew he was on the cusp of something great. "As you wish, my friend," Besner said. "I will call upon you later this week with some sketches."

Three months later, the bracelets were complete, and Rosman was able to present them as a surprise to Hélène. He couldn't have imagined, when he was a younger man, how full his heart would feel when he looked upon his children and their beautiful, raven-haired mother; he sometimes felt as if he might burst with love, though he found it hard to say such things aloud. The bracelets, however, told the story that his words could not. They symbolized his devotion to Hélène, and his hope for the future of Ruth and Daniel.

It was 1927. The world was his for the taking. Paris was alive with possibility and hope, with music and culture, with art and fashion.

Just thirteen years later, the light would go out in that very same city, plunging it into despair. Still, Salomon and Hélène had their two beautiful children, who were growing up bright and re-silient, kind and strong. Together, they would survive. Together, they would weather the storm.

And then, one night in July 1942, there was a banging on the Rosmans' door and the world changed forever. Three Germans loomed at the threshold, there to take the family away.

"These arrests are usually the work of the French police," said an officer named Möckel as he stepped into the opulent parlor of their apartment. He looked around, sniffing like a dog picking up a scent. "But I heard that you have beautiful things. I knew I needed to see for myself." His gaze lingered on Hélène. "I see the rumors are correct."

"We are French citizens," Rosman said stiffly. "We have com-mitted no crime."

The German sniffed again. "Ah, but you're Jews," he said simply, as if that explained everything. "Go now, children, get your things ready. You won't be returning."

"Papa?" Ruth said softly, glancing at her father.

He could hardly meet his daughter's eye, for he understood now exactly what was happening. "We are going on a trip, children," he said, trying to keep his tone light. He looked into his wife's eyes and could see there that she, too, understood the truth, and knew, as did he, that their children must be shielded from it as long as possible. They were fifteen, nearly adults, but he would protect them as long as he could. "Take your warmest coats. Hurry, my dears."

Ruth and Daniel exchanged worried looks but did as they were told. While they hastily packed, Möckel cheerfully relieved Hélène of all the jewels she was wearing, from her diamond engagement ring to the interlocking butterfly bracelets on her wrist, which she had worn every day since her husband had given them to her a decade and a half before. "Designed by Max Besner, if I'm not mistaken?" Möckel asked.

In the years since Rosman had ordered the bracelets, Besner had become a bit of a celebrity in the jewelry industry, but still, Rosman was startled to realize that his friend's reputation had reached the Germans. "Yes, that's correct," he said stiffly.

"They're extraordinary," Möckel said, holding them up to the light. They twinkled and danced, as if showing off for the German. "The way they link together, there's nothing like them."

"Please, when will I get them back?" Hélène asked in a small voice, though certainly she had to have known the answer.

Möckel just laughed and directed his men to go through all the drawers in the house to uncover whatever other treasures the Rosmans might be hiding.

Salomon Rosman would not survive the year, nor would his wife Hélène. Never again would the apartment in the eleventh arrondissement belong to their family; never would the children smell the sweet smoke of their father's pipe or hear the timbre of his laughter. Never would they taste the challah their mother labored over each week or hear the soothing sound of her voice as she sang softly to herself in the kitchen.

But just as the jeweler had promised, the bracelets would live on. Diamonds always do.

CHAPTER ONE

2018

As the canary diamond across the room caught the light, Colette Marceau's fingertips itched, just as they always did before a score. *Patience*, she reminded herself. *Steady, girl*. She was nearly ninety, for goodness' sake, too old for this, too wise. But age brought with it some advantages. Yes, it would be harder to make a fast getaway with a bad back, and the arthritis that had begun to stiffen her fingers as the decades passed made it more difficult to undo complicated clasps. But should she ever be caught, claiming senility would be an easy defense. After all, perhaps she hadn't known what she was doing when she slipped a Rolex from a man's wrist or relieved a woman of her diamond studs.

"Ladies and gentlemen, may I have your attention?" The voice of the evening's host, Massachusetts state senator John Nierling, boomed out from the speakers at the front of the elegant Cherry Blossom Ballroom. Overhead, crystal chandeliers twinkled and threw the light, but they couldn't compete with the piece Colette was here for, a cushion-cut 8.07-carat yellow diamond ring worth $90,000. "I'd like to introduce my longtime friend and colleague," Nierling continued as the chatter in the room began to subside and heads turned toward the podium. "Please welcome Linda Clyborn, the president of the Boston Orchestral Education Consortium."

There was a smattering of applause from the hundred or so attendees, all orchestra donors dressed to the nines, most clutching wineglasses that made it difficult to clap. As a result, Linda Clyborn's walk to the podium felt oddly subdued. She teetered a bit on heels too narrow to balance her wide hips, and her hair was an unflattering shade of blond, though she surely had access to the best colorists in Boston. These were things Colette noticed without trying to, the way that even the wealthiest people often didn't quite fit into the social circles they aspired to. Those who came from old money were born into the ways of moving and dressing and speaking that came with family inheritance. Those who had worked hard and found success were often quiet and humble. But those who had clambered their way into wealth often lacked polish, the way an uncut diamond lacked shine.

"Thank you, my friends," Linda said, slurring the *s* ever so slightly. Colette could feel the corners of her lips twitching. The more the woman drank, the easier it would be to slip the pale yellow diamond from her finger.

Rings were tricky. In fact, though Colette had been relieving unpleasant people of their jewels since she was ten years old, she hadn't become truly comfortable with rings until she was nearly thirty. Bracelets were easy; she could unhook a clasp with a firm but gentle lift of her thumb as she brushed against an unsuspecting donor. Necklaces, too, often fell easily with a graceful move Colette had come to think of as a syncopated chassé; she could unfasten the most complicated closures with a flick of her right wrist just as she turned and brushed against the person, apologizing with her eyes downcast in feigned embarrassment as she let the jewels tumble into her left hand. Men's watches were the easiest of all; the fold-over clasp of a Patek Philippe was no more challenging than the ardillon buckle of a Piaget, though it had taken her countless hours of training to release both without directly touching the wrist of the wearer.

Rings, however, were a different story. It was feasible to steal them only when they were visibly loose, which eliminated a fair number of potential scores. It was also impossible to steal a ring without a fair amount of physical contact. The key, therefore, was distraction. Her favorite move for a female mark was to wait until there was a visibly inebriated man, or at the very least a visibly pompous one, in the vicinity. Colette would reach out and give the mark a sharp pinch in the side with her right hand while grabbing the mark's hand with her left, pretending to help steady her while expressing indignation. In the millisecond during which their hands were touching and the mark was distracted, she would reach over with her right hand and slide the ring off, something that had taken Colette years of practice to perfect. The woman would always be so incensed by the pinch, and so intent on finding the offender, that she wouldn't feel the ring being slipped off. Later, when she reported the loss of the jewelry to the police, she would almost inevitably mention the pinch, but never the small-framed woman who had come to her aid before melting back into the crowd. Most of the time, the marks never saw Colette's face at all.

Up at the podium, Linda was thanking a laundry list of fellow millionaires for their support. No one ever thanked the underpaid assistant who kept things running behind the scenes or the third-grade teacher who'd once told them they could be anything they wanted to be. No one thanked the second-chair bassoonist or the play's understudy, the stagehands or the ushers. If a mark ever broke protocol and, for instance, addressed a member of the catering staff with genuine respect, or held a door for a hotel housekeeper, Colette would abort her mission and assume she'd gotten things wrong.

That had never happened, though, because Colette never chose her targets carelessly. No decent person deserved to have their possessions taken. It would go against the code Colette had sworn allegiance to as a little girl.

She had lived her life by that code. Her own mother had died by it.

And now, Linda Clyborn's number was up. Not only had she maneuvered to block her husband's three daughters from inheriting anything from his estate after his untimely—and some said suspicious—death at the age of sixty, but she had also been linked definitively to a neo-Nazi group, which she was helping to fund using the proceeds from her late husband's substantial estate.

Colette had experienced enough Nazis to last a lifetime, thank you very much. Having lived in Occupied France seven and a half decades earlier, she simply had no room for them here in Boston in the year 2018.

"And finally," Linda Clyborn was saying as Colette continued to slip unnoticed through the crowd, "I'd like to thank all of you here tonight. Your support has made it possible for the Boston Orchestral Education Consortium to continue providing programs for both our valuable professional musicians and for the children who might one day wish to pursue careers in the arts. Enjoy the evening, and don't forget to bid on the silent auction items."

She waved to the crowd and descended from the stage to

another underwhelming round of applause. She greeted the oily Senator Nierling, whom Colette planned to relieve of his own Rolex at some point in the future. But not tonight.

Linda Clyborn teetered through the crowd, shaking hands and kissing cheeks, and when the deejay started playing hits from the 1980s and the crowd began gyrating awkwardly, Colette straightened her wig—an unassuming gray bob with curtain bangs—and commenced her approach.

She glided through the throng until she was a foot away from her target. A trio of fortysomething men approached from the opposite direction, one of them visibly drunk, sloshing beer from a pint glass as he walked. Just then, Linda glanced in Colette's direction, and Colette froze. If Linda noticed her, she would need to abort the mission for the evening. But Linda looked right through her, in search of someone more important than a small, modestly dressed octogenarian. Colette rolled her eyes. To people like Linda Clyborn, the elderly were invisible. Really, it made scores like this almost too easy.

As Linda shook hands with another woman and set off through the crowd again, Colette made her move. Just as the trio of men passed, Colette reached out and pinched Linda, simultaneously grasping the woman's hand, feigning aid while sliding the ring smoothly from the woman's left middle finger. She felt it slip into her own palm with a satisfying plunk, all eight-plus carats now liberated.

She quickly closed her hand around the prize and slid it into her pocket as Linda Clyborn whipped around, focusing her rage on the drunkest of the three men, who was stammering a confused apology, unsure what he was being accused of. As the pitch of the woman's voice rose, Colette melted backward into the crowd.

Later, when Linda Clyborn discovered that her ring was gone, no one would remember a small, gray-haired woman in a nondescript black cocktail dress, making her way casually toward the exit as her mark's aggrieved shrieks rose from the dance floor.

CHAPTER TWO

1934

Annabel Clement was born to be a thief, just like her mother, her grandmother, and her great-grandfather before her. It was a responsibility she had taken seriously from the very first time her own mother had sat her down to explain that she was descended from the real Robin Hood—and that she was expected to carry on the family tradition. When she became a mother herself, she knew that as soon as her daughter was old enough to understand, she would share the legacy with her, too.

"It is who we are," Annabel explained a few days after Colette's sixth birthday, pulling her close in their apartment in the eleventh arrondissement of Paris, miles away from the West Yorkshire village where she'd been raised. She had fallen in love at eighteen and followed her new husband across the Channel to his native France. On this evening, Roger, a school headmaster who had never warmed to Annabel's calling, was working late, leaving Colette and Annabel alone. "It is who you are born to be. When you turn ten, I'll teach you how to steal, just as my mother taught me at that age."

"But stealing is wrong, Mum," Colette said in a small voice. "Isn't it?"

Annabel loved that the girl addressed her with the British term of endearment rather than the French *Maman*. It made her feel a bit less homesick for her own hometown, tucked into England's Barnsdale Forest. "It is only wrong in a world that is black and white, darling. If you can take from people who are cruel and unkind and use what you've taken to make the world a better place, then what you have done is heroic, not criminal. It is your destiny, Colette."

Colette's face scrunched in concentration. "Then why can't I learn to steal *now*?"

Annabel chuckled. "It's important that you understand first why we do what we do. That's why we always start with the history in our family. The stories are who we are."

Colette sighed. "Very well, Mum."

Annabel smiled down at her. "Once upon a time, in the village of Wentbridge, lived a man named Robin Hood. He felt strongly, as do I, that no one who has earned his money or his worldly possessions honestly should be parted from them, even if he's far richer than anyone should be. But he who has evil in his heart, or has used his fortune to bring harm to others, no longer has a claim on his property. Those are the people Robin stole from then, and they're the people we steal from now."

"But why did he steal, Mum?" Colette asked, looking up at Annabel with wide eyes. "What happened to him?"

"You see, the king at the time was a bad man, who was making life worse and worse for his subjects. Robin and his friends tried to get by, but the taxes grew and grew, and soon, the local sheriff started to imprison those who didn't have the ability to pay. 'We must make a change, then,' Robin decided, and he began to free those who'd been falsely imprisoned and to take back the things that had been stolen from the townspeople."

"He was a hero, then."

"That he was, my darling. And do you want to hear my favorite part of the story?"

Colette nodded. "Yes, Mum."

Annabel smiled and pulled Colette closer. "High above the Barnsdale Forest, near Wentbridge, where Robin lived, flew a white-tailed eagle who believed in Robin's quest for justice. He looked over Robin and his men, keeping them safe. When there was danger, he called out, '*Kyi-kyi-kyi!*' Can you say that?"

"*Kyi-kyi-kyi!*" Colette repeated with a grin.

Annabel threw her head back and trilled, "*Ko-ko-ko.*" She smiled down at Colette. "That's how the eagle always ended every call. To this day, that's the way a white-tailed eagle sounds, if you listen closely enough. I've always thought it sounded a bit like, 'Come, come, come,' as if the descendants of that first eagle are urging us to follow him into adventure."

"Did you hear the eagle?" Colette asked. "When you were my age?"

Annabel nodded, a wave of homesickness washing over her. She loved Paris, and of course she loved Roger, but there would always be a piece of her heart in England. "Every day of my childhood, my darling. You'll hear it one day, too."

Four years later, on the day Colette turned ten, Annabel sat her down again, just as her own mother had done with her a generation before.

"I've told you stories of your forefather since you were old enough to understand," Annabel said gently, staring into the wide green eyes of her firstborn. Annabel and Roger had just welcomed their second child, a daughter named Liliane, who lay sleeping beside them in her bassinet. One day, Annabel would teach her about her legacy, too. "Now it is time for you to begin following in his footsteps."

"I'm ready, Mum."

"You must promise me, my sweet Colette," Annabel said, "that wherever you go, you will never forget who you were born to be."

Colette nodded solemnly. "I promise."

"And," Annabel had said, leaning in to whisper, "you mustn't tell Papa." She felt guilty asking Colette to keep secrets, but she knew that Roger would put a stop to Colette's training if he knew. Over the years, he had tolerated Annabel's need to steal, but he had never approved of it. Early in their marriage, she had often come home with a new piece to fence, wanting to tell him about all the good she would do with the proceeds, but his face always hardened into a scowl, and he held up his hands to stop her from speaking, saying that the less he knew, the better. As time had gone on, she had mostly stopped trying. "You must keep this between just the two of us."

"I know," Colette said, casting a nervous glance toward their apartment door, through which her father might enter at any moment. "But why doesn't he care for what you do, Mum?"

A lump rose in Annabel's throat. "To some people, stealing is a crime, no matter the reason. But I firmly believe that as long as we ensure that we only take from those who are cruel, and we always find a way to help those who are kind, we are on the side of God."

"Then Papa will understand one day. He has to."

"I hope you're right, Colette. But enough of that. Let's begin with our training, shall we?"

Annabel started not with lessons about undoing clasps and distracting marks, but rather with etiquette sessions so that Colette would easily blend in wherever she went. She taught her daughter everything from the correct forks to use to how to politely exit a conversation without giving up any personal information. On weekends, they took long walks to the Bois de Boulogne, the closest thing Paris had to the Barnsdale Forest, so that Colette could learn to run long distances over rough terrain, to forage, and to climb trees, all things that would help her to survive should a robbery ever go wrong.

On the afternoons when Roger worked late, Colette and Annabel huddled at the kitchen table, their heads bent together, practicing how to unhook all types of jewelry clasps, how to free cuff links, even how to jostle people so that in their startlement, they wouldn't notice rings being slipped from their fingers.

Colette stole her first piece in the summer of 1938, an elegant Longines pocket watch slipped from the vest of a Swiss banker named Vallotton who had swindled dozens of Parisians out of their life savings. He had a few friends high up in the police prefecture, and he had become untouchable; the authorities simply looked the other way while he destroyed people's lives.

"I'm nervous, Mum," Colette said softly as they finished their drinks—a glass of wine for Annabel, a *citron pressé* for Colette—at the café Vallotton frequented. He was a creature of routine—he ordered a Ricard on the terrace of the same café each day at precisely five o'clock—which made him very easy to target. He was the perfect mark for Colette's first score.

"Don't be worried, my dear," Annabel said, putting her hand over her daughter's and giving a comforting squeeze. "Vallotton is notoriously self-absorbed. He's the easiest type of person to steal from, for he won't even notice your existence."

At five o'clock on the dot, Vallotton strode up to the café, sliding like an oil slick into his usual chair. Annabel's heart thudded as she watched her daughter study the man. Colette's eyes were sharp and calculating, but her hands trembled.

"Steady, my darling," Annabel murmured. "Remember, this is who you were born to be."

Taking a deep breath, Colette nodded and stood from the table. Annabel stood, too, leaving a bit of money for the waiter, and the two of them began to exit the café, weaving by Vallotton's table. As Annabel watched, her little girl squared her shoulders and jostled against Vallotton as they passed.

"Hey!" the man exclaimed, whirling around in his seat. "Watch where you're going!"

"I'm very sorry, sir, very sorry," Colette said quickly, keeping her eyes downcast just in case Vallotton tried to get a good look at her face, but as Annabel knew would be the case, he hardly looked at her at all. While Colette continued to stammer an apology, she simultaneously unhooked the watch and slipped it from Vallotton's front pocket into the folds of her dress in one fluid motion.

"They shouldn't allow children in cafés, I've always said," Vallotton grumbled, shooting an accusatory glare at Annabel, who turned her head and looked away to ensure that Vallotton wouldn't be able to describe her later, if it came to that.

"Oh, yes, sir, quite right, sir," she said cheerfully. "They're the scourge of the earth." And then, without looking back, she and Colette strolled casually out to the sidewalk and turned right, heading away from the café.

"Mum," Colette said the moment they'd turned the corner. "I did it! I really did it!" Her cheeks were pink with excitement, her eyes glistening. "Do you think Robin Hood would be proud, Mum?"

"I know he would be," Annabel said, blinking back tears of pride. "And so am I. You're going to do so much good in the world, my love. I can't wait to see what the future brings."

CHAPTER THREE

2018

The morning after the theft of Linda Clyborn's ring, Colette sat at her kitchen table in the Boston suburb of Quincy, admiring the way the pale yellow diamond caught the light, throwing beams across the room in a glittering rainbow. She never tired of the jewels themselves, the meticulous cuts, the razor-sharp lines, the prisms of color they held within their hearts.

When had Clyborn noticed it missing? Had it been during the cocktail party, or had she been too drunk on her own power to register the lack of weight on her finger? Had she flashed her hand deliberately to show it off, only to realize it was no longer there? Had theft been her first guess when she'd realized the ring was gone? Or did a part of her think that she'd lost it herself?

Colette hoped for the latter; when a person believed she had mislaid her own jewels, she tended to be defensive with the police rather than truly trying to recall every face she'd seen the night before. Not that the woman had registered her existence anyhow.

Colette slid the ring onto her bare left ring finger, where she'd never worn a ring of her own. She sighed at the perfect fit, the way it looked like it was meant to be there. If only she could keep a piece here and there, enjoying the jewels for herself, but that would subvert the family tradition, the one her mother and her uncle Leo had raised her to firmly uphold.

By her count, over the nearly eight decades she'd been stealing, interrupted only briefly during the Second World War, she'd funneled well over $30 million in stolen jewels to deserving organizations, a figure that made her heart swell with pride. Typically, she simply made anonymous contributions to established foundations, but the thing she was proudest of—and the only organization she had funded every single year since its establishment—was the Boston Center for Holocaust Education, which she had anonymously founded herself in 1972 as a way to continue the work she and her mother were doing when her mother's life was cut brutally short.

No one—not even the center's founding director, Rachel Haskell, or her daughter, Aviva, who had both become like family to Colette—had any idea that it was Colette who'd provided the seed money for the center; they knew her merely as a dedicated volunteer, one who had helped the organization open a second branch of the center in New York in 1980. *You're going to do so much good in the world*, her mother had said just after Colette had stolen her first piece, and all these years later, Colette still hoped she would be proud.

Colette's phone buzzed on the table in front of her, jolting her out of her thoughts. The older she got, the more prone she was to wandering down memory lane. Her mother and sister had been gone for three-quarters of a century, and yet she could see them both so clearly. Most nights, she had nightmares of shadowy figures stealing them away, but sometimes, she dreamed vividly of the three of them snuggled together in bed, Mum reading stories to her two daughters. Colette could still hear the sound of her sweet voice, her round British accent.

She pushed the thoughts away and glanced down at her phone screen. *Aviva.* The girl, now an attorney in her late thirties and still a volunteer for the center, was like the daughter Colette had never had. She smiled and answered.

"Colette?" Aviva's voice was hushed and muffled.

"Aviva, I can hardly hear you," Colette said, pressing the phone to her ear as she cursed the way her hearing had deteriorated with age. The more years one lived, the more indignities one was forced to endure.

"Colette," Aviva repeated more firmly. "Were you at a gala last night for the Boston Orchestral Education Consortium?"

Colette's mouth went dry. "Why would you ask that, dear?"

"There was a theft there last night," Aviva said. "There are a few pictures in the paper today, and there's a woman in the crowd, just beside the woman whose ring was stolen, and she looks exactly like you, but with a wig."

"Now why would I go to an orchestra gala, darling?" Colette asked, trying to keep her voice steady, even as she mentally cursed her bad luck. Obviously, Linda Clyborn had reported the theft immediately, which meant that Colette would need to wait to fence the piece. It was terribly inconvenient. "What was stolen?" she asked innocently.

"A ring," Aviva said. Colette could hear the rustling of a newspaper, and she imagined Aviva sitting at her office desk, overlooking Tremont Street and the Boston Common below. "Worth more than one hundred twenty-five thousand dollars, according to the paper."

Colette guffawed before she could stop herself. The ring wasn't worth a penny more than $90,000, though she shouldn't have been surprised that a person like Mrs. Clyborn would lie about such a thing. She imagined that the vile woman was already waiting with her hand outstretched for a check from her insurance company. "You do know, dear, that Linda Clyborn is a neo-Nazi, which is quite a ridiculous thing to be. It's hard to find much pity for her."

Aviva was silent for a second. "How do you know the name of the person the ring was stolen from?"

Colette shook her head at her own carelessness. "I have my paper open, too," she lied. "I'm reading along with you now."

"And you don't think the woman in the picture beneath the headline looks just like you?"

Colette's newspaper was still on her front doorstep; she hadn't made it that far yet. "Oh, I can see a passing resemblance."

"It's more than passing, Colette. Are you sure you weren't there?"

Sometimes, the best deflection was to go on the offensive. "Really, dear, if you're accusing me of something, just come out and say it."

"No, I'm sorry," Aviva said right away, sounding embarrassed. "But how do you know that Linda Clyborn is a neo-Nazi, anyhow?"

"You know me, darling," Colette said. "I like to keep up with the gossip." Really, what was wrong with her this morning? Nothing could be farther from the truth, actually, and from Aviva's noncommittal grunt, it was clear Aviva knew that, too. "In any case, she isn't someone I'd waste time feeling concerned about. Not a particularly good human being."

Aviva was silent for a few seconds. "Why do I have the feeling that you know more about this than you're letting on?"

Colette forced a tinkling laugh. "Now you're treating me like a hostile witness. Forget about it, dear. But since I have you, would you like to come over for dinner tonight? I'm making your favorite." Perhaps it was a mistake to invite Aviva over when the younger woman was obviously suspicious. But Colette felt a sudden loneliness, a sense that the years were slipping away before she'd righted any of the wrongs of the past. Being around Aviva always made her feel a bit more centered, like she had a purpose. Besides, she needed to change the subject somehow.

"Dijon chicken?"

"Of course." It was Colette's specialty, a dish she remembered her mother making before the war, chicken breast cooked in a thyme-laced Dijon cream sauce. "Say, seven o'clock?"

Aviva hesitated before sighing. "You know your chicken is the way to my heart. I'll be there."

Colette hung up and then shuffled to her own front door to grab the newspaper that awaited her there. Flipping to the local section, she stared in disbelief at the photograph below the fold on the front page. It was indeed a picture of her, as clear as day, as she moved in on Linda Clyborn. If the photographer had taken it thirty seconds later, he would have caught her in the act. How had she not realized that there was someone there snapping photos of the crowd? Her heart thudded as she contemplated just how close she had come to being caught this time.

Her phone rang again, and this time, it was Marty's name on the caller ID.

"Hey, kid," he said when she answered, and she smiled at the term of endearment, which should have felt ridiculous at her age, but which warmed her heart just as it had since the first day she'd met him sixty-six years before. She'd been twenty-four then to Marty's twenty-six, but he'd made her feel like a schoolgirl. In a different life, she imagined that they might even have fallen in love. "Have you seen today's paper yet?" he asked.

"I have," she said, glaring at the offending picture once more.

He chuckled. "Am I to assume, then, that you have a delivery for me?" He was being cautious, as he always was, in case there was a tap on either of their lines, but it felt ridiculous at this point; they'd been doing business together for six decades, and neither had ever fallen under suspicion; who was going to suspect an eighty-nine-year-old woman and a ninety-one-year-old man of running a massive jewelry theft and black market resale operation?

"Maybe," she said. "But only for safekeeping."

"Only for safekeeping," Marty agreed immediately. They both knew that the piece would be too hot to move for at least a couple of weeks. "But I'll reach out to my contacts to begin gauging interest. Could you bring it by in a bit? Are you free for lunch today?"

He knew as well as she did that she was free for lunch nearly *every* day, unless she was volunteering at the center. With no relatives other than Aviva—the closest thing to family she had—there was no one to need her. "I'll have to check my calendar," she deadpanned, and Marty laughed, as she knew he would.

"Why don't you come by at noon?"

"I'll see you then." Colette hung up with a smile on her face and snuck one last look at the newspaper before crumpling it up and shoving it straight into the recycling bin.

After she'd had her coffee and gone for her morning walk—she walked three miles daily to keep her blood flowing—Colette got dressed for the day, chiding herself for the care she took in selecting the perfect outfit.

Though she'd been in the States since 1952, Paris would always be a piece of who Colette was. Her wardrobe was full of Breton stripes, smart black trousers, crisp button-downs, and simple black dresses for the nights she needed to blend in with upscale crowds. Her hair was cut into a short French bob, and when it began to lose its dark color two decades ago, she'd let it. Now, it was the color of snow, the perfect shade to make her signature red lipstick pop. That was another secret of hers; when she went on missions to steal jewels, she kept her makeup understated and natural and her wigs the color of dishwater, all the better to blend into a crowd. But at all other times, her red lips were her trademark.

Now, she tried on three different pairs of wide-leg trousers before she settled on one with a high waist that accentuated her slim figure. She pulled on a cream-colored, narrow-cut silk blouse and carefully tucked it in before slipping into her favorite pair of cap-toe ballet flats and assessing herself in the mirror. Some days, she wondered where the time had gone. The pages had turned too quickly, leaving her somehow at the end of her story in the blink of an eye.

She didn't suppose it mattered to Marty how she looked. There had been a time in the past when he had cared—she *knew* he had cared—but that had been long ago. She'd had her chance. She'd had many chances. It was far too late now, but she'd be lying if she said she didn't get a little thrill out of the way his eyes still traveled up and down her body every time she saw him. It was habit, she supposed, but it made her blush yet the same.

The drive to Marty's store on Washington Street took twenty-three minutes, and after Colette parked a half block away, she sat in the car for a few minutes, scanning the other vehicles in the area. One could never be too careful; she had driven away in the past after seeing what looked like undercover police vehicles parked nearby. But today, neither the other cars nor the passersby looked suspicious, so Colette grabbed her handbag, got out of the car, and strode purposefully into Weaver's Diamond Exchange, the store Marty's grandfather, Joseph Weaver, had founded a hundred years ago, passing it down to his son, Joseph Jr., who then passed it to Marty back in 1967.

Colette could still remember the first time she saw Marty fifteen years before that, when she accompanied Uncle Leo on a trip to fence a pair of emerald-and-sapphire earrings. They had just moved to the States from England, after Uncle Leo had gotten into a bit of trouble with the law, and it was Marty's father who had sponsored their hasty citizenship application.

Uncle Leo had introduced Colette to Marty, and for the first time in her life, she'd been unable to formulate words. "Cat got your tongue?" Uncle Leo had asked, amused, while Colette's cheeks blazed. Marty's hair was golden, his eyes a brilliant blue, and his strong jaw and high cheekbones looked like they'd been carved from marble.

But he'd saved her from her embarrassment by extending a palm for the earrings, which she placed there with a shaking hand. "I'm not sure I can give you an accurate estimate until I've seen them on someone," he'd said, winking at her. "Would you do the honors, Colette? Then we can talk price."

Nodding, she had taken the earrings back and slipped the right one in, but when she fumbled with the left, Marty had reached out to help her. Her skin tingled where he touched it, and she could have sworn he'd lingered for a second longer than he needed to, brushing her cheek with the back of his hand as he withdrew. "Perfect," he'd murmured, and then he'd quoted Uncle Leo a price that was 10 percent higher than she would have asked for. Uncle Leo had eagerly accepted and then hurried Colette out before Marty could withdraw the offer, but as they left the store, she couldn't help but glance back over her shoulder at him. He was watching her, just as she'd somehow known he would be, and he raised one hand in farewell, giving her another amused smile.

"I think that young man was smitten with you," Uncle Leo had said in the car with a chuckle. "But you watch out for him, Colette, do you understand? Too dangerous to get connected to anyone who works in the business." When she'd looked at him questioningly, he'd added, "A jewel thief and the person who sells the thief's loot? It's a recipe for disaster, Colette. Just get it out of your mind."

But she hadn't been able to, and since Uncle Leo used Weaver's Diamond Exchange as a fence the majority of the time, it had been impossible to forget Marty because she saw him at least a dozen times a year. Once she began executing bigger scores on her own, she preferred using Weaver's, too. They still had to use other fences so that they didn't leave breadcrumbs for the police to follow, but the Weavers were the only ones who knew what they were up to—and why it mattered. Colette trusted Marty and his father with her life—which was why, the year she turned twenty-six and Marty asked her on a date, she'd said no. Uncle Leo was right; it was too dangerous.

But that wasn't the only reason she'd declined. After all, what did dating lead to but marriage and children? And Colette had already sworn that she would never have a child. How on earth could she be trusted to keep anyone safe after everything that had happened in Paris?

He had asked her out on a date seven times more—she'd counted—and on the seventh time, he'd asked, "Do I ever have a chance with you, kid?" It had broken her heart to tell him no, but she had, and that was that. Six months later, he'd begun going steady with a girl named Kay Rhodes, and a year after that, he'd married her. They'd never had children, and Colette had learned just how bitter regret tasted.

Kay had died nearly twenty years ago, and by then, she and Marty had been platonic friends for most of their lives. Sometimes, she wondered what would happen if she confessed now that she'd said no because she hadn't wanted children—and because Uncle Leo had forbidden it. Would Marty think she was mad to be digging up things from the past that didn't need to be discussed? Would he have forgotten he had ever asked her out in the first place?

"Well, well, if it isn't the most beautiful Parisian in Boston," Marty said, a grin spreading across his handsome face as she walked into his empty store. He still looked just like Robert Redford all these years later. Why was time so much more generous to men than to women?

"Flattery will get you everywhere," she said, smiling back. There was something charming in the idea that they shared this routine.

"I thought I'd make lunch today," he said, and if she hadn't known better, she would have suspected he was nervous.

"Make me lunch? Well, that would be a first."

"I'd make you lunch every day if I could, kid." Marty was an old flirt, always had been. She wasn't foolish enough to think that his attentions were reserved just for her.

He came around the counter and gave her a quick peck on the cheek, then he locked the front door and turned the CLOSED sign around. "Let's go in the back."

Five minutes later, they were sitting across the table from each other, sharing torn pieces of baguette, a hunk of Brie cheese, and an apple Marty had sliced up. "So the orchestra benefit last night?" he asked as he poured her a glass of Chablis from a bottle he'd just pulled from the fridge. "That was you?"

She held his gaze as she took a sip of wine. "Suppose it was?"

"Then I'd say you have a valuable piece on your hands. And the beneficiary this time?"

"The Holocaust center, of course. The woman is a dedicated neo-Nazi."

Marty chuckled. "You are a marvel, Colette. I wonder how the people at the center would feel if they knew their most dedicated volunteer was also the one who's been keeping them in the black for more than forty years?"

She shrugged. "You know the rules." No descendant of Robin Hood could ever take public credit for the good he or she was doing in the world. It was too dangerous, and it would subvert the meaning of their work.

"But *I* know what you're doing." He took a sip of his wine and raised his eyebrows pointedly at her.

"You know all my secrets." She said it lightly, but the words felt heavy the moment they were out of her mouth. The truth was, there was no one in the world who knew her better. She wondered sometimes what Uncle Leo would have thought of the friendship that had developed between Marty and her over the years. She was certain he wouldn't approve, but that didn't mean he was right; knowing that Marty was ever only a phone call away had kept her afloat through her darkest times. The fact that they were both still here, still looking out for each other, was remarkable.

Marty sliced off a sliver of Brie and handed it to Colette on a piece of baguette. "I'll have to wait a few weeks, until the interest cools down."

"I know." She took a bite, followed by a sip of wine, and her taste buds sang.

"You could retire, you know," he said after a moment. "I hate to think of something happening to you."

"I've made it this far, haven't I?"

Marty smiled. "We're both too old to go to jail. Do you ever think about hanging up your hat?"

She bit into an apple slice and chewed slowly without breaking eye contact. "Do *you*?"

He leaned closer. "You're the whole reason I'm still in business, kid."

She felt a pang of guilt. "You don't have to keep working with me, Marty. I have other brokers I can bring the pieces to."

He put his hands over his heart and feigned injury. "Are you trying to kill me?"

She couldn't help but laugh. "What I mean is that you don't owe me anything, Marty. You've done more than enough over the years. If you want to hang up *your* hat . . ."

"Ah, but I look dashing in a hat." He grinned. "Besides, you're the best part of the business."

She basked in the words for a second, though she knew they'd been just another line of throwaway flirtation. "Then I guess we're stuck with each other."

He smiled. "Just the way I like it, kid. Now let's take a look at that piece."

Colette reached into the hidden inner pocket of her handbag and withdrew the ring, enjoying the way Marty's eyes widened slightly as he looked at it for the first time. He reached for the piece, then carried it across the room to his desk, where he flicked on a lamp. He pulled out his jeweler's loupe and examined the diamond for a few seconds in silence before looking back up at

Colette. "It's perfect," he said. "I think I can probably get between seventy-two and eighty for it."

Colette did the mental math. Marty would take his standard 15 percent of the sale, which would leave her with somewhere in the neighborhood of $65,000, more than enough to make the risk worthwhile.

"Marty," she said, trying to mute the voice in her head, "you are a prince among men."

"And you, kid, are my princess." He gave her that sparkling, flirtatious grin again, the one that she knew meant nothing. "Want me to hang on to the ring for you here?"

She nodded, feeling relieved as she watched him lock it into the safe. As much as she loved admiring the jewels, it always made her uneasy to keep stolen goods at her own house. If anyone ever suspected her and called the police, how would she explain what she was doing with them? Marty, at least, always had plausible deniability. He had bought the pieces from a stranger and had no idea they were hot, but gee, he was sorry for the mistake. "Marty?" she asked after he'd returned to the table and poured them both a bit more wine. "Do you ever regret going into business with me?"

He looked at her blankly. "I can hardly remember a time before my dad and I worked with you and your uncle."

"But just because you've been doing something for a long time doesn't necessarily make it right. Your business could be one hundred percent on the up-and-up, Marty. And because of me—"

"Because of you," he interrupted firmly, "I get to feel like I'm playing a small role in doing some good in the world. Is what we're doing illegal? You bet. But is it *wrong*? I don't think it is, do you?"

"Of course not." Colette wouldn't be able to live with herself.

"Colette, I don't have a single regret about any of it," he said firmly. He raised his wineglass and waited until she looked him in the eye. "Here's to the best partnership I've ever had."

She hesitated and then clinked her glass against his. "Cheers," she said, and then she looked away, because she couldn't stand the way it suddenly felt as if he could see right through her.

CHAPTER FOUR

1938

Throughout the summer and early autumn of 1938, Colette worked alongside her mother, lifting pieces here and there from people who were cruel and unkind. She felt a zing of pride with every successful theft, and each time her mother sold one of her stolen pieces to a jewelry broker, she knew she was making a difference. "That's my girl," her mother said whenever they walked away with a stack of banknotes to donate to one of their favorite causes, and Colette loved the way her mother's face glowed with love when she looked at her daughter, her protégée.

One afternoon that fall, Colette came home from school to find Mum waiting for her in the parlor.

"Where's Liliane?" Colette asked, looking around for her little sister, who was nearly eight months old now.

"Your uncle Frederic and aunt Marie are looking after her for the night, and Papa has gone to a teachers' meeting in Lyon for the next few days," Mum said. "You and I have the whole evening to ourselves, and we have something important to do."

"What is it, Mum?"

Mum's eyes twinkled. "Your first major score, my darling. It's time."

A shiver of excitement ran down Colette's spine. "Where are we going?"

"To the Opéra. I've bought you a new dress."

"The Opéra?" Colette had never even been to the theater, never mind to the magnificent Palais Garnier, the grandest opera house in the world, with its soaring pillars and its gilded statues of Harmony and Poetry looking down on the avenue below.

"There's a German production on tonight, and there will be plenty of those aligned with the Germans in the audience," Mum said, her jaw tight.

Colette blinked at her, trying to catch up. "Are the Germans bad?"

Mum smiled. "Sometimes I forget you're only ten." She seemed to be searching for words. "No, my darling, there are many wonderful German people, but the German chancellor is a man named Hitler who destroys anyone who stands in his way. He's threatening to invade Czechoslovakia, and in Germany, he has begun doing terrible things to Jews."

"But . . . why?" Colette's best friend, Sarah, was Jewish, and she was the nicest girl in the whole class. What could Germany's chancellor have against people like her?

"Because Hitler is a very bad man. And those who are complicit in taking rights away from their fellow citizens are just the kind of people who deserve to have their jewels stolen. If my sources are correct, the wife of Ernst Balkenhol, the second-in-command to Hitler's propaganda minister, will be in attendance, wearing a very expensive diamond choker."

"She's our mark?" Colette asked.

"Ingrid Balkenhol is *your* mark, my darling," Mum said. "Now go change, and I'll tell you more on our way there."

Thirty minutes later, Colette had slipped into the simple, short-sleeved black cocktail dress Mum had laid out for her. In the mirror, fastening the pearls Mum had loaned her, she appeared at least twelve or thirteen. She nodded to her reflection on the way out the door, whispering to herself, "You can do this."

"The key," Mum murmured as they walked west on the rue Réaumur through a crisp fall evening, "is to act aloof, like you couldn't possibly care less about anyone's opinion. Don't look anyone in the eye. Always appear to be searching the crowd for someone. Don't make yourself memorable in any way."

"But this dress . . ." Colette looked like a film star, complete with a fur stole around her shoulders, on loan from Mum.

"You look beautiful in it, my dear," Mum said, "but you'll be two a penny in this crowd—which is exactly as it should be."

Mum had explained that they would need to sit through the entire production before making their move; to arrive after it had begun would be to make a spectacle of themselves, and to depart early would put them at risk of being noticed. "Besides," Mum said with a smile as they crossed the rue Louis-le-Grand and emerged into the Place de l'Opéra, "the production tonight is Wagner's *Tristan und Isolde*, one of the most beautiful operas in existence."

"You've seen it before?"

"A long time ago. And this version is supposed to be even more beautiful. It premiered in Paris just last Thursday with a Norwegian soprano named Kirsten Flagstad in the role of Isolde, the forbidden love of the hero, Tristan. She's a soloist for a big opera company in America, and she's quite famous. The critics say that no one has ever performed the role better. I can't think of a better way for you to experience your first night at the opera, my darling."

Colette was stunned at first by the sea of elegant people, dressed in their finest, wearing a king's fortune in jewels. And the Palais Garnier itself! It was like nothing Colette had ever seen, with its enormous white marble staircase, colorful mosaics, and countless chandeliers lighting the way. It was hard not to be overwhelmed by the sheer decadence of it all. But as she and Mum moved through the crowd, her palms were sweating. It was one thing to steal small pieces here and there at cafés, as she'd been doing, but another thing entirely to lift a very expensive diamond choker from the wife of a powerful man in a packed theater.

"Mum, what if I can't reach Frau Balkenhol's neck?" she whispered in a sudden panic as she and Mum headed for their seats twenty rows back from the stage. "What if I'm not tall enough?"

Mum squeezed her hand and nodded to a blonde on the arm of a uniformed man near the front of the audience. The woman barely came to her husband's shoulder; her features were sharp and thin, her frame childlike. "*That* is Frau Balkenhol," she said. The woman was hardly taller than Colette. "You'll be able to reach just fine, darling."

"And a woman that size would be accustomed to being jostled," Colette murmured, thinking of all the times she'd been jabbed in the shoulder or elbowed in the head by people who didn't bother looking down. The world was not built to accommodate small people.

"Exactly," Mum said, smiling down at her, and Colette understood that, in fact, this had been part of the plan all along. Her first major score—a necklace from the diminutive wife of a bad man—had been designed especially for her.

The production was longer than Colette ever would have imagined—more than four hours, including two intermissions—but Colette found she couldn't look away. In fact, she found herself completely forgetting that she was here for a mission rather than to be swept away by the most beautiful story she'd ever seen.

She watched in awe as the main character, Isolde, intent on killing a knight named Tristan who was taking her to marry a king she didn't want to marry, mistakenly gave him a love potion rather than the deadly poison she had intended. She drank the potion, too, meaning to meet her death, but instead, the two fell deeply in love with each other, though it was a forbidden passion. In the second act, Colette's heart thudded as Tristan and Isolde found ways to be together, even as those who forbade it tried to tear them apart. They declared their passion for each other, but then an ally of the king stabbed Tristan, which made Colette gasp and cover her mouth in shock as tears ran down her cheeks. In the third act, Tristan struggled for his life as Isolde rushed to be by his side, and then, as Colette watched with wide eyes, holding her breath, he died with Isolde's name on his lips. At the end, Isolde joined her forbidden love in death.

As the lights went up and the performers took their bows, Colette found that she was sobbing. The opera had been a tragedy, but also the most romantic thing she'd ever seen. Despite all that stood against them, Tristan and Isolde were ready to sacrifice everything for each other.

"You must get ahold of yourself, darling," Mum said as they stood to applaud. Her tone was amused, her eyes warm as she looked down at Colette.

"But there was so much sadness, and yet it was all so beautiful." Colette was clapping so hard that her hands hurt. "Is love really like that?"

"Like what, my darling?" Mum asked as the curtain finally went down and the crowd began to filter out.

Colette searched for words. "Like something you'd give your life for. Like something you'd do anything for, despite the odds against you. Like something that stays with you your whole life through."

She looked up at her mother just in time to see tears in her eyes. "I think," Mum said, her voice wobbling strangely, "that very few people are lucky enough to have love like that." The crowd was moving toward the exit now, and Mum put a hand on Colette's shoulder, nodding in the direction of Ingrid Balkenhol, who had begun to make her way toward the exit. "It's time, my darling. Go get in position. I'll meet you outside, as we planned."

Heart racing, Colette nodded and slipped away, letting the crowd swallow her. There would be time to think about the against-all-odds love story of Tristan and Isolde later. For now she had to focus. As she slid through the surge of people toward the top of the grand marble staircase, her doubt faded, replaced by steely resolve. She was good at this. She had trained for this moment. As Frau Balkenhol appeared through a theater door and moved toward Colette, deep in conversation with another woman, Colette zeroed in on the diamond choker around the German woman's slender neck. Necklaces were easy to steal, but still, her palms were sweaty again as she glided through the crowd.

She could feel Mum's eyes on her from across the grand foyer. The crowd nudged and pushed along as a thousand patrons made their way to the stairs. The window was closing fast; the theft had to happen in close quarters, when everyone was jostling against one another.

Colette took a deep breath. And then, just as Frau Balkenhol passed, she reached up with her left hand and, gentle as a whisper, flicked the uncomplicated clasp at the woman's neck, sweeping her right hand out to catch the diamond as it fell. The moment it hit her palm, Colette closed her fist around it and deliberately stumbled forward, knocking into the man in front of her, who then knocked into Frau Balkenhol, while Colette pretended she had thrown out her hand only to catch her balance. The man turned, but by the time he had said, "Excuse me, madame," to Frau Balkenhol, and by the time the German woman began yelping in aggrieved protest, Colette was already melting back into the crowd.

Across the foyer, Mum nodded her approval and vanished into the sea of departing operagoers, leaving Colette to casually make her own way outside. As she exited the Palais Garnier and the night air wrapped its icy fingers around her, she pulled her fur stole a bit tighter to shield herself against the chill. Keeping her right hand closed in a fist around a fortune in diamonds, she ducked her head and hid a small smile of triumph as she hurried away, resisting the urge to look back.

CHAPTER FIVE

2018

Aviva arrived for dinner promptly at 7:00 p.m., and when Colette answered the door, she noticed first that the younger woman had brought a nice bottle of Napa sauvignon blanc—and belatedly, that Aviva was also clutching a folded section of the newspaper. Colette forced a smile and gave Aviva a quick hug and a peck on the cheek.

"Come in, dear, come in," she said, and as Aviva stepped over her threshold, Colette snuck a look at the newspaper in her hands. Indeed, it was the same offending piece of garbage that she had thrown out once already.

Colette accepted the bottle of wine but turned her back on the paper, striding down the hall toward her kitchen with Aviva trailing behind her. Aviva's mother had died more than twenty years earlier, when Aviva was just eighteen, and for a time, Colette had taken Aviva in. They'd been close since then, and Aviva knew nearly everything about her—except for her hobby of jewel theft. "My favorite wine," Colette said over her shoulder. "Thank you for remembering."

"Of course. I brought the *Globe*, too."

"I told you I'd already seen it." Colette didn't meet Aviva's gaze as she reached into her cabinet for two wineglasses. She made quick work of the bottle's cork with her wine key and poured them each a healthy splash. Finally, as they toasted, Colette could avoid Aviva's gaze no longer; to refuse to look at the other person while clinking glasses was an invitation for bad luck, and she couldn't afford that.

"I know," Aviva said, taking a small sip of her wine. "But you were so cagey earlier that I wanted to see your reaction for myself."

"Is that right?"

"It is," Aviva continued, though Colette couldn't tell whether the girl was amused or annoyed. "And now I can see that you're acting even weirder than you sounded on the phone today."

Colette took a long sip of wine and then hazarded a glance at the newspaper, which very clearly featured a photo of her. "Is there a reason you're treating me like a criminal?"

Finally, Aviva softened. "Colette, I'm just trying to understand what happened. Why would you lie to me about being at the benefit?"

"I don't have to keep you apprised of all my comings and goings."

"Of course not. But you also don't need to be untruthful about them. This *is* you." She jabbed her finger at the newspaper. "Also, sidenote, I like that dress on you. But what's with the wig?"

Colette decided to be at least partially honest. "The truth is, I did go to the benefit. As I mentioned, Linda Clyborn is a neo-Nazi. I personally don't think they should be allowed to run around Boston unchecked, do you?"

Aviva blinked at her. "So what was your plan, exactly? To confront her?"

"No." Colette took another sip of wine. "Just to observe."

"And while you were busy observing, did you happen to see anyone steal her hundred-twenty-five-thousand-dollar ring?"

"Ninety thousand, tops," Colette mumbled into her wineglass.

"Pardon?"

"Nothing." She turned and reached for the large wooden bowl on the kitchen island. "Would you mind tossing the salad, dear? I've already made the champagne vinaigrette, just as you like it. It's in the cruet over there."

Aviva nodded and went to work with the pair of wooden tongs Colette handed over. For a moment, she was distracted by the bowl of greens while Colette pulled the Dijon chicken breasts from a skillet and plated them alongside rice pilaf. She drizzled a lemon-tinged cream sauce over everything and picked up the dishes.

"Shall we?" Colette asked, gesturing to the kitchen table, which she had already set.

"You're not getting out of this just because you're feeding me," Aviva grumbled, but as they ate their salads in silence, Colette began to think that the trick of plying the girl with her favorite foods had worked after all. She had just begun to relax when Aviva spoke again.

"Does this have to do with Marty?" she asked abruptly. "Were you at the gala with him? Is he involved in stealing jewels?"

Colette choked out a laugh. "Darling, Marty is the most unsubtle man I've ever met. I don't think he could steal a piece of jewelry if he tried. He would be too busy trying to flirt with the item's owner."

Aviva smiled at this. "Okay, yeah, you're right. I just thought since he's in the jewelry business . . ."

"That he must be a thief?"

"No. I'm just trying to understand why you were inches away from the victim of a crime right before that crime occurred."

"In court, I believe that would be considered circumstantial evidence," Colette said.

"Who said anything about court?" Aviva shot back.

Colette had just opened her mouth to reply when the doorbell rang. Colette excused herself to answer, grateful for the moment away from Aviva to collect her thoughts. Aviva had always been like a dog with a bone, which had served her well in her professional life; she never rested until she got to the bottom of things. But Colette had never been on the receiving end of one of her interrogations before, and she realized she didn't particularly like it, though she couldn't help but feel a bit proud of Aviva for her persistence.

Just as she was rolling her eyes at the instinct to replace her annoyance with pride when it came to the girl she considered family, she looked through the peephole and registered with a start that the stranger there in an ill-fitting suit was holding up a badge. She hesitated, and then pulled the door open.

"Boston Police Department, ma'am," the man said as she stared at him, wordless. In all her years of jewel theft, this was only the second time the police had shown up at her door—and the first time, during the war so many years ago, had ended in tragedy. "I'm Detective Aldo Damien. Do you have a moment?"

"Um" was all Colette could manage, and she and the detective stared at each other for a moment in what Colette imagined was a face-off, though the detective likely only registered that he was staring down a confused old lady.

"Ma'am?" the detective asked with some concern when Colette still hadn't unfrozen.

"Can I help you?" Aviva's voice came from behind Colette,

and Colette turned to see Aviva approaching, her gaze steely as she regarded the detective. She put a hand on Colette's shoulder.

"Yes, ma'am, I'm Detective Damien with the Boston PD." He held up his badge again, and Aviva studied it for a second, then nodded. "I'm looking for Colette Marceau."

"For what purpose?" Aviva asked.

The detective raised an eyebrow. "And you are?"

"I'm her friend," she said, "*And* her attorney."

"I see." The detective's expression hardened slightly. "I just have a few questions for Ms. Marceau."

"Pertaining to?" Aviva asked. Colette hid a smile.

"Pertaining to a theft that occurred last night at a benefit Ms. Marceau attended." The detective stared at Aviva for a moment before dropping his gaze. "Look, ma'am, we're just trying to talk to anyone who might have seen something. A very expensive piece of jewelry went missing." He turned to Colette. "I just need a moment of your time."

"Of course," Colette said, recovering herself. "Come in, won't you?"

"Colette, you don't need to—" Aviva began, but Colette waved a hand to cut her off.

"I have nothing to hide, dear. I'm happy to answer the detective's questions."

Aviva grumbled her disapproval, but she followed Colette and a triumphant-looking Detective Damien down the hall to the formal living room anyhow. Colette gestured to the armchair as she took a seat on the couch, and she was relieved when Aviva settled next to her and reached for her hand. From the concerned glance Aviva cut her way a moment later, Colette realized she was shaking, and she quickly withdrew her hand and placed it in her lap.

"Let's get to it, young man," she said to the detective. "Aviva and I were just in the middle of dinner."

"It smells good," the detective said, smiling at her.

"It is good. And now it's getting cold," Colette said. "Now what can we do for you?"

The detective looked flustered. "You see, a very expensive ring was stolen from a woman at the gala you attended last night."

"And what makes you think Colette was at this gala?" Aviva cut in.

The detective scratched his head. "We showed some photographs to a handful of witnesses, and one of them mentioned that they knew her from the Boston Center for Holocaust Education." He turned back to Colette. "You volunteer there, right, ma'am?"

"I do." Colette silently cursed her lousy luck; what were the odds that someone associated with the center would be in attendance at the gala?

"And you're a retired librarian?"

"I am." She had always loved books, and she had needed to make a living somehow, given that her family's code of honor expressly forbade her from profiting from theft. "Though I'm not sure what bearing my former job has on your investigation." It made her uneasy that the detective had looked into her past enough to know about a job she'd left two decades ago.

"Ma'am," the detective said, a hint of annoyance creeping into his tone. "In case I wasn't clear, you're merely being questioned as a potential witness. This should take only a few minutes."

"Go ahead, then," Aviva answered for her, and they both looked at Colette.

"Yes, I was there," Colette said slowly. "I do love the orchestra."

Aviva nodded heartily and said, "Yes, she does," which Colette felt sure was overdoing it, but the detective didn't seem to notice.

"And, ma'am, did you see anyone suspicious in the vicinity of Linda Clyborn? She was the woman who spoke from the podium last night." Obviously he thought that Colette was a dolt. Oh, well—she could use that to her advantage.

"A speech," she said slowly, pretending to think about it. "Hmm, I wasn't paying much attention."

Aviva shrugged and gave the detective a look of faux sympathy.

"Would you mind if I show you a few photos?" He didn't wait for an answer before pulling out three mug shots, all of men who appeared to be in their forties or fifties, from a manila folder. "Did you see any of these people at the gala last night?"

She looked down at the unfamiliar faces. "Who are they?"

"Jewel thieves known to operate in this area."

"Jewel thieves. Oh my." Well, that would make it easier to deflect attention. "Why, yes, I do believe I saw that young man," she said, pointing at random to one of the photographs. "Yes, I'm almost certain I did."

The detective looked relieved. "Thank you, Ms. Marceau. That's very helpful." He stood, slid the photos back into the folder, and smiled patronizingly at Colette. "See? That wasn't so hard, was it?"

"Oh, very easy," she agreed like the old bat he thought she was. "I do hope you catch the thief. Aviva, would you mind showing the nice detective out?"

"My pleasure," Aviva said. The detective smiled again at Colette, and then Aviva marched him to the front door, opened it pointedly, and slammed it behind him.

"You didn't need to be rude," Colette said when Aviva returned to the living room.

But Aviva didn't answer. She was staring at Colette like she'd never seen her before. "You took that ring," she said in awe. It was a statement, not a question.

"That's ridiculous," Colette said, looking away.

"Is it? Then look me in the eye and tell me it wasn't you."

Colette swallowed hard and returned her gaze to Aviva, but she didn't say a thing.

"*You took that ring,*" Aviva repeated slowly. "Colette, why would you do such a thing?"

Perhaps this was the universe giving her an opportunity. "Attorney-client privilege?" she asked, and when Aviva nodded slowly, Colette drew a deep breath and blurted out the words she'd been wanting to say for so long. "I've been a jewel thief since I was a child, as was my mother before me, and her mother before her."

Aviva stared at her as if Colette was speaking a language she didn't understand. "*What?*"

"Come, dear. The chicken is getting cold." She started back toward the table. "I'll tell you everything, but I can't do it without a glass of wine."

That night, after Aviva had left with a dazed expression, Colette stood at her bathroom sink and stared at her reflection in the mirror.

She had taken off all her makeup in preparation for sleep, and the woman who stared back at her appeared exhausted. Without her armor of lipstick, mascara, and blush, she looked every one of her eighty-nine years, though she hardly felt that age.

Sometimes, she was tempted to rue the way her features had dropped, the way her neck had creased like a fan, the way the years stripped women of the right to be noticed in the world. But each time she started down that road, she reminded herself that her mother hadn't grown old at all. She had died at the age of thirty-six at the hands of the Nazis. And how could Colette turn her nose up at years her mother hadn't had the chance to live?

She sighed and turned away from the mirror, flicking off the bathroom light.

"I told her, Mum," Colette said aloud as she climbed into bed and turned out the light. "I told Aviva the truth, and now I have to wait and see if it changes things between us."

Colette didn't speak to her mother often—she was no fool, and she knew that her mother had been dead for seventy-six years. But on nights like tonight, when she felt the past catching up with the present and forcing her hand, it brought her comfort to speak her thoughts into the silence and to imagine that her mother was out there somewhere, still listening, even after all this time.

"A detective came to the door tonight; I suppose you saw that," Colette added after a long pause. "Maybe Marty's right and I should quit while I'm ahead. You were always so much better at this than I."

The only reply was the same crushing silence that always surrounded her. Sometimes, she wondered if the reason she never felt her mother's presence was because her mother was still disappointed in her.

The final promise Colette had made to her mother was that she would find Liliane and bring her home. Colette had failed in this last sacred task, and she had never forgiven herself for it. Her father hadn't forgiven her, either. She had spent her entire life trying to atone, but there was no coming back from a sin like that.

She closed her eyes and tried to let sleep take her, but slumber proved just as elusive as forgiveness. Finally, she flicked the light back on, got out of bed, and walked over to the safe tucked into the back of her closet.

She didn't like to keep pieces in the house, for fear that they could be used against her if the police ever showed up for a raid. Marty insisted that here in the United States, the police needed probable cause to get a warrant, but his rationalization had fallen upon deaf ears. Colette knew all too well that the authorities could simply show up and take you away whenever they pleased.

But the small safe in her bedroom closet contained the one thing she couldn't live without: the diamond-studded bracelet her mother had sewn into the hem of Colette's nightgown just a few nights before it all ended. It was half of a pair Mum had stolen from a German—the theft that had gotten her arrested. Mum had sewn the other half into the hem of Liliane's gown, and it had gone missing forever the night Liliane was taken. Colette had enlisted Marty's help years ago in tracking it down, but to her great regret, the piece had never resurfaced. Colette had become more and more certain over the years that it never would. For all she knew, it was lying at the bottom of the Seine.

Now, Colette pulled her half out, opened the clasp, and slipped it onto her narrow wrist. To anyone who hadn't seen the matching bracelet, the one she wore now looked like two lilies swaying in the breeze. Four golden veins ran through each flower, each made of a constellation of flawless colorless diamonds set on a gold filigree web and tipped with tiny black diamonds. Colette's half alone was worth hundreds of thousands of dollars. Together, the bracelets, which came together to form a butterfly, would be worth nearly a million.

Colette knew that her mother had never intended to keep the bracelets. She normally sold her stolen pieces to finance the French Resistance, but this set had had special meaning; she had taken them because they'd been stolen from her friend, a woman named Hélène Rosman. "One day," her mother had said, "I will return the bracelets to Madame Rosman. In the meantime, you and Liliane will each keep half, just in case. If the worst comes to pass, having the bracelets to bargain with will keep you safe."

But the bracelets hadn't kept them safe at all.

And now, the single bejeweled wing that sparkled in the dim bedroom light on Colette's age-speckled wrist was all that remained of Colette's mother and sister, who had lost their lives so many years before.

CHAPTER SIX

1939

In September 1939, Germany invaded Poland, and everything in Colette's world changed in an instant. "We must be careful," her mother began saying tersely, giving Colette fewer and fewer opportunities to steal. "It's getting more dangerous."

Although France's borders hadn't been breached, the world was at war. "But surely we can help people, can't we?" Colette had asked just before Christmas. "Our work is more important than ever."

"Indeed," her mother said. "But Paris is no longer safe, my darling. It's only a matter of time before the Germans are here, one way or another."

And then, in May of 1940, her words came true. The Germans poured easily into the Netherlands and Belgium, and then over the French border. By the first week of June, they were closing in on Paris.

Colette, her little sister, Liliane, and her parents were among the hundreds of thousands who fled the capital, fearing that there would be heavy casualties as the Germans tried to take the city. The roads were crowded with those trying to escape, pockmarked with recent bomb craters and lined with bodies; Mum kept Liliane's eyes shielded from the chaos as much as she could, but Colette knew none of them would ever forget the things they'd seen.

They made it as far as Valençay, some 250 kilometers south, where they found temporary lodging in a barn owned by a sympathetic farmer, but there was never enough to eat, and anyhow, word soon reached them that Paris had fallen to the Germans. There was no longer a threat of warfare in the streets, now that the French had capitulated, so in the last week of July, like so many others, they returned to the capital, defiant but ready to resume their lives.

A swastika flag now hung from the Arc de Triomphe; the clocks had been set forward an hour to German time; the museums and libraries had been stripped bare. French soldiers were marched through the streets, their uniforms in tatters, on the way to prison camps, and German soldiers now filled the cafés that Colette and her family had once frequented.

"We must do *something*," Colette whispered to her mother on the night they returned to their apartment, which had gone musty and stale in their absence. Mum was tucking Colette and Liliane into the bed they shared, and beside Colette, under the covers, Liliane was already drifting off to sleep, her breathing slow and even. She was only two years old, too young to understand what was happening, which Colette supposed was a blessing. "I want to help, Mum. Surely there are Germans we could steal from."

"Darling, I cannot permit it," Mum said firmly. "There was danger before, but at worst, you might have had to spend a night in jail. The penalties should you be caught stealing from a German now would be much, much worse."

"Does that mean you'll stop stealing, too, then?"

Mum bit her lip. "No," she said with a sigh. "It is in the times of greatest danger that we must summon our greatest courage. It is what I have trained for all my life."

"But I have, too, Mum."

Mum's eyes glistened with tears. "My darling, I cannot put you in harm's way. You will have the rest of your life to do good, but now, your most important job is to survive."

For two years, Colette reluctantly followed her mother's orders. For two years, her fingers itched each time she passed a German sympathizer wearing an expensive piece. For two years, her heart twisted with shame each time she saw someone who needed help. She had felt so powerful when her mother had trusted her to steal, and now, she felt a terrible sense of not mattering at all.

Mum had begun working with a clandestine organization based in the neighborhood, run by a man she knew only as *Le Paon*, the Peacock. It was a loose group, hastily formed, but it was filled with people trying to help the cause, and it gave Mum purpose. The more Mum threw herself into the work of stealing to fund the underground, the more useless Colette felt. But each time she asked to help, her mother's answer was firm and un-equivocal. "I simply cannot risk losing you, Colette," she would say. "I cannot permit it."

But by the time Colette turned fourteen in the summer of 1942, things had gotten much worse for all of them, and Co-lette could no longer ignore her urge to do something, *anything*. The Germans had begun arresting Jewish men, women, and chil-dren in mass roundups, and Colette knew that Le Paon's network was now helping to fund escape lines that would save lives. She wanted desperately to help, too. She had the skills and the train-ing to make a difference, and it was high time she tried.

She knew enough, though, not to tell her mother, and to wait for the right mark, the right opening. Mum had taught her well.

For her first target in two years, Colette settled on Madame Virlogeux, a dressmaker who had become quite wealthy in the last several months fabricating designer knockoffs for German officers to send home to their mothers and wives or, more often, to give to their French girlfriends. Madame Virlogeux had a stable of eight women who cut and sewed patterns, and the rumor was that she had them beaten by one of her henchmen when a dress didn't come out exactly to her liking. That wasn't Colette's concern, however, nor was the money Madame Virlogeux was making from the Germans, though both repulsed her.

No, what had triggered Colette's interest was the knowledge that the dressmaker had betrayed at least three Jewish families in her building, making false accusations to the Germans so that she could take over their apartments. In this manner, she had secured for herself the entire second floor of a building on the rue Saint-Sébastien. Her betrayals had, so far, resulted in the arrests and deportations of several adults and six innocent children, two of them just four years old, Liliane's age.

For weeks now, Colette had been taking the long way home from school, weaving a few blocks out of her way so that her route would take her down the rue Saint-Sébastien. She hadn't been lucky enough to spot Madame Virlogeux on any of her previous passes, but today, as Colette rounded the corner, she saw the portly dressmaker standing outside the front door to her building, smoking a cigarette as she talked to two German officers, a narrow diamond-and onyx bangle twinkling on her right wrist. Her platinum hair was in a severe twist, and her immaculate lipstick was blood red. Hatred sizzled within Colette, and before she could talk herself out of it, she crossed the street and slipped into a throng of people walking past the dressmaker's building.

Colette hardly had time to consider what she was going to do, and though she hadn't stolen anything in ages, instinct took over as she approached. There were seven other people moving by in a group, including three young women and two older men. Heart thudding, she reached out and grabbed the purse strap of one of the women, giving it a hard tug to create a distraction. It was a move she and Mum had practiced several times before the war; she could easily create a confused commotion if she involved not one but *two* strangers at the same time.

The woman shrieked, spinning around and immediately spitting accusations at the two old men behind her. The melee distracted Madame Virlogeux and her Germans, and as the little knot of people passed, Colette used the opportunity to jostle one of the men into Madame Virlogeux at the very same moment Colette herself slipped the bangle from the dressmaker's wrist. Madame Virlogeux yelped and began to hurl obscenities at the man as Colette melted back into the crowd, her heart thudding.

She had done it. She had taken a diamond bangle from one of the cruelest women in Paris, exactly the kind of theft her storied ancestor would have cheered on.

But as Madame Virlogeux continued to rant at the now-cowering old man, one of the Germans she'd been in conversation with was peering around, and as Colette hurried away, his gaze landed on her. When their eyes met, his expression hardened and he took a step forward, and that's when she made her mistake. Instead of continuing on her way as if nothing was amiss, as she'd been trained to do, her flight instinct kicked in, and she took off running.

She knew instantly that she'd reacted incorrectly, but it was too late. Heavy footsteps sounded behind her, and then the soldier called out in German, ordering her to halt immediately. But he was an older, slightly overweight man, and his speed was no match for hers, propelled as she was by sheer terror. She circled her own block a few times before she was certain that she'd lost him. Finally, she turned onto the rue Pasteur, where she had lived since the day she was born, and stopped across the street from her own apartment building. She was breathing hard, and it wasn't until she stopped running that she realized she was shaking uncontrollably. Suddenly, the German came around the corner from out of nowhere, panting heavily. Colette gasped and quickly backed into a doorway, pressing herself into the shadows as she held her breath. If the man continued down the block, he'd pass her hiding space in less than two minutes. There was nowhere left for her to go. What had she done?

The German paused at the corner and then began walking again, more slowly now, his eyes narrowed as he scanned the doorways along the street. Any moment now, he would see her. She put her hand over her own mouth to stifle a gasp and shrank back as far as she could go.

From the opposite direction, a boy she recognized vaguely from the neighborhood was hurrying toward them. He was about her age, with thick, dark hair and long lashes, and he wore a yellow, six-pointed star outlined in black—it had just been announced a few days earlier, on the first of June, that Jews must wear them everywhere. For a few seconds, Colette forgot all about her own predicament. *Go back*, she wanted to cry out. As perilous as the city was for all Parisians now, it was ten times more dangerous for Jews, who could be arrested and even executed without cause.

But the boy only quickened his pace, as if he hadn't noticed the danger at all, finally drawing to a halt just a few meters away from the frowning soldier. Slowly, deliberately, the boy bent to tie his shoe, right in the path of the German. *What was he thinking?*

The German stopped short, glowering down at the boy in his path. "Who do you think you are?" he barked in thickly accented French.

"Pardon?" The boy looked up, his face expressionless. It was as if he hadn't noticed the massive German approaching, and even now, he didn't seem particularly ruffled.

The German sneered down at him. "Well? Where did the girl go?"

"Who's that?" the boy asked just as blankly, sounding far calmer than he should have.

"There was a girl, you stupid Jew. She was running."

"I'm afraid I haven't seen anyone," the boy said.

"Sir," the German said coldly, assessing the boy.

"Pardon?"

"You haven't seen anyone, *sir*. You will address me with respect, Jew."

"Yes, sir, of course, sir. I'll let you know, sir, if I spot anything suspicious. Sir."

"Yes, well," the German said as he looked around the street, where a handful of passersby were hurrying past him nervously. Colette shrank further into the shadows. "Watch yourself," the German added gruffly before turning on his heel and striding away.

The boy waited until the German had been gone for a full minute before he turned and looked right at Colette. He gave her a small smile and jerked his head, beckoning her to come out from her hiding place. Still he didn't move; it was as if he was rooted to the spot. Slowly, Colette unfolded herself from the shadows and made her way down the block and across the street until she was standing just a meter away from him.

"I believe you may have dropped something," he said by way of greeting, holding her gaze.

Colette patted her pocket and felt the breath go out of her when she realized it was empty. At that moment, the boy moved his foot slightly to reveal what he'd been standing on, and she gasped. Beneath the scuffed sole of his right shoe was the bangle she'd stolen.

Cheeks flaming, she bent quickly to grab the bangle and straightened, shoving it deep into her pocket. "Why did you help me?"

He shrugged. "I was already heading this way when I saw you drop it."

"But you could have been arrested. Things are terribly dangerous now for—" She swallowed the end of her sentence, for things were dangerous for all Parisians, but they both knew what she'd meant.

But the boy just shrugged. "One should always help if one can."

The words did something to her, for it was just how she felt, too. "Indeed."

"Forgive me for asking, but is the piece yours, mademoiselle?"

"Not exactly." She hesitated. "But the woman it belonged to is a collaborator." He looked confused, so she added, "Think of this as a redistribution of riches."

He chuckled, then his expression melted into one of concern. He stared at her for a moment, and she had the sense he was assessing her. "You shouldn't be caught with something that has gone missing. Not until the Germans have stopped looking."

He was right. What would happen if she brought the bangle home to her mother, and the Germans came door-to-door looking for it? No, she would need to hide it somewhere until the threat had passed. "But where will I keep it?"

"I have an idea." He gestured for her to follow, and after a second, she started after him. He led her halfway down the block to a building with a dark green door and pushed it open.

"But this isn't where you live, is it?" she asked as she followed him through an archway into a small courtyard. The space was surrounded on all four sides by the building, but above, it was open to the sky. Someone had planted a small garden here, and in the midst of bricks and stone, several rows of flowers reached for the sun. "I've lived on this street my whole life. I would know you if you lived here."

"You're right. I live a few blocks away, but there's no lock on the door here—I suppose because it only leads into this courtyard. You must enter through that door over there to get inside the building itself," he said, pointing to another dark green door on the other side of the garden. "I come here sometimes when I need a moment of peace. There's something about seeing these flowers survive against the odds that makes me feel hopeful."

Colette's gaze flashed to the yellow star on the boy's shirt, and as their eyes met again, his cheeks turned pink. "It's beautiful," Colette said after a moment, looking back at the flowers. "But I'm not sure it would be safe to hide something here, out in the open."

He smiled. "I very much agree. But you haven't seen this yet." He walked to the wall on the left side of the courtyard and paused, looking up at the windows above. He scanned them quickly and then, seemingly satisfied that no one was watching, he moved so that his body was blocking the wall and quickly slid a brick out. "Here," he said, his voice low.

She gaped; the gap behind the brick was the size of a jewelry box—large enough to secret away a few small treasures. "But how . . . ?"

He smiled. "I noticed the loose brick last month. I've been watching. I don't think anyone knows but me."

"You would share your spot with me?"

The boy nodded.

"But . . . why?"

"Because the best secrets are meant to be shared, don't you think?"

He held her gaze. Maybe one day, she would tell him her secrets, too: that this wasn't an isolated incident, that she was a jewel thief, that she was determined to risk everything to restore justice. But for now, it was enough to feel that she was the keeper of his confidence, and so she pulled the bangle from her pocket and they both looked at it as it sparkled in the sunlight. "It's beautiful, isn't it?" she asked after a moment.

But when she looked back at the boy, he was no longer looking at the bracelet. He was looking right at her. "I think perhaps it's the loveliest thing I've ever seen."

CHAPTER SEVEN

2018

Colette thought often of the boy from Paris, the one with the yellow star who had shown her the hiding place in the courtyard. He had not survived the war, but his words that day had stayed with her, imprinted on her soul. *One should always help if one can*, he'd said. It was a principle that had guided her life since then.

The morning after the detective's visit, Colette woke before dawn after a mostly sleepless night, her stomach knotted with worry, and the visions from her nightmares—ghosts and demons stealing her mother and sister away—still dancing in front of her eyes. What if Aviva couldn't accept Colette for who she really was? What if she didn't understand that Colette had only ever tried to do good in the world? And what if the detective came back, triggered by Colette's unease during their interview? What if he realized that she wasn't simply a confused old lady, but rather a cunning thief whose arrest would close decades of open cases?

It felt to Colette as she got out of bed and shuffled to the bathroom that she was standing on a precipice, and she didn't know yet whether the ground would stay solid beneath her feet or would crumble to dust, sending her plunging into the deep unknown.

She washed her face, made herself a cup of coffee, and got dressed, taking care with her makeup as she always did, adding her signature red lipstick and black mascara, though she expected no visitors today.

She was just preparing some eggs for breakfast when her doorbell rang. She looked at the clock on the wall, her heart hammering. It was barely seven o'clock in the morning, and nothing good arrived at one's door so early. Could it be the detective, returning to confront her with evidence? Her throat started to close, but then she realized that it could equally be Aviva, here to say that she'd thought about Colette's words overnight and that she understood. She forced herself to breathe normally as she hurried to peer through the peephole.

But it was neither the detective nor Aviva standing there. It was Marty, his face oddly pale. She wasn't sure what unsettled her more—his strange expression, or the fact that he was here at all.

"Marty?" she asked after she'd opened the door, just in case she was seeing things. They always stayed away from meeting anywhere except the store—or at a neutral location such as a restaurant downtown—just in case he was ever followed. "Are you all right?"

"I need to talk to you," he said, not answering the question, and her stomach began to churn.

"If this is about me being careless at the benefit, I've already gotten an earful from Aviva, not to mention the detective who dropped by yesterday."

"What?" He looked horrified enough that she knew instantly that wasn't what he was here to discuss. "There was a *detective* here?"

He turned to scan the street, and Colette did the same. What if the detective was out there watching? But neither could see any vehicle that looked like an unmarked police car.

"I don't think he knew anything," Colette said as Marty turned back to her, his eyebrows raised. "He showed me mug shots of three known thieves and asked if I'd seen any of them at the benefit."

Marty's eyebrows went up even further. "And I assume you pointed one out."

"Of course."

Marty laughed, his face relaxing. "Poor bastard."

Colette shrugged. "He shouldn't have gotten himself nabbed in the first place."

Marty shook his head, the smile falling from his face. "Look, kid, I'm not here to talk about the benefit. It's something else. Can I come in?"

Colette nodded and moved aside, closing the door behind him after he'd stepped over the threshold. Her nerves were jangling, but she busied herself with pouring Marty a cup of coffee and fixing it just the way he liked it—cream and two sugars. He had always been the sweet to her bitter, the light to her dark.

"So?" she asked, trying to keep the worry out of her voice as she handed him his coffee. "What is it, Marty? Don't tell me you're in some kind of trouble."

"No, nothing like that." He cleared his throat. "I've found it."

She looked at him blankly. "Found what?"

"The bracelet, Colette. I found the bracelet you've been looking for all these years."

She was certain she'd misunderstood. "*Which* bracelet, Marty?" She needed to hear him say it.

He held up a copy of the glossy *Boston Monthly* magazine, folded open to a story about an upcoming jewelry exhibit. "*The bracelet, Colette.*"

The world around Colette seemed to go still. Marty continued to speak, but it sounded as if his voice was coming from very far away. There, on the page of the magazine, was the bracelet she'd last seen in August 1942, just before her mother sewed it into the lining of little Liliane's nightgown, and less than forty-eight hours before the Gestapo showed up at her family's door.

Colette grabbed the magazine from Marty and stared. She had been looking for the bracelet for seventy-six years, but the longer a piece was missing, the smaller the chances of its return. She had come to believe that she would never see it again, and yet here it was, its diamonds sparkling even in the full-color photograph from the magazine spread, its shape unmistakable. The caption described its design as "an abstract swirl, or perhaps a pair of flowers," and for a moment, she could clearly hear Liliane's voice saying, *It's a blob.* But Colette knew that it was half of a whole, a broken butterfly with only one wing.

"I have always thought," she said carefully, hearing the tremble in her own voice, "that if I found the bracelet, I would find the person who took my sister." The words still hurt to say.

"Now's your chance," Marty said quietly.

"But don't you see?" She looked up at him. "It's too late. It's been seventy-six years, Marty. Whoever took Liliane would be long dead by now. The bracelet may be here, but the answers won't be."

Marty reached to pull her into a hug and spoke gently as she laid her head on his shoulder and wept. "You don't know that," he said. "*Someone* owns this bracelet. Someone knows where it came from. Maybe the monster who took your sister made a deathbed confession to a son or daughter. Maybe they can be persuaded to tell you what they know."

Colette sniffled and pulled away. He was selling a pipe dream, and she wanted so badly to buy it. "Where is the bracelet, Marty?"

"The Diamond Museum." Colette knew the place; it was a small, seasonal museum just a few blocks from Marty's store, housed in what had once been an opulent private home, built in the 1790s and donated a decade ago by a wealthy jewel collector named James Franklin Cash III. He had left explicit instructions in his will asking that his soaring historic house be turned into a museum that celebrated the gemstones he had loved all his life. "It's in an exhibit on early-twentieth-century European jewelry that's opening in a few days," he added.

"But where did it come from?" Colette whispered, more to herself than to Marty. "How did the bracelet get here? Where has it been all these years?"

"We'll find out, Colette," Marty said, pulling her back into his arms. "I promise you, we'll find out."

After he'd finished his cup of coffee, Marty offered to stay, but Colette needed time to think, and besides, if the detective returned, having a jewel broker on hand wouldn't exactly help her case. Marty departed with regret etched across his face, leaving the magazine with her. After he was gone, she read and reread the brief article that accompanied the picture, but it told her very little; there was no indication of where the bracelet had originated. *As with previous exhibits at the Diamond Museum,* the article said, *most of the pieces are on loan from private collections in deals secured by museum director Lucas O'Mara.*

She'd never met O'Mara, though his name was familiar; the *Boston Globe* had run a nice feature on him last year, and Marty had mentioned him a few times in glowing terms. O'Mara was in his mid-forties, and he'd had a career as an engineer early on before changing course and enrolling at the Savannah College of Art and Design to study jewelry design. And while he'd never made it as a professional designer, he had been hired as the founding director of the museum after a short stint at the Boston Museum of Fine Arts. Now, he curated rotating collections of jewels in partnership with the New England Diamond Alliance. Instead of making jewels, O'Mara had figured out how to celebrate them.

Surely this O'Mara was the kind of person who understood just how much jewels could mean to a family's history. Could he be the key to finding out where the bracelet had been all these years? Could it be as simple as approaching him to ask? But of course, if she questioned O'Mara herself, it would be impossible for her to later steal the bracelet without being at the top of the suspect list, if it came to that. And she couldn't send Marty in to do it; as a jewelry broker, asking questions about a piece that subsequently went missing would be career suicide—and it would risk exposing decades worth of illegal jewel sales.

But then something occurred to her. What about Aviva? Aviva could question O'Mara without raising suspicion, especially if she could frame it as part of a mission for the Holocaust center. With his walls down, maybe he'd admit what he knew.

Before she could second-guess herself, she picked up the phone and tried Aviva, first on her cell, and then, when she didn't answer, at her office.

"I'm afraid she isn't in yet, Colette," said Marilyn, who'd been Aviva's legal assistant for the last decade. "It's still quite early, even for Aviva."

Colette checked her watch and realized that, although it felt like she'd already lived several days since she'd gotten out of bed this morning, it was only a few minutes after eight o'clock.

"What are you doing there already, Marilyn?" Colette asked, flustered.

Marilyn laughed. "My granddaughter has a baseball game this afternoon. I figured I'd get a jump start on the day so I could leave early."

Colette closed her eyes for a second. What would it be like to have grandchildren to shape one's life around? It had been entirely her decision not to have children, but it still stung sometimes to realize how much she had missed. "I hope her game goes well, Marilyn. Can you tell Aviva I'm coming in to see her?"

"Is she expecting you?"

"Probably," Colette replied, for Aviva would know very well that she wouldn't be able to leave their conversation last night unfinished.

"Great. We'll see you in a bit, then."

Colette disconnected and picked up the magazine again in disbelief. The bracelet twinkled back at her, even as her eyes clouded over with tears.

When Aviva arrived at work that morning, her assistant, Marilyn, looked up with a smile. "Colette called," she chirped, and Aviva resisted the urge to scream.

"Thanks, Marilyn," she said with a polite smile, breezing past her without asking if Colette had left a message. She couldn't handle thinking about it before she was on at least her second cup of coffee.

Aviva's office was on the seventeenth floor of a high-rise downtown. When she'd graduated from law school in her early twenties, it had initially been her plan to begin a career here as an attorney specializing in copyright law, but it had taken her only a few years to drift back to the life she'd led with her mother before the accident.

The Boston Center for Holocaust Education had been her mother's first child, and Aviva found that when she began to volunteer there she could still feel the ghost of her mother with her. She had expected the constant reminder to hurt, but it had done the opposite; it had been a balm for her pain.

Now, the senior partners knew that Aviva was as dedicated to her hours at the center as she was to her legal work, which meant that they gave her some leeway to volunteer but also that she would probably never make partner. Surprisingly, that was just fine with her, and as a result, she spent nearly as much time volunteering with Colette as she did working with clients.

But apparently, she had never really known Colette at all. How was it that the woman who'd become like a second mother to her had actually been *stealing jewels* for nearly her entire life? The words had spilled out of Colette last night like water from a broken dam, and Aviva hadn't known what to say. She was an attorney, charged with upholding the law. And while she understood that Colette's motives were good, theft was theft, wasn't it? Stealing was a crime, and from the sounds of it, Colette had no plans to stop. Where did that leave Aviva?

Marilyn buzzed Aviva fifteen minutes after she arrived at the office that morning to tell her that Colette was in the waiting area, hoping to speak with her.

"I don't want to see her," Aviva said stiffly.

"That's what she said you'd say," Marilyn replied. "She also said she's brought apples and a nice big hunk of cheddar and is prepared to wait you out."

Aviva closed her eyes and shook her head. Of course Colette would arrive to an ambush with her own personal picnic. "Tell her she'll be waiting for a while."

"Will do," Marilyn chirped. Then, in a lower voice, she added, "Though whatever's going on, Aviva, I'm certain Colette means well. You know that."

"I don't know anything anymore, Marilyn."

She hung up and spent fifteen minutes reading through a contract one of her clients had received the day before, but the words swam before her eyes. Finally, she picked up her phone again. "Marilyn?" she asked when her longtime assistant answered. "Exactly how determined does Colette look?"

"What do you mean?"

"Like is she I've-brought-my-little-French-lunch-to-make-a-point determined? Or I'm-staying-until-security-drags-me-out-of-the-building-kicking-and-screaming determined?"

"Oh, well, the latter if I had to guess," Marilyn replied cheerfully.

Aviva sighed. "No use delaying the inevitable, then. Can you send her in?"

"Sure thing."

Aviva hung up and lowered her forehead to the desk with a groan. That was the position she was in a few seconds later as Marilyn showed Colette in. "She's all yours," Marilyn murmured before backing out and pulling the door closed behind her.

Aviva didn't bother raising her head. "If you've come to apologize—" she began.

"Apologize?" Colette repeated in disbelief. "Aviva, I regret putting you in a difficult position, but I can't say I'm sorry for a lifetime of trying to do some good."

Aviva finally raised her head, narrowing her eyes at Colette, who, despite the vehemence of her tone, looked guilty and nervous. "Some good?" Aviva repeated. "People do good by volunteering for nonprofits or creating scholarship funds. *Not* by becoming criminals."

"People do good in many different ways."

"Not in that way!" Aviva shot back. "Colette, laws exist for a reason! What if everyone in society decided they could just steal from one another whenever they wanted to?"

"That's why my family has always lived by the strictest of codes," Colette said. "I have never once stolen for personal gain."

"Yes, and I'm sure that would hold up in court."

Colette shrugged. "They'd have to arrest me first."

Aviva stared at her like she was crazy. "Have you already forgotten the visit from the detective last night? They're the ones who arrest people, you know."

Colette held up her wrists. "Do you see handcuffs here?"

Aviva exhaled in annoyance. "Not *yet*."

"May I have a seat?" Colette asked. "Or are you going to make me stand the whole time?"

"I don't remember asking you to stay," Aviva muttered, but when Colette just raised an eyebrow, Aviva gestured to one of the chairs across from her desk, and Colette took a few steps forward and sat down, wiggling her narrow hips around a bit until she was settled in the seat. "Comfortable?" Aviva asked without bothering to keep the edge from her voice.

"Very much so," Colette said agreeably. "I've always liked these chairs."

"I'm so happy I can accommodate you." Aviva leaned back in her chair and crossed her arms. She didn't even know where to begin. "So tell me. Stealing. How exactly have you been able to 'do some good'?" She made air quotes around the words.

Colette looked hurt. "I see you don't believe me."

"I believe that *you* believe it," Aviva conceded. "But how much good can you actually do by stealing a few trinkets here and there?"

"They're hardly trinkets."

"Fine, then—baubles? What would you call them?"

"I'd call them more than thirty million dollars' worth of jewels that have gone to charity over the years, straight from the wrists, necks, fingers, and pockets of cruel people," Colette said, sitting up a little straighter in her chair and looking Aviva right in the eye.

Aviva felt her jaw fall open. "Thirty *million*?" she repeated, aware that her voice had gone up an octave. "Please tell me you're joking."

Colette shrugged. "It's been a long career, dear."

Aviva stared at her for a long time, trying to put the pieces together. If Colette was telling her the truth, she was surely one of the most successful jewel thieves in America—not to mention someone whose illegal activities would land her in prison for the rest of her life if she was caught. It put Aviva in a terrible position. "Colette," she finally said, trying to stay calm, "if you have really stolen thirty million dollars in jewels over the years, you're in a huge amount of trouble."

"If they can pin anything on me. Which they won't be able to. I'm very careful."

Aviva could feel a headache coming on. "Colette . . ."

"Yes?"

"I mean . . . Again, assuming that you're not exaggerating, how much good have you really been able to do, balanced with the amount of risk you've taken?"

"Ah," Colette said, sitting back in her chair. She seemed to be considering something.

"What is it?" Aviva finally asked when Colette still hadn't spoken.

"I never told your mother," Colette said slowly, "because I always worried that she wouldn't understand."

"Understand *what*?"

"Aviva, I suppose it's time you know that it was stolen jewels that funded the opening of the Holocaust center."

Aviva blinked at Colette rapidly, trying to process what the woman was saying.

"You look a bit like you're having a stroke," Colette said mildly.

"I'm sorry, but I could have sworn that you just said the Holocaust center was founded by money that came from illegal criminal activity. The center that my mother dedicated her life to, and that I've worked for since I was a teenager."

"That's right, dear," Colette said calmly. "It's how I continue to fund it, too. It's vital you understand, though, that the only money I've ever funneled to the center comes from avowed Nazis and neo-Nazis. If they're foolish enough to align themselves with such an abhorrent way of thinking, it's only fair to use their money to fund Holocaust remembrance."

"But . . ." Aviva couldn't think of a single thing to say.

"I know it's a lot to absorb. I was up all night worrying about it, thinking about whether to tell you. But then something happened this morning, and it forced my hand. I need to ask you a favor, and I don't feel I can do that without being honest with you."

Aviva felt dazed. "A *favor*? You want me to do you a favor?"

Colette nodded. "Marty came over this morning with some news and—"

"Marty," Aviva interrupted. "Does he know about this? Your career as a thief? Your founding of the Holocaust center with the proceeds from stolen jewels?" It still didn't feel real.

"Of course he does. I probably should have told you sooner, too. And there will be plenty of time to talk about this later, dear, but for now, I need your help." Colette took a deep breath. "You see, there's a bracelet in an exhibit about to open at the Diamond Museum, and—"

"If you think I'm going to lift a finger to help you steal—"

"No, no," Colette said quickly. "I would never ask you to do that. This isn't about taking the bracelet. It's about finding out where it came from."

Aviva narrowed her eyes. "Why?"

"Because it disappeared the same night my sister was kidnapped and murdered."

For the second time this morning, Aviva felt like someone had knocked the wind out of her. "*Murdered*?" When Colette's eyes filled and she nodded, Aviva added, "But you've never even told me you had a sister."

"Yes, well, I did. Her name was Liliane. It's very painful for me to talk about, you see. The last thing my mother ever asked me was to go back for her, to find her." Colette took a deep breath. "I promised her, Aviva. I failed, and I've lived with that for seventy-six years. But if I can find out where the bracelet has been for all these years, maybe, at the very least, I can learn who took it—and who took Liliane."

Aviva gaped at Colette for a moment. The woman felt like a stranger to her now, but she had still been Aviva's rock through thick and thin over the past two decades. Regardless of what she had done, Aviva owed it to her to listen. "You're telling me the truth? This isn't just an elaborate way to get me to stop being mad at you?"

"Dear, I'm not that clever, I assure you." Colette drew a deep breath. "The night my mother was arrested, Liliane was taken through our bedroom window, and she never came home. She was just four years old."

Aviva put a hand over her mouth. "And you have no idea what became of her?"

Colette looked down at her lap. "No, I'm afraid I *do* know. Her body was found floating in the Seine a few days later. You see, Aviva, it's my fault. When the police came that night, I was worried about my mother, and I left Liliane alone. Never did I imagine that she'd be stolen right from our home."

"You were just a child yourself."

"I was fourteen." Colette choked on the last word, which came out wrapped in a sob. "Old enough. I was supposed to protect her."

"Colette, I'm so sorry," Aviva said, standing and reaching for her, but Colette shook her hand away.

"This is the bracelet she had with her, sewn into the lining of her nightgown, the night she was taken." She held up the magazine she'd been clutching since she came in the door, and after one more long look at it, she passed it to Aviva. "When her body was found in the Seine . . . Liliane's nightgown . . . The hem was ripped open. The bracelet was gone."

"Oh, Colette. And now the bracelet is here? In Boston? How can you be certain it's the same one?"

"Because," she said, rolling up her sleeve, "I have the other half."

Aviva leaned forward to stare at the delicate bracelet on Colette's wrist. It was shaped like a pair of flowers, studded with what looked like a hundred diamonds, all of which twinkled in the light.

"Aviva, I need you to go to the Diamond Museum," Colette said. "I need you to talk to the museum director and find out where this bracelet has been all these years. He must know who owns it and where it came from."

"But don't you want to go and ask him about the bracelet yourself?" Aviva asked, confused. Colette had never been one to hand tasks off to others; she was defiantly self-sufficient. But as Colette looked at her, unblinking, realization dawned. "I see. You can't go in case you want to steal the bracelet."

"I hope it doesn't come to that," Colette said. "But you see, I have no legal claim on it. My mother stole it from a German officer in order to return it to her friend, who perished in the Holocaust. So even if we can establish where it has been all these years, I may not be able to claim it through official channels. I might have no choice."

"Colette, I want to help you," Aviva said. "But I can't aid and abet a crime."

"I'm not planning a crime right now, Aviva," Colette said. "I'm trying to find out who betrayed my mother and murdered my little sister. I just need you to go in and explain to the museum director that you do pro bono work with the Boston Center for Holocaust Education and are hoping to feature the bracelet in a newsletter article about jewels lost during the Second World War."

"Why not just be honest?" Aviva asked. "Why not tell him what happened to your sister?"

"You don't think he'd be immediately defensive? Or try to protect the wealthy patron who has shared the jewels with the museum? The rich look out for their own, Aviva, and we know nothing about this O'Mara character or where his allegiances lie."

Aviva groaned. "So you want me to lie to this poor guy?"

"Would it actually *be* a lie if you did write an article for the newsletter?"

"Do we even *have* a newsletter?"

Colette gave her a look. "It goes out electronically to both the Boston center and the sister center in New York. Are you not signed up?"

Aviva rolled her eyes.

Colette sat back. "Look, I know I'm probably the last person you want to help right now. If you aren't comfortable with this . . ."

She let the words hang there. Finally, Aviva sighed. "I'm your family. Let's see what I can find out from the museum director, and we'll go from there."

CHAPTER EIGHT

1942

When Colette came back for the diamond-and-onyx bangle a week after the boy showed her the hiding space, she half expected that it wouldn't be there anymore. After all, she didn't know the boy, and she hadn't seen him since the day he showed her the loose brick in the wall. Had it all been a trick? Had he absconded with the piece and sold it himself? Maybe she'd been too quick to trust a stranger.

The worst part was that it was too risky to check on the bangle right away. What if the German had somehow seen her hide it? She could be walking into a trap.

"What are you doing?" asked her sister, Liliane, on the seventh day she caught Colette staring out the window of the bedroom they shared, her palms pressed to the glass. They lived on the ground floor, which didn't afford the best view of the neighborhood, but she could easily see the front door to the building down the street, the one with the boy's hidden garden.

"Looking for someone."

"Who?" Liliane was four years old now, and she followed Colette around like a shadow. Most of the time Colette didn't mind, but today, she didn't want to explain herself to a child.

"You don't know him," Colette answered impatiently.

"I know everybody you know!" Liliane protested.

"You do not." Finally, Colette turned and bent to her sister. "Liliane, sometimes people have secrets that they don't tell anyone."

Liliane's eyes went wide. "You have a secret from *me*?"

"I have lots of secrets from you," Colette said, but she regretted the words instantly, for Liliane's big green eyes filled with tears.

"But I don't keep any secrets from *you*!" Liliane said indignantly, her lower lip wobbling.

"You're four. What secrets could you possibly have?"

"I don't know!" Liliane shot back, crossing her arms and glaring at her sister. "But if I had any, I'd tell you!"

"Fine." Colette turned back to the window. "I'm looking for a boy, if you must know."

"Well, what is his name?"

"I don't know."

"Well, why are you looking for him if you don't know his name?" Liliane pressed.

Colette clenched her hands into fists. "He has something that belongs to me, okay?"

"What does he have?" Liliane persisted.

Finally, Colette spun around and put her hands on her hips. "Liliane, sometimes you have to leave a person to herself!" She didn't wait for her little sister's reply before striding out of the room.

"Colette!" Liliane called after her, but Colette had had it. It was time to see if the boy had kept his promise.

Outside her apartment building, she scanned the street, and then, satisfied that no one was watching, she hurried across the way to the big green door. She glanced around once more before pushing it open and slipping inside.

The inner courtyard was deserted, just as it had been when she'd been here with the boy the week before. Just as he'd done, she looked up at the building to make sure no one was peering down from one of the windows above, and then she moved quickly to the wall. She reached for the brick, eleven rows up, five across, heart thudding, as she wondered what on earth she'd do if she found the space behind it empty. She couldn't even confront the boy, for she had no idea where he lived.

When she slid the brick out and peered into the wall, she thought for a second that the bracelet had indeed disappeared, for all she could see there was a folded piece of paper. Heart hammering, she reached for it—and realized immediately that it was wrapped around something. She slid the paper out and glanced nervously around once more. Then, she unfolded it and breathed a sigh of relief as the bangle slid into her hand. Not only was it still there, but it appeared that the boy had returned at some point to conceal it even better. Why would he take another risk to help her?

She was about to shove the paper back into the hole when she realized that there was something written on it. She pocketed the bangle and looked at the note, her eyes widening as she read the four short lines.

Comme un port dans la tempête
Elle est mon refuge dans le conflit.
Elle scintille et brille
Comme tous les diamants de Paris.

She stared, her heart thudding. No one had ever written her a poem before, and she could feel herself blushing at the thought that a boy she barely knew had done so now. She read it again and again, a slow smile of disbelief creeping over her face. *Like a port in the storm / She is my shelter in the conflict. / She sparkles and shines / Like all the diamonds in Paris.*

He had signed the note *Tristan*. His parents must have been quite cultured, to have named him after the heroic main character of the Wagner opera she'd seen a few years earlier—though didn't they realize he'd died at the end? Or perhaps they'd named him for the Breton lai "Chevrefoil," which Colette's class had studied last year; it was where the tragic tale of Tristan and Isolde had originated, but in "Chevrefoil," the focus wasn't on Tristan's death, but rather on the love he and Isolde shared, described by the poet as "so true, so pure." Ever since the night she'd gone to the Opéra with Mum, Tristan had been Colette's favorite literary hero, so it felt a bit like fate that a boy with that name would be writing her poetry now.

Folding the note quickly into her pocket beside the bangle, she slid the brick back into place and hurried away.

For the next two days, she kept watch at the window, waiting for Tristan to return to the courtyard. As she stared out through the glass, she repeated the poem softly to herself. "*Comme un port dans la tempête / Elle est mon refuge dans le conflit. / Elle scintille et brille / Comme tous les diamants de Paris.*"

"What're you doing, Colette?" Liliane interrupted at one point. "Mummy says you're acting very odd."

"I'm looking for the boy I told you about."

"But why? You don't even know his name."

"Yes I do. It's Tristan."

"That's a very strange name."

"It's just old-fashioned. Literary." Colette bit her lip. "Anyhow, he wrote something for me, okay?"

Liliane shrugged. "Well, why don't you write something for *him*, then, silly?" Then she bounced away, singing to herself, before Colette could reply.

Write him something in return? Of course. She was no poet. But maybe she didn't need to be. Maybe she just needed to speak from the heart.

She went into her parents' room and pulled a piece of paper and a pen from Papa's desk, bringing them back to her room.

Dearest Tristan, Thank you for your beautiful poem, she wrote. *I wish I was a poet, too, because there are things I would like to say to you. Thank you for keeping my secret safe.* She hesitated, then signed it, *Isolde.* Was that too much? She considered crossing it out, starting again, but anonymity made her brave. In "Chevrefoil," Isolde—sometimes spelled *Iseult*—was the forbidden lover of Tristan, who left verses written on hazelwood for her, and she hoped that he would understand what she was saying—that he had tugged at her heart in a way no one had before, even if it would be impossible for her to be with him right now. In the opera, Tristan and Isolde had both consumed a love potion, and as Colette read her Tristan's poem once more, she felt a bit as if she'd had a sip of one now, too.

Before she could second-guess herself, she tucked the paper into her pocket and hurried out the front door of the apartment. Five minutes later, she had placed her folded note behind the brick.

She gave the bangle to her mother that night, while Mum bathed Liliane.

"Colette, please, you could have been caught!" Mum exclaimed, even as she took the bangle and quickly slipped it into her own pocket.

"But I was not," Colette pointed out.

Tears glistened in Mum's eyes. "My darling, I cannot lose you. Please, I beg of you; no more until after the war."

"You put yourself in danger, too," Colette replied. "I thought that maybe if I helped . . ."

Mum folded her hands, wet from Liliane's bath, around Colette's. "My sweet Colette, it is my job to take such risks, not yours."

Colette held her mother's gaze. "It is my duty as much as it is yours. It is who we both are," she said. Then, she glanced at Liliane and added, "It is who we *all* are."

Liliane smiled up at her from the tub. "*Kyi-kyi-kyi,*" she said softly.

Colette grinned, her heart lifting. Even Liliane understood. They both loved their mother's bedtime stories of their ancestor and the eagle who flew high above him in the forest, protecting him and urging him on to greater adventure. "*Kyi-kyi-kyi,*" Colette replied.

"*Ko-ko-ko!*" Liliane concluded excitedly, splashing water out of the tub.

Mum made a noise in the back of her throat and looked away, but she said no more. The conversation was done and the bangle was in her possession. Colette knew that it would find its way to the underground and that maybe, maybe, it would enable lives to be spared.

Colette returned to the wall two days later and was surprised to find a new note waiting for her.

Dearest Isolde, Tristan had written. *One needn't be a poet to express one's heart. I find that saying what you mean is always the best way to proceed.* Then, beneath those two lines, he had written another rhyming verse.

Elle brille comme le soleil.

Elle risque beaucoup pour redistribuer les richesses.

C'est une héroïne quand personne ne la regarde.

Quand je la vois, je goûte sa gentillesse.

She put a fist to her mouth to cover her smile. *She shines like the sun. / She risks much to redistribute riches.* She shook her head in delighted disbelief; he had used her own words about the bangle in his latest poem! *She is a heroine when no one is watching. / When I see her, I can feel her kindness.*

He could feel her kindness? And he had called her a heroine. Her heart swelled with pride. She vowed that she would do all she could to live up to the brave young woman he believed her to be.

For the next month, Colette felt like herself again, and it was glorious. Stealing from Madame Virlogeux had made her bold; knowing that the proceeds of her theft might do some good in the fight against the Germans had made her proud. Many in Paris had hurried to cozy up with the Germans, betraying their neighbors for a bit of favored treatment, which meant that there were plenty of marks for Colette to choose from.

She stole a diamond ring from a wealthy housewife who had cheerfully denounced her neighbors for using forged ration cards. She lifted a pocket watch from a government functionary who was eagerly working with the Germans to identify unregistered Jews. She took a necklace from a shopkeeper who informed police about an illegal printing press in the building's basement, and she slid a signet ring from the finger of a lawyer active in the Parti

Populaire Français, the fascist and antisemitic political party that had eagerly aligned itself with the Germans.

Colette knew her mother didn't approve of what she was doing, but neither did she turn away when Colette slipped pieces into her hand. She always murmured warnings about their luck running out, but it hadn't happened yet.

Besides, the underground group Mum was working with was doing the most important job in Paris, and Colette desperately wanted to help. They had begun in 1940 by distributing a clandestine newspaper urging resistance, but gradually, their purpose had transformed. Since the mass Jewish roundups in the eleventh arrondissement the previous August, their main focus had become the relocation of Jews to the Free Zone.

Perhaps you and your family should leave Paris, she wrote boldly one day to Tristan. *I can't bear the thought of anything happening to you. I know people who can help you, if you want.*

He replied, *Never fear, my Isolde. We will be safe.*

She had been tempted to leave pieces of jewelry in the wall, too, for safekeeping, but to do so would be to put Tristan in danger, and she couldn't do that. Besides, what if he didn't understand why she felt the need to steal? No, it was better to use the secret spot only to pass messages, and she and Tristan wrote back and forth nearly every day, leaving scraps of paper for each other in the hiding space.

Sometimes she passed him on the street, but though they held each other's gazes and exchanged small, secret smiles, they never spoke. Not only would Colette's father forbid it, but a flirtation between a Jew and a Gentile could easily land them both in trouble if a German or a collaborator spotted them. They were just as star-crossed as the original Tristan and Isolde. It was better to save their deepest thoughts and feelings for paper. Besides, there was something terribly romantic about an epistolary love affair.

One day, the boy wrote five and a half weeks after they'd first met, *I will be able to hold your hand. One day, we will be defined by more than just our religions. One day, all that will matter is that you are you, and I am me, and that will be enough.*

That night, as Liliane slept soundly in the bed they shared, Colette sat at her desk, reading the notes the boy had sent her. *One needn't be a poet to express one's heart,* he had said in one of his first missives. *I find that saying what you mean is always the best way to proceed.*

She took a deep breath. She knew that she was no poet, but mere prose no longer seemed like enough to express how she was beginning to feel. So she wrote line after line, crossing words out here and there, crumpling pieces of paper when the rhythm didn't land right, until she settled on four lines that reflected what was in her heart.

Je pense à ce que ça ferait
Avoir ta main dans la mienne.
Un jour nous traverserons ce qui nous divise.
Tu seras mon roi, et moi, ta reine.

I think of what it would feel like, she had written, *to have your hand in mine. / One day we will cross that which divides us. / You will be my king, and I, your queen.*

She felt bold writing such things, the heroine of her own story at last. She had never had a beau before, but she imagined that this was what it might feel like to fall in love, a slow opening of the heart like cracking a window on a warm spring day to let the sunshine in.

I hope I haven't been too forward, she added at the bottom of the note, *but I think that in times of darkness, we must find a way to be daring, don't you agree? Your Isolde.*

She slipped the poem into the wall the next afternoon, her heart thudding. The poems and the notes had brought her to life in a way she couldn't have imagined, filling her with purpose, reminding her that she was valiant and strong and could change the world. *She is a heroine when no one is watching,* the boy had written.

His words had lit a fire within her, and she vowed to be the girl the boy believed her to be, someone heroic and courageous. What would he think when he read her poem? Would it touch his heart the way his words had touched hers? They were writing their own love story, and how else could it end but happily ever after?

As her family passed a quiet Bastille Day at home that evening, toasting to the resilience of France, she found herself thinking only of Tristan, and wondering where he was, whether he was safe, and how soon she might hear from him again.

CHAPTER NINE

2018

The historic home that housed the Boston Diamond Museum was a soaring, three-story colonial mansion with a small bronze sign out front. Aviva parked a block away and approached the entrance, hyping herself up for a professional pitch to the museum's director, a man named Lucas O'Mara. She still couldn't believe she'd agreed to this.

Squaring her shoulders, she tried the front door but deflated when she found it locked. She shouldn't have been surprised; the exhibit's grand opening wasn't for another two nights, so there was no reason to think it would be open to the public yet. Still, certainly Lucas O'Mara and his team had to be inside, setting up. And she wasn't doing anything wrong, was she? It wasn't as if *she* planned to steal the bracelet, and finding out information wasn't a crime. As Colette had pointed out, there actually *was* a newsletter for the Boston Center for Holocaust Education, and now Aviva was even signed up for it. Colette had apparently already put in a call to Chana Baruch, the director of the center, who also edited the newsletter, asking if Aviva might contribute a piece.

"Chana was thrilled," Colette had chirped on the phone just this morning. "She asked if you could take photos of any Holocaust-related pieces, too."

"Sure, why not," Aviva had deadpanned. "Maybe I could sing and tap-dance on the museum floor while I'm at it."

"Whatever feels right to you, dear," Colette said, refusing to take the bait. "Just make sure you take pictures of the bracelet."

Aviva had rolled her eyes and hung up.

Now, she would just need to figure out how to spin her visit to the diamond museum into a newsletter story, while subtly asking questions about the only piece she cared about. She knocked on the front door, and when there was no answer, she pounded harder.

A moment later, the door swung open, and Aviva found herself face-to-face with a tall, broad-shouldered man with gray-flecked dark hair, a few days of salt-and-pepper stubble, and the greenest eyes she'd ever seen. She recognized him from the About Us section of the museum's website as Lucas O'Mara, though the photo hadn't done him justice. "Can I help you?" he asked, looking down at her. His pale blue T-shirt was streaked with what looked like grease, and his dark jeans were tucked into scuffed work boots. "We're not open to the public yet, I'm afraid."

"I know," Aviva said quickly, casually planting a foot in the doorway, a trick from her early days working in the district attorney's office. It was harder—both physically and mentally—to close a door on someone if that person had already taken a step inside. "I'm Aviva Haskell, and I'm with the Boston Center for Holocaust Education. We have a monthly newsletter with a *vast* readership." Was she overselling it? She cleared her throat. "I was hoping to talk to you about your exhibit for a few minutes. Our members are very interested in jewels that may have come through Europe during the Second World War."

The man looked down at her foot as if he knew she was hiding something. As his gaze traveled up the length of her body to her face, she could feel herself blushing. Was it because he was ridiculously good-looking, or because she was, in fact, up to no good?

"Our PR agency didn't let me know you were coming, Aviva Haskell from the Boston Center for Holocaust Education's newsletter," he said.

"I didn't go through them." Aviva hadn't realized the museum was represented by anyone. She would have looked much less suspicious if she'd gone through the proper channels. "The truth is, I'm a volunteer for the center. I, um, don't want to let the boss down, you know?" Could she sound like any more of an incompetent idiot? "You must be Lucas O'Mara, the director?" She framed it like a question, though she already knew the answer.

"I must be." The man was still staring as if he was trying to read her but couldn't quite pin down the language she was written in. "So after nearly ten years on this same block, and after I've pitched the Boston Center for Holocaust Education about collaborating on our last three twentieth-century European exhibits and haven't gotten a response, you appear out of the blue?"

She silently cursed whoever had ignored O'Mara's overtures in the past. She hesitated and then settled on the truth, or a version of it. "To be honest, I saw the photograph of the diamond bracelet from your upcoming exhibit in *Boston Monthly*, and I was intrigued."

"Were you?"

"It's a beautiful bracelet. I wondered where it had come from."

"Did you?"

"Just out of curiosity, are you planning to answer every one of my statements with a question? Because I could do this all day."

Lucas finally cracked a smile. "Could you?" he asked, but when his smile widened a second later, she realized he was teasing her, and she smiled slightly in return.

"May I see it?" she asked, cutting to the chase. "The bracelet?"

He raised an eyebrow, then stepped aside. "Who am I to stand in the way of a journalistic mission?"

Aviva followed him in and waited as he locked the door behind them, noting as he did so that the display cases lining the hall were all empty. "Don't you need jewels for a jewel exhibit?" she asked as he joined her.

He followed her eyes to the blank spaces. "Ah, you truly are an intrepid reporter."

"Okay, full confession? This is, uh, the first time I've written for the newsletter."

"And what is it you do when you're not penning riveting newsletter features, Ms. Haskell?"

"Call me Aviva. And I'm an attorney."

He arched an eyebrow. "Well, that explains all the questions."

"But I've volunteered for the center for years. My mother was the founding director, so it's a place that means a great deal to me." She cleared her throat. "So, um, the jewels?"

"Ah. Yes, well, once the museum opens, we'll have security guards twenty-four hours a day, along with a rotation of off-duty police officers. But until then, it's just me, so having the pieces in the cases now would be like an invitation to jewel thieves to come and help themselves."

"Right, of course, wouldn't want that, Mr. O'Mara." Aviva swallowed hard and forced herself to maintain eye contact with him. What would he say if he knew that the newly minted attorney for Boston's oldest jewel thief was standing right in front of him?

Fortunately, Lucas was the one to look away first. "Come on. Safe is in the back. And you can call me Lucas."

He led her through a darkened room filled with more empty display cases toward a narrow stairway down a hall at the back of the building. "How long have you worked here, Lucas?" Aviva asked as they walked to the second floor.

"Since the museum opened," Lucas answered, not giving her more. He unlocked the office at the top of the stairs and held the door open for her.

"Have you always been interested in jewels?" she asked as he flicked the light on, illuminating a small space with an antique-looking wooden desk and walls lined with bookshelves. She glanced at the shelf closest to her and was surprised that the volumes weren't about gems; they seemed to be his personal collection, everything from Hemingway to Louise Penny, Fitzgerald to Lisa Scottoline. She ran her fingers along a few of the spines. He had good taste.

"I have," he replied, crossing to open a closet in the back. In it, there were five massive safes built into the wall. They were so large and imposing they looked like bank vaults, but she supposed that was just the kind of security a diamond museum would need. "When I was working at the Boston Museum of Fine Arts, I brought in a traveling exhibit of gems from Amsterdam's Diamant Museum, and the New England Diamond Alliance took notice."

"The New England Diamond Alliance?" Aviva asked, though she already knew what it was; Marty was a member. But it was good to get a witness talking about innocuous things he was comfortable with; it made him an easier nut to crack when the hard questions rolled around. Not that Lucas O'Mara was a hostile witness, she reminded herself.

"A trade group of jewelers and jewel brokers in this part of the country," Lucas explained. "They hired me on to host a rotating collection of exhibits from around the world."

"So there's no permanent collection?" she asked sweetly, though she knew this, too.

Lucas shook his head as he bent to spin the dial of the second safe from the left, his broad shoulders blocking Aviva's view of the numbers. "No. It's why we're not open year-round; we host an exhibit for a month or two, and then I go back to negotiating shows for the year ahead. We rely on the generosity of collectors, who share items for a few months at a time."

The safe popped open, and Lucas reached inside, pulled out a velvet bag, and shut the safe behind him. He turned to Aviva, pulled a handkerchief out of his pocket, and used it to slip the bracelet from the bag and place it into his palm. "Voilà," he said as Aviva stared.

Aviva could feel her heart thudding in recognition. Of course she'd seen a picture of the bracelet the night before, in the magazine Colette had handed her, but seeing it in person—an obvious match to the piece Colette had been wearing—took her breath away. It was hewn of the same delicate filigree attached to a thick rope of gold, had the same narrow golden veins, and had a constellation of diamonds that shone like a twinkling spill of stars. It was clearly a mirror image of Colette's piece. She pulled out her phone and snapped a few pictures. These would have to do for the newsletter.

"Lilies," Lucas said quietly, and Aviva looked up to see that he'd been studying her while she studied the bracelet.

"Pardon?"

"They're lilies, made of diamonds," he said. "Here, do you want to hold it?"

Aviva took the bracelet from him as carefully as she could. It sparkled, even in the pale light of Lucas's office, and it felt heavy in her hand. Did it carry the weight of what it had witnessed? Had it seen what became of Colette's sister? "Where did you come from?" she murmured as she turned the piece side to side, admiring the way the gems caught the light.

"Are you talking to the bracelet?" Lucas asked, sounding amused.

Aviva looked up, feeling foolish. "Er, I was just saying that it's very unique."

"It's one of a kind," Lucas said, his voice suddenly tender, and Aviva had to bite her tongue to stop herself from telling him that no, actually, it was *two* of a kind. "When we mount themed exhibits, like the one we're about to open, we often reach out to collectors who have pieces that fit. In this case, as you probably know, the show that opens Friday features pieces from Europe, handcrafted around the turn of the last century. This piece was made in the 1920s, between the two world wars."

"Fascinating. Who loaned it to the museum?" Aviva asked, trying to keep her tone casual.

Lucas's eyes moved from the bracelet to her face, and he lingered there for a second, like he was still trying to figure something out. "I'm afraid the owner wishes to remain anonymous."

"Off the record," Aviva said, trying a conspiratorial wink, which only earned her a frown of confusion.

Lucas plucked the bracelet from her hand, and she resisted the urge to grab it back. "I'm afraid I can't reveal that."

"Are they from France?" she persisted, knowing immediately that she'd gone too far.

He didn't answer her until after he had slipped the bracelet gently back into the velvet bag, returned it to the safe, and locked the door. "What makes you say that?" he asked, turning back to her.

"Just a guess. It looks like something someone would wear in Paris." Okay, now she just sounded like an idiot.

He stared at her for a moment. "The owner is originally from France, yes," he conceded, not quite an answer, but she knew it was all she was going to get. "Is there anything else?"

She knew she had to somehow salvage this situation. She hadn't been subtle enough in asking about the bracelet, and now he was suspicious. "Uh, blood diamonds!" she blurted out, and the second the words were out of her mouth, she knew it had been the wrong thing to say. She tried to recover. "What I mean is, how do you make sure the newer diamonds in your pieces are ethically sourced? For the newsletter."

Lucas's expression grew even colder. "What on earth does that have to do with the Boston Center for Holocaust Education?"

"Well, I—"

"Look, that's something I take very seriously, okay?" Lucas said. "Diamonds come from the earth itself, and when they're sourced ethically, and cut expertly, they're beautiful and enduring. But when there's blood on the hands of the companies that mine the diamonds, it stains the jewels forever. Yes, some of the older pieces we have were almost certainly mined irresponsibly, but it's important to me—to this museum—to work with the Natural Diamond Council, which ensures that diamonds are now mined both ethically and sustainably going forward. Okay?"

"Right, sure, of course," Aviva said quietly. "I didn't mean to suggest—"

"The council makes sure not only that diamond mining is done correctly, but that it also supports more than ten million people worldwide through things like local employment, taxes, education, and social programs. It's not a perfect system, but it's very important to me to try to play a role in doing right by the people who bring these stones up from the earth."

"I believe you," Aviva said. "This isn't a smear piece, I promise. We're, ah—not really a hard-hitting newsletter."

They stared at each other for a moment, and slowly, Lucas's face relaxed. "I'm sorry," he said. "I didn't mean to get so defensive. I've had a few bad experiences with journalists with ulterior motives."

"I'm not exactly a journalist."

"My experiences with attorneys haven't been much better. Nor have my experiences with people who show up unannounced asking strange questions." He raised his eyebrows at her.

Aviva forced a smile. "I'm just interested in where the pieces of jewelry have come from. I think the ones like the bracelet, the ones that have traveled through decades and across oceans, must have really interesting stories."

"Yes, they do."

"And the truth is, my mom was a Holocaust survivor. She was born in Belgium in 1940 and survived the war there in hiding with her parents." Aviva rarely shared that with people, and she wasn't sure why she was telling him now. "Sometimes I get too emotional when I think about all the things taken from people like her."

"I'm very sorry she went through that. Truly. But I don't have any reason to believe the bracelet was stolen, Aviva." He paused and pulled a business card from his wallet, handing it to her. "Look, our opening night gala is tomorrow. Why don't you come? Bring a date if you want." His gaze flicked to her empty ring finger and back up. "You can get a better sense of what we're doing here, and maybe that will help with your news story."

She pocketed his card. "The bracelet will be on display?"

He smiled slightly. "That's the plan. As someone wise recently pointed out, you do, in fact, need jewels for a jewel exhibit."

She couldn't help but smile. "Then I know just who I'll bring."

Colette had saved Aviva's life. Aviva had never said those words aloud, but she hoped the older woman knew how much it had meant to her that she had stepped in without hesitation when Aviva's mother had died.

Losing your only parent at eighteen was a strange thing. At eighteen, you were legally an adult, so there was no one from the state insisting that you be cared for. But Aviva had still been in high school; how was she supposed to live, never mind survive the grief?

It wasn't the first time she'd been left behind. The difference was that her father—whom she barely remembered—had left by choice when she was three, walking away from her mother and from her because he'd met another woman he wanted to start a family with. She had found him on social media a few years ago, smiling out from a photograph on his daughter Sharlene's Facebook page, sandwiched between his three adult children. "Happy Father's Day to the best dad!" Sharlene had captioned the photo, and Aviva had wanted to throw up.

She had reached out to him just once, and the memory of it still mortified her. It had been the day after her mother had died. She hadn't been able to bring herself to leave the hospital waiting room, for where was there to go? Her mother was here, and her mother was all she had. Her mother's sister, Jan, who Aviva had called when her mother had been brought in the night before, had arrived around nine o'clock in the morning. Jan's eyes were dry, though she had just been informed that her sister was dead. "Time to go home, honey," she had said loudly, like a savior, putting an arm around Aviva as Aviva stood.

"To your home?" Aviva had whimpered, forgetting for a moment that her mother and Jan didn't get along, that she hadn't actually seen her aunt in more than a year, though Jan and her husband Robert lived only fifteen minutes away.

Jan pulled her arm from Aviva's shoulders, like she'd been burned. "Well, no, hon. To yours."

"But . . . I can't be there. Not without my mom," Aviva had said. "My mom's dead," she added, trying the words on for size, though they didn't yet feel real.

Jan's bright smile was performative and didn't reach her eyes. "I think you'll be better off with your house and your things," she'd said. "You know how your uncle Robert is about unannounced company."

Aviva had known then that her aunt and uncle would not be taking her in, and since they were her only living relatives aside from her father and three half sisters she'd never met, she knew exactly where that left her. Alone. Eighteen and completely, utterly by herself.

"I'm going to stay," she said, taking a step back from Jan.

"Here?" Jan glanced around, the phony smile still plastered on her face. "You can't stay here, hon. It's a hospital waiting room."

Aviva sat defiantly down in one of the uncomfortable plastic seats and crossed her arms. "Thanks for coming," she said, refusing to even look at Jan.

Jan stood there for a moment, muttered something about Aviva being ungrateful and rude, and left without another word.

Aviva hadn't realized she was crying until a grandfatherly man who'd been reading a book nearby moved to sit beside her and handed her a tissue. "I couldn't help but overhear about your mother. I'm so sorry," the man said gently. "Is there someone else you can call, dear?"

Aviva racked her brain and came up pitifully empty. "I don't—"

"What about your father?" the man asked, and Aviva found herself nodding.

"I'll call my father," Aviva said, and the man smiled in satisfaction, as if he had solved a complex mystery. That's how Aviva had come to wander, in a daze, to a pay phone, to pick up the well-worn copy of the white pages beneath it, and to look up a man she knew had lived across town for all of these years but had never come to see her.

"Hello?"

She knew his voice the moment he answered the phone, on the third ring, and she was unprepared for how hard the familiarity would hit her. *Daddy*, she wanted to say, even though she knew he'd left her without looking back. Instead, she said, "Um, hi, it's Aviva. Your daughter."

There was silence on the other end for a very long time. "Aviva," he finally said, like it was a foreign word he didn't know.

"My mom died," she blurted out.

More silence. "I'm very sorry to hear that, Aviva." He didn't offer anything more. Had she really expected him to? That after all these years, he'd fling open the doors to his house and invite her in? That he'd be a father once again? She could hear noise in the background, then his muffled voice telling someone that he was on the phone, to give him a minute. When he returned, he spoke more quietly. "Sorry, Aviva. That was one of my daughters."

I'm one of your daughters, she wanted to remind him, but it seemed he had already forgotten. "What am I supposed to do?" she asked, feeling pathetic.

"I'll send you some money if you need it," he said finally. "Is that why you're calling?" That's when she had hung up and promised herself that she would never speak to him again, because what kind of father left in the first place, and then, when given a second chance he didn't deserve, made sure that his daughter knew once and for all that she meant nothing to him?

She'd been sitting alone in the waiting room three hours later when Colette Marceau, one of the longtime volunteers at the Holocaust education center that Aviva's mother ran, had swept in, breathless, her eyes red from crying.

"I just saw the story of your mother's car accident on the news, Aviva," Colette had said, rushing over and wrapping her arms around her. Aviva wasn't that close to Colette, but she knew that the older woman—nearly a generation older than Rachel— was one of her mom's favorite people. On the days Aviva had to stop by the center after school, Colette was the only one who seemed to take a genuine interest in her, asking her questions about school and friends and her plans for college.

"How did you know I'd still be here?" Aviva had asked, not hugging back but not rejecting the hug either. Finally, Colette released her and sat down next to her.

"Because I lost my mother, too, and I remember not wanting to leave the last place I'd been with her. Like there was a piece of her still there. But there wasn't, Aviva. The pieces of her were all already inside me, like the pieces of your mom are for you. You'll carry her with you wherever you go."

Aviva's tears had begun to flow for the first time since the doctor had come out hours before to tell her that her mother had died on the operating table. "How will I do that?" she asked.

"By being yourself," Colette said. "Your mother raised you. She already poured herself into you, into who you are. Just stay true to that path, and she'll be with you always."

Colette put an arm around Aviva as she sobbed, and after a while, she said, "We don't have to leave until you want to, but when you're ready, I'll take you home."

"I don't want to go home." Aviva sniffled. "I can't. Not yet."

Colette didn't look thrown by this in the least. "Of course, Aviva. What I meant is that you are welcome to come home with me."

At this, Aviva had looked up. "With you?"

"For as long as you'd like," Colette said.

"But . . . why?"

"Because I know what it's like when your whole world disappears in an instant. I won't sit here and pretend to understand everything you're feeling, but I do know what loss feels like, and I was fortunate enough to have people offer me a home when I needed one most. It would be my honor to do that for your mother, to do that for you."

Aviva wasn't sure what to make of Colette at that moment; it was the most they'd ever said to each other. "I don't want you to feel obligated just because you and my mom were friends."

"I don't do anything I don't want to do, Aviva." Colette held her gaze. "And I don't make offers I don't mean."

Aviva stared back for a long time, and in Colette's green eyes, she saw strength and determination and the hope that if she could, like Colette, survive the worst, maybe one day she'd be strong enough to stand on her own, too. "Okay. Thank you."

Colette had patted her hand, but she hadn't gotten up, nor had she suggested that Aviva follow her. Instead, she had waited another two hours, quietly, her hand resting on Aviva's, until Aviva had stood on her own and said that maybe she was ready to leave. It was in those two hours, during which Colette had simply allowed her to be, that Aviva understood that caring for someone wasn't about fitting them into spaces that you'd already cut out. It was about allowing them to exist in their own way.

That was why she owed it to Colette to do all she could to find the answers the older woman sought. After more than twenty years of Colette's generosity, maybe she could finally begin to return the favor. She could hardly wait to tell her that she'd be able to see the bracelet for herself the following night.

CHAPTER TEN

1942

I think Colette has a beau," Annabel confided to her friend Hélène Rosman the day after Bastille Day. They were sitting in the parlor of Hélène's apartment near the Jardin May-Picqueray, just a few blocks from Annabel's home, drinking ersatz coffee and discussing the future.

"At a time like this?" Hélène asked, taking a small sip. She was a few years older than Annabel, a slender, statuesque woman with a chic, dark bob and impeccable style, whose wrists and fingers twinkled with the jewels given to her over the years by her husband, Salomon, a diamond merchant who was now forbidden to work due to the mounting Jewish restrictions.

Annabel and Hélène had met less than a year earlier, at a meeting for Le Paon's underground network, but Annabel felt as if she'd known the other woman for much longer than that. They were kindred spirits, the only two mothers in their small group.

"Perhaps I should be worried," Annabel said. "But there's a glow to her, Hélène. She's in love, I think."

Hélène smiled, her expression wistful. "Ah, to be young again."

Annabel sighed. "It's beautiful to watch, but young love makes one reckless, doesn't it? I can't help but worry."

"You've told me what a smart girl she is, Annabel," Hélène said, patting her friend's hand. "She won't do anything rash." She leaned in a bit closer, her eyes twinkling. "Who's the lucky boy, then?"

"A boy named Tristan, it seems. I've found scraps of letters she has started to him. She sits at the desk in her bedroom for hours each night, crossing out her words, and starting over. I've never seen her like this. I'm certain she thinks I don't notice, that she's being discreet."

Hélène laughed softly. "She's not old enough yet to realize that mothers see everything." Annabel had met Hélène's twins, Daniel and Ruth, during a visit to the Rosmans' apartment last month, and she had found them both polite and kind. She worried about them constantly, just as she worried about Hélène and her husband.

"Are you certain you won't let Le Paon help move you to the Free Zone?" Annabel asked now, changing the subject abruptly. It was why she had come, to try once more to convince Hélène to leave Paris. Just the day before, they'd been called to an emergency meeting of the underground group. Le Paon had received a tract in Yiddish from the Jewish Communists, warning that files on thirty thousand Jews had been handed over to the Germans. The report spoke of a possible mass deportation, but Le Paon was skeptical. *They've already done their worst*, he'd said with a frown. *They're more bark than bite.*

How many people could the Germans realistically take, anyhow? Previous warnings of raids had been wildly exaggerated. What reason was there to expect that this roundup would be any different? Still, Annabel felt a sense of foreboding she couldn't explain, and she wished that Hélène would take the danger more seriously. "He has promised to get you false papers, and then—"

"No, Annabel," Hélène said, interrupting. "Salomon and I have discussed it, and we are in agreement. We were not raised to run from our problems."

"My friend," Annabel said, reaching for Hélène's hands and waiting until the other woman looked her in the eye. "There's no shame in doing what you can to protect your family. I wish you'd consider it."

Hélène shook her head and looked away. "Our minds are made up. Besides, Salomon says the war will be over within the year. We must hold on just a little longer."

"I'm afraid he may well be wrong," Annabel said. "Le Paon says—"

"Le Paon means well," Hélène said, interrupting once more, as if she couldn't bear to absorb the logic Annabel was compelled to deliver. "But he is very caught up in the glory of leading an underground group, isn't he? Haven't you seen the way his eyes twinkle with each new tragedy?"

Annabel had to admit this was true, but she didn't interpret Le Paon's zeal quite the same way; he wasn't delighted by the mounting catastrophes but rather energized by them, inspired to do more to help. "I think," Annabel said carefully, "that he simply believes we have a long way to go before dawn."

"Perhaps," Hélène said, and for a moment, the two women sipped in easy silence, Annabel trying hard not to wrinkle her nose at the acrid aftertaste of acorn and chicory with each sip. What she wouldn't give for a real cup of coffee.

"Annabel?" Hélène asked sometime later. "Do you worry about what would happen to Colette and Liliane should you be caught stealing?"

Annabel felt a surge of fear at the question. "Every moment of every day."

"But then, why do you continue to do it?" Hélène asked gently, no judgment in her tone.

"Because," Annabel said, her eyes downcast, "the underground needs money, and I can get it for them. How do I turn my back on that?"

"Don't you see? That is how Salomon and I feel," Hélène said. "As long as we stay here in Paris, we can help. But every decision you and I make shapes the course of our children's lives in ways we can't yet see, doesn't it?"

"There is both exquisite joy and boundless heartache in being a mother," Annabel agreed. "I would do nearly anything to protect my girls, but I cannot abandon my country in its moment of need."

Hélène nodded, tears in her eyes. "If something were to happen to you, though, what would become of them?"

"Roger has no involvement in my activities," Annabel said, trying not to sound bitter. After all, Roger's aversion to helping the underground didn't make him a bad man; it simply made him a cautious one. "He would look out for the girls until I came home, should I be arrested. I also sew pieces of jewelry into the linings of their clothing to protect them."

Hélène raised an eyebrow. "The linings of their clothing?"

Annabel allowed herself a small smile of pride. "I'm stealing more than you can imagine, my friend, new pieces nearly every day. I can't move them right away, for risk of being caught, so I hide them in the hems of their skirts and nightgowns. They are perfect spots for safekeeping, and if the girls ever find themselves in a jam, they'll always have something with which to buy their way out."

"And the girls know of these hidden treasures?"

Annabel nodded. "Even Liliane understands our family's heritage, and she knows never to tell anyone about the jewels unless her life is in danger."

Hélène looked down at her own hands, adorned with three beautiful rings: a wedding band and a diamond solitaire on her left ring finger, and a ring studded with emeralds and diamonds on her right. After a pause, she slid the emerald ring off and held it out to Annabel. "Then in that case, would you keep this ring safe for me, Annabel?"

Annabel looked at the ring and then at her friend. "You'll keep it safe yourself, Hélène."

Hélène's eyes filled with tears as she placed the ring on the table between them and waited for Annabel to take it. "But what if I can't? What if you're right, and the worst is coming? What if staying is a terrible mistake? What if something happens to me or to Salomon? I want the children to have something to remember me by. This was a tenth-anniversary present from Salomon; he designed it himself. Please, Annabel, take it. You'll return it at the end of the war one day, over a real cup of coffee, surrounded by people who don't want to erase my very existence."

"My friend—"

"Sew it into one of your daughters' dresses. And if they need to use it one day to keep themselves safe, I would be proud to know that I'd played a role in protecting them. Jewels are just jewels, Annabel. They mean nothing and everything, all at once. But I have to believe that reason will prevail, and that this will all be over soon."

"God willing," Annabel replied, but then she pushed the ring back across the table and waited until Hélène looked up and met her eye. "I won't take this from you, my friend. Taking it would be an admission that we think something will happen to you. And I don't believe that. I can't. You'll be fine, and so will Salomon and your children."

Hélène looked at the ring for a long time before picking it up and sliding it back onto her right ring finger with a small nod. Then she gently touched the bracelets on her right wrist, intertwined lilies that together formed a butterfly, crafted from hundreds of tiny diamonds and delicate strands of gold filigree. Annabel had never seen Hélène without them.

"You're right," Hélène said, her voice hollow. "I can't part with any of these pieces. They are all a part of me."

"I know," Annabel said. Jewels carried the hopes and dreams of those who had crafted them, given them, worn them, and the twin bracelets were, to Hélène Rosman, a piece of who she was. Annabel understood, too, the urge to carry on as normally as possible, because refusing to be cowed was an act of resistance in and of itself.

The front door of the Rosmans' apartment opened then, and Daniel and Ruth tumbled in, laughing, their heads bent together. They straightened when they spotted Annabel at their table, and they both greeted her with a formal, "*Bonjour*, Madame Marceau."

"Bonjour, Daniel. Bonjour, Ruth. How lovely it is to see you both again." And though the words were true, Annabel also found it painful to see them, for they both sported the yellow stars that marked them as *Juifs*, and the pieces of fabric were a stark reminder of the danger the two children were in all the time. Annabel forced a smile and stood to exchange *bises* with the children. "I really should be heading home," she said.

Hélène stood, too, and embraced her. "Thank you for these moments of commiseration, Annabel," she said. "They give me hope."

"They do the same for me," Annabel said. She smiled once more at the children and then turned back to Hélène. "I'll call on you next week."

"*Au revoir*," Hélène said, returning the smile as she opened the door for Annabel. "I'll see you soon."

"God willing, my friend," Annabel said, but she couldn't shake the heavy feeling that settled over her as Hélène closed the door behind her, leaving Annabel alone in the hall.

CHAPTER ELEVEN

2018

Aviva rang Colette's doorbell at 9:00 a.m. on the dot, as if she'd been waiting in the driveway until the exact moment it would be appropriate to show up.

"I'm up most mornings before six, dear," Colette said after she and Aviva had hugged hello and they were walking down the hall to her kitchen. "You could have come earlier."

Aviva yawned and Colette noticed the dark circles under her eyes. "I almost called you last night, actually, but I figured you might be asleep."

Colette harumphed, because back when Aviva had lived with her after Rachel's death some twenty years earlier, they had stayed up to all hours, watching old black-and-white movies, escaping to worlds that were less painful than the one they inhabited. "What makes you think I was sleeping?" Colette asked tartly.

Aviva bit her lip. "Um . . ."

"You can say it. You think I'm old."

"I would never say that." Aviva looked uncomfortable.

Colette cracked a smile. "Fine, you win. I was asleep on the couch before nine. I think my movie-marathon days are in the past." She could still close her eyes on the sofa sometimes and imagine the shape of Aviva there beside her, breathing in and out in the darkness, her face illuminated as she disappeared to Casablanca with Humphrey Bogart or to St. Louis with Judy Garland.

"Do you think you could manage one more late night?" Aviva asked as Colette put a kettle on to boil and scooped grinds into her French press. It was the only way she made coffee, dark and smooth and strong.

Colette's heart thudded, for she suspected that this had to do with the reemergence of the bracelet into the world. "Are we going clubbing?" she asked lightly.

Aviva laughed. "Clubbing?"

The kettle was ready, and Colette removed it from the heat and poured it into the French press, drawing a deep breath in as the scent of coffee filled the kitchen. "I was a regular at Studio 54, I'll have you know," she said. She'd been in her late forties when the disco opened in 1977, but many of the celebrities who came to be associated with the club were older than she. It also became a popular hangout for people obsessed with social climbing. The dance floor there throbbed with some two thousand guests each night, and Colette loved getting lost among them, looking for marks she had researched in advance, slipping bracelets and watches from the wrists of people who would assume they'd lost them, and then checking into the Drake Hotel before the sun came up.

"Sure, Studio 54," Aviva said, smiling at Colette, who simply shrugged. Even Aviva, who knew her too well to underestimate her, saw her as nothing more than an old woman who couldn't possibly have led an exciting life before she came along. "No, I wasn't thinking clubbing. I was thinking maybe an invitation to the opening night of the exhibit at the Diamond Museum."

Colette dropped the spoon she was holding, sending it clattering to the floor. As she bent to pick it up, waving off Aviva's help, she blinked a few times, hard, trying to get control of herself and of her shaking hands. By the time she straightened and began to stir the coffee grinds in the French press, she was trembling only a little. "So you've been there?" she asked, keeping her voice even.

"Colette," Aviva said, "I saw the bracelet."

Colette forced herself to continue through the motions of making Aviva's coffee. She slowly depressed the plunger knob, watching the black liquid clarify through the glass. "I see." She busied herself with plucking two mugs from the cabinet and pouring the coffee so that she wouldn't have to meet Aviva's gaze. "Was anyone at the museum able to tell you where the bracelet came from?"

Aviva retrieved cream from the refrigerator, poured a long drizzle into her coffee, and stirred. "Only that the owner is from France. I met with the museum director, who wasn't very forthcoming. Apparently he's not a fan of people showing up asking awkward questions."

"Yes, well, he's going to have to get used to it," Colette said.

Aviva peered at Colette suspiciously over the rim of her mug. "You can't steal it, Colette." The girl could apparently read minds now. "Not from a museum. Not from a man who seemed decent and kind."

"I wouldn't really be taking it from him," Colette said, hedging.

"But Lucas would be on the hook for it," Aviva said.

"Lucas?" Colette asked. "You're already on a first-name basis?" That boded poorly, too, as did the way Aviva's cheeks got just a bit pinker at the question.

"He invited us to the opening tonight," Aviva said, recovering. "I thought it might be an opportunity for you to get a look at the bracelet and to ask some questions. They'll sound less suspicious coming from you than from me."

"Because I'm an old lady?" Colette asked sweetly, taking a sip of her bitter coffee.

"*Because* I've already told him I'm writing an article about the exhibit," Aviva corrected. "But if you don't want to go . . ."

"Of course I do," Colette said firmly, forcing herself to take another sip of her coffee. She would need all the stamina she could muster. "What time do we leave?"

Aviva left after finishing her cup of coffee, perhaps sensing that Colette desperately needed some time to herself. And Colette did need that, of course, but instead of using it to get ahold of her runaway emotions, she spent it getting even more worked up as she googled the name of the museum director. Perhaps she would have to come clean about why the bracelet meant so much to her if she had any hope of learning its secrets. First, though, she needed to know who she was dealing with. Where did O'Mara's loyalties lie?

But an online search turned up only a handful of glowing profiles of Lucas O'Mara—some featuring photographs. Colette could see how he'd made the typically unflappable Aviva blush, what with that square jaw and deep green eyes.

Fine, she thought with some annoyance as she closed a window including yet another image of the handsome museum director. *Let's see what skeletons are hiding in your closet.* But after entering his name into all the databases she had access to, including the ones that would tell her if he had ever been arrested for a crime or named in a lawsuit, she still came up empty. Surely it wasn't possible that the man was clean as a whistle. Perhaps he just excelled at covering his tracks.

Finally, she called Marty. "What do you know about the man who runs the Diamond Museum?" she asked.

"Good morning to you, too, Colette," Marty said, sounding amused. "Lucas O'Mara?"

"Yes." She didn't have time for pleasantries; this was too important. "Do you know him?"

"We've met a handful of times, yes. Nice boy."

"He's in his forties, Marty."

"That's still a child to you and me."

Colette couldn't argue with that. She could be O'Mara's mother, maybe even his grandmother. "So who's he in bed with? The Irish mob? The Italians? A European jewel-fencing ring?"

Marty laughed. "Last I checked, his only allegiance was to his daughter."

"His daughter?"

"Mindy or Millie or something like that. Off to college now, I think. The mom died a few years ago, when the daughter was in high school."

"Oh." That stopped Colette in her tracks. A widower who had been raising a daughter alone? She couldn't steal from someone from whom life had already stolen so much. Her heart sank.

"He's aboveboard, kiddo," Marty said, an apology in his voice. He knew exactly what she'd been asking, and that he'd just thrown up an impassable roadblock. "Though I do think the amount of pomade he uses in his hair borders on criminal."

Colette laughed, despite herself. "Marty?" she asked after a moment. "What do I do if I can't take the bracelet back?"

"You want me to give O'Mara a call? Jeweler to jeweler?" Marty asked, and Colette almost dropped the phone.

"Absolutely not!" She'd sounded sharper than intended. "What I meant to say is that Aviva is taking me to the exhibition's opening tonight. I can speak with him myself. I'd appreciate if you could continue to keep my confidence."

"Of course." Marty hesitated. "Are you all right, Colette? I mean, with the bracelet turning up after all these years . . ."

"Certainly," Colette snapped, resenting the implication that she was *ever* anything less than fully in control. "Goodbye, Marty."

"Good luck tonight, kid." He sounded sad as he hung up.

Colette set her phone on the counter and stared at it for a few minutes, wishing it could tell her what to do. She felt antsy, itchy, her fingers twitching of their own accord as if they wanted to be anywhere but here. She clasped her hands to still them, but she could feel it, the urge in her bones to steal.

Her mother had spent so much of her short life trying to do good for others, as had her uncle Leo, who took her in after the war. Colette had tried so hard to follow in the footsteps they laid out for her, to honor her family tradition, but did it all come to naught if she failed at this most important test? Over the years, she had anonymously funded women's shelters, drug rehab centers, food banks, children's hospitals, cancer research, nursing homes for Holocaust survivors, and programs for foster children who had aged out of the system. She knew she had brought honor to her family, though she had failed at producing an heir to carry on. Robin Hood's centuries-old bloodline would die with her, but perhaps it was time.

Colette had always believed if she had a chance to get some form of justice for her murdered sister, it would make up, in part, for her failings. She would give anything to turn the clock back to that terrible night, but that was impossible. Would finding out where the bracelet had been all these years clear her conscience, or just make things more complicated?

Colette shook her head. Enough of that. The only way to cure a mood like this was to steal.

Colette had had her eye on Franklin Gorich for more than a year now. She rarely stole from someone without months and months of research, to ensure that she was taking only from people who deserved it, whose choices had led them to the kind of justice her family had spent hundreds of years dispensing.

She hadn't planned to move so soon, but she knew exactly where she would find Gorich this time of day, and at the very least, he'd be wearing his Rolex Submariner. Today called for the salve of a satisfying score, and Gorich was the closest target.

Gorich had been indicted last year for his role in a scheme to bribe a United States senator. The senator had been convicted of taking payoffs in exchange for approving the sale of arms to a foreign government, but Gorich, the go-between, had cut a deal in exchange for his testimony. He had gone back to his job at the high-powered PR firm he co-owned without missing a beat, and the firm had lost only a handful of clients as a result.

As Colette waited outside his office building on Beacon Street, her fingers itched with purpose. He'd almost certainly be emerging soon for the short walk over to Parker's, where he ordered the clam chowder and baked Boston scrod every Tuesday.

He exited his building at 11:50 on the dot, briefcase in his left hand, cell phone in his right. He was so busy FaceTiming with someone on his screen that he crossed a lane of traffic without realizing he'd nearly been hit. Colette rolled her eyes as she followed a half block behind him, but she had to admit, his complete lack of regard for anyone else made her task exponentially easier.

At the restaurant, he sat at his usual table near the window, not bothering to lower either his voice or the volume of his phone's speaker. Colette sat at the bar and pretended to read a menu while Gorich ordered his usual and then—as she knew he would—got up from the table to use the bathroom. She, too, excused herself from the bar with a polite smile, telling the bartender she'd be back in a moment after she'd used the ladies' room. She sauntered slowly toward the restrooms and was just in time to collide with Gorich as he made his way back to his table a moment later, once again absorbed in a loud FaceTime call on his phone.

The force of their collision knocked the phone out of his hands, and, as she had counted on, his annoyance about having his call interrupted outweighed everything else. "Watch it, lady," he barked in her general direction, without bothering to give her even a glance, which worked out just fine, because it meant he didn't see her at all as she feigned a momentary injury, which allowed her to lean on him long enough to slip the Rolex from his wrist as he bent to retrieve his phone.

"Some old lady ran into me," he explained to the person on his phone screen as he brushed her off and returned to his seat. Colette shook her head, pocketed his Rolex, continued to the restroom, and returned to the bar a few moments later for a glass of white wine. Leaving early would only make her look suspicious, but what thief in her right mind would stay for a drink after ripping off a ten-thousand-dollar watch?

She observed from the bar as Gorich continued to talk on his phone, berated his waitress, and finally departed after leaving the same meager tip he always did—five dollars on a $55 meal. Colette, on the other hand, left a 25 percent tip on a $16 tab and slipped out, her head down. As usual, her age acted as a cloak of invisibility. Later, when Gorich realized his watch was gone, not a soul would remember her face. She had her doubts that he would even put two and two together and realize the old lady from outside the bathroom might have been the one to relieve him of his property.

In the meantime, though, the proceeds from his watch would fund another few months of assistance for families who used the Boston Food Pantry—and Colette could hold off the nightmares for another evening or two before they came roaring back in, like they always did.

CHAPTER TWELVE

1942

Early in the morning on the 16th of July, Annabel awoke to the sounds of squealing brakes and slamming doors outside. She sat up with a start. "Roger? Darling, wake up, something's happening."

Beside her, her husband stirred. "It's nothing, Annabel," he mumbled into his pillow. "Go back to sleep. It's the middle of the night."

Annabel hesitated. Perhaps he was right. But after Le Paon's warnings two days earlier, she had to see for herself that nothing was amiss, so she got out of bed and crept to the window. She pulled open the corner of the blackout curtain and peered out, putting a hand over her mouth to stifle a scream when she realized what she was seeing.

On the street outside sat three large police trucks. The building across the way teemed with French police officers, and as Annabel watched, six of them emerged dragging a family of four—two parents and two little boys—toward one of the vehicles. The mother and father both wore jackets with yellow stars stitched on, and they were each carrying a valise. As the mother helped the children—both of whom were around Liliane's age—into the back of one of the big trucks, a police officer shoved her so hard that she fell to the ground. When her husband cried out and reached down to help her, he earned himself a blow on the head from a rifle butt.

A moment later, another family wearing the yellow star—two parents, an elderly grandmother, and a toddler—were shoved from the same building and up into the truck by another batch of policemen.

"Roger," Annabel said again, turning from the window. "There's a roundup happening outside. They're taking children."

"Children?" Roger repeatedly groggily, sitting up in bed. "But that doesn't make sense. The Germans are after able-bodied adults who can labor for the Reich."

The vehicle filled with Annabel's neighbors was pulling away now, and down the block, she could see another Jewish family meeting the same fate. "Roger, I don't think this is about free labor."

Roger got out of bed and crossed to stand behind Annabel. Together, they peered out the window in stunned silence.

"What could they want with the children?" Roger asked after a while, his voice hollow.

The only answer Annabel could think of was one she didn't dare say aloud. "I have to warn Hélène," she said softly, turning from the window.

"They won't be on the deportation list," he said confidently. "The Rosmans are French, aren't they? Certainly they're only taking foreigners."

"I don't think it matters tonight."

"You'll go see them first thing in the morning," he said after a moment. "It's too dangerous right now—you can't be caught breaking curfew. Not with police about."

"I know," Annabel said, biting her lip to stop herself from crying. Never had she felt more helpless; she had stolen at least two hundred pieces since the start of the Occupation and had funneled an enormous amount of money to the underground, but at this moment, none of that mattered at all. It hadn't been enough to save her neighbors, and it meant nothing if Hélène Rosman and her family had been arrested, too.

Sleep was impossible, so Roger and Annabel sat in the parlor, holding hands and listening to the sounds of distant screams, as they waited for the sun to rise on a city that would never be the same.

On the morning of July 16, Colette awoke into a nightmare.

When she made her way, yawning, out of the bedroom she shared with Liliane, she found her parents side by side on the sofa, staring at the wall and looking as if they hadn't slept a wink.

"Mum, Papa, what is it?" she asked, her stomach suddenly knotted with fear. Had Papa discovered that Colette had been stealing? Were they waiting for her to awaken so that they could punish her and forbid her from working with the underground?

But that wasn't it at all. "It seems there has been another Jewish roundup overnight, my darling," Annabel said, her voice breaking. "We watched from the window as several families were taken."

"Families?" Colette repeated blankly.

"They were taking everyone," Papa said when her mother seemed unable to reply. "Children, too."

"But . . . why?" Colette asked, her heart beginning to thud. If they were taking whole families, did that mean Tristan was in danger? She bit her lip before she spoke rashly. Though she suspected her mother knew she had a beau—could she call him that?—she was certain neither of her parents would guess the boy was Jewish. Her Tristan was just as forbidden as Isolde's lover had been.

"I'm going to see what I can find out in just a little while," Mum replied. "I'm not sure the police are done with the raids, and it might not be safe yet."

"The *French* police?" Colette asked.

Her mother's eyes were watery as she focused on Colette. "I'm afraid so."

Colette's heart sank like a stone. "But if the French police were carrying out the raids," she said slowly, "that would mean they were able to arrest far more people, far more quickly, than if Germans were going door-to-door." When her mother nodded, the knots in Colette's stomach tightened. But suddenly, she realized that they had someone they could call to find out more. "Papa, what about Monsieur Charpentier?"

Her father looked at her blankly. "Who?"

"The policeman who used to be your student," she said. "He always says hello to Liliane and me, remember?" He was a relatively young man, perhaps in his twenties, and seemed pleasant enough, though his face reminded Colette of a weasel's. "Perhaps he knows something."

Papa's forehead creased in concentration, and then his expression cleared. "Ah, yes, Guillaume Charpentier. 'Charpentier, Charpentier, *celui aux grandes oreilles*,' his schoolmates used to say."

It bothered her that her father was so casual about his students mocking the size of the young man's ears, but that didn't matter now. "Could you call on him, Papa? Perhaps he can tell you what has happened."

With a grunt, her father nodded, and twenty minutes later, he had left the apartment in search of news. He returned quickly to report that Monsieur Charpentier hadn't yet come home from the police prefecture, and that his wife knew nothing about the raids.

"I'll go see the Rosmans," said Mum. "And then we'll speak with Le Paon. I'll return with news."

While she waited for her mother to come home, Colette slipped across the street to the hiding place she shared with Tristan, but when she moved the brick aside, she found only her own poem there, still untouched. That meant nothing, she reminded herself. She had left it just two days ago; he simply hadn't had time to claim it yet. He would be here. But a lump of fear rose in her throat, threatening to choke her. What if something had happened to him?

Two hours later, Mum returned, her face ashen. "Thousands of Jews have been taken across the city," she reported, her voice trembling. "They are being held in the Vél' d'Hiv."

Colette had been to the cycling stadium near the Eiffel Tower; the place wasn't large at all. "Thousands? But surely they can't fit."

"Any word on Madame Rosman?" Papa asked, coming into the room.

Mum shook her head, her eyes filling. "There was no answer at their door, and no one I've spoken with has heard from them. I fear they've been seized."

"Or maybe they fled," Papa said. "Perhaps they were warned."

"They *were* warned," Mum said in a small voice. "Le Paon warned her, and I tried to persuade her, but Hélène didn't believe they were at risk."

A silence fell over the three of them as the truth sank in. "Mum?" Colette said a moment later, summoning her courage.

"There is a boy named Tristan who lives in our neighborhood. How would I find out if something happened to him?"

Papa frowned and looked at Mum. "Who is this Tristan?"

"A boy Colette has been writing letters to," Mum said. She turned back to Colette, concern in her eyes. "Darling, only Jews were taken last night."

"I know," Colette mumbled.

Papa turned to peer at her suspiciously, and when she didn't say anything, his eyebrows slowly rose. "Colette, is this boy you've been writing letters to *Jewish*?"

"He is." She looked down at her toes.

"Colette!"

"You don't understand, Papa!"

He took a step toward her. "Relationships with Jews are forbidden by the Germans! Do you know what could happen to you—to your mother, to our family—if your activities brought suspicion to our door?"

Colette cowered for a second before the boy's words came back to her. *She is a heroine . . . She is brave.* She took a deep breath and pulled herself up to her full height, forcing herself to look her father in the eye. "I have only followed my heart, Papa. If we let them tell us how to feel, we've already lost, haven't we? Tristan and his family are no different than we are. We're all humans, we're all—"

Her father interrupted her by slapping her hard across the face, and then, muttering under his breath, he strode out of the room. Colette put her hand to her burning cheek, too shocked to feel the sting, as Mum approached with tears in her eyes and wrapped Colette in a hug.

"I will do what I can to find this boy," Mum promised.

But as Colette cried into her mother's shoulder, she knew it was already a lost cause. She didn't know Tristan's last name or where, exactly, he lived. How on earth could her mother find out a thing?

For two days after the mass roundups, Colette drifted around the apartment, aimless and bereft. She returned to the wall four times, hoping against hope that Tristan had returned to read her poem, but each day, her piece of paper still sat there, undisturbed.

"You're sad," Liliane said in a small voice as Colette put her to bed two nights after the arrests. "Why?"

Mum was out at a meeting of her underground organization, and Papa was so upset that Colette had been corresponding with a Jewish boy that he refused to talk with her. She was glad for the excuse to close herself away in the bedroom she shared with her sister.

"Some very bad things are happening in Paris right now," Colette said.

"Is that why Mummy is sad, too?"

Colette sighed. "Her friends were taken away by the police. And so was the boy I write letters to, I think."

"Why did the police take them away?" Liliane bit her lip. "Aren't policemen supposed to help people?"

Colette didn't know how to answer that. Of course a four-year-old should trust the police; what if she got lost and needed help? Wasn't that the job of the authorities, to keep them all safe? But the fact that the French police had been complicit in the roundups changed everything, didn't it? That wasn't something she could explain to Liliane, though, so she settled for saying, "If something bad happens, Liliane, it's okay to ask a policeman for help. You can trust them."

Liliane scrunched her face like she was considering Colette's words, and finally she nodded, her features relaxing. "Okay," she agreed. "Will you tell me a story, Colette?"

"I don't feel much like stories tonight, Liliane."

"Please?" Liliane pleaded. "At least tell me the one about Robin Hood! And his eagle!"

"You've heard that one a hundred times." But Colette couldn't help but smile slightly. As depleted and hopeless as she felt, she knew she'd find solace in the familiar tale, too.

"*S'te plait?* Pretty please?"

"Very well." Colette smoothed Liliane's curls from her forehead and leaned in to begin the tale they both knew by heart. "Once upon a time in Wentbridge . . ."

"Near Mummy's forest!" said Liliane.

"Yes, exactly," Colette said with a smile. And as she began to tell the familiar tale of their ancestor, she was reminded that even in the darkest of times, one could make a difference. She could feel hope rising up within her like a zeppelin, and as she finished the story ten minutes later and tucked the sheets around her drowsy sister, she knew that she must redouble her efforts to steal for the underground, for the sooner the Germans were driven out of France, the better the chances that her Tristan—and her mother's friends—would return.

"*Kyi-kyi-kyi,*" she finished the story, as she always did.

"*Kyi-kyi-kyi,*" Liliane replied with a yawn, already drifting off to sleep.

"*Ko-ko-ko,*" Colette concluded softly, and Liliane's eyelids fluttered.

"I love you, Colette," Liliane murmured, and Colette bent to place a kiss on her forehead.

"I love you, too," she said. "Sweet dreams, little sister."

CHAPTER THIRTEEN

2018

The opening of the European Masters of the Twentieth Century exhibit at the Diamond Museum was just the kind of event Colette was accustomed to attending for the purposes of jewel theft, so to arrive dressed to the nines without that sort of mission left her feeling unmoored.

"You okay?" Aviva asked as they walked up to the museum's front door, which stood open, the sound of classical music drifting out into a crisp Boston evening.

"Honestly?" Colette said. "Not at all."

"We don't have to go in," Aviva said.

Colette took a deep breath. "Of course we do." She took Aviva's hand, drawing strength from the contact, and together, they walked through the door.

The party was already in full swing, jewel brokers and wealthy donors sporting formal wear and sipping champagne. Waiters circulated with trays of hors d'oeuvres while a string trio played Bach in the corner.

But for the dozen security cameras blinking overhead and the two black-clad guards circling the room, this would be a jewel thief's dream. Everyone in the room appeared to have pulled out the very best from their personal collections; diamonds, emeralds, and sapphires glittered everywhere in big, gaudy pieces made to show off. Around the room, behind the security glass of display cases, sat another two dozen twinkling pieces, each bathed in its own pool of light. There was a ring that featured the largest ruby Colette had ever seen, a diamond choker with a sapphire heart, and even a silver-filigree tiara dotted with hundreds of tiny diamonds and amethysts.

Colette and Aviva took a quick lap around the room, peering into each case, and when they had finished, Colette felt exhausted. "Where's the bracelet?" she asked Aviva.

Aviva opened her mouth to answer, but her reply was cut off by the arrival of a handsome young man a bit older than Aviva, with gray-streaked dark hair, a square, stubbled jaw, and eyes the color of sunlit emeralds. Colette recognized him immediately from his photographs.

"Aviva, I'm glad you came," he said in a deep voice that matched his rugged good looks, and Colette had to put a hand over her mouth to cover the laugh that bubbled up within her. No wonder Aviva had acted so evasive the day before when Colette had asked her about the museum. In person, Lucas O'Mara looked like a *Superman*-era Christopher Reeve.

"Lucas," Aviva said, her tone even but a flush creeping up her cheeks, "this is my friend Colette."

Lucas turned his gaze on her, and Colette searched his eyes, trying to figure him out. She prided herself on her ability to read people, a trick of the trade she'd had to develop long ago. She had expected someone with a guarded expression, his smile hiding some level of cunning. But he didn't look like that at all.

"Colette," he said warmly. "Welcome. I'm Lucas O'Mara, the museum director."

"So I hear," Colette said. Lucas's apparent kindness had thrown her, as had the way he felt instantly familiar. "Forgive me, but have we met before, Mr. O'Mara?"

Lucas searched her face. "I don't think so. Are you in the industry, Ms. . . . ?"

"Colette is fine," she said quickly, because it was bad enough that he knew her first name.

"Colette, then. And please, call me Lucas." He smiled at her, and she liked him even more for treating her like an equal, not like an old lady, as so many others did.

"Lucas," Aviva cut in, "we know you're busy and don't want to keep you. But Colette and I were wondering if you might be able to point us toward the bracelet you showed me yesterday. The one from the magazine."

He smiled again, revealing deep dimples. Of course he had dimples. "Certainly. Right this way."

Aviva gave Colette a wide-eyed look as they trailed after Lucas, who strode purposefully through the crowd, smiling and greeting guests as he led them toward the entrance to another exhibit room. Colette was still trying to puzzle out where she'd seen him before. She tended to stay away from gatherings of jewelers, so as not to become a familiar face, but perhaps she'd spotted him in passing at Marty's shop, or at one of the handful of other stores where she occasionally sold pieces.

"Here we are, ladies," Lucas said, gesturing into the back room. "The exhibit's cornerstone pieces are on display in here. You'll find your bracelet along the back wall."

Your bracelet. The words felt oddly accurate, and Colette did her best not to react.

"Thanks, Lucas," Aviva said, and Colette noticed that the two held each other's gazes a beat longer than necessary. "Ready?" Aviva asked after Lucas finally smiled at them and walked away to mingle.

But Colette barely heard her, for the couple standing near the back wall of the secondary exhibit room had shifted, revealing the jewelry case behind them. Even from across the room, she could see it, glimmering in the light, beckoning to her like a beacon to the past. Hardly aware of Aviva hurrying after her, she floated across the room.

And then, at once, she was standing in front of the bracelet she had last seen seventy-six years ago, separated from it by merely a barrier of glass. It was just as she remembered it, a near mirror image of the bracelet she'd kept all these years, its diamonds beckoning to her.

She could feel the low moan that rose from her throat but hadn't realized she had grown unsteady on her feet until Aviva put a hand on her back to brace her. "It's all right," Aviva whispered in her ear.

"No," Colette said softly, staring at the bracelet. "It isn't all right at all." To the bracelet, she whispered, "Where have you been? What did you see?" The couple who'd been admiring the piece gave her a pitying look; she knew she sounded like an old bat who'd lost her marbles.

But one thing was certain: if the bracelet could talk, it would tell Colette where it had come from—and what had happened to her sister all those years ago. Now that the bracelet was here, really here, she was more determined than ever to find the answers—and to reunite the butterfly wing with its other half at last. It was one final thing she could do for her mother and sister. Perhaps then she could find some peace.

"Colette?" The museum director had appeared at her side at some point, and when he touched her elbow, she jumped, snapping out of her reverie. "Are you all right, ma'am?"

She looked into his eyes and there was something about the penetrating concern in his gaze that reached inside her, to a well of grief she hadn't known was so deep. Before she knew it, she was crying, tears sliding down her cheeks.

"To whom does this bracelet belong?" she asked, and something changed in his expression then, a shuttering, like the curtains had been drawn and they were standing in darkness.

"The owner has asked to remain anonymous," he said, the warmth gone from his tone.

"Please. I must know." Her voice was raspy with desperation.

"I'm afraid I can't break that confidence." He was watching her now, appraising her, and she felt unsettled by it. And then, all at once, she could see it; there was something personal about the bracelet to him, and he was bothered that she was asking questions.

"Is it *yours*, Lucas?"

He blinked a few times. "Why would you ask that?"

She stared at him, trying to see through him. But the uneasy silence dragged on too long, and Aviva broke it by stepping between them, clearing her throat, and saying something to Lucas in a voice too low for Colette to hear.

Lucas gave her one last look, a strange blend of defensiveness and pity, before mumbling an excuse and drifting away.

"Colette?" Aviva asked after a moment of silence.

"The museum director," she said flatly, not taking her eyes off the bracelet. "Lucas O'Mara. He's hiding something."

And then, while the party swirled around her, Colette simply stood and stared, her palms pressed to the glass, studying the piece of her past she had been certain was gone forever.

Aviva sat at her desk the next morning, her head pounding. She'd been rattled by seeing the normally unflappable Colette so anguished and insisted upon sleeping in Colette's guest room, just in case Colette needed her. But Colette hadn't said a word, hadn't even mustered an objection to Aviva's attempts to dote on her, and that worried Aviva as much as anything else. Never in the whole time Aviva had known the older woman had Colette allowed herself to be taken care of, but last night, she'd stared mutely at the wall while Aviva laid out pajamas for her, put toothpaste on her toothbrush, and tucked her into bed like a small child.

Aviva hadn't slept a wink, and around 5:00 a.m., she had pulled out her laptop, settled in at the kitchen counter, and, yawning, wrote up a quick article for the center's newsletter. She'd emailed it, along with a few photographs of the bracelet, to Chana just before seven o'clock.

Thirty minutes later, Colette had shuffled into the kitchen, hair mussed and dark circles under her eyes, looking as if she hadn't had a moment of sleep, either. "How about I take the day off and hang out with you?" Aviva had offered as she made coffee.

Colette looked at her dully. "Thank you, dear, but I'd prefer to be alone."

Now, Aviva gazed at the monitor of her office computer, frowning. Colette's words last night about Lucas O'Mara knowing something had rattled her. Colette was never wrong about people.

She bit her lip as she opened a search window and typed in Lucas's name. She had looked him up to get a sense of him before she turned up at the gallery, but her search had been cursory: a standard background check to verify that he didn't have a criminal record, and a Google search to see if his name had popped up in any articles related to the jewels he featured at the museum.

Now, though, she was looking for something different. The bracelet couldn't actually be *his*, as Colette had suggested. Colette had placed its worth at hundreds of thousands of dollars, and knowing that he had raised a daughter by himself, she couldn't imagine he had saved enough to buy it on his museum salary.

So what possibilities did that leave? Could the bracelet belong to someone in Lucas's family? She puzzled that over for a moment as she pulled up a LexisNexis search through her law firm's account. She found a few articles that seemed to match, including a decades-old paragraph in the *Patriot Ledger* listing him as the valedictorian of his graduating class at Pembroke South High School, and noting that he was the grandson of a well-known South Shore contractor. Could the construction business have been lucrative enough that Lucas's grandfather had been the one to purchase the bracelet, maybe for his wife, years ago? Could it have been passed along to Lucas when his grandparents had passed away?

Or perhaps Aviva was looking at the wrong branch of his family. Marty had mentioned that Lucas was widowed; could it be that his defensiveness over the bracelet wasn't because he was hiding something, but because it was connected to his deceased wife's family? Certainly that would make a person feel guarded, wouldn't it?

She searched for Lucas's name in the *Globe*'s wedding announcements and felt a bit guilty when she found him. He had married a woman named Vanessa Verdier twenty years before in a ceremony at the Peabody Country Club.

Verdier. It was a French name. Could his wife's family have come from France, bringing the bracelet with them? Aviva leaned forward, her gut telling her she was on the right track.

Another search found an obituary for Vanessa Verdier O'Mara, who had died four years earlier of ovarian cancer, leaving behind her husband, Lucas, and their daughter, Millie. Aviva felt a surge of sadness as she recalled how it had felt to lose her own mother; she wasn't sure how old Millie had been when Vanessa died, but losing one's mother was devastating at any age.

The obituary said that Vanessa had been predeceased by her parents, Jean-Paul and Carole Verdier, and her grandmother, Odile Verdier, but that her grandfather, Hubert Verdier, was still alive. A quick search found an article about Hubert Verdier from just two months ago in the *Patriot Ledger*, a fluff piece about South Shore centenarians. Verdier, it seemed, was residing in an assisted-living home in Braintree and had just turned 102—and in the article, the writer called him "an immigrant from Paris who arrived in the Boston area just after the Second World War."

Aviva stared at the screen. Was this her answer? Could Hubert Verdier—the grandfather of Lucas O'Mara's dead wife—have brought the bracelet from France to the United States? And if so, had he also been involved in taking it, along with Colette's sister?

Before she could stop herself, she picked up her phone and dialed Lucas's number. "Hi, it's Aviva from the Boston Center for Holocaust Education," she said when he answered, her words falling out in a tumble.

"Hello, Aviva from the Boston Center for Holocaust Education." Lucas's deep voice sounded amused. "Have you called with more hard-hitting questions about blood diamonds?"

She cleared her throat. "Actually, I'm hoping that the question I have will be easy for you. It's just that, well, I'm afraid I might be crossing a line."

"Is that so?" He sounded guarded now.

"Look, I'm going to be honest with you," she said. "I have a personal interest in the bracelet—the one we talked about in your exhibit—because I have reason to believe it was stolen during the Holocaust."

"What?" His tone sounded both defensive and confused. "But that can't be true."

"I'm afraid it is." When he said no more, she took a deep breath and blurted out, "It belongs to your wife's grandfather, doesn't it? Hubert Verdier?"

He didn't speak for so long that she was afraid he'd hung up.

"Lucas?" she prompted.

"You looked up my family?" He sounded angry.

She felt a surge of guilt. "I just did a search of old newspaper articles—and I found the one about South Shore centenarians. It said that your wife's grandfather had come from Paris, and that he's one hundred and two years old now, which would have made him twenty-six years old the summer the bracelet was stolen."

"You're not accusing Hubert of stealing the bracelet, are you?" he asked finally, his tone defensive. "He's had it for as long as I've known him. I'm sure he didn't take it from anyone. He's not that kind of man."

"Of course," Aviva said instantly, her heart suddenly racing. "But if he bought it from someone before he left France, perhaps he can give us a lead that will help track its provenance . . ."

"As you so astutely pointed out, Aviva, he's one hundred and two. I doubt very much that he's going to be able to remember where he purchased a bracelet seventy years ago."

"Anything would help. Please. It's vital we find out."

She could hear him breathing.

"Lucas, you work with jewels," she said when the quiet had gone on too long. "You understand how much they can mean to people. The bracelet in your exhibit once belonged to a Jewish family in Paris. It was taken from them by the German who sent them away to their deaths—and then it disappeared." It wasn't the whole truth, but it would do. "I'm just trying to find some answers." She held her breath. "Please, I'd really like to speak with him."

"Look, Aviva, the story you're telling is tragic, and I'm very sorry to hear it—I really am. My own grandparents lived through the Second World War, too, and I know how painful those memories are. But Hubert has had two heart attacks in the last year. I understand that it's important to you to get some answers, but I can't agree to that at the risk of his health."

"Please. This is just a chat to see what he knows. It's very important to Colette."

"The woman you brought to the opening?"

"The people the bracelet was stolen from were friends of her family." She bit her lip. Again, it wasn't the full story, but it wasn't as if she could casually tell him that she suspected Hubert Verdier of murder.

Lucas went silent again. "Just a conversation?" he said finally.

"Just a conversation."

"Fine, but only if I go with you."

"You don't need to do that. I wouldn't want to inconvenience you."

"Aviva, you seem like a nice person, but Hubert isn't in the best of health, and I'm concerned about him getting agitated. I think he'll be more relaxed if I'm there. In any case, it's the only way I'll agree to this."

"Right, of course." Though it might be harder to ask Verdier tough questions in front of Lucas, perhaps it would also make the older man comfortable enough to be honest.

Lucas exhaled. "Look, if the bracelet was stolen, and Hubert knows something, I agree that you and your friend Colette deserve to know. Just go easy on him, okay?"

"I promise. Thank you." But as Aviva hung up after arranging to meet Lucas in a few hours at Verdier's assisted-living home, she wondered if that promise would be impossible to keep. If Hubert Verdier was somehow involved in the death of Colette's sister, he had given up his right to be left in peace a long time ago.

CHAPTER FOURTEEN

1942

In the days following the roundups of July 16 and 17, the details trickled in through Mum's contacts in the underground. In all, more than thirteen thousand Jews had been seized across the city. More than eight thousand were being held in the Vélodrome d'Hiver, the small covered stadium near the Eiffel Tower, while single adults and couples without children had already been sent on to the Drancy transit camp on the edge of town.

"We must do something," Colette's mother had said again and again since the morning after the raid, and she looked as if she hadn't slept a wink. While Papa quickly went back to business as usual, heading into his office to prepare for the commencement of a new school year, Mum disappeared for hours at a time, coming back with her eyes bloodshot.

"There was a transport yesterday," Mum said on the fourth morning after the roundups, as Colette and Liliane ate breakfast in silence. Papa had already gone to work; Mum was floating around in a fog, opening and closing drawers like she couldn't remember what she was looking for.

"A transport?" Colette repeated.

Mum turned and looked at her, her gaze unfocused. "Probably a thousand people, moved out of the Vél' d'Hiv on buses. I stood there and watched, Colette. It was terrible. The children were crying, there were elderly people who could barely walk . . ." Her voice trailed off.

"But . . . where were they taking them? Surely those who are very young or very old aren't able to work for Germany."

Her mother's eyes filled. "I don't know, Colette. I can't imagine that the Germans have anything good in mind for them. And at the rate they were moving them, my guess is that they intend for the entire population of the Vél' d'Hiv to be sent away in the next few days."

"Did you see Madame Rosman there?" Colette asked. "Or her family?"

"I was too far away. But perhaps if there's another transport today . . ."

"Let's go," Colette said instantly. When her mother looked at her blankly, she added, "Perhaps we can find Tristan, too."

Mum rubbed her temples. "I can't bring you and Liliane there, darling. The conditions inside . . ." Mum trailed off and drew a ragged breath. "One of the members of Le Paon's group went in as a Red Cross volunteer, and she says there's barely room to move. People are desperate. They can't breathe. They're starving. Illness is spreading like wildfire, children are screaming, and there are no toilet facilities. It's hell on earth, and it's so crowded that it's impossible to know *who's* in there."

"Certainly those guarding the Vél' d'Hiv must have a list," Colette said, her voice small.

Mum shook her head sadly. "It's chaos. Le Paon is doing his best to find the names of those who were arrested, but so far, we have nothing, no confirmation that the Rosmans were taken at all. But they aren't in their apartment, and Madame Rosman wouldn't have fled without leaving word." She hesitated and added, "I persuaded the Rosmans' concierge to let me into their apartment yesterday, Colette. Everything is gone, all of Madame Rosman's beautiful jewels, all of Monsieur Rosman's diamonds."

Colette bowed her head. "Please," she said. "Let's try the Vél' d'Hiv today. Maybe we'll find them this time. Maybe we can catch sight of them if they're scheduled for a transport."

Mum looked like she was wavering. "Very well. But you and your sister must stay by my side the whole time, and if I have any sense that we're in danger, we'll leave immediately. Do you understand?"

Colette nodded vigorously. "Thank you, Mum."

"Don't thank me yet, Colette," her mother replied, tears shining once more in her eyes. "I suspect that what we see there today will haunt us for the rest of our lives."

The scene at the Vél' d'Hiv was even worse than Colette had imagined. When she, Mum, and Liliane drew closer to the stadium, a fifteen-minute walk from the La Motte-Picquet metro station, the odor of sweat, fear, and human waste greeted them several blocks before they caught sight of the building.

"How can the police treat the arrestees like this?" Colette asked as they drew closer and the smell grew more pungent. "It's inhumane."

"The world has gone mad," Mum said, her voice hushed with horror. "*Kyi-kyi-kyi*," she murmured as they rounded the final corner, the high brick façade coming into view.

"*Kyi-kyi-kyi*," Liliane replied, equally subdued. Though the little girl was too young to understand everything that was happening, it was clear she could sense the distress of her mother and sister.

"*Ko-ko-ko*," Colette concluded their familiar call, and as she caught Mum's eye, she wondered if her mother was thinking, as was she, about the way that descendants of Robin Hood had always been called to great adventure, in service of a greater good. Both she and Mum had been doing their best to make a difference here in Paris, but the din rising from the stadium ahead of them, clearly the voices of thousands, was a signal that their work had been largely for naught.

There were five large buses idling outside the Vél' d'Hiv's gates as they approached the front of the stadium, and Colette's stomach twisted in knots. "You were right," she said. "They're taking them somewhere."

"It looks that way." Mum hesitated and then bent to Liliane. "I want you to stay right here, holding Colette's hand, my love." Then she straightened and said to Colette, "Don't move. I'm going to see what I can find out."

Before Colette could protest, her mother had slipped away and was hurrying across the street to the front of the massive building. Colette watched as Mum exchanged words with one of the French policemen out front, a baby-faced fellow who looked hardly older than Colette. His cheeks were pink, and he was shaking his head vehemently as Mum peppered him with questions.

Just then, an older officer emerged from the stadium, his uniform pristine, his scowl plainly visible even from across the street. He barked something at Mum, shooing her away from the door, and when she tried to stand her ground, he shoved her, hard, sending her stumbling backward. Colette gasped and took a step forward out of instinct, but her mother looked up, met Colette's gaze, and shook her head firmly. Colette forced herself to stay still, holding Liliane's hand, though every molecule in her body wanted to cross the street to defend her mother.

Mum said something to the senior officer, who sneered and raised his hand as if to strike her, lowering it a second later with a look of disgust. He muttered something back, and Mum nodded and hurried back across the street to her daughters.

"Are you all right?" Colette asked, rushing forward as Mum rejoined them.

"I'm fine," Mum said, her words clipped. "They're about to move some of the prisoners."

No sooner had she said the words than the large doors of the Vél' d'Hiv opened, and people began to shuffle out toward the buses, surrounded by a line of police officers, who looked on menacingly and shoved those who weren't moving quickly enough. Colette's mouth went dry with panic and grief; it was clear that the prisoners had suffered greatly during their four days in captivity. Most looked weak, disheveled, and frightened. Children's nightclothes were filthy; many adults wore fine dresses and smart trousers that had been soiled and torn. Some were crying; some looked dazed; some appeared stoic, others furious.

Colette, Liliane, and their mother inched closer, made anonymous now by the crowd of Parisians around them who had stopped to watch the show. Some looked on with pity, some reached out to touch the hands of prisoners, perhaps to give those poor souls the comfort of human contact, but others sneered and barked out taunts and slurs.

"Go back to where you came from, Jew!" yelled a teenage boy who'd shuffled up beside Colette, and before she could stop herself, she spun into him and kneed him hard in the groin. When he grunted and doubled over in pain, she feigned embarrassment.

"I'm so very sorry!" she exclaimed sweetly. "I must have stumbled. Perhaps you'd be better off if you went back to where *you* came from."

"Colette," her mother hissed through gritted teeth. "This is not the time to make a scene."

Colette glanced at the boy, whose face was still red, and who was backing away from her and muttering obscenities under his breath. "I'm sorry, Mum," she said. "But I don't think *I* was the one making the scene."

Her mother sighed and shook her head. A second later, she gasped and started forward. "Hélène!"

Colette followed her mother's gaze to the middle-aged woman who'd just emerged from the Vél' d'Hiv. She was tall and thin with bobbed hair that hung limp and lifeless. There were dark circles under her eyes, her face was pale, and her violet dress was filthy. She looked up dully at the sound of her name.

"Hélène!" Mum cried again, her tone anguished. Colette clutched Liliane's hand and followed her mother forward.

"Mum, be careful," Colette said as they drew closer to the prisoners. "Please, you'll get yourself in trouble."

But Mum ignored her. "Hélène!" she said for a third time, and the woman finally found Mum in the crowd, her eyes glassy and unfocused.

"Hélène, where are your children?" Mum called out desperately. "And your husband? Aren't they with you?"

Madame Rosman shook her head. "The children—taken yesterday," she called back quickly, which earned her a shove from a police officer. "Salomon—" Her voice broke. "Already gone."

"Keep moving," the officer barked.

"Gone?" Mum repeated, her voice hoarse with emotion.

"The Germans," Madame Rosman choked out.

"Mum, please, you must be careful," Colette said, still holding tight to a trembling Liliane with her right hand while trying to pull her mother back with her left. Mum shook her off and surged forward.

"Here," Madame Rosman said as the nearest officer turned his attention momentarily to a wailing toddler shuffling forward alone. She tripped forward, seeming to lose her balance, but at the last second, she tossed something small to Mum, and Colette realized that the stumble hadn't been an accident. "It's all I have," Madame Rosman said, locking eyes with Mum. "Sewn into the hem of my dress, just like you said. They took everything else."

"Even the bracelets?" Mum asked.

"All of it." Her tone was hollow. "It's why they came for us." She was almost to the bus door. "An officer named Möckel. He knew exactly who we were."

"I'll find the bracelets, Hélène!" Mum called out, her voice shaking. "I'll find them, and you'll have them back when you return. I promise."

Madame Rosman gave a small nod as she was shoved onto the bus, where she disappeared from view. Mum finally allowed Colette to pull her back into the crowd surging behind them. A moment later, the bus's door slammed closed and it pulled away.

"She'll be back, Mum," Colette said, trying to project a confidence she didn't feel. She'd been searching faces desperately for any sign of Tristan, but so far, she hadn't seen him. Her heart felt heavy. "The Rosmans will be back."

"Will they?" Mum asked as the bus turned the corner and disappeared from their view. The next bus in line was pulling out now, puffs of black choking from its tailpipe, the wails of its passengers muted by the closed windows.

"Of course they will," Colette said, but as the third bus pulled away and she locked eyes with a crying child whose face and palms were pressed to the glass, the last of her hope went up like the exhaust from the bus, disappearing into the air. "Won't they?"

"I don't know," Mum said, her voice hushed, and then the street fell quiet, the last of the buses gone, the passengers on their way out of the city they'd thought was safe, the city they'd called home, the city that had turned its back on them. "I honestly don't know, my darling."

Then, and only then, did Colette begin to cry.

"*Kyi-kyi-kyi*," Liliane said, her voice small. She squeezed Colette's hand more tightly. "*Kyi-kyi-kyi*, Colette. Say the thing, Colette. It'll make you feel better."

"*Ko-ko-ko*," Colette replied through her tears, not feeling better at all.

Three weeks later, Le Paon obtained a list of all the Jews arrested in the roundup, and among them were all four members of the Rosman family, as well as a boy named Tristan Berousek, aged fifteen, who lived on the rue Ternaux, just a five-minute walk from Colette's apartment. Tristan was such an unusual name in France that when her mother gently gave her the news, the last of Colette's hope vanished. The boy who wrote her beautiful poems had undoubtedly been taken, along with more than thirteen thousand others on that terrible summer's day.

Those who'd been held in the Vél' d'Hiv had been moved over the course of four days to camps in the department of Le Loiret, including Pithiviers and Beaune-la-Rolande. In the first week of August, mothers had been separated from their crying children and been sent east, most to the camp of Auschwitz; the children had followed on trains a week or two later.

Years later, Colette would learn that of the more than seventy-six thousand Jews sent from across France to death camps during the war, a mere twenty-five hundred survived. A decade after the war, Colette was heartbroken to find Tristan Berousek's name on a list of deportees who had died at Auschwitz in the autumn of 1942.

She had known him for barely a month, but his memory was with her always, along with the memory of losing her mother and sister, all of them reminders of why it was so important to remember the past and try to do good in the world, for in doing so, it might just be possible to turn back the darkness.

CHAPTER FIFTEEN

2018

Colette was absently washing dishes at the sink early in the afternoon when the doorbell rang.

She set the mug she'd been scrubbing in the drying rack, turned off the water, and wiped her hands on a dish towel, then she walked to the front door in a fog. She was unsurprised to see Aviva standing at the door, but she wasn't prepared for what the younger woman had come to tell her.

"Colette," Aviva said, something dark and disturbing and unreadable in her expression. Her voice cracked as she said, "I've found him."

Colette's throat went dry. "Found who?"

"The man who owns the bracelet." Aviva pulled a piece of paper out of her purse. "Does the name Hubert Verdier ring a bell?"

Colette searched her memory and put a hand over her mouth as realization dawned. "*Verdier*," she whispered. "There was a policeman named Verdier in my old neighborhood. Aviva, I spoke with him once, after the war . . ." She trailed off. Remembering the brief interaction so long ago felt like recalling a scene from someone else's life. "Could it be the same man?"

Colette peered down at the printout Aviva handed her. On it was a grainy newspaper photo of an old man staring right at the camera from a slouched position in a recliner, his eyes rheumy, his expression annoyed, defiant, righteous. Colette searched his face for evidence of someone she remembered, but all she could see was an old, hunched man. "Hubert Verdier," Colette repeated in disbelief.

"He's the grandfather of Lucas O'Mara's wife, the one who died a few years ago," Aviva said. "Lucas told me today that the bracelet is Verdier's, and that he lived in Paris during the Second World War. It could be him, Colette."

Colette stared at the photograph, trying to see evil beneath the wrinkles and jowls and white hair. "Did you take my sister?" Colette whispered to the man in the image.

Aviva put a hand on Colette's back, trying to comfort her, but the contact only made Colette jump. She couldn't bring herself to look away from the man's face, though. If he had been the man to murder Liliane, it was desperately unfair that he had lived more than a century while her sister had died at the age of four. And had she really been face-to-face with her mother's betrayer, her sister's murderer, all those years before? Had she let a killer simply walk away because she'd been too foolish to see him for what he was? Colette didn't know she was crying until she felt a tear slip down her right cheek. "We have to go talk to him, Aviva."

Aviva exhaled slowly. "I know. I've already called Lucas."

Colette stared at Aviva. "He's fine with us confronting his family member about the fact that he's quite possibly a murderer?"

"I didn't exactly tell him about what happened to your sister. Just that the bracelet had once belonged to friends of your family, and you wanted to understand where it had been all these years."

"I see." Colette frowned. "You and Lucas seem to be getting awfully close."

Aviva's gaze slid away. "He's kind, Colette. He was genuinely upset when I mentioned that the bracelet had disappeared during the Holocaust. He offered to come with us to speak with Verdier."

"He's coming *with* us?"

"It was the only way we were going to get in to see him, Colette," Aviva said with a sigh. "Maybe I should be the one to question Verdier. It might be hard for you. And if it turns out he's not the same man . . ."

"I'll be all right, Aviva. Please stop treating me like a fragile old lady."

"Fine," Aviva said. "But I'm calling Marty, too."

"Marty? Whatever for?"

"Because he'd do anything to protect you. You know that, right?"

Colette's cheeks felt warm. "Well, of course. I'd do anything for him, too. He's my oldest friend."

Aviva smiled. "You really don't see it?"

"See what?"

"He's in love with you, Colette."

"What are you talking about?" Colette said in astonishment. "Marty is like a brother to me."

Aviva rolled her eyes. "Believe me, the way he looks at you is extremely unbrotherly."

Colette's cheeks felt warm. "That can't possibly be true."

"For someone so good at reading people," Aviva said with a smile, "you're awfully blind when it comes to yourself."

The assisted-living facility in Braintree was painted a cheery yellow with white trim, like a lemony cake piped with buttercream. It sat on the corner of a busy intersection near South Shore Plaza, which Colette had driven through a dozen times in the last year alone.

She had been searching her memory since Aviva said the name Verdier, but she couldn't reconcile the vague image of a pasty, shifty-eyed man with the reality that he might have killed her sister. She could barely remember their interaction, but she recalled that he'd struck her as a greedy, manipulative man, not a killer. Had she somehow read him incorrectly? How could she forgive herself if it turned out that she'd had the chance to bring him to justice more than seventy years before—and had foolishly missed it?

Then again, maybe this wasn't the same man. Verdier wasn't a terribly uncommon name in France. But his ownership of the bracelet couldn't be coincidence.

Marty met them in the parking lot. "You don't have to go in there," he said, once he'd greeted both Aviva and Colette with kisses on the cheek. "I can take care of it for you."

Colette searched his face for evidence that he might secretly be in love with her, but he looked just the same as he always did. What on earth was Aviva talking about?

"Thank you, but I have waited nearly eighty years for answers," Colette replied, surprised by the steeliness in her own voice. "If this is the monster who murdered Liliane, I can handle it. I owe it to my family."

Aviva and Marty exchanged looks. "Of course," Marty said, reaching for her hand and giving it a squeeze. "But we're right here with you, okay?"

"I appreciate that," she said, looking down at their intertwined fingers and then back up at him. Was it her imagination that he looked flustered as he dropped her hand?

A moment later, they were walking toward the front desk, where, true to his word, Lucas O'Mara was waiting for them, chatting with the receptionist.

"How nice that you could all come!" the woman chirped. "Mr. Verdier doesn't get many visitors anymore, aside from Lucas here, of course." From the way the woman fluttered her eyelashes at him, it was clear that she looked forward to his visits. "Are you family?"

The three of them mumbled noncommittal answers—it wasn't as if they could tell her they were dropping in to ask the old man if he'd murdered a child more than seventy years ago.

The woman jotted four numbers down on a piece of paper, which she handed to Lucas, who accepted it with a smile and a nod. "Today's door code," she said.

"Door code?" Aviva repeated.

"For the memory-care unit," the woman confirmed. "It changes every day."

She beamed at them, and Colette's heart plummeted like a stone. "Memory care?" Of course she shouldn't be surprised; the man was 102 years old, for goodness' sake. But exactly how far gone was he?

In the elevator, Aviva hastily introduced Marty to Lucas, who smiled politely and said, "Yes, I think we've met a few times at New England Diamond Alliance gatherings. Nice to see you again, Mr. Weaver. How do you know Aviva and Colette?"

Marty fixed Lucas with a steely look. "They're both family to me," he said. "I'd do anything for them. And I mean *anything*."

Colette felt her cheeks warm, and Lucas barked out an uneasy laugh.

"Easy, Marty," Aviva murmured.

The elevator pinged, the door opened, and the four of them stepped out. Lucas entered the four-digit code at the door on the fourth floor and held it open for Aviva, Colette, and Marty to enter. Inside, the place was brightly lit and clean, with care workers in teal shirts and nurses in scrubs hurrying around. There was a spacious gathering room just to the right, where *The Price Is Right* played loudly on a large television, entertaining the half-dozen residents who were gathered around. Printed schedules taped to walls announced crafting classes, bingo, and an evening social hour, and Colette shook her head at the unfairness of it all, the fact that this man who may well have destroyed Colette's family was not only still alive after all these years, but apparently accessing all sorts of engaging activities.

They followed Lucas down a series of hallways until they came to a door marked *423*. "Here he is," Lucas said, raising his hand to knock.

At first, there was no response, and Colette wondered whether the monster who'd stolen her life was now one of the glassy-eyed residents watching the Showcase Showdown in the other room. But then Lucas knocked again, more loudly this time, and they could hear a shuffling inside, followed by footsteps.

The door was yanked open a moment later, revealing a hunched, white-haired man with cloudy eyes and a deeply lined face set in a scowl. "What's all the racket?" he asked, and even in those few words, Colette could recognize the edges of a French accent, as unmistakable as her own. It was remarkable that after so many years in another country, the curves of one's mother tongue always remained. She sought in his features the police-man she'd spoken with so many years before, but he looked only like an old man, not familiar at all. His eyes darted from Aviva to Colette to Marty before finally landing on Lucas. "I know you."

"Yes, Hubert, it's me, Lucas. I come to visit you every week. Remember? I'm your granddaughter's husband?"

"I know *that*," Verdier said irritably. "So where's my granddaughter?"

"She's not here, Hubert," Lucas said gently, and Colette and Aviva exchanged concerned glances.

"She never visits me anymore," Verdier grumbled. "Bring her next time, will you?"

Lucas's voice sounded thick with emotion as he replied, "You know what? I'll bring Millie along the next time she's home from college."

"Millie?" Verdier seemed to be searching his memory, and Colette's heart sank further. "In college? But she's just a little girl."

"She's nineteen now, Hubert," Lucas replied lightly. "They grow up in the blink of an eye, don't they?"

Verdier looked troubled. "If you say so." His eyes moved back to the three strangers standing behind Lucas. "You've brought friends."

"Yes, sir. Meet Aviva, Colette, and Marty."

Verdier reached out and shook each of their hands. Colette could feel a tremble running through him, and as their palms touched, she shuddered. Were these the hands that had killed her sister?

Verdier squinted at Marty. "This one's very old."

"Have you looked in the mirror lately, buddy?" Marty shot back, and Colette elbowed him.

"Can we come in for a quick chat, Hubert?" Lucas cut in before Verdier could reply. The old man shrugged, turned his back, and began to shuffle down the hall of his apartment. The four of them followed, Lucas closing the door behind them.

Verdier led them into a room on the left, which was flooded with light from large windows overlooking the parking lot. "Home sweet home," he said wryly, gesturing to a stiff brown couch against the far wall. He lowered himself into one of the two worn recliners on the other side of the room, wincing as he did, and Colette sat gingerly on the couch, Aviva settling on one side of her and Marty on the other. Lucas sat in the other recliner, and the old chair creaked in protest. "Now what is this all about?" Verdier asked.

"Hubert, these folks here would like to ask you a few friendly questions," Lucas said. Colette detected an emphasis on the word *friendly*.

At Hubert's nod, Colette took a deep breath and said as calmly as possible, "We met once, I think, you and I."

Verdier narrowed his eyes at her. "I don't remember that."

"I do. There was a man named Le Paon, who sometimes slipped you bribes for information. He set up a meeting between us."

"Le Paon?" Something in Verdier's eyes flickered and his nostrils flared. As he darted a nervous glance at Lucas, Colette's skin tingled. She'd struck a chord. "I don't know anything about bribes."

"I think you do," Colette replied, trying to keep her tone calm. "But this isn't about bribes."

"Then what is it about?" Verdier replied, shooting another look at Lucas, who was frowning now.

"You were a policeman in Paris during the war?"

"If you say so," Verdier grunted, but Lucas gave Colette a small nod of affirmation, his brow furrowed, and her heart lurched. It had to be the same man she'd met years ago. But did that mean he'd been the one to take the bracelet himself?

"I need to know how you came to have a piece of jewelry that once belonged to my mother," Colette said. "Annabel Marceau." She watched his face for a sign of recognition, but there was nothing. "She lived in the eleventh arrondissement."

He nodded slowly. "The eleventh. Yes. I knew it well."

"And you knew my mother?"

He shook his head. "I didn't say that."

"So how did you get the bracelet that disappeared the night she was arrested in 1942?"

He blinked at her a few times, his expression suddenly shuttering. "I've stolen nothing," he snapped, which made Colette's heart beat a bit faster, because she hadn't mentioned theft. She was about to respond when he barked, "Who told you that?"

"We're very sorry. We didn't mean to insult you," Aviva cut in quickly, her tone as smooth and sweet as honey, and some of the anger seemed to drain from the old man. Lucas's frown had deepened, but he hadn't yet stepped in.

"Yes, well, what's all this about a bracelet?" Verdier asked, his eyes darting to Lucas and then back to Colette. "I don't even know which bracelet you mean."

"The one you gave me for the exhibit at my museum, Hubert," Lucas said, peering at the old man with concern. "The family heirloom with all the diamonds."

Colette held her breath as several emotions flickered across Verdier's face: surprise, guilt, anger. He didn't say anything at first, but his eyes darted nervously to Lucas before coming back to rest on Colette. "I wanted to sell it, but she said she'd never forgive me," he said, his gaze turning suddenly distant. "She wore it like it was nothing, like she didn't notice the value. I think she was showing off."

"Who do you mean, Hubert?" Lucas prompted.

Verdier looked off into the space behind Colette. "She was beautiful, you know. He didn't see it, but she was beautiful and she loved me."

"Your wife?" Colette guessed.

He jerked his head toward her, snapping out of his reverie. "You don't know her!" he barked. "You don't know anything about her!"

"No, of course, you're right, we don't," she said soothingly.

"She *loved* me," he repeated, his voice small.

"Of course she did," Colette said. She was relieved to see his shoulders relax a bit more. Lucas, too, sat back in his chair, though he looked concerned. "And the little girl?" she asked, keeping her voice as light as possible. "Can you remind me what happened to her that night in the summer of 1942?"

Anger flashed across the man's face once more, and he bared his teeth at Colette. "You know perfectly well that we don't talk about that! Who do you think you are?"

"I think it's time we leave Hubert alone," Lucas cut in as he stood up from the low-sunken recliner. He was glaring at Colette now, but she wasn't finished. Verdier had reacted like a guilty man, and she hadn't gotten this close after seventy-six years only to turn away.

"Tell me what happened that night, Mr. Verdier," she said.

"Colette," Lucas said in a warning tone.

But Verdier didn't seem to hear Lucas. Instead, he looked up and met Colette's eye. "You already know."

"But I don't. Please." She could feel herself starting to cry. "Why did you take her? Why did you kill her?"

The man reared back. "You're accusing *me*?"

"But you said—"

"I was a policeman! Doesn't that mean anything to you? I upheld the law!"

"All right," Lucas said firmly, stepping directly in front of Colette, blocking her view of the old man. "It's time to go."

"You killed my sister, didn't you?" Colette cried, tears running down her face, but Lucas was already firmly guiding her out of the room, pushing her away from Verdier and the truth.

"Please, Lucas," Aviva said in a low tone, rushing to Colette's side as Lucas propelled her to the door. "She deserves answers."

"You promised me you'd go easy on him," Lucas snapped at Aviva as Marty appeared at Colette's other side. "And you come here accusing him of *murder*?"

"Lucas, if he did this—" Aviva began.

"He didn't," Lucas shot back. "He may be a lot of things, but he's not a murderer. I can't believe you'd attack him like this."

"But—" Aviva said.

"Out, now," Lucas said firmly. "All of you."

And with that, he opened the door to Hubert Verdier's apartment and practically pushed the three of them into the hall, slamming the door in their faces.

When Colette looked up at Aviva, the girl's face was red. "Lucas is right," Aviva said softly. "We pushed too far."

"But he was about to tell us—" Colette began, but Aviva cut her off.

"He wasn't," she said, pulling Colette into a hug. Marty put a hand on Colette's back as Aviva continued. "He was frantic. He was losing his grip on reality. He's had two heart attacks already, Lucas said. We can't give him a third."

"But—" Colette protested.

"I'll talk to Lucas, okay?" Aviva stepped back and exchanged a concerned look with Marty. "We'll come back. But if he's the man who took your sister, we need him to live long enough to tell us what he did—and to face justice after all these years."

Colette nodded, the fight draining out of her, leaving her exhausted. Marty put his arm around her shoulders, and in silence, the three of them made their way back to the elevator, every step taking them further away from the truth.

CHAPTER SIXTEEN

1942

Four weeks after the Vél' d'Hiv roundup, Hélène Rosman's twin bracelets resurfaced on the wrist of Octavie Duplessis, a former prostitute who was proudly sharing a bed with Sturm- bannführer Gustav Möckel, the German whose name Hélène had mentioned outside the stadium before she disappeared.

According to Le Paon's sources, the Rosmans hadn't been on the initial list for deportation, likely due to Monsieur Ros- man's role as the longtime diamond broker to several French government officials, but then word of their large jewelry collection had reached Möckel, the deputy advisor for Jewish affairs at the German embassy, one of the architects of the massive roundup. Rumor had it that he was an avid jewelry collector, and that the addition of the Rosmans to the roundup list was almost certainly because of his hunger to get his hands on their valuable pieces.

In other words, the bracelets that now gleamed on the wrist of Möckel's French mistress had been the reason the Rosmans were now in German custody. Annabel simply couldn't let that stand.

No, she had to take the bracelets back, despite the risks. She knew better than to make theft personal, of course, and she was being reckless by doing so now. But it was all she could do to fight back on behalf of her friend, and so she ignored the warning bells that rang in her head as she slipped into the bustling Brasserie Roye on the rue des Lombards, where she'd been told she could find Möckel and Mademoiselle Duplessis.

It made Annabel's blood boil to see what had become of the place. The owner, a flabby man named Maurice Grivel, had been obsequious before the war, always fawning at the table of some socialite or another, but he'd seemed harmless enough.

But then, after Paris's occupation in the summer of 1940, something changed. Grivel had turned his toadying toward the invaders and, almost overnight, had transformed his brasserie into a place of warm welcome for the Germans. While other restaurant owners struggled to survive, cobbling together meals from ingredients that grew ever sparser, Monsieur Grivel was thriving. And although Annabel was not here for Monsieur Grivel tonight, she couldn't help but pause in the entryway to glower at him across the room.

Focus, Annabel, she thought, shaking herself. Emotion had no place in a thief's arsenal; her anger would need to take a back seat for the next few minutes. She reminded herself of her mission as she melted into the crowd. *Be invisible. Take the bracelets. Disappear into the night.* Monsieur Grivel would get his due when the war ended.

"Mademoiselle? Une coupe de champagne?" a passing waiter asked, his gaze flat with distaste. Ordinarily, Annabel would be worried that she'd been singled out and spoken to, but she knew, from sliding in and out of the Brasserie Roye over the last month, that this was just the way the place did business. She was a woman alone, thus she was presumed to have come here in hopes of an advantageous liaison with a German officer. Perhaps it was easier to fall into bed with a Nazi if one could somehow drown out the voice of conscience.

She declined the offer of bubbly and glided across the room, her gaze cast downward. People sometimes remembered you when they'd looked you in the eye; they tended to forget when you were simply a shadow.

Conversations wafted by in German as she passed. *Sieg. Neue Regelungen. Die überlegene Rasse.* Victory. New regulations. The superior race. She knew only a little German, but these were words she'd come to recognize, tossed casually around in conversation at places like this, as men in crisp uniforms patted one another's backs and bragged of their exploits, pompously giving voice to secrets that surely weren't meant to be mentioned in public. Annabel knew that more than once, the underground had been able to warn members of imminent arrest thanks to spies in places like this, people who pretended to be fawning German sympathizers but would blow the place up in a heartbeat if given the opportunity.

But tonight, Annabel saw no friendly faces—just Germans and French police, whose eager embrace of the occupiers made Annabel physically ill.

She moved toward the back of the restaurant, head down, until at last she spotted her target. The vile *collaboratrice horizontale*—the name the French called those who went to bed with the enemy— stood in the corner, clutching a coupe of champagne with her right hand and the arm of her German lover with her left. The interlocked bracelets twinkled like crystalline snowdrops on her left wrist, too close to the sleeve of the German, so Annabel would need a distraction to induce the woman into pulling her arm away.

Annabel quickly assessed the layout of the crowd, settling on a younger German officer, barely old enough to shave, who stood just two paces away from Mademoiselle Duplessis, his back turned to her, clutching a beer and deep in conversation with a French woman whose cleavage spilled dangerously from her blouse.

Annabel knew just what she needed to do. Head still down, she slid toward the young officer, angling her right shoulder into his before quickly ducking away in the opposite direction. Beer sloshed from his glass as he regained his footing by taking a step backward, directly onto the feet of Mademoiselle Duplessis, who shrieked dramatically. Möckel turned to see the cause of her distress, advancing menacingly on the younger officer, who was holding up his hands in defense, one still clutching his beer. At that moment, Annabel made her move, swiftly unhooking the dual clasps of the bracelets on the whore's wrist with two flicks of her right thumb and middle finger and reaching up to catch the jewels with her left palm as they fell.

She closed her hand around the bracelets, feeling their cool weight, and melted back into the crowd before Mademoiselle Duplessis realized the pieces were no longer on her wrist.

All had gone according to plan—an easy get if there ever was one. So why, then, was the hair on the back of Annabel's neck suddenly standing on end? She looked furtively around, and her eyes locked with those of a broad-shouldered French policeman, his dark uniform perfectly pressed, his eyes black and burning. Perhaps he hadn't been staring at her after all. She glanced behind her, her heart thudding. But there was no one there, and when she turned back around, he was already advancing on her, walking swiftly through the crowd.

Annabel's breath caught in her throat, but she didn't hesitate. She spun on her heel and strode as quickly as she could toward the exit while forcing herself not to break into a run. As she moved, she reached up and, while pretending to loosen her collar, slid the pair of bracelets into the right cup of her brassiere.

When she reached the door, she chanced a glance over her right shoulder and saw the policeman still plowing through the crowd in her direction, his eyes locked on her.

"Damn it," she muttered under her breath, turning away. She pushed through the door into the warm Paris evening. It was nearing curfew, which meant that there were fewer people on the streets, fewer chances to blend in. She took a sharp right down the rue Saint-Martin just as she heard the door to the brasserie behind her burst open. There was no time to lose; she broke into a run, turning first down the rue Pernelle and then down the rue Saint-Bon.

"Please, God," she murmured as she slid through the shadows. "Please let me make it home to my girls."

Annabel took the long way home, weaving through the back streets of the Marais, just in case the thick-necked policeman had managed to match her pace, but she couldn't hear footsteps behind her, and she was fairly certain he hadn't been able to keep up. But he had seen her face, which was nearly as alarming, and if he hadn't realized immediately that she'd taken the bracelets, he was sure to put two and two together once news of the brazen theft circulated.

How had she been so careless? As she turned left onto the rue Bréguet and right onto the Boulevard Voltaire, she could feel tears stinging her eyes. Never had she made such a mistake! One did not simply steal from the Germans and escape with a slap on the wrist. If she'd been caught tonight, she would likely be sent to a labor camp, perhaps even executed as an example to others.

A chill ran down her spine as she finally rounded the corner onto the rue Pasteur. She checked behind her once more to ensure that she was alone, and finally, satisfied that she was the only person foolish enough to be out on the street after curfew, she let herself relax a little.

She let herself into the building and slipped into her apartment. Roger was in the parlor, reading the newspaper, and he looked up when she entered, still panting.

"Annabel, again?" he asked, his tone exasperated as he took in her disheveled state. "Another theft?"

She avoided his gaze as she reached into her brassiere and pulled out the bracelets. She held them up, marveling at the way the diamonds caught the light of the candles in their foyer. "These are different, Roger. They're not for the underground. They belong to Hélène Rosman."

"The Rosmans are gone, Annabel. Why would you risk it?"

"Because they'll be back. I know they will."

"And then what? You think that giving them back a couple of pieces of jewelry will change anything?"

She blinked back tears. "So much has been taken from them, Roger, don't you understand? So much has been taken from all the Jews of Paris. It's why my work is more important now than ever!"

"You think you're making a difference, but these pieces you take, Annabel, they're just things!"

"But they're not! When I steal for the underground, I buy favors and safe passage to the Unoccupied Zone for people who are being persecuted. What I'm doing matters. Can't you see that?"

"I can see that you think you're some kind of savior, Annabel," Roger said. "But it's lunacy to think you can make a difference."

"No, Roger, it would be lunacy if I were content to watch the world crumble around me without trying to help." They stared at each other for a long moment, on two different sides of a divide that Annabel feared she could not cross. Finally, she sighed and changed the subject. "Where are the girls?" she asked.

He looked pointedly at the clock in the corner. "In bed, Annabel."

Heat rose to her cheeks. "Of course. I didn't mean to be so late."

"Yes, well." He was exasperated with her.

"Roger—" she began, not knowing quite what she wanted to say but realizing she owed him an apology. She also desperately wanted to feel his arms around her. She was weary and frightened, and wasn't she supposed to be able to draw comfort from her husband in times like these?

"Annabel, I'm tired," he said, cutting her off. "We'll discuss everything tomorrow, but for now, please leave me in peace."

It felt like a slap. "Yes, of course. Very well."

He softened a bit. "Why don't you go kiss the girls good night? If they're still awake, I know it would bring them comfort to see you." He didn't wait for a reply; he snapped his newspaper open again, already taking his leave of the conversation.

Annabel stood there for a moment, bracelets clutched in her hand, watching him. And then she backed out of the room, her heart heavy with regret.

The room the girls shared was dark when she entered, but she could see their sleeping forms in the dim light that spilled in from the hall.

Annabel sat gently on the edge of the bed the girls shared and placed a kiss on Liliane's forehead first, smoothing back her curls, and a second on Colette's, brushing away a ringlet. The girls were fast asleep, their long lashes fluttering against their cheeks as they dreamed. Tonight, they were in their yellow nightgowns, an *L* embroidered on the front of Liliane's, a *C* on Colette's. Their blue gowns—just the same as the ones they were wearing but for their color—hung in the wardrobe.

The matching nightgowns were more than just beautiful reminders of Annabel's native England, though they were sewn by her friend Frédéric's wife, Marie, from English cotton and lace that Annabel's mother had sent from England three years earlier, just before she passed away. They were also the girls' security, the guarantee that if anything ever happened to her, they would have money to survive. Into the hem of each of their gowns, she always sewed the most recent pieces she had stolen, and the pieces stayed there until she sold them. It was vital to wait for at least a few weeks, until interest in the missing jewels had cooled.

There was now a diamond choker in the hem of Liliane's yellow gown, a ruby ring in the hem of Colette's. The blue nightgowns in the closet held jewels, too: a pair of diamond earrings in Liliane's, a diamond wedding band in Colette's. The girls knew the jewels were there, knew that they were only to be mentioned in case of emergency. Even Liliane, at the age of four, understood the importance of keeping the secret.

Tomorrow, Annabel would carefully open up the hems of the blue nightgowns and add the two bracelets she'd stolen tonight—one in each gown, connecting the girls. The bracelets, she imagined, would be safe there until Hélène Rosman came home. And if, in the meantime, something happened to Annabel and the girls needed to trade the pieces away to protect themselves, Hélène would understand that, too. At least they would not wind up back in the hands of the monstrous Möckel.

"Sleep tight, my angels," she said, giving each of her daughters another kiss. "I will protect you always."

CHAPTER SEVENTEEN

2018

The morning after the visit to Hubert Verdier's assisted-living facility, Lucas was waiting in the reception area of Aviva's office when she arrived to work just before eight thirty. He stood up, glaring at her, when she emerged from the elevator.

"Lucas," she said, trying to sound calm and not cornered. "What are you doing here?"

His eyebrows shot up. "Really, Aviva? You thought you could just question my grandfather-in-law about a *murder* and I wouldn't want to have a conversation with you about it?"

"Aviva?" Marilyn cut in, standing up from her place behind the reception desk. "Should I call security?"

"No," Aviva said quickly. "Lucas is a friend. This is just a misunderstanding, right?"

"You have a strange definition of misunderstanding." Lucas glanced at Marilyn. "Look, I'm sorry, ma'am. I didn't mean to worry you. Aviva caught me off guard yesterday and—"

"Come on," Aviva said before any more of this conversation played out in public. Marilyn reluctantly buzzed them into the office, concern still written across her face, and Lucas didn't say another word until Aviva had closed the door to her office and gestured to one of the chairs opposite her desk. He didn't sit down; he just stood there, glaring at her.

"Fine," Aviva said, taking a seat behind her desk and trying to sound unruffled. "Say what you came here to say."

"I thought you just had some innocuous questions about the provenance of the bracelet!" he snapped. "This is about a *murder*? Exactly what game are you playing here, Aviva?"

"It's not a game, Lucas."

"You can say that again. Hubert is a very old man, Aviva. Are you trying to kill him?"

"Of course not," Aviva shot back. "We're just trying to find out the truth, and he obviously has some answers. You saw how agitated he became when we mentioned the bracelet and the little girl. Unless you want me to involve the police, I need to go back and see him again."

Lucas's eyes bulged. "The *police*? Aviva, he had a *cardiac episode* after you left and the home had to call an *ambulance*. You think I'm going to give you my blessing to *repeat* that?"

Aviva felt a surge of guilt. "Is he okay?"

"Like you care."

"Of course I care, Lucas!" She took a deep breath. "Look, I'm very sorry that we upset him so much. But if he's the man who kidnapped and murdered Colette's sister . . ." She let her voice trail off. "Please tell me he's all right."

"He's all right," Lucas said reluctantly. "It wasn't a heart attack."

"Thank goodness," Aviva said.

Some of the fight seemed to drain out of Lucas. "I think it's time you tell me the whole story, Aviva."

Aviva hesitated, trying to decide what she could tell him. Certainly no good would come of her revealing that Colette was a jewel thief. "Colette and her mother were both active in the French Resistance," Aviva said carefully. "Someone betrayed Colette's mother, and the night the Germans came for them, Colette's younger sister, Liliane, disappeared. She was later found dead, and the bracelet that had been sewn into the hem of her nightgown for safekeeping has been missing for nearly eighty years. Until it turned up in your museum."

Lucas's eyes went wide, and she was certain from his expression that he hadn't known about the old man's past. "And you think Hubert somehow betrayed your friend Colette's family?" he asked, sinking into one of the seats across from her desk, his anger melting into bewilderment. "This is the Jewish family you mentioned the bracelets belonging to?"

"No, not exactly. Colette's mother took the bracelets back from the German who stole them. And then she was betrayed by someone who may have been a French police officer—and who we think now might be Hubert Verdier."

"Aviva, it just isn't possible that Hubert did something to the little girl. I've known him my whole life. He and his wife were my grandparents' closest friends when I was growing up."

"That's how you met your wife? Through your grandparents?"

He turned a bit red. "We were the only grandchildren on both sides, and we were the same age. It was always just sort of expected that we'd wind up together."

Aviva studied him, feeling a surge of pity. Not that she knew much about marriage, but his didn't sound like a match made in heaven so much as a foregone conclusion. It also meant that when he'd lost his wife, he'd lost someone he'd known his whole life. "I'm very sorry you lost her."

He sighed. "I am, too. It's had a huge impact on our daughter's life, and I worry about her every day."

Aviva softened. "I'm so sorry. You said she's nineteen?"

"Yeah. She was a freshman in high school when Vanessa passed four years ago. I'm so thankful that my grandfather lived just down the block from us; he really stepped in and helped raise her when I was still trying to get my bearings. And with my own mother gone . . ." His voice trailed off, and he shook his head.

Aviva blinked back tears. "Your grandfather was still alive then?"

"He's still alive *now*," Lucas said with a small smile. "Nearly a hundred years old, and still sharp as a tack. He likes to say he's like the Energizer Bunny. He keeps going and going."

"And your mother? You said she's gone?"

He smiled slightly. "Is this part of the inquisition? Or have we transitioned into the friendly conversation part of this meeting?"

"Friendly conversation," Aviva answered honestly. "I lost my mom when I was eighteen and my dad was never in the picture, so I know what it's like to be without parents."

He held her gaze in a way that made her stomach do a little flip. "I—" he said, and then cut himself off with a slight shake of his head. "I'm very sorry, Aviva. What happened to your mom?"

"Car accident." It was still hard to say the words after all these years.

"God, I'm sorry."

"I don't know what I would have done without Colette," she said, sinking into the strange sense of camaraderie she felt with others who had suffered such a formative loss. "She made me feel loved when my whole world had fallen down."

"So you feel especially protective of her. I get that. I feel protective over Vanessa's grandfather, too—I think that being responsible for Hubert now makes both Millie and me feel like we're honoring Vanessa's memory, you know?"

Aviva nodded. "I'm sorry I didn't tell you what we suspected before we went to see him. I really am. I still think he knows something about the bracelet, and about what happened to Colette's family, but it wasn't fair to blindside you like that." She could feel heat creeping up her neck. "I should also add that your daughter is really lucky to have you. I wish my dad had stuck around long enough to play a role in my life—but he was long gone way before I lost my mom."

Lucas leaned forward and folded his hands around hers. "That is very much your father's loss." He looked into her eyes for long enough that she had to look away. "So," he said, clearing his throat. "Do you have time for a cup of coffee? Playing verbal chess makes me thirsty." He smiled at her.

"Coffee? Does that mean you don't hate me?"

"It means I understand where you're coming from. It means that I'll try to talk to Hubert myself. And it means that now that we have all that out of the way, it might be nice to just talk with you. That is, if you want to."

Aviva smiled. She had forty-five minutes before her first appointment of the day. "I think I would like that very much."

Two days later, during a volunteer shift at the Holocaust center, Aviva was still thinking about the coffee she'd had with Lucas. She couldn't remember the last time she'd felt so listened to; he had seemed genuinely intrigued by everything she'd had to say, and he'd offered stories of his own—about how proud he was of his daughter, about how thrilled he was with the museum's success, and about his concern over his own elderly grandfather living alone—and by the time they parted ways, she felt almost as if she'd been on a date.

He was a genuinely nice guy, and that complicated things. She could see the wheels turning in Colette's head; she wanted the bracelet back. Now that Aviva knew Lucas better, though, she couldn't let that happen. If an enormously valuable piece disappeared while on loan, the Diamond Museum's reputation would be tarnished, and Lucas would be ruined.

"Okay, out with it," she said to Colette once they were alone in the Holocaust center's copy room, stuffing mailers for an outreach campaign.

"Out with what?" Colette asked innocently as she folded a flyer into an envelope and sealed it.

"Out with whatever it is you wanted to talk to me about."

"Who said I wanted to talk with you about anything?" Colette said, avoiding Aviva's gaze as she stuffed another mailer.

"Come on. You're thinking about stealing that bracelet, aren't you?"

"But that would be illegal, dear," Colette said sweetly. "I certainly wouldn't mention it to an attorney if I had plans to do something like that."

"Colette," Aviva said firmly, "you can't steal from Lucas."

Colette was quiet for a moment as she filled and sealed a few more envelopes. "Getting attached to Lucas O'Mara is a bad idea, Aviva."

"Why?" Aviva demanded. "I finally meet someone who seems kind and decent, and you want me to forget about it so that you can steal from him?"

"Please keep your voice down, dear," Colette said, finally looking up. "And no, Aviva. It's that I wonder whether he really is the decent, kind man you think he is. That family is hiding something, and he's right at the center of it."

"He's not," Aviva insisted. "Colette, this isn't like the Robin Hood stuff you told me about. You don't know why his family has the bracelet or where it came from. You can't take it without knowing those things. Besides, didn't we already tip our hand when we went to see Hubert Verdier? And stealing from Lucas would be—"

They were interrupted by the center's director, Chana, poking her head into the copy room. "Call for you, Aviva," she said.

"Call for me?" Aviva shot Colette a puzzled look. "But I don't work here. Who would call me here?"

"It's one of the volunteers at the New York center," Chana said with a shrug. "He read your article in the newsletter and assumed you were on staff. I told him he was lucky you were around this evening."

"I told you people read the newsletter," Colette singsonged.

Aviva ignored her. "What does he want?"

"He said he wanted to talk to you about the bracelet you mentioned in the article," Chana said. "Says he knows who it belonged to before the war."

Aviva turned to Colette with wide eyes.

Colette cleared her throat. "Can we take the call at your desk, Chana?" Colette asked. "On speakerphone?"

"Anything for our center's longest-serving volunteer." Chana turned away and headed back for her desk, while Colette and Aviva followed. "Sir, you're on with Aviva Haskell and Colette Marceau, both of whom are volunteers here at the center," Chana said after pushing a few buttons on her phone. "Can you hear us?"

"Clear as day, ma'am," boomed a man's French-accented deep voice. "Ms. Haskell, Ms. Marceau, thanks for taking my call. I realize this is a bit unusual."

Chana picked up her water bottle, gestured for Colette to take her seat, and walked away.

"Chana said you were interested in the bracelet in the newsletter?" Aviva said, cutting to the chase.

"Very much so," the man said. "The bracelet in the newsletter, you see, belonged to my mother." He spoke slowly, his voice trembling.

"To your mother?" Colette asked dubiously, exchanging looks with Aviva.

"Yes." He hesitated. "You may not know this, but the bracelet was one of a pair."

Colette went completely still as he continued.

"They fit together, you see. My father commissioned them for her when my sister and I were born. My mother wore them each day, two halves of the same whole, just like us. Apart, the bracelets appear to be lilies. Together, they form a butterfly."

"How could he know that?" Colette asked in a whisper.

"May I ask your name, sir?" Aviva asked.

"Of course. Forgive me for not introducing myself sooner. It's Daniel Rosman."

"Daniel *Rosman*?" Colette gasped and gripped the desk. "Mr. Rosman, what was your mother's name?"

"My mother?" He sounded startled. "Hélène. Hélène Rosman. Why?"

"And your father was Salomon, if I'm not mistaken," Colette said.

There was a long stretch of silence. The man sounded choked up when he answered. "How on earth did you know that?"

"My—my mother knew your family. She was a friend of your mother's. Her name was Annabel Marceau."

More silence. "My mother knew a Madame Marceau who lived in our neighborhood. The wife of a schoolteacher, I think. I met her once or twice in our apartment."

Colette closed her eyes. "Yes. Those were my parents, Mr. Rosman. My mother was heartbroken when you and your family were arrested. I thought you had all died."

"My parents did, I'm afraid." His voice sounded hollow. "My father was fifty-two when he was executed by firing squad, and my mother just forty-two when she died in Auschwitz. My twin sister and I both survived, though Ruth has been gone for nearly twenty years now. I never had children, nor did she, and it has haunted me for many years to think that there would be no one to carry on the search for the bracelets after I was gone. Did—did your family survive the war, Ms. Marceau?"

"My father did," Colette replied. "My mother and sister— both gone."

Rosman exhaled. "I'm very sorry to hear that. My mother was very fond of your mother; that would have broken her heart."

"My mother's heart would have broken to know what happened to your parents, too. Forgive me for asking, Mr. Rosman, but can you tell me about the clasp of the missing bracelets? Just so that I'm certain you are who you say you are?"

Daniel was silent for a second, and Aviva and Colette exchanged looks. Had Colette asked a question that had tripped him up? But then they could hear him exhale, and when he spoke again, his tone was both sad and firm.

"Of course," he said. "The clasps of the bracelets are different. The one in the museum exhibit Ms. Haskell wrote about, I believe, is the butterfly's left wing, and the clasp of that one has four tiny diamonds on it, and the letter *R* etched into the metal. The stones are for the four of us in my family—my parents, my sister, and me—and the *R* is for Ruth, my sister's name. The other, the one that is still missing, is the butterfly's right wing. That one has four tiny diamonds for the same reason—to represent my family—and the letter etched into the metal is a *D*, for Daniel, my own name."

"A *D* for Daniel," Colette said softly. "I always believed it was a half-moon, and that the diamonds were stars."

"You've seen the other bracelet, Ms. Marceau?"

Colette blinked a few times. "I have."

For a moment, Aviva thought that Colette was going to admit to having the other half. Instead, she said, "My mother took them back, you see. She hoped to return them to your mother at the end of the war."

"She—took them?" He sounded confused. "From whom?"

"The German officer who stole them from you."

"Möckel?" Rosman said slowly.

"Möckel." Colette drew a shaky breath. "He was the one who came to take my family, too, Mr. Rosman."

When Aviva reached over to squeeze Colette's hand, she noticed for the first time that Colette was crying. "Mr. Rosman," Aviva cut in. "Do you think you could come to Boston? This feels like a conversation we should be having in person—and I imagine you'd like to see the bracelet in the museum."

"I'm very eager to see it, Ms. Haskell," Rosman said. "I can be on the first train out of Penn Station tomorrow morning. I think that puts me in Boston by nine."

"We'll meet you at the offices of the Boston Center for Holocaust Education," Aviva said. After agreeing to the details and exchanging numbers, she ended the call and turned to Colette, whose face was in her hands. "You knew who he was?"

Colette nodded slowly. "I never knew Daniel Rosman or his sister, but I saw his mother once—only for a few seconds—as she was being led away from the Vélodrome d'Hiver in Paris—on her way to being deported to Auschwitz. My mother knew her well, though—so well that she risked her own life to take back the things that belonged to her. I—I can't believe that her son is still alive. And that he's *here*. In the United States. Just a few hours away."

"You're certain he is who he says he is?" Aviva asked. "It's hard not to be skeptical when it comes to something so valuable."

"But how else would he know about the clasp? And the fact that the bracelet was one of a pair? Plus the fact that he knew the name Möckel . . ." Colette shuddered. "There's no doubt in my mind, Aviva."

"It's extraordinary, isn't it?" Aviva asked after a pause. "The way that these diamonds have resurfaced like this and set everything into motion?"

"It is," Colette agreed. "But this means that it's more important than ever to get the bracelet back. It's time to finish what my mother started so many years ago."

CHAPTER EIGHTEEN

1942

The night it all ended had begun just like any other.

Mum had made dinner—a watery soup of rutabaga and carrots—and helped Liliane change into her blue nightgown, reminding her, as she always did, of the treasures sewn into the lining, just in case. "Remember, my dear girls, you must only tell a grown-up you trust about the jewels, and even then, only in an emergency."

"I know, Mum," Liliane murmured as Mum leaned forward, breathing in the sweet, spun-sugar scent of her younger daughter's curls. "It's our secret."

Colette lingered after Liliane had trotted out to the other room, neighing like a horse, in search of her father to beg him to play a game involving knights and princesses. "Mum?"

"Yes, my darling?"

Colette's stomach swam with unease. "Things are getting more dangerous, aren't they?"

Mum put her arm around Colette. "Oh, my darling, we'll be all right." She paused. "But if something should happen to me, you must promise me you will look out for your sister."

Colette studied Mum's face. Was there something she wasn't saying? "Of course, Mum. I promise. I'll always protect her."

Mum blinked a few times, and Colette could see the tears in her eyes. "I know you will, my sweet girl."

From the other room, they could hear Papa snapping at Liliane that he was busy and didn't have time to play. He acted as if the very existence of his children was an inconvenience these days, and Colette could see how upset he was that Mum had continued to steal. He didn't understand that what she was doing was more important now than ever. Colette could hardly imagine his rage if he discovered that she, too, had been taking jewels from Germans and collaborators.

As Papa's tone of annoyance drifted in from the parlor, Mum pressed her fingers to her temples and took a deep breath. "Liliane!" she called brightly. "Come here, darling! Colette and I will play with you!"

Liliane horse-trotted back into the room, and Colette jumped up and grabbed her little sister's hand. "Come on," she said, forcing a bright smile. "We get to be knights of the Round Table, and Mum is our horse."

"*Neigh!*" Mum replied solemnly, and Colette laughed and pulled her little sister in for a hug.

Later that evening, Colette played quietly with Liliane in their shared bedroom, pretending that Liliane's dolls were ballerinas, while Mum washed the dishes and Papa read the newspaper on the sofa. As they made the rag dolls dip and dance, Colette's mind wandered to Madame Rosman's bracelets in the hems of their gowns. Was that why Mum had been acting so unsettled? Was it worry for her friend? Or concern about keeping such valuable pieces safe for the duration of the war?

The theft of the bracelets a week earlier, Colette knew, went against her mother's usual moral code, for she hadn't stolen them to fund justice; she had stolen them to avenge a friend. Then again, perhaps the theft had been right in line with Mum's ideals after all, for she'd clearly been trying to right a wrong. But was that even possible with the Rosmans already in German custody? They'd already lost so much, and the return of the bracelets would surely do little to soothe the horror they'd endured after they returned.

Colette understood the need to do something, *anything*, to restore some sense of justice. It was just what she'd been doing for the last several weeks, stealing frequently, almost desperately, in an attempt to balance out the disappearance of Tristan. She hadn't even told her mother about most of the pieces yet. Mum would scold her for being reckless, but if avenging something so terrible didn't justify a response, what did?

As Liliane made her dolls pirouette and leap on the imaginary stage of the bed, Colette absently fingered the hem of her own nightgown, which was cleverly lined with an extra layer of cotton to prevent anyone from being able to feel the pieces hidden there. Colette could just barely make out the weight of her half of the bracelet pair, and of Hélène Rosman's emerald ring, which her mother had also placed there for safekeeping. *We will protect them for her until she returns*, her mother had said, not meeting Colette's eye, and Colette wondered if Mum even believed her own words about Madame Rosman coming back.

"Colette," Liliane chirped, cutting into her thoughts, "you aren't paying attention! It's time for the grand finale!"

"Of course," Colette said, forcing a smile as she picked up her doll. She had just returned her ballerina to the makeshift stage when, suddenly, there was a loud pounding on their front door.

"Open up!" called a deep, German-accented voice from the hall.

"Mum?" Colette cried out, leaping up. The Germans were *here*! At her family's door! Was it because of her? Had she been careless in her stealing? Had she put her family at risk?

"Go out the bedroom window now, Colette!" Mum shouted back, her voice high with panic as the man with a German accent shouted from the other side of the apartment door again. "Take Liliane! Run!"

Colette hesitated, paralyzed by indecision. If they fled now, who would look out for Mum? She couldn't trust Papa to do so.

"Go, Colette! Now!" her mother cried again, and it was the impetus Colette needed to grab Liliane's hand and head for the window. She opened it quickly and stuck her head out to make sure there weren't any soldiers waiting for them outside. There was a German truck idling by the curb, but it was empty. The coast was clear.

"Come on, Liliane, hurry," she said urgently, pulling her sister toward the window. They were on the ground floor, so there would be only a small drop to the sidewalk once she hoisted Liliane out.

She had just lifted her sister up when there was a loud, splintering sound from the outer room, and suddenly, heavy footsteps sounded in the apartment, along with several German-accented voices, all yelling commands to Mum and Papa at once. There was the sound of a slap, and Mum screamed a bloodcurdling scream, and something in Colette snapped. She couldn't abandon her mother.

"Wait here, Liliane," she said quickly.

"Don't go!" Liliane whimpered. "I'm scared."

"I'll be right back, I promise. I just have to help Mum."

"All right," Liliane agreed in a hushed voice, tears pooling in her eyes. "*Kyi-kyi-kyi*," she whimpered under her breath, but Colette had no time to respond.

Colette ran from the bedroom and burst into the parlor, where four uniformed Germans seemed to take up all the space in the room. One was holding her father; another had her mother's hands twisted behind her back, and the remaining two were opening drawers and cupboards, pulling all the contents out and tossing them onto the floor. "Let them go!" Colette cried before she could stop herself.

"No, Colette, no!" her mother cried, locking eyes with Colette, and Colette knew that her mother was telling her to turn around, to go back, to protect Liliane. But it was already too late; one of the Germans who'd been pulling out drawers had turned and was advancing on her menacingly now.

"And who do we have here?" he asked in thickly accented French, grabbing Colette's arm with such force that she yelped in pain.

"Don't hurt her!" Mum screamed, which earned her a backhand across the face from one of the Germans.

"Mummy!" Colette whimpered as the German twisted her arm, sending pain ricocheting up her shoulder.

At that moment, a middle-aged German officer with close-cropped hair and ice-blue eyes stepped through splintered remains of the doorway, and the men who'd seized the family promptly snapped to attention. Mum gasped, shooting a terrified glance at Colette.

The man strode into their apartment like he owned the place, stopping just a foot away from Mum. "Annabel Marceau," he said flatly, as if he was disappointed in her very name. "At last we meet."

"I—I don't know who you are," Mum said. In response, the German holding her shook her a little, and the officer laughed, his face devoid of humor.

"Oh, now, I don't think that is true at all," he said, his perfect French tainted by his German accent. "We would have met last week, in fact, had you stopped to say hello. Or was there not time while you were committing your theft?"

Papa's head snapped around and he glared at Mum. Colette could feel his fury across the room—not anger with the Germans, but anger at Mum for putting them in this situation.

"Roger, I—" Mum said softly, tears in her eyes. But he looked away in disgust and muttered something to the German holding him.

"In case you need a reminder, Frau Marceau, I'm Sturmbann-führer Gustav Möckel," the officer said, his voice a practiced purr. "But perhaps you'll remember me better as the owner of the two bracelets you stole."

"I don't know what you're talking about," Annabel said, holding her chin high.

Möckel took a step closer, his nose nearly touching Mum's now. And then, he lifted his palm and slapped her once, hard, across the right cheek. Mum gasped in pain, and Colette yelped, which only made the German holding her twist her arm more tightly.

"Then allow me to refresh your memory," Möckel said. "But let's talk at my place rather than yours, shall we?" He snapped his fingers and gestured to the door. The Germans holding Mum, Papa, and Colette began shoving them in that direction, but Co-lette summoned her courage, kicked the man holding her in the shin, and twisted away, running for the door to her bedroom. All she could think about was getting to Liliane.

But when she flew into the bedroom, it was empty, the window wide open, the curtains fluttering in the breeze. "Lili-ane?" she screamed, throwing open the wardrobe and ducking to check under the bed, but her sister wasn't there. There was nowhere else to hide. "Liliane!" she shouted again, rushing to the window and craning her head to look out. She could just make out the figure of a man in a dark uniform hurrying off, a shadowy bundle over his shoulder. "Liliane!" she screamed at the top of her lungs, but the Germans were already in the room, already dragging her away, and she watched helplessly as the man dashed around the corner, still clutching Liliane, without looking back.

"A man took Liliane!" Colette called out frantically to Mum and Papa as the Germans dragged her back into the parlor.

"What?" Mum demanded. "That's impossible. Who would take her?" She turned to the cold German officer. "Please. I know I'm in trouble, but if something has happened to my daughter . . ."

Her voice trailed off as Möckel smiled at her, his eyes hard. "How careless of you to misplace a child."

"Please," Mum whispered.

Möckel chuckled and turned to Colette. "Your mother is a criminal," he said gleefully. "Did you know that? She's a thief, and I will make her pay."

"Mum?" Colette whimpered.

"Oh, my dear," Möckel said, lowering his voice to a purr. "Your mother cannot help you now, and if your sister somehow escaped? Then she is the lucky one." He straightened up and gestured to one of the officers.

"Wait! Please! Wait!" Mum cried, but Möckel was already gone, and the younger Germans, with their blank expressions, were clearly here to do whatever he asked. "Liliane!" But there was no reply as the Gestapo pulled the three remaining Marceaus kicking and screaming down the hall.

As they arrived at the headquarters of the Sûreté Nationale on the rue des Saussaies, Annabel knew she should be thinking of how to get them all out of this, but all she could think about was Liliane. Who was the man who'd taken her from the window? Was it a neighbor who'd seen the Germans arrive and had thought he might be able to help? Or someone with bad intentions who'd spotted an opportunity? Could it have been someone who suspected Liliane's dress was lined with hidden jewels? And if so, would the man release her once he'd taken her treasures? She was only four years old; she didn't know the way to the homes of any of the Marceaus' friends; she didn't even know how to get into their building. What if someone hurt her? What if something terrible happened to her? What if she didn't find her way to safety and starved to death on the street or was hit by a car? The further Annabel went down the road of possible outcomes, the more her throat closed in panic.

The Germans separated the family in the low-ceilinged hallway of the building, shoving Roger and Colette roughly away. Colette was still sobbing inconsolably, but Annabel was heartened to see that Roger seemed to have snapped out of it and was trying to comfort his daughter.

"There's been a mistake," he said over his shoulder as he was shoved by a uniformed German toward a door down the hall. "We don't belong here. We've done nothing. My wife is British!"

The German guffawed. "Today," he said, his accent thick and heavy, "the only thing that matters is that she's *caught*."

He and Colette were pushed through a doorway, and it was the last glimpse Annabel had of them before she was shoved up a flight of stairs, down a hall, and into an office, where Möckel was seated behind a desk, not a hair out of place, his uniform buttons glinting in the too-bright light. He nodded to the officer who'd brought her in, and the man deposited her roughly into a chair and then backed out, leaving the two of them alone.

In the heavy silence, Möckel came out from behind his desk to stand in front of Annabel's chair, and for a few seconds, he just studied her, as he had done in her apartment.

"Please," she said, her voice cracking. "My younger daughter is missing, and I—"

"It really is remarkable," he said, cutting her off.

She waited for him to elaborate, but he didn't, so finally, she swallowed hard and ventured, "What is?"

"Oh, well, that a mother would be so foolish." His tone was cheerful, chummy, and it made her stomach hurt. "And so careless. How does one misplace a child?"

"She was taken from her bedroom during the raid," Annabel whispered. "You know that. She's only four years old, and she must be very frightened."

"As she should be. These are dangerous times. Dangerous to be a foreigner in Paris. Dangerous to be a child on the streets alone. Dangerous to be a *thief*."

He leaned in close, searching her eyes, and Annabel forced herself to remain still.

"It is even *more* dangerous," he added, his voice low, "to steal from someone like me."

Still, Annabel said nothing. Her silence seemed to unsettle him.

"Where are they?" he asked abruptly, all traces of artificial saccharine vanishing. "Where are my bracelets?"

"I don't know what you mean." Annabel fought to keep her voice from wobbling.

"That's a shame," he said. "You see, I know that it was you. You were spotted at the Brasserie Roye by a French police captain, who described you in detail to a police artist. And it seems that the wife of one of our esteemed Parisian officers recognized you immediately. Very careless of you to be seen, wasn't it?"

Perhaps he was bluffing. "She was wrong," Annabel said. "I've never been to the Brasserie Roye."

"Ah, well, I might be persuaded to believe that, were it not for the king's ransom in jewels my men found in your cupboards. I see you have a nasty little habit of collecting other people's valuables, Madame Marceau."

Annabel stared at him, the world tumbling down around her in slow motion.

"Now, you see, I'm a generous man, Madame Marceau. And as you also might imagine, my friend is very disappointed to have lost two items of jewelry she loves. I worked very hard to bring them to her. They're quite unique, you see, but I don't need to tell you that, do I? If you tell me where the bracelets are . . ."

She looked into his eyes and could see the lie there. When he had the bracelets, he would also want her life in exchange for his troubles. She understood with a sinking sense of certainty that her death was predetermined, but there was still hope for Roger and the girls.

"My husband and daughters had nothing to do with this," she said after a long moment. "Let them go, and I will give you all the answers you need."

Möckel studied her, and his expression slowly melted into a sneer of disbelief. "You are not the only one who can read people, madame," he said. "You don't have the pieces anymore, do you?"

She blinked. "Why are they so important to you anyhow?"

"Because they are *mine*. No one has any right to take what belongs to me, do you understand?"

"They belong," Annabel said, summoning all her courage, "to the Rosman family."

His expression went stone-cold. "The Rosman family? They were Jews. They're all thieves and liars. They had no right to anything. Now what have you done with them?"

A great swell of sadness washed over her. Hatred simmered in his eyes as he looked down at her, and she could see it then, the way the Nazi party had brainwashed men just like Möckel who were neither intelligent nor charismatic. He was a lackluster nobody, and Hitler's minions had whispered in his ear that his deficiencies weren't his fault after all. If the Jews were to blame for everything, Möckel and men like him could believe themselves entitled to everything they'd ever wanted. They'd been made into puppets, as stupid men often were, and still they had no idea.

She had thought until this very moment that the war would surely be over within the year, but she understood now, as she looked into Möckel's cold eyes, that it would last for much longer than that. The strings of men like him were pulled by a faraway puppet master, a tale as old as war itself.

"I see you do not agree with me," Möckel said when the silence had gone on for too much time. "Am I right, then? Are you a Jew, too?"

Annabel looked up. "What does my religion matter? I'm a human. Just as you are, though you seem to have forgotten."

He backhanded her hard across the face, and she bit her lip to stop herself from screaming. "Salomon Rosman said the same, just before I had him executed."

Her heart stopped for a second. He had confirmed what she feared—that at least one of the Rosmans wouldn't be coming home. "Yet you remember his name," she said. This abhorrent man had a conscience, even if it was buried deep. "Salomon Rosman was a man with a family and a life and his future, and deep down, you know that. You feel guilt for what you did."

Möckel struck her again, and this time, she cried out before she could stop herself. The sound of her pain seemed to delight him. He smiled coldly. "I feel nothing at all, Madame Marceau." He leaned in close. "And I'll remember your name, too, after I've taken your life."

CHAPTER NINETEEN

2018

The morning after the call with Daniel Rosman, Colette awoke before dawn, her head pounding. Never had she imagined that at nearly ninety, she'd be reuniting with someone her mother once knew, someone she had long believed dead.

What might her mother have thought if she'd known that one day, Colette would have the chance to return at least one of Madame Rosman's bracelets? She imagined that she might be very proud—but she would also wonder what was taking Colette so long to seize the bracelet's other half. After all, it was nearly within her grasp, and didn't she have an obligation to finish what her mother had started?

Colette shook her head and got out of bed. None of that would be solved today. But seeing Daniel Rosman was something she would need to brace herself for. She was grateful Aviva would be with her.

But then her phone rang just past seven, Aviva's name popping up on the caller ID. "Colette, you're going to kill me," Aviva said, "but a hearing on my schedule was moved to nine a.m. Do you think we can reschedule with Daniel Rosman?"

Colette checked her watch. Rosman's train had to have left New York two hours ago. "I'm afraid he's probably already on his way, dear."

Aviva groaned. "Colette, I'm so sorry. Do you want to call Marty and ask him to meet you?"

Colette considered it for a moment, but what would she need his company for? The ghost of her mother would be with her. "No, dear. I'll be fine."

"Are you sure?"

Colette could hear the worry in Aviva's tone. "Darling, you're doing it again. Treating me like a child rather than a perfectly capable woman who has survived nearly everything life could possibly throw her way."

Aviva sighed. "Right. I know. But do you promise to call me after you've seen him?"

"I promise." And with that, Colette ended the call and went to her closet to figure out exactly what one should wear when coming face-to-face with the past.

When Daniel Rosman walked through the door of the Boston Center for Holocaust Education at half past nine, Colette knew him immediately; she was certain she had seen him before, though she had never met him in Paris.

He solved the mystery quickly. "You must be Colette," he said with a smile after he'd approached, his gait confident and even. "I know you, don't I? Have we volunteered together in the past?"

"You look familiar to me, too," Colette admitted, standing and shaking his hand. His grip was warm and firm, and when his fingers closed around hers and he looked her in the eye, Colette registered with some surprise that he was a very good-looking man. He had to be around her age, but his back was straight, his shoulders broad, his silver hair thick, and the deep wrinkles around his eyes a sign of a life lived smiling. "Perhaps the Holocaust education symposium the New York center put on in 1985? Or 1986, was it?"

He beamed at her. "'Eighty-six, yes! I was the chair of that event. You were there, too?"

She nodded in astonishment. She remembered hearing the name Rosman at the time—it had struck her because of her mother's friend—but Rosman wasn't an uncommon name, and she hadn't given it a second thought. Not in a million years would she have imagined that it belonged to Hélène Rosman's son.

Chana spotted them from across the room and hurried over. "Well, if it isn't two of the center's longest-serving volunteers," she said, beaming. "Don't tell me the two of you are only just meeting for the first time!"

Daniel smiled at Colette. "It appears that way. In fact, Ms. Marceau and I were just recalling an event we both attended some thirty years ago."

"Please, Mr. Rosman, you must call me Colette."

"Only if you'll call me Daniel."

Chana looked amused. "Daniel, Colette here was one of our very first volunteers, way before my time, back when the center opened in 1972." Turning to Colette, she added, "And Daniel has been active with our New York branch since its inception in 1980. You've probably been in a half dozen cross-training sessions together over the years."

"What a small world." Colette smiled.

"Shall we walk, Colette?" Daniel asked, offering the crook of his arm and smiling down at her. "Since we're evidently old friends?"

"We shall." With a smile at Chana, she allowed Daniel Rosman to escort her out the rear door of the center, which opened into a small private rose garden.

They didn't say another word until they were seated on a stone bench in the corner of the green space.

"Might I be so bold as to ask what drew you to volunteering for the center, Colette?" Daniel asked. "Are you Jewish?"

She looked down. It was the question she received most often in reference to her work here, and still, it never failed to surprise her. She was human, and as far as she was concerned, every person who had lived through the war—whatever role they'd played—should be working tirelessly to keep alive the memories of the six million people who'd lost their lives in the Holocaust, so that such atrocities could never ever happen again. She could feel a familiar tide of defensiveness rising within her.

But when she looked up, Daniel's smile was open and friendly, and after a few seconds, she relaxed into it. "No. I'm not Jewish. But during the war, my mother worked with an underground organization to protect Jewish citizens. Being here feels a bit like keeping that work alive. Had my mother lived, I think she would have continued to help for as long as she could."

"Your mother sounds like a tremendous woman," Daniel said.

"She was. And I know she thought the world of your mother."

"May her memory be a blessing," Daniel murmured. "And your father, Colette? What was he like?"

Colette shook her head, surprised that the grief of his abandonment still stung after all these years. "Not nearly as incredible. What about your parents?"

"Both extraordinary people. My sister and I were so lucky to have them for the short time we did. My father was a sixth-generation diamond broker whose family was originally from Amsterdam. My mother was whip-smart, and she had a sly sort of humor about her. My father adored her; he would have done anything for her. I can only imagine that he must have gone to his death feeling most of all that he had failed to save her."

"But the fault was not his!" Colette said instantly.

"And yet, don't we all feel that way when we fail to save those we love the most?"

Colette looked at her hands. "It is certainly how I feel about my sister."

He held her gaze. "You mentioned on the phone that she died during the war. Do you mind if I ask what happened to her?"

She looked away. "She disappeared the night we were all arrested in 1942. Her body was found floating in the Seine soon after. She was only four."

"Oh, Colette." Daniel surprised her by putting a hand on her shoulder. "I'm very sorry to hear that."

"Yes, well, the bracelet from the exhibit . . ." She trailed off, drawing a deep beath. "It disappeared with her. And now that it has turned up . . ."

Understanding flickered across Daniel's face. "You might finally discover what happened to her if you can trace its journey. Of course."

She studied her hands. "You can see why it means a great deal to me."

"You know, my mother always said that jewels carry a piece of anyone who has touched them," he said. "I'd like to think, therefore, that there are pieces of my parents in that bracelet, and pieces of your mother and sister, too. And I know my mother would want you to find some peace."

"I'm not sure I deserve that." She didn't know why she was being so frank with a virtual stranger. "I turned my back for a second, Daniel. It's my fault she disappeared."

"Colette, if I may be so bold, none of us bears the responsibility for those we lost in those terrible times."

"Thank you for that, even if I can't quite believe it." She finally met his gaze. "I know the bracelets are yours, Daniel. My mother would want you to have them back."

"They?" he asked quietly. "You don't know where the other one is, do you?"

Her breath snagged in her throat. Every piece of her wanted to tell him no, to keep the bracelet for herself. It was the last thing she had to remember her mother and sister by. But it had never really been hers. And giving it back to the Rosmans was what her mother had always wanted. So after a brief moment of hesitation, she slowly rolled up the sleeve of her silk blouse and held out her wrist full of diamonds so that they sparkled in the morning sunlight like stars.

Daniel didn't say anything at first; he simply stared as if he couldn't quite believe what he was seeing. Finally, he reached out to touch her wrist, sending a jolt through her. "Colette," he breathed, still staring at the diamonds.

"My mother sewed it into the hem of my nightgown to keep it safe, just before she was arrested," she said. "The other half was with Liliane. I've had it all these years, Daniel. It was the last thing she gave to me, you see. But if I had known you survived . . ." She felt the crushing weight of regret; what had she done by keeping the piece from the Rosman family for so long? Why had she simply accepted that they were dead? Why hadn't she looked harder for them? It was her fault that he had gone nearly his whole life without knowing the pieces were safe. "This belongs to you."

Finally, he looked up. "My father always said that diamonds never really belong to anyone. They'll witness births and deaths, war and peace, feast and famine, and yet they'll live on, for millions of years. They have witnessed the past, and they will witness a future we can't begin to imagine."

"He sounds like a wise man." She began to unclasp the bracelet, but Daniel reached out and folded his hand over hers, stopping her.

"No, Colette," he said.

"But it's yours. I insist. My mother stole it so that she could give it back to your family, and I think she'd be very glad that her wish is finally coming to pass, albeit many years too late."

Daniel hesitated, but after a long pause, he nodded, tears in his eyes. "In that case, thank you, Colette."

She smiled weakly and reached again for the clasp, sliding the constellation of jewels from her wrist.

Tentatively, he accepted the bracelet, staring at it for a long time before folding his palm around it. He looked up at her. "Now, do we have any idea where the half in the museum came from?"

"I think we've found the man who took it," Colette said, already missing the bracelet but knowing she'd done what her mother would have wanted her to do. "Who may well have taken my sister. Now I just have to get him to remember the past." To his look of confusion, she clarified. "He's in an assisted-living facility about a half hour outside Boston. Aviva and I, along with our friend Marty, went to speak with him a few days ago, but he wasn't very lucid. I'm not sure if I'm setting myself up for failure, but I'd like to try again."

"Well, then." He stood and held out his arm. "Shall we?"

She looked up at him, confused.

"Let's go remind him." He looked once again into her eyes, as if he was searching for something. "Let's go find out the truth."

The drive to the facility where Hubert Verdier lived was quiet, but the silence that fell over Colette and Daniel as she drove was comfortable. Colette couldn't remember the last time she hadn't felt the need to fill the space with words, even when she was with Aviva or Marty. But there was something about Daniel—perhaps their shared backgrounds as children of long-dead parents, immigrants from France, survivors of a war—that made her feel as if she'd known him forever.

Still, as they approached the facility, she found herself wanting to explain something. "You may as well know that the article in the newsletter was part of Aviva's cover. When she went to the museum asking about the bracelet, she had to tell the museum director something."

Daniel chuckled. "And then he would have grown suspicious if she never wrote about it."

"Perhaps not the best-laid plan. Nor was my plan to barge in on Hubert Verdier and accuse him of murder." She cleared her throat. "I know you don't know me very well, but I'd like you to know that I'm not the type of woman who ordinarily goes around accosting old men."

"Who could blame you, Colette? After all this time, to be face-to-face with the man who may have taken something so precious from you? I can't say I wouldn't do the same." He smiled slyly at her. "In fact, I can't promise I won't do the same right alongside you in just a few minutes."

"But you can't, you see. You must let him believe that we're both friends of his. Coming at him aggressively before only made him shut down. If he believes he knows us, that we're on his side, perhaps he'll come clean."

"Or perhaps, Colette, he has managed to erase the past entirely." She could feel his eyes on her as he continued. "My sister had dementia; the doctors said that her time in Auschwitz had likely hastened the disease's onset, because she was only in her sixties when she was diagnosed. There was a period when all she could talk about was the horrors of the past. And then, the past was gone for her, too, like a vanishing act, up in smoke."

"That must have been very difficult for you."

"It was. It was a feeling of losing her slowly, by inches. And then all at once, she was gone. It leaves one with a question: Is the past as you remember it if you're the only one left with the memories?"

Colette's heart lurched; she often wondered the same, much like the old riddle about the tree falling in the forest with no one around to hear. If you'd sustained great tragedy, but all those who'd been with you were now dead, did your recollections become less valid? Less real? "You and I have both had to carry our memories alone for a great while. We are fortunate to have lived so long, I think, but there's a particular curse to surviving with one's memory entirely intact, isn't there?"

They slipped into an easy silence once more, and Colette didn't speak again until she'd taken the exit to Braintree. "Do you ever wonder how different the world would have been if the people we loved hadn't been taken from us?"

"Even a single death changes the world forever. And in the Second World War, it was millions. The thought is staggering." He paused. "I do think often about how different my own life would have been. My sister and I had to fend for ourselves after the war. We had to wrestle with grief we couldn't process. And the guilt of living while they died, it never really leaves you, does it?"

"No, it doesn't." Colette pulled the car into the parking lot of the assisted-living facility and cut the ignition. They both sat for a moment without moving. "I think I've wasted a great many years not knowing how to move on. How to forgive myself for surviving." She felt suddenly choked up.

"I feel just the same." He reached over and folded a hand over hers. "But it's not the end of the road for us yet, Colette. And being here with you reminds me that as isolated as we might feel, perhaps we're not so alone after all." He paused and drew his hand back. "Now, shall we see what we can find out?"

"Are you certain you want to be a part of this?"

"It is part of the story of the bracelet," he said, reaching for the door handle, "and that means it is my story, too."

CHAPTER TWENTY

1942

Annabel knew this was the end. She could see it in the way Möckel looked at her, like a shark circling his next meal. She knew, too, that he was not the sort to make empty threats; when he had promised to take her life, he meant it.

In her small, windowless cell at the Cherche-Midi prison, she paced, her heart hammering. She would die for this, for the family legacy she had tried so hard to honor. But her husband and daughters should not meet the same fate. They simply couldn't.

"Have they found my daughter yet?" Annabel asked the German woman who seemed to be in charge of the female prisoners. The large, broad-shouldered woman, who wore a black shirt emblazoned with the Nazi symbol, was obsequious to the Gestapo officers, but there was a hard glint in her steely gray eyes, and Annabel knew better than to trust her. Still, she was desperate for news. "My younger one? Liliane?"

"No," the woman said, the word clipped.

"You're certain?" Annabel asked, bile rising in her throat.

"I expect she's safe and sound." The German overseer already sounded bored with the conversation.

"Why do you say that? Have you heard something?"

"It is just that with the situation you're in . . . well, God couldn't possibly be so cruel."

"Oh," Annabel said, her heart sinking. She tried to remind herself that at least the lack of news meant that nothing terrible had been confirmed yet. "I don't believe in that, you see."

The woman narrowed her eyes. "You don't believe in God?"

"That isn't what I meant. It is just that God is not the one doing such terrible things in the world right now. I believe in God very much."

"Well, let us see if he gets you out of this one."

Annabel swallowed down her anger at the woman's indifference. "And what of my husband, Roger, and my older daughter, Colette? Please, can you tell me anything?"

The German woman made a face like she'd just tasted something sour. "They are here," she said after a moment.

"Here? In Cherche-Midi?" Annabel's heart squeezed with fear. "Are they safe?"

"For now."

"Are they hurt?" Annabel felt as if she might throw up, though she hadn't eaten since her arrest.

"Not the girl," the German said quickly, and Annabel exhaled. "But your husband . . ."

"Is he all right?"

"He's alive, anyhow. The Gestapo had some questions for him." She smirked.

Annabel's stomach lurched with horror and guilt. "They didn't hurt Colette?"

"Not as far as I know." The woman seemed to be considering something before she leaned in and whispered, "Word is they will be released tomorrow. They know nothing."

Annabel blinked back tears of relief. "Oh, thank goodness. Please, you must let me see them."

"You know I can't do that."

"Please. I—I know what's coming for me, and I just want to say . . ." She drew in a trembling breath. "I want to say goodbye. I will reward you handsomely, I promise."

"You must know that the Gestapo have confiscated everything of value in your apartment," the woman said, clearly unmoved by the tears spilling down Annabel's cheeks.

"Yes, but there are other pieces, you see." Annabel knew she was taking a chance. If the German woman reported her offer to the Gestapo, she would lose all her leverage. "Pieces that could make you rich."

The Nazi woman studied her for a long time, her pudgy face a theater of conflicting emotions. Annabel watched as guilt and greed, compassion and fear waged war there, until finally, the woman's expression went slack. "And how will you get these pieces to me?"

Annabel sagged in relief. "After they're safe, I'll tell you—"

"No." The woman cut her off. "What if you're lying? Or if they do not keep you alive that long? If you want me to help you, you must tell me now."

She knew she couldn't do that, for to tell the overseer the location of her hidden jewels, her insurance policy, would leave her with nothing to bargain with. And she would take to her grave the secret of the bracelet sewn into Colette's gown; if Möckel had any idea that the piece he desperately wanted was right here, beneath his nose, Annabel had no doubt that he'd punish Colette for harboring it, and she couldn't let that happen. No, the pieces would have to come from the outside. "If you bring me to them, I will give my husband a letter," Annabel said at last. "He will bring it to the person who is holding some of my valuables for me."

"And what is it you are promising me?" Greed burned in the overseer's eyes.

"A diamond ring with a stone as big as the pit of a cherry." It was a piece Annabel had stolen just last week from a jewelry store that sold to Germans, owned by a collaborator who had betrayed several Jewish families in his neighborhood.

The woman stared at her. "This will not buy your freedom, you understand. You would give me something of such value simply for a chance to see your husband and daughter one last time?"

Annabel bowed her head. "Please. I must know they're safe, see it with my own eyes. I never intended for them to be caught up in this."

"Why did you do it, then? Why would you do things that put your family in so much danger?"

"I thought I was making a difference," she replied, an answer that was true but that sounded foolish now.

"Mankind was not bettered by your thievery, then?" the woman asked, sounding amused. It turned Annabel's stomach. "You give me your word that I will receive the ring?"

"Bring me a pen and paper, and I will write the letter now."

The woman stared at her for a long time. "I will make trouble for your husband and child if you have misled me. They'll be the ones to pay for your lie."

Her heart skipped, but she forced herself to remain calm. "I understand."

"Very well. Let me see what I can do."

The German overseer came to Annabel's cell sometime in the middle of the night, her face barely visible in the inky blackness. Annabel hadn't slept a wink, for she'd been determined to stay awake in case the woman came. Now, the steely-eyed jailer put a finger to her lips, unlocked Annabel's door, and beckoned for her to follow.

As the woman led Annabel through the darkened building, she said in a low voice, "Do you have the letter?"

Annabel nodded and held it up.

The overseer snatched it from her and mumbled something about reading it outside, and then she grabbed Annabel's arm and squeezed. "You make any move to run, and I'll shoot your daughter."

"I understand."

The woman brought Annabel into the back alley through a door at the rear of the building, and for a second, she was afraid that this had all been a trap. But then she saw Roger and Colette huddled by the door. Roger's face was swollen, his lip split, his left eye blackened.

"My darlings," she breathed.

Colette whimpered, "Mum!" But Roger just stared at her, not moving a muscle.

"You have one minute," the guard said tersely.

Annabel pulled Colette to her, holding tight. "Roger, my dear," she said as he continued to glare at her. "I'm so very sorry. I never intended for any of this to happen."

A muscle in his jaw twitched. "And yet here we are."

She blinked away the coldness in his tone. "I'm told you'll be released soon," she said. "You'll find Liliane, Roger? You give me your word?"

He looked puzzled. "Of course, Annabel. I am her father."

"You must take this letter to Frédéric, who has some of my things. The diamond ring is to go to the guard, by anonymous courier."

Anger flickered in Roger's expression as he pulled back. "To her?" he asked, glaring at the overseer, who glowered right back.

"Please. They'll come for you if she doesn't get the ring."

"Fine. I'll take care of it."

"And once you've found Liliane, you all must leave our apartment immediately, in case the Germans return for you."

"But it is *my* apartment," Roger protested. "It was handed down to me by my parents, Annabel."

"And it is the first place they will look for you and the children if they have more questions for you, Roger. Talk to Frédéric; he will help you find somewhere else to spend the remainder of the war."

He looked into her eyes for a long time, and she forced herself not to look away. As they stood there, she could so clearly see a time not so long ago when they stood just like this, gazing at each other, waiting to say their vows. They had been so naïve, so happy, with no idea of what was coming. She hadn't known just how much the years could change a person. Or was this who he'd always been, and it was just that, at last, the veneer had fallen away?

"Very well," he said finally.

She had been holding Colette the whole time they talked, and now, as the overseer cleared her throat pointedly, Annabel turned to her older daughter.

"You and your father must find Liliane as soon as you're released," Annabel said, doing her best not to cry. "Promise me, my love."

"I promise," Colette said, her voice small. "But aren't you coming with us?"

Annabel shook her head, her heart aching for all the things she would miss. She wouldn't get to see her daughters grow up; she wouldn't get to tell them every day how proud she was to be their mother; she wouldn't get to hold grandchildren in her arms. "I will always be with you, my love," she said. "Teach your children to be brave and strong and good, as you are, and I will be there in your every moment."

"It's time," the overseer grunted.

Annabel pulled Colette close once more, for what she knew would be the last time. "Find your sister," she repeated, "and know that I will love you both for all eternity."

"*Kyi-kyi-kyi*," Colette whispered through tears.

"*Ko-ko-ko*, my love," Annabel replied, her throat closing. "I'll be with you always."

Colette was crying as the overseer shoved her roughly away, but there was no time to comfort her because the woman was already dragging Annabel back toward the door.

"Back to your cells," the overseer barked at Roger. "You'll be released in the morning."

"What about my mother?" Colette asked.

The overseer just shook her head, and a shiver ran through Annabel as she saw understanding spark in her daughter's eyes. Colette's horrified gaze turned to her, and it nearly broke Annabel.

"I'm so sorry, Colette," Annabel said, her voice cracking, but then Roger grabbed Colette's hand and began to pull her away. "I love you, my darling."

"I love you, too, Mum." Colette kept her eyes fixed on Annabel until they disappeared into the darkness, but Roger didn't look back even once.

 CHAPTER TWENTY-ONE

2018

As Colette and Daniel walked through the front door of Hubert Verdier's assisted-living facility, Colette braced herself to be turned away—perhaps their visit a few days earlier had been too disruptive, or perhaps O'Mara had left word that she wasn't to be allowed to visit Verdier again. But the same receptionist sat at the desk, and when she looked up and saw Colette, she smiled.

"Lucas's friend, right?" she asked before Colette had a chance to speak. As Colette managed a startled nod, the woman's smile widened. "It's wonderful to see you visiting again, ma'am. Our residents get so much out of interactions with loved ones."

"How . . . lovely," Colette choked out.

Giving her the day's code to the memory-care floor, the receptionist cheerfully waved both Colette and Daniel through. "You may want to check the dining room first," the woman called after them as they headed to the elevator. "They should just be finishing up midmorning coffee and sweets. The residents love it!"

"Of course," Colette managed weakly.

"Are you all right?" Daniel asked a moment later as they rode up to the fourth floor.

"Not particularly. The idea of the man who may have killed my sister sitting upstairs enjoying coffee in his tenth decade of life while my sister died at the age of four . . ."

He put a hand on her lower back, steadying her. "I'm right here with you."

"Daniel, what if he's the man who did this? What if I sat across the table from the man who killed my sister more than seventy years ago, and just let him walk away?" She had been scouring her memory, but as far as she could recall, there was no sign then that he was anything but a police officer who was easily bought.

"How would you have known, Colette?" Daniel asked gently.

She didn't have an answer for that. She closed her eyes briefly and did her best to push the guilt away as the elevator door finally dinged and slid open. "Can you imagine what our mothers would say to see us together now?"

"I think they'd be very happy," Daniel said with a small smile as they stepped out onto the fourth floor.

Colette entered the security code, and once inside, they followed the sound of clattering dishes down a long hall into a dining area, where a few dozen residents were scattered around tables with mugs of coffee in front of them. A member of the staff walked around with a carafe, pouring refills and distributing cookies. "Here goes," Colette said softly as she spotted Hubert Verdier sitting alone at a table in the corner, looking into space with a frown.

"Hubert!" Colette said, sweeping toward him with a smile as Daniel trailed behind her. "How lovely to see you, my friend."

Verdier looked up at the two of them blankly. "Do I know you?"

She forced another smile. "Of course. We knew each other long ago, in Paris."

"I don't recognize you." He looked at Daniel. "Or you."

"We almost didn't recognize you either," Daniel replied without missing a beat. "How wonderful it is to see you."

He studied her. "What did you say your names are?"

"Daniel and Colette."

"What, you don't have last names?"

"Oh, we know each other far too well for those kinds of formalities, don't we?" Colette forced another bright smile. "We won't stay long anyhow. It will be nice to just reminisce about the past with you for a few minutes."

"I don't like to talk about the past," Verdier grumbled, but after a second, he gestured toward the chairs across the table. Daniel pulled out one of them for Colette, and they both sat.

"Oh, but this will be fun, Hubert," Colette said. As Verdier scowled at her, she forced herself to keep smiling brightly at him. "Remember? We know you from the old neighborhood," she continued kindly. "Paris was so different before the war, wasn't it? Do you remember the Square Maurice Gardette nearby? Or the Canal Saint-Martin?"

"Who wouldn't?"

"But then the Germans got there," she continued, "and everything changed."

He grunted, but he was paying attention, his eyes following her every movement.

"It was difficult to get by without working with them, wasn't it?" she went on with faux cheer, though every word tasted sour and strange. "What I mean to say is that I certainly understand that some people had no choice but to . . . collaborate."

"Are you accusing me of something?"

"Certainly not." She feigned shock and glanced at Daniel, who murmured his agreement. "I'm simply saying that I understand that some people—especially policemen, for example—might not have had a choice."

He looked at Daniel and then at Colette, brow furrowing. "What do you know about policemen?"

"Well, not as much as you, sir."

He looked at Daniel again. "What's the lady going on about?" he asked.

"Oh, just the authority you had back then," Daniel answered smoothly, and Colette wanted to kiss him. He was playing his role perfectly.

"I remember you clearly," she added quickly. Hubert's eyes flicked back to her, but he was beginning to look bored with the conversation. "You were so handsome in your uniform. I was just a girl, but I knew a good-looking gentleman when I saw one."

He puffed out his chest, suddenly a bit more interested. "Well, don't let Francine hear you talking that way."

"Francine? Was that your wife?"

Suddenly, whatever camaraderie had existed between them evaporated. "You know very well that my wife was Odile!" he snapped. He muttered something to himself. "You sound like her now, trying to trip me up."

"I sound like Odile? Your wife?"

"Who are you again?" He was beginning to become visibly agitated, his cheeks turning pinker, his eyes watering. "Do I know you?"

"I'm an old friend." It was time to cut to the chase. "Hubert, we've come to ask you about the night you tipped the Germans off about Annabel Marceau."

A storm seemed to flicker across his face—shadows, clouds, electricity, all in quick succession. "The Germans?" he repeated.

"You told the Germans about the stolen jewels in our apartment, didn't you? How did you know what my mother had done? How did you know where to find the bracelets? Why did you take my sister?" The words poured out with the sting of acid.

He stared at her. The silence seemed to swirl around them, heavy and dark. Her heart hammered as she waited for his reply.

"The Germans," he finally repeated once again, and then, to her surprise, he started to sob.

Daniel reached for her hand and squeezed. When she looked at him, he nodded toward the exit. He clearly thought she should stop, but she couldn't. Not when she was so close.

"Why are *you* crying?" she asked, pulling her hand from Daniel's and trying to keep the hatred out of her voice. How dare *he* shed tears over the past when he'd been the one to take everything?

"It is my greatest shame," he said. His tears continued to fall, marking the collar of his shirt, but he seemed not to notice. "My greatest shame, you see."

"The way you betrayed my family? What you did to my sister?"

He blinked at her. "The things I did under orders from the Germans . . ."

"*What* did you do? I need to hear you say it."

He banged his fist on the table, making both Colette and Daniel jump. "The deportation orders. So many Jewish families . . . I didn't know where we were sending them, I swear. I never would have . . ."

And then, as he trailed off, she understood what he was saying. He had been one of the many French policemen who had followed instructions from the Germans to arrest Jewish citizens, ultimately sending them to their deaths.

"I forget so many things," he concluded as he stared out the window. "But this, I remember clearly, like it was yesterday."

"Good," said Daniel. When Verdier turned to glare at him, he added, "You should remember the role you played in the mass murder of innocent people. If only a few of you had stood up to try to stop it . . . "

Verdier turned back to Colette, his face a mask of misery. "You think I'm not haunted by those ghosts every day?"

"What about my sister?" Colette pressed. She got out of her chair and walked closer to him. He flinched and cowered, as if he was afraid she was going to attack him. *No*, she wanted to say, *you're the monster, not I.* "Are you haunted by her ghost, too?"

"Was she one of the Jews?" he asked in a small voice. "They all haunt me, you see. The nightmares I have . . ."

"She was the girl you stole from our apartment window and murdered in August of 1942." She was running out of patience for this guilt trip down memory lane. "It was you, wasn't it? She was the girl whose bracelet you stole and kept for all these years."

His expression hardened, and his tears stopped instantly, like a faucet had been turned suddenly off. "The bracelet," he rasped. "This is about that damned bracelet?"

Her heartbeat accelerated. "Did you take my sister?" she asked, enunciating each word even as her voice cracked. "Did you take my sister from our bedroom and throw her into the Seine after you'd taken the bracelet?"

He opened and closed his mouth. Colette leaned in for a confession, but instead, he hissed, "Only a devil would do such a thing."

"And you're that devil!" she shot back.

"It isn't true!"

"Then how did you get it?"

He coughed and turned to Daniel, his expression suddenly calm, as if he'd forgotten the heated discussion they were in the middle of. "The Eiffel Tower sparkles now like a shop full of diamonds," he said pleasantly. "Did you know that? They've put lights on it, and the lights dance every night, sparkle, sparkle, sparkle."

"Answer her," Daniel said, his voice low and steady.

Colette touched Hubert's arm, and he jerked away from her as if he'd been burned. "Please," she said. "The diamond bracelet. The one that looks like a pair of lilies made of stars. I need you to tell me how you got it."

He was silent for a long time, and then finally, after a glance at Daniel, he turned to her, his expression suddenly sad and guileless. "I promised never to tell."

"You promised *who*?" She felt a shiver of doubt. Was there someone else involved? Was it possible that Verdier wasn't Liliane's killer after all?

"Did she send you?" he cried. "She sent you, didn't she? I told her to stop torturing me! Enough already!"

"Please. I'm begging you." She could feel her desperation creeping in, could hear it in her voice. "Please tell me what you did. Did you betray my mother? Did you kill my sister? Or was there someone else?"

He stared at her. "I am very tired now," he said after a long pause. "I'd like you to leave."

"But—"

"Nurse!" he cried suddenly, startling her.

"Please, no."

"Nurse!" he cried again. "Nurse! Help! I'm being harassed!"

In an instant, there were three nurses around him, consoling him, and before she knew it, a fourth nurse had arrived and was shooing her and Daniel away.

"No, please," Colette protested as Daniel grabbed her hand. "I just need him to answer my question. Please."

"You are agitating him, ma'am!" the nurse snapped. "I need you both to leave."

"Come on," Daniel said in a low voice. "We'll come back. But we have to go."

The nurse hustled them down the hall, toward the elevator. "I'll have to report this to Mr. Verdier's family."

"Please, you don't understand . . ." Colette tried to protest, but already, the nurse was turning away, and the door to the memory-care unit was closing behind them. "I've waited seventy-six years for the truth!"

But there was no reply. The door was already closed, and Colette watched helplessly through the window as the nurses soothed the man who may well have taken her sister's life.

 CHAPTER TWENTY-TWO

1942

Colette hurried along the Boulevard Raspail beside her father, doing her best to keep her head down and her mouth shut.

"I don't want to hear a word from you until we're home," he'd growled as he tugged her away from the Cherche-Midi prison, where Mum was still being held. The two of them had been unceremoniously released just before noon.

"But what about Mum?" she had asked, already knowing the answer. Tears slid down her cheeks as she struggled to glance over her shoulder.

Her father responded by yanking on her arm so hard it felt as if it might just pop free of her socket. "Don't look back."

She did her best to keep up with him as he tightened his vise-like grip on her hand and pulled her along. "Please slow down."

"Quiet, I said."

"What about Liliane?" she asked as they turned the final corner onto their street. "How will we find her?"

"I don't know," Papa spat. "I don't know, Colette, all right?"

"Maybe she's already come back," Colette ventured. But when they entered through their unlocked front door, their apartment was still and dark, a table overturned, a chair leaning haphazardly against a window, no sign of life. The Germans had pawed through everything, emptying drawers, overturning furniture, ripping even their mattresses apart. It looked like a wasteland. "Liliane?" Colette called out when her father remained mute, and when there was no answer, she cried her sister's name a bit more loudly. "Liliane!"

She hurried into the bedroom they shared and found it as still and dark as the parlor. "Liliane?" she asked once more into the silence, but she already knew that her sister wasn't there.

Her father was still standing in the parlor, just where she'd left him, when she ran back into the room. "Papa, we must find her." She couldn't keep the tremor out of her voice.

There was a knock then on the door, startling them both. "Liliane!" Colette cried, already racing for the door, but her father grabbed her and held her back.

"Wait," he said. He looked through the peephole and then opened the door, revealing Madame Nadaud, the building's concierge. Madame Nadaud was perfectly suited for the job of looking after the building, for she was a snoop who always knew everyone else's business. Usually, the way her gaze followed Colette and Liliane with suspicion was an annoyance, but today, Colette was profoundly grateful to see her, for if anyone knew where Liliane was, it would be the nosy Madame Nadaud.

"Madame!" she said before either of the adults could speak. "Is Liliane with you?"

Madame Nadaud opened and closed her mouth without a sound before turning to say something soft and indecipherable to Colette's father, whose face drained of color.

He glanced at Colette and then, with a frown, said to Madame Nadaud, "Perhaps we should speak in the hall."

"Do you know where my sister is?" Colette demanded, ignoring her father.

Madame Nadaud looked at Papa, who hesitated, then nodded and turned away. Madame Nadaud regarded Colette, the gleam in her eyes belying the carefully arranged false compassion plastered across her face. "My dear," she said, "I'm afraid your sister is gone."

Colette shook her head, not understanding, as Papa let out a low moan. "What do you mean, *gone?*"

Madame Nadaud looked once again to Colette's father, but his head was in his hands; he was no help.

"No," Colette whispered, a thick panic rising in her throat as understanding settled over her.

When Madame Nadaud spoke again, her words were directed to Papa. "There was a body found in the river. A child."

"No. No, no, no," he said. "It couldn't be her."

"Yes," Madame Nadaud said, sounding just a shade too satisfied to be relaying the worst news possible. "At first we assumed that it was just another Jew, thrown to her death."

Even through her grief, Colette felt a flash of white-hot rage toward Madame Nadaud for the casual disdain in her words. She couldn't protest, though, because she needed to hear what Madame Nadaud was about to say. She had the strange sense of the walls closing in around them.

"But it wasn't a Jew," Madame Nadaud continued excitedly, her faux sympathy nudged aside now by her eagerness to deliver gossip. "I saw the body myself, you see. I recognized her instantly."

"No, it isn't possible," Colette said.

"Oh, but I'm afraid it is, dear," Madame Nadaud said. "She was wearing a nightgown just like the one you have on now."

Colette looked down at her filthy blue nightgown, which she'd been wearing when the Germans dragged them off two nights ago. "But . . ."

"I'm quite certain. I saw her with my own two eyes. What a tragedy for our building. The neighbors are very upset. So many people to console! It's all been very exhausting for me."

Colette's heart was hammering. Her palms were sweaty. Her skin suddenly felt like it was on fire, a fire that would never be extinguished, and Colette wanted to claw her way out of her own body, to scream at the sky, to demand that God return her sister, for there had been a mistake, a terrible mistake. Before she knew what she was doing, she had rushed at Madame Nadaud, hammering the smug woman with her fists and screaming, "No, no, no, no!" until finally, Papa pulled her off and held her tight.

"I'm very sorry," he said to Madame Nadaud, his voice cracking as Colette wailed.

"Well, I never!" Madame Nadaud said indignantly, glaring at Colette as she brushed her clothes off. "You should really learn to control your children."

"Child," Papa corrected miserably.

"Pardon?" Madame Nadaud said.

"Child, not children," he said. "Now, I have only one."

Annabel passed three more days in Cherche-Midi, knowing she was living on borrowed time. The German overseer spoke not another word to her, and Annabel's tiny cell—no bigger than a broom closet—felt smaller and more claustrophobic by the hour.

The lumps of brown bread slipped through her door were hardly enough to subsist on; the small sips of water she took from the jug in her cell made her stomach rumble in protest.

At night, she could hear other prisoners whispering, and the realization that there were others around her in a similar predicament both saddened her and brought her the comfort of knowing she wasn't alone. On her second night in prison, after another visit from Möckel in which he'd demanded to know if she was working with an underground group and then watched with a smile as one of his men beat her so savagely that she lost both of her top front teeth, she heard the distant strains of other prisoners singing "La Marseillaise," which made her heart ache. She joined in softly, tears in her eyes. Even in this terrible prison, even with all of them facing death or deportation, the spirit of France was alive and well, and when the song concluded with a hushed but enthusiastic chorus of "*Vive le general de Gaulle*," Annabel began to sob.

There was hope for this country's future yet, even if she wouldn't live long enough to see it. As long as there were men and women willing to risk their reputations, their safety, their lives for what was right, there was the promise of a better tomorrow for her daughters.

"*Notre France vivra*," the other prisoners chanted each night at seven o'clock, three times over, and on the third night, Annabel joined in with the refrain. *Our France will live*. The words were true; Annabel could feel it in her bones.

She could no longer sleep, and at night, she closed her eyes and imagined Colette, Liliane, and Roger safe and well, perhaps on their way out of Paris. They would make it through the war. They would survive losing her. They would understand one day why it had been impossible for her to sit idly by while evil seeped into Paris. Her girls would grow into adults, and they'd become the kind of women who stood up for others, too. She was sure of it.

On the fourth morning, two Gestapo came for her, and she knew just from looking at the younger one's averted eyes that this was the end. Möckel would have more questions for her, she would again refuse to answer, and he would decide that since he wasn't going to get the bracelets back, he might as well take her life.

Later, as Möckel's henchmen beat Annabel, the world went blurry before her, and she felt her life slipping through her fingers like sand from a cracked hourglass. She had done what she thought was right, but for the first time, she understood that the price was too high.

She had made a mistake in thinking she could reclaim her friend's dignity by stealing back her jewels. Still, she knew that having the bracelets back would restore a piece of Hélène Rosman when she came home. She closed her eyes now and tried to find solace in imagining how Hélène's face would look when Colette and Liliane reunited her with the jewels hidden away in the linings of their gowns. She had to believe that this part of the story, at least, would have a happy ending.

"I told you that you would regret this," Möckel said at one point, swimming into view. The world had gone hazy; she knew many of her bones had been broken; her mouth was full of blood, and the ringing in her ears made him sound very far away.

"I regret nothing," she replied, but she wasn't certain Möckel could understand her, for her teeth were cracked, her jaw broken beyond all possibility of repair. "*Je ne regrette rien.*"

"Finish her," Möckel said. She could hear his footsteps receding, and the beating began again.

She closed her eyes, and as she released the last threads that connected her soul to her body, she saw an image in her mind, clear as day: her two daughters, old women now, holding hands under the shade of hazel trees that reminded her of the forest of her own childhood. There were children there, too, a promise that her family's legacy would live on. She would never know them, but God willing, she would watch over them always.

As she moved forward into death, she was smiling, for she had seen the future, and it was beautiful.

CHAPTER TWENTY-THREE

2018

Aviva, I need to talk to you about your friend Colette."
Those were the first words out of Lucas O'Mara's mouth
when Aviva answered a call from him on Friday morning.

"Um . . ." It was all Aviva could muster, for she couldn't
imagine what Colette had done this time, though it certainly had
to do with the bracelet. But hadn't Colette spent yesterday with
Daniel Rosman? Aviva had tried calling her after work, but Colette had merely texted back saying that they were on their way to
the museum so that Mr. Rosman could see the bracelet in person.
Surely she hadn't undertaken a heist while she was there, had she?
"What did she do?" She gritted her teeth while she waited for the
answer.

"She showed up at the assisted-living facility again," Lucas
said.

"That's all? Oh, thank God."

"That's *all*? I thought you and I talked about this! The staff
said she brought an older man with her this time, and they harassed my wife's grandfather in the dining room."

Aviva closed her eyes. "She brought Daniel Rosman with her?"

"Who's Daniel Rosman?" Lucas asked.

Aviva hesitated. "It's a long story. But it seems that the bracelet belonged to his family before it belonged to Colette. You didn't meet him at the museum yesterday?"

"I left as soon as Hubert's home called me to tell me what happened. This Rosman is from the family you said it was stolen from?"

"Yes."

Lucas was silent for a moment. "You do know that I had no idea about any of this, right? That as far as I knew, the bracelet was a Verdier family heirloom?"

"I believe you. But Lucas, as much as I understand where you're coming from in wanting to protect your wife's grandfather, Colette and Mr. Rosman should have the opportunity to ask how the bracelet wound up here, in his possession."

Lucas was silent for a moment. "Hubert has fewer and fewer lucid moments these days, Aviva. It might be too late to expect him to remember anything."

"But if there's a chance he might—"

"The assisted-living facility is insisting that your friend Colette be banned. They're concerned about her repeatedly agitating a patient."

"Please don't let them ban her."

"It's not up to me, Aviva. But there's someone else who might know what happened. Someone whose memories might be clearer anyhow."

"Who?"

"My grandfather. He's known Hubert since before they both immigrated to the States. He's still sharp as a tack. If Hubert told him where the bracelet came from, he'll remember it."

"Have you asked him about it?"

"Hubert and my grandfather had a falling-out a number of years ago. He's made it clear several times that he has no desire to talk about anything having to do with Hubert."

"So what makes you think he'll tell you anything now?" Aviva asked.

"Well—he probably won't."

Aviva's heart sank. "Okay . . ."

"But he may tell *you*."

"Me?"

"Look, you have a good reason for wanting answers here. My grandfather's a decent man, and if he can give your friend Colette some peace, I think he'd want to do that. Why don't you come with me to his house tonight for dinner?"

"Lucas, are you sure?" Aviva asked.

"I have plans with him already, and he won't mind if I bring a guest. I'm very aware that someone I consider family might have deeply hurt someone you consider family. I'm doing the best I can to make it right."

Aviva's heart squeezed. "I know. Thank you, Lucas."

It wasn't a date. Aviva knew that, of course, but she would be lying if she said she hadn't lingered a bit longer than usual in her closet before picking out a navy dress that dipped low in the front—but not too low—and hugged her curves—but not too much.

She called Colette on her walk back to the office and was frustrated when it rang through to voicemail. "Call me back, Colette," she said. "I heard what you did at the assisted-living facility, and we're going to talk about that. But in the meantime,

I'm seeing Lucas O'Mara's grandfather tonight. I'll tell you if I find anything out. In the meantime, don't do anything stupid, okay?"

But Colette didn't return the call, and the rest of the afternoon fell away in a blur of drafting motions and briefs.

Aviva was waiting in the lobby of her building when Lucas arrived five minutes before five in charcoal pants and a crisp forest-green button-down. "You look beautiful," he said, looking her in the eye. Then something in his expression changed, and he cleared his throat. "I mean, if that's okay to say."

"Thank you. You look great, too."

He smiled at her. "I suppose it's too late to ditch my grandfather and just take you out to dinner?"

She could feel herself blushing. "Can I take a rain check on that?"

"You name the day," he said, holding her gaze.

"Does your grandfather know I'm coming?"

"I called ahead and said I was bringing a friend. I didn't tell him why, though."

"Oh, great," Aviva said. "It's an ambush."

Lucas shrugged. "I don't think he would have agreed to see us if he knew we were coming to ask him about Hubert. It's . . . complicated. It's better this way."

On their drive out to Weymouth, where Lucas's grandfather lived, Aviva told the story of Daniel Rosman's arrival and his claim on the bracelet, as well as Colette's. By the time they pulled into his grandfather's driveway, Lucas's face was pale, his expression grave.

"No wonder it's so important to you to find out how it got here," he said as he helped her out of the car. "I have a hard time believing that Hubert is the person you seem to think he is, but what happened to Colette and Daniel is horrendous. The brace-let's in my possession, which means I owe it to you to help."

"You don't owe me anything."

"But Colette deserves answers, Aviva. I know that. I'll do what I can to help you get to the bottom of this."

She nodded, a lump in her throat. It took her a few seconds before she was able to say, "I just want to bring Colette some peace."

Lucas led her up the winding front walkway to his grandfather's house, a large, white two-story with black trim. "What a beautiful home," Aviva said.

"It's where I grew up," he said with a smile. "When I was little and my mom and I moved back to Boston, we lived with my grandparents."

He rang the bell, and a moment later, the front door swung open to reveal a tall, white-haired man with slightly stooped shoulders. He stepped forward to hug Lucas and then turned to smile at Aviva. "Lucas," he said warmly, a French accent still coating his words. "Who have you brought with you this evening?"

"This is my friend Aviva," Lucas said. "Aviva, this is my grandfather."

When Aviva reached out to shake hands with him, she was surprised to find his grip strong, though she could feel a tremble in his arm. "Nice to meet you, sir."

"Call me Bill, young lady," he said. "And please, come in."

Aviva smiled at Lucas as they followed his grandfather down a long hallway that opened into a dining room. He used a walker, but otherwise, he seemed in good health.

"You'll forgive me for the early dining hour, young lady," he said, throwing Aviva a smile over his shoulder as they entered the dining room. The table had already been set, and his housekeeper was bustling around, filling glasses with water. She smiled at Lucas, nodded at Aviva, and then headed for the kitchen. "Back in my younger days, I didn't eat until nine o'clock most nights. But now, I'm sorry to say, I'm fast asleep by then. Ah, the indignities of age."

Aviva returned the smile. "Don't tell anyone, but I love a good early bird special."

Bill chuckled. "To be honest, I've found that as long as the meal includes a nice glass of wine, it doesn't really matter what time you take it."

"A man after my own heart," Aviva said.

"Excuse me, Bill," the woman cut in, reemerging into the dining room. "Would you like me to uncork a bottle of the Artemis?"

"That would be lovely, Sondra, thank you." He glanced at Aviva. "Aviva, this is Sondra, who's been with me for many, many years. Sondra, this is Lucas's friend, Aviva."

Sondra smiled. "It's nice to meet a friend of Lucas's," she said. "I can't remember the last time he brought someone home."

"Please, sit, sit," Bill said, sitting down and gesturing to the two seats across from him. "Sondra, we'll have that wine now."

The woman bustled off as Lucas and Aviva took their seats. "Sondra is a wonderful cook, isn't she, Lucas?"

"She makes the best meat loaf in the world," Lucas said.

"Well, we are not having meat loaf tonight." Bill winked at his grandson. "It has been a long time since Lucas has brought home a young lady. This deserves a special meal."

"Granddad—" Lucas began, shooting Aviva an apologetic look.

"No, no, you don't have to explain," his grandfather said, raising his palms. "To be honest, Aviva, it means a lot to me when

Lucas includes me in his life. It gets rather lonely around here. If I didn't have Sondra, I fear I'd lose my mind."

Aviva swallowed hard and shot Lucas a guilty look. "Maybe we should—"

But Lucas reached for her hand under the table and squeezed. "What Aviva is trying to say is that we're very glad to be here with you, Granddad. And we do look forward to just talking. But first, we had some questions we want to ask you."

Concern flickered in Bill's expression. "Questions?"

Sondra bustled back in then with an open bottle of wine, and no one said anything as she went around the table, filling each of their glasses. When she was done, she nodded at Bill, who gave her a distracted half smile.

"To Lucas," Bill said, raising his glass as Sondra disappeared back into the kitchen. Lucas and Aviva exchanged looks and raised theirs, too. "Now what's this all about? I was under the impression that this was to be a friendly meal with a new friend of yours."

"It is, Granddad, I promise. But we hoped you might be able to help us with something." Lucas squeezed Aviva's hand again. "We've come to ask you about the bracelet that belongs to Vanessa's grandfather." A storm cloud moved across the older man's face as Lucas continued. "Like I said on the phone, there's a woman who's been asking Hubert a lot of questions."

"What do I care about Hubert?" his grandfather snapped.

"I know that the two of you had a falling-out—" Lucas said.

"You don't know anything about it, son," his grandfather interrupted. "And to air our dirty laundry in front of a guest? What were you thinking?"

"Sir, I'm sorry, I didn't mean to—" Aviva began, but the color was rising in Bill's face, and he seemed not to hear her as he leaned across the table to speak directly to Lucas.

"It isn't enough that you displayed that damned bracelet without asking me, and now this?" he demanded. "Questions that have no place being asked in front of a stranger?"

Lucas blinked a few times. "But why would I ask you about displaying the bracelet, Granddad? It belongs to Hubert, doesn't it?"

"Yes, of course it does. But . . ."

"But what, Granddad?"

"But there's so much you don't know."

"Okay," Lucas said. "So tell us."

Instead of answering, his grandfather stood and walked with difficulty to the mantel, where an old black-and-white family picture was displayed in a silver frame. Aviva had noticed it on the way in; it was a couple in their thirties with a girl who looked to be around eleven or twelve—Bill and his wife with Lucas's mother, she assumed.

Now, Bill stared at the image for a long time before picking it up. He glanced at Aviva and then back at Lucas, a look of resignation on his face. "Did you know that your grandmother had an affair, Lucas?"

Aviva choked on a sip of wine and glanced at Lucas, whose eyes had widened.

"Grandma?" he asked.

His grandfather nodded. "For many years. I suspect that even when this photograph was taken in 1950, the affair had already begun."

"Are you sure?" Lucas asked. Aviva wanted to slip out of the room and leave them to their private family conversation, but then Lucas's grandfather spoke again.

"It was the bracelet that gave it away, you see," he said, and suddenly, Aviva understood. Just as the bracelet had played a role

in the downfall of Daniel Rosman's family members, and Colette's, it had been involved in a betrayal of Lucas's grandfather,
too. Perhaps the piece was cursed.

"Wait, wait, wait," Lucas said, his voice stiff, "you're saying
that Grandma had an affair with *Hubert*?"

His grandfather looked him in the eye and nodded, seemingly
waiting for him to put the rest of the pieces together.

"And that's why you and Hubert had a falling-out? Because
you found out?" Lucas put a hand to his forehead. "Did Vanessa
know?"

"I don't think Hubert told a soul, but what do I know? I
wouldn't have thought him capable of carrying on an affair
with my wife beneath my nose—and his wife's—for decades,
either."

"*Decades*? My grandmother and my wife's grandfather were
having an affair for decades? How did you find out?"

His grandfather finally put the photograph down, turning it
away as if he couldn't bear to look at the evidence that they'd
once been a happy family. "She came home wearing the bracelet
one day."

Lucas shot a confused look at Aviva and then turned back
to his grandfather. "But that's not exactly evidence of an affair,
is it?"

His grandfather sighed. "I had suspected for a long time that
she was carrying on with someone, Lucas. I just never imagined it
was with one of our oldest friends. Apparently . . ." He trailed off
and drew a deep breath. "Apparently, he let her wear it each time
they . . ." He shook his head in disgust.

"That's why you're so upset that I'm displaying it."

His grandfather hesitated. "Yes. And if I didn't know better,
I might think that Hubert had given it to you deliberately, to

ruffle my feathers." His gaze flicked to Aviva. "And what is your friend's involvement in all of this?"

"The woman who was asking Hubert all those questions is a good friend of Aviva's."

Aviva gave him a guilty smile, and he glowered at her and then at Lucas.

Sondra bustled back in then with three small salads, which she set in front of each of them before glancing around and registering the chill that had fallen over the room. "Is everything all right?" she asked.

"Just fine, Sondra," Bill said stiffly. "Though I fear I'm losing my appetite." He turned to Aviva as Sondra went back into the kitchen. "So this isn't a friendly visit after all."

"It *is* a friendly visit, sir," Aviva said. "I'm sorry to upset you. It's just that my friend Colette has been looking for the bracelet for more than seventy-five years, since the day her mother was arrested and her sister was murdered."

Bill stared at her. "Murdered? I don't understand."

"The bracelet disappeared the same night Colette's sister was kidnapped," Aviva continued, "and we believe that if we can understand why Mr. Verdier had it, perhaps we'll be a bit closer to discovering what happened to her sister."

The color had drained from Bill's face, and he tugged at his collar. "There was certainly no murder. Hubert isn't—" He stopped abruptly.

"With all due respect, Granddad, how can you be so sure that Hubert was truthful with you about anything?" Lucas asked. "If he was dishonest enough to have an affair—"

"I *told* you I don't want to talk about that!" Bill snapped, tugging at his collar once more. Aviva was beginning to worry about him; it was clear he was becoming agitated.

"I know, I know," Lucas said, holding up his hands. "I'm sorry. I am. But Granddad, we need to get to the bottom of this. Aviva's friend deserves to find some peace."

"Peace?" He choked out a laugh. "The ghosts of the past sneak up on us all. You aren't old enough yet to know that."

"Granddad—" Lucas said, but his grandfather cut him off.

"Who is this friend of yours?" his grandfather asked, his gaze flicking to Aviva. "You say her sister was taken?"

"From her bedroom window," Aviva said. "The same night the Germans came to arrest her family in 1942."

He stared at her. "But this can't be true."

"Please, Granddad," Lucas said. "Anything Hubert told you might help."

"You think answers to decades-old questions will change a thing?" Bill was still staring at Aviva. "And you, young lady. I know you must think you're helping this friend of yours, but stirring up the past only hurts those who lived through it. It's all very entertaining to try to solve a mystery, isn't it? But do you understand that when old wounds are reopened, they hurt very deeply?"

"I think, sir," Aviva said gently, "that my friend's wounds never closed. She has lived her whole life feeling that her sister's death was her fault. I think that learning the truth about what happened would bring her some peace, at last."

Bill looked at his plate for a very long time. None of them had touched their salads yet. In the silence, they could hear pans banging in the kitchen and the sound of running water.

"What became of your friend's mother?" he asked at last. Aviva and Lucas exchanged glances; it wasn't at all what she had expected him to say. "The one who was arrested."

"Colette's mother? She was executed by the Germans, sir," Aviva said.

Bill made a noise in the back of his throat, but he didn't say anything.

"Please, Granddad," Lucas said. "If you know anything, we're begging you to tell us. Help us bring Ms. Marceau some peace."

Bill coughed sharply, and then silence descended once more as he continued to stare at his plate. "It's too late," he said, his voice thin and raspy.

"Too late for what, Granddad?" Lucas asked.

Bill didn't answer right away. "Too late to change the past," he said at last. "It's done. Settled. Over. It's a mistake to try to dig it up. A mistake for everyone."

"I'm afraid, sir, that it's being dug up anyhow," Aviva said gently. When Bill turned to her, she said, "A man whose family it originally belonged to is planning to claim it, which will likely mean a legal inquiry about its provenance."

Bill's expression shuttered. "I know nothing about any of it."

"Granddad—" Lucas said, but his grandfather cut him off.

"I'd like the two of you to go now," he said calmly. "I'm sorry, young lady. I know I must seem quite rude. But I'm very tired all of a sudden."

"Granddad!"

But Bill held up a hand to stop him. "Sondra!" he called, and Aviva couldn't help but notice that he didn't sound tired at all.

Sondra hurried back in and looked uncertainly at their untouched plates. "Sir?"

"We're done with dinner, Sondra," Bill said. "I'd like you to show Lucas and his friend to the door."

Lucas stood, his jaw clenched. "Granddad, if you can think of anything else . . ."

"You'll be the first to know, Lucas." He looked at Aviva as she stood from the table.

"Come on," Sondra said firmly. "I'll walk you two out."

As Sondra led them out of the room, murmuring an apology, Aviva could feel Bill's eyes following her, and a shiver of certainty ran down her spine. He knew something. And that meant she was one step closer to the truth.

 CHAPTER TWENTY-FOUR

1942

Two days after they'd been released from Cherche-Midi, Papa took Colette to see Mum's closest friends, Uncle Frédéric and Aunt Marie.

"We've had some news from our concierge," Colette's father said stiffly to Uncle Frédéric after they'd greeted each other. Uncle Frédéric was not really Colette's uncle, but rather the jewel broker her mother had been using in Paris since before Colette was born. Colette had never met Mum's brother, Leo, who lived in England, and Papa had no living relatives. Frédéric and his wife Marie were the closest thing she had to extended family.

"Roger, I know," Uncle Frédéric said, his voice thick with grief. "I heard the rumor but I did not believe it, so I went to the river where they were pulling the body up . . ." He drew a shuddering breath and glanced at Colette. "I hoped to be able to tell you that the rumors were wrong, but . . ."

"But what, Uncle Frédéric?" Colette prompted, her voice small.

"But," Uncle Frédéric said, his voice cracking, "I recognized the nightgown. With the *L* stitched across the front. It is the one my Marie made for Liliane." He reached out for Colette's hand. "The nightgown that matches yours."

"And you're certain?" Roger asked.

Uncle Frédéric nodded. "I sat beside Marie each night as she sewed the gowns. I would recognize it anywhere."

"And the bracelet sewn into the lining?" Roger asked. Colette couldn't understand why that mattered, but her father's jaw was rigid with anger.

"Gone," Uncle Frédéric said. "The hem had been ripped open."

Colette's father put a hand over his mouth.

"Papa, what is it?" Colette ventured after a few seconds.

"It means that the man who took your sister knew about the jewels," he said, his voice flat. "It means that she was likely taken by someone who knew your mother, who knew what she was up to."

"But . . ." Colette said, her stomach turning. A life for a meaningless piece of gold, studded with a few sparkling gemstones? "What about my half of the bracelet?"

It wasn't what she had intended to ask—and when the question came out, it came out all wrong. She didn't care about the bracelet itself. She was asking what she was supposed to do with a piece that would never be complete again, but more than that, she wanted someone to tell her what *she* was supposed to do knowing that she would never again be whole. How would she live in a world without her sister?

Her father fixed her with a look so cold that she could feel the ice inside her. "I don't give a damn what you do with it," he said.

"But—"

"Your sister is *dead*, Colette."

As if she didn't know. As if she didn't feel in the very depths of her soul that it was her fault for turning her back. As if she wouldn't blame herself for it forever. "I'm so sorry, Papa," she said. "I'm so sorry."

"You should be," he spat. "You were responsible for her! You left her alone, and then when you saw someone taking her away, you weren't even clever enough to go after her! You just stood there!"

"But the Germans—"

"Bah! You could have run from them if you wanted to!" Papa shot back. "But you were too frightened, Colette, and now your sister is *dead*."

The words sliced into her like knife blades. "I know." Her eyes welled with tears.

"Roger, it isn't her fault," Uncle Frédéric said, his tone suddenly clipped. "Leave the child alone!"

Papa whirled on Uncle Frédéric. "Leave her alone? She didn't even get a good look at the man who took her sister! Perhaps we would have found her in time if we knew more about him other than the fact he was apparently wearing a uniform of some sort."

"I'm so sorry," Colette sobbed, but her father waved her words away.

"As far as I'm concerned, you can take that bracelet—and every other damned thing your mother stole—and throw it in the Seine," he said. "I want nothing to do with any of it."

"Now, Roger—" Uncle Frédéric said, a flush creeping up his neck.

"Don't 'Now, Roger' me," her father said, turning on Uncle Frédéric again. "It's over, Frédéric. I should have put a stop to this madness long ago. I should have forbidden Annabel from doing what she did. I knew it was a mistake, and now I have to live with the fact that I did nothing about it."

"She's a grown woman, Roger!" Uncle Frédéric exclaimed. "She didn't need your permission. She was doing what she felt was right. She was trying to make a difference in the world, like those who came before her."

Colette's father's eyes blazed. "A difference, you say? Look where it got her. Her daughter is dead, and she soon will be, too, if she isn't already."

Colette gasped. "Papa, what do you mean?"

Uncle Frédéric glared at Colette's father and put his arm around Colette, as if he could protect her from the blow that was coming.

"I mean," Colette's father said, his voice dripping with disdain as he turned to her, "that your mother took things too far. And they will kill her for it, Colette. Is that clear enough?"

Colette closed her eyes. "No. It can't be."

"Roger, to speak this way in front of your daughter—" Uncle Frédéric said, his voice cracking.

But Colette's father interrupted. "I'm finished, Frédéric. With all of it." He began to move toward the door, but Uncle Frédéric released Colette and stepped into his path.

"Now wait just a moment," Uncle Frédéric said. "I know that times are difficult right now, but you have a daughter who needs you, and—"

But Colette's father shoved him aside, barely breaking his stride. At the door, he turned. "I'll bring you the rest of Annabel's jewels tomorrow, the ones that the Germans missed beneath our floorboards. It should be enough to get Colette out of Paris. Annabel has a brother, Leo, in England. You can send her there."

And then, without a look back, he was gone, taking all semblance of normalcy with him. Colette buried her head against Uncle Frédéric's shoulder and wept.

Colette had been certain, at first, that her father would return for her. He was grieving just as she was, and he blamed her for Liliane's death, just as she knew she would always blame herself.

It was true that at fourteen, she wasn't a little girl anymore, and that all across Europe, children her age had lost their parents and were having to learn to fend for themselves. But Colette was no orphan; her father was still very much alive. Surely he would remember that he still had one child who needed him. She knew how he felt about jewel theft, and she imagined that his feelings had only hardened after what had happened to Mum, so she did her best to ignore her urge to steal.

"He'll come back, won't he?" she asked one night over dinner with Uncle Frédéric and Aunt Marie. They were kind people, people who had loved her mother, people who had known Colette and Liliane since they'd been born. They had taken Colette in without hesitation when her father had deposited her there three weeks before.

When he answered, Uncle Frédéric looked her in the eye, which she appreciated; he treated her not as a burden or a child, but as someone intelligent he was glad to share a table with. "I fear not, my dear girl," he said gently. "I've had word that he has left Paris."

"But . . . where did he go?"

"North, I've heard. That's all I know, I'm afraid."

Colette glanced at Marie, whose head was bowed, then she looked back at Uncle Frédéric. "Surely my father won't abandon me, though," Colette said into the silence. "Surely he'll come back."

"Before the war, my dear, I would have thought the same. But this conflict—all the fear and death and tragedy—has changed us all."

"It is because he blames me for Liliane," Colette said quietly. "As well he should. If I hadn't turned my back—"

"Nonsense, Colette," Uncle Frédéric cut in. "You are not responsible, no matter what your papa says. Please, my dear, this burden is not yours to carry."

But Colette knew he was wrong. How else could her own father have abandoned her so easily? No, she had done something terribly wrong, and now, she was getting what she deserved.

"I'm very sorry," she said after a while as she picked at the food in front of her: a watery bowl of turnip soup, a piece of bread made from questionable grain. She had lost her appetite weeks ago, and it still hadn't returned. "I shouldn't be your responsibility. Another mouth to feed at a time like this . . ."

This time, it was Marie who answered. "My dear girl," she said, "you are here because you are our family. We loved your mother, and we love you, too. We will continue trying to reach your uncle in England, but in the meantime, you have a home with us as long as you need it."

Two months after she'd come to stay with Uncle Frédéric and Aunt Marie, Colette slipped away one afternoon to make sure that her father was really gone, tracing a lifetime of familiar steps to the rue Pasteur. But she found the door to her old apartment locked and boarded, and when she rapped on the door to the concierge's apartment, the sullen old woman barked at her to get out.

"Your father said to tell anyone who asked that you were both dead, I suppose so that the Germans don't come back sniffing around the place," she said. "Do you mean to put me in danger by returning here?"

"Of course not, Madame Nadaud. I'm very sorry, but has my father really moved away?"

"Are you deaf? Of course he has. He couldn't very well play dead in his own home, could he?"

Colette swallowed hard. "But what will become of the apartment?"

Madame Nadaud puffed up her chest. "He has paid me handsomely to keep it for him until the end of the war. He will pay me more upon his return."

"I see." He had evidently kept some of her mother's stolen jewels for himself, using them to bribe the concierge. So much for wanting nothing to do with them. "Do you know where he's gone?"

She jutted out her chin. "To Brittany, that's all I know. But if I were you, I'd forget about him. Aren't you the one who abandoned your sister? A father doesn't forgive a thing like that."

It felt like the woman had slapped her. "But—"

"Now get out before I call the authorities." She slammed her door, leaving Colette frozen in the hall.

She went next to the police prefecture, summoning all her confidence before she approached the desk.

"I'm looking for Monsieur Charpentier," she said, trying to sound casual and not as if she was terrified of the men in uniform, who she now knew were capable of destroying people's lives. "He's an officer here."

The man sniffed as if he'd smelled something foul. "Guillaume Charpentier? He's gone."

"Gone?"

"He got a transfer to somewhere in the south. Lucky bastard."

Colette's heart sank. He was the last person she knew who might be able to help her find answers. "Thank you," she whispered. She made it to the street outside before she began to cry.

Over the next few months, Uncle Frédéric wrote repeatedly to Uncle Leo, but they never received a reply. They had no way of knowing whether Leo was still alive, whether he had received any of Frédéric's correspondence, and whether he might find it within his heart to welcome his sister's teenage daughter.

One night early in the new year, after Colette had been living with Uncle Frédéric and Aunt Marie for several months, they sat her down beside the fireplace for a talk. She was nearly fifteen, and she had gone in an instant from being a child to being a woman who had no choice but to stand on her own two feet. She still hadn't returned to stealing, though, for what if her father came back for her? She couldn't give him a reason to walk away again. But with each passing day, she began to understand that she was turning her back on those who needed her help, turning her back on her heritage, turning her back on what her mother had lived—and died—for. It would break Mum's heart to see what had become of her.

"There are some things we'd like to speak with you about," Uncle Frédéric said once they were all settled, the heat from the dying embers not nearly enough to warm the bitter cold that had set in.

"It is time for me to leave, isn't it?" Colette guessed. "I'm sorry. I have overstayed my welcome—"

"No," Uncle Frédéric cut in swiftly. "Not at all, my dear. Your home is here for now. It is clear enough that there will be no travel to England in the midst of a war."

"Thank you," she said, looking from Frédéric to Marie, who looked uneasy. "But then, what is it?"

"I know we have all long suspected, but we have received definitive word about your mother," Aunt Marie answered, her tone gentle. "We weren't sure whether to tell you, but, well, you deserve to know what happened."

"She's dead, isn't she?" Colette said, for she had felt it in her soul. Liliane's absence had felt different, but of course that was because it was cloaked in her guilt.

"Yes," Uncle Frédéric said without hesitation. He looked Colette squarely in the eye, addressing her once again as an adult. "I'm very sorry, Colette. As it turns out, the man she stole those bracelets from is well known for being both cruel and vindictive. She couldn't have chosen a worse target."

"It was very important to her to take those bracelets back, though," Colette said. "They belonged to her friend."

"Yes, I know," Uncle Frédéric said. "I knew the Rosmans, too, and I was as upset about what happened to them as your mother was. Your mother was trying to do the right thing, to save a pair of pieces that meant the world to that family. But I imagine the German responsible for her death felt humiliated by the theft. He is probably furious that despite punishing her, the bracelets are not back in his possession."

Colette thought about her half of the piece, which she'd carefully sewn into the lining of her brassiere. She wore it over her heart each day, and she vowed that whatever happened, she would make sure that Möckel never laid eyes on it again. She would keep it safe until Hélène Rosman returned, just as her mother had wanted. "Do you think Liliane's half of the bracelet will resurface?"

"One day. If the man who took her life took the jewels, too, it was almost certainly because he intended to sell them, not because he intended to enjoy them for himself. I have inquiries out to every jeweler I know. When the bracelet appears again, we will know."

 # CHAPTER TWENTY-FIVE

2018

"Are you okay?" Aviva asked as she and Lucas drove back to Boston. Lucas's knuckles were white from gripping the wheel, his expression unreadable in the darkness.

He glanced at her and then looked back at the road. "I'm mortified that my grandfather talked to us like that. It's very unlike him. I'm really sorry."

"It's me who should be apologizing to you. It was my questions that stirred all of this up."

"But you had every right to ask them."

"Still, I'm so sorry you had to find out about your grandmother that way."

Lucas sighed. "To be honest, knowing she had an affair doesn't surprise me. I loved her—she was my family—but she was the most self-centered person I've ever known. When I was a kid, she'd get angry if my grandfather paid attention to me instead of her, even if it was only for a few minutes. I think my mom really struggled with that, too. Things were really rocky between her and my grandmother. I don't know how my grandfather lived with her all those years."

"Relationships are complicated," Aviva said softly.

Lucas choked out a laugh. "I'd say that's the understatement of the evening. You must feel like you've stepped into a soap opera—my grandmother having an affair with my wife's grandfather? Honestly, Aviva, I'm very embarrassed."

"Hey," she said, reaching out to touch his arm. "None of this is your fault."

Lucas's voice was rough. "You have to admit, it's pretty screwed up."

"Eh, we're all a little screwed up," she said. "That's what makes us interesting."

He laughed and then sobered. "How am I going to tell Millie? She never knew my grandmother, but she's always had a great relationship with her great-grandpa Hubert. He's the last piece of her mother's side of the family left. This is going to break her heart."

Aviva shrugged. "Maybe she doesn't need to know. It's hard enough losing your mom when you're young. I think that this would feel like another profound loss."

"Maybe you're right. I try so hard to do the right thing with her, but it's hard to know what that is sometimes, you know? I worry a hundred times a day that I'm screwing it all up."

"I think," Aviva said, "that just being there for her, loving her, is the best thing you could be doing. I didn't have that after my mom died. I had Colette, but that wasn't the same as having a parent. I have the feeling that you're an incredible dad, Lucas. It's not about getting it right one hundred percent of the time. It's about showing up and trying."

Lucas gave her a small, sad smile. "Thanks for that."

"Anytime."

Lucas was quiet for a moment. "Listen, I know tonight was a complete train wreck, but since my grandfather kicked us out before we had a chance to eat, do you have any interest in having dinner with me now?"

Aviva turned to him in surprise. "Are you sure you want to? After everything that happened tonight?"

"Very sure—if you're up for it. In fact, I can't think of a better way to turn the evening around. Unless, of course, you're completely alienated and want nothing to do with me, which, by the way, I would totally understand, too."

Aviva's heart fluttered. "I'd love to join you for dinner," she said with a smile.

His eyes were warm as he turned to her. "Good. How does Italian sound? There's a great little place right by the museum."

"Italian sounds perfect."

Five minutes later, Lucas had just pulled into a spot along the street and cut the ignition when his cell phone rang, startling them both. "Sorry," he said, digging in his pocket. "I just have to make sure it's not Millie."

"Never apologize for being a good dad." She watched as he looked down at his phone, blinked a few times, and then shot her an indecipherable look before picking up.

"Hello?" he answered, and then he was silent for a second as the person on the other line spoke. "What happened?" he asked, and then, a moment later, "Okay. I'll be right there."

"What is it?" she asked after he'd hung up. "It wasn't your daughter, was it?"

Lucas ran a hand through his hair. "No. It was the assisted-living facility."

Aviva groaned. "Oh, no. Not Colette again."

"No." Lucas took a deep breath. "Apparently, Hubert collapsed in the hallway on the way back to his room after dinner. They called an ambulance, and he's being taken to the hospital now. They think it was a heart attack—he's not conscious. I—I have to go."

"I'll come with you," Aviva said instantly. "I mean, if you want me to."

Lucas held her gaze. "I do. If you're sure."

She nodded, and as he turned the car back on and pulled away from the curb, she found herself praying hard that Hubert would survive long enough for Colette to get her answers.

Colette sat across the table from Marty, a candle flickering between them in the low light of the Edgewater, Colette's favorite restaurant on the South Shore. She had called Marty earlier in the day to ask how soon he could sell the ring he was holding for her, and told him there was something else she wanted to discuss, too. He'd told her that he had a busy day, but that he'd make a reservation somewhere for dinner that evening.

She hadn't expected this, though. When he picked her up, he'd seemed uncharacteristically nervous, and he hadn't told her where he was taking her until they were a block away.

"What on earth made you choose someplace so nice?" she asked him as they waited at a stoplight. Usually, she and Marty dined in the back of his shop or at one of the casual restaurants nearby.

"No reason," Marty said, his eyes darting quickly to her and then back to the road as the light changed.

"If I didn't know better," she said, "I would think you were trying to woo me."

Marty just laughed as he pulled up to the valet stand at the Edgewater, but she could see color creeping up his neck. She imagined that she must be blushing, too.

Now, as the waiter delivered a first course of oysters, Colette had the strangest feeling that they were on a date, and she wasn't sure how she felt about that.

"You know, Colette," Marty ventured after slurping an oyster and washing it down with a sip of the sauvignon blanc they'd ordered, "I've been wanting to do this for years."

"Do what?" she asked, taking a sip of her wine.

"Take you out properly."

"Then why haven't you?" She couldn't stop herself from asking the question. After Marty's wife had died some twenty years ago and he'd begun to date again, she had wondered whether he might ask her out, but he never had. He had opted for younger women, and she'd felt like a bottle of milk past its expiration date.

"I should have," he said. "Is it too late now?"

Colette touched her bare wrist, thinking of the bracelet that had glimmered there just a day before, the bracelet she'd given back to Daniel Rosman, fulfilling her mother's decades-old wish. Daniel's appearance in her life had upended everything. She'd felt like herself with him in a way she hadn't felt in many years with anyone, even Marty.

After leaving Hubert's assisted-living facility a few days earlier, and after seeing the other half of the bracelet in the museum, Daniel had come home with Colette for a few hours, and the two of them had simply talked, sharing stories about their mothers, and about their memories of early childhood in Paris in the 1930s, before the war. When he'd hugged her goodbye before heading back to his hotel, she'd had the strangest sense of wanting to hang on just a little while longer, and she'd been relieved when he told her he planned to stay in Boston for at least a few more days.

After he'd departed, she'd sat in silence for several minutes in her living room, trying to put a finger on what she was feeling. It was, she realized, a sense of belonging. It was a feeling of being exactly who she was. And it was the knowledge that for this man whose life had always been woven into hers, that was enough.

With Marty, she had always felt the opposite. She knew he cared for her as deeply as she cared for him. But when they were younger, making it past her defenses would have been hard work, and he'd opted out. Later, when they might have had another chance, he had chosen women young enough to be his daughters. "Yes," she said now. "I do believe it is too late."

He looked genuinely mournful as he twisted his napkin in his lap. "I've been a fool for a long time, Colette."

"Yes," she said with a smile, "you have been. But it never would have been a fit, Marty. I'm glad we never tried, because it might have ruined a beautiful friendship. And Marty, I *am* deeply grateful to call you my dearest friend."

Marty looked up. "I'm grateful, too." He cleared his throat and took a long sip of his wine. "Well, now that we have that out of the way . . ." He trailed off and loosened his tie. "What did you want to see me about? You said you had a question?"

She nodded, grateful to have moved into safer territory. "Do you remember the first ring you ever sold for me?"

"Sure I do, kid. As I recall, it featured six emeralds, each flanked by six pave-set diamonds."

"Your memory is astonishing."

He smiled. "How could I forget? It was one of the pieces that helped fund the opening of the Holocaust center, wasn't it?"

"It was." She took a deep breath. "And now I'd like to buy it back."

He stared at her. "Colette, it would have to cost upward of fifty grand, if it's even still out there."

"I'm hoping," she replied, "that the proceeds from the sale of Linda Clyborn's ring will be enough not only to cover the cost, but to give the owner incentive to sell it."

He seemed to consider this. "Let me see what I can do. If I recall, we sold it to a diamond broker who was a collector himself; it's possible that he, or his descendants, still have possession of it. Can I ask why you want it back?"

She looked at her hands. "Because when I sold it, I was doing so to honor the people it had been stolen from. I thought the whole family was dead—but the son survived. And now he's here. The ring belonged to his mother, and I'd like to return it to him."

"This is about that man in town from New York? Daniel Rosman? The one whose family owned the bracelets?" he asked, and when she looked up in surprise, he shrugged. "Aviva called. She was concerned about you."

Colette exhaled. "Yes," she said. "It's about Daniel Rosman."

Marty studied her face, and she had the sense he was reading her like a diary. "This is important to you."

"Very," she said.

"I see." Marty cleared his throat, and she wondered if he could see in her eyes why this meant so much to her. She wasn't sure she understood it herself. "I'll see what I can do, kid. I promise."

"Thank you, Marty."

The waiter interrupted to refill their wineglasses and to tell them that their entrees should be out shortly, and just as Colette was reaching for a final oyster, she felt her cell phone vibrate in her handbag, which was hanging from the arm of her chair.

"Excuse me," she said, pulling her phone out to see who could be calling at this hour. She was surprised to see Aviva's name there; the girl called this late only if something was wrong. "Marty, it's Aviva. I have to take this."

"Of course." He took a sip of his wine and watched with concern as she answered.

"Aviva, dear, is everything okay?" Colette asked.

"No," Aviva said, her voice sounding far away and hollow. "I'm on my way to the hospital."

Colette sat straight up in her chair, her heart racing. "The hospital? What happened? Are you hurt, dear?" Marty leaned forward, worried.

"No, no, nothing like that. It's Hubert Verdier, Colette. He's had a heart attack."

Colette put a hand over her mouth. "No. It isn't possible. After all this time . . ." She trailed off. "Did they say he'd be all right?"

"The home didn't know anything other than he'd been unconscious when the paramedics arrived. They took him to South Shore Hospital. I'm with Lucas and we're headed there now."

"You're with Lucas? I see." Hadn't she told Aviva that getting involved with the museum director was a bad idea? "Keep me updated, will you?"

"Yeah. I just wanted to let you know." Aviva hesitated. "I'm sorry, Colette."

"I am, too." Colette ended the call and looked at Marty in disbelief. "Hubert Verdier has had a heart attack. Aviva is headed to South Shore Hospital with Lucas O'Mara now."

"Damn it." Marty stood up and pulled several twenties out of his wallet.

"What are you doing?" Colette asked as he put the money down on the table and beckoned for the waiter.

"I'm driving you to the hospital," he said, offering her the crook of his arm. "And I'm going to stay there with you until we get some answers."

When she and Marty walked into the waiting room of South Shore Hospital's emergency room twenty minutes later, Colette spotted Aviva and Lucas O'Mara right away. They were sitting side by side near the door leading into the operating room, and Lucas's head was in his hands. Aviva's eyes widened when she saw Colette, and she nudged Lucas, who looked up, his eyes bleary. Colette swallowed down a lump of guilt. She shouldn't be here, in this moment of worry for Lucas. But how could she not be?

"Colette?" Lucas said, blinking a few times as if he wasn't sure if his eyes were deceiving him. "Marty?"

"We were at dinner together when we heard the news," Colette said. "I know I'm probably the last person you want to see right now."

Lucas cocked his head and looked at her, his expression confused.

Colette cleared her throat. "Because of the interactions I've had with your grandfather-in-law. I would understand if you blamed me for what's happened—"

Lucas's face cleared and he cut her off. "I don't, Colette. He has a bad heart. This isn't your fault."

"But—"

"I understand why you felt you had to question him. I really do." He glanced at Aviva, who was nodding, and when he looked back at Colette, he appeared suddenly exhausted. "I just hope he survives this. You deserve some answers. We all do. Please, sit down."

He gestured to the two seats across from him and Aviva, and Colette and Marty slid into them. "Thank you," Colette said, though the words didn't feel like enough.

Lucas merely nodded and looked away. Aviva rubbed his back, and after a moment, Marty folded his hand over Colette's.

Twenty minutes later, a young doctor in scrubs emerged from the door to the OR and asked for the family of Hubert Verdier.

Colette lurched to her feet. "Is he awake?"

The doctor reached out and gently touched Colette's arm. "I'm very sorry, ma'am, but we weren't able to save him."

Colette's knees went out, and Marty caught her, pulling her close before she could go down. She buried her face in his chest for a second before taking a deep breath and returning her attention to the doctor.

Lucas exhaled and took a step forward. "I'm the next of kin," he said, and the doctor turned to him after giving Colette a confused look.

"Oh. All right, then. I'm afraid Mr. Verdier stopped breathing in the ambulance on the way here," the doctor said, pronouncing the name *Verdeer*, rather than the French *Ver-dee-ay*, though no one corrected her. "We tried to resuscitate him, but he was already gone. I'm very sorry."

"He didn't . . . say anything?" Colette asked, her voice small, and the doctor glanced at her with concern.

"He wasn't conscious, ma'am. Again, I'm very sorry." She nodded at Lucas and turned away, heading back into the OR.

"Of course," Colette murmured as the last of her hope went up in smoke. She turned to Lucas. "I'm sorry, Lucas. I'm sorry for your loss."

She was surprised when he reached out and squeezed both her hands. "And I'm sorry for yours. I know how much it meant to you to get some answers about the bracelet. I promise, I'll keep trying to get to the bottom of it."

"But this was the bottom," Colette said. "He took all his secrets with him."

"Or maybe," Lucas said, glancing at Aviva, "there's still someone out there who knows enough to give you some peace after all these years."

CHAPTER TWENTY-SIX

1943

As the bitterly cold winter of early 1943 wore on, Colette came back to life.

It began when she was standing in a lengthy queue for Uncle Frédéric's and Aunt Marie's allotment of bread. Teeth chattering from the icy freeze, she had been lost in thought about the night Liliane was taken when, suddenly, she heard a familiar name spoken in a hushed voice by one of the two women queued in front of her.

"Le Paon is holding a meeting this afternoon," said the younger woman, who was wearing a red wool coat. The declaration was followed by something unintelligible, and then Colette heard the woman add, "—trouble paying for documents."

"I thought funding was the least of our problems," said the other woman, who was around the age Mum had been, her forehead creasing in concern.

"Apparently there's been a disruption," the younger woman replied. "Anyhow, I'm going to the meeting. Are you?" And then they bent their heads together and began speaking in voices so low that Colette could no longer hear them without making her eavesdropping obvious. But she had heard *Le Paon*, the leader of her mother's underground group.

Colette had been thinking for months about stealing again, now that it had really sunk in that Papa wasn't coming back for her. But she didn't have any idea how to find her way to a trust-worthy member of the Resistance, and each time she had asked Uncle Frédéric and Aunt Marie for help, they had rebuffed her. *You don't need to be stealing*, Aunt Marie had said firmly just the week before. *I would never forgive myself if you were arrested again.* Colette had bitten her tongue, but she wanted to say that she couldn't forgive *herself* for sitting idly by while the world crumbled.

But now fate had delivered an opportunity. Not only were these two women apparently planning to attend a meeting with Mum's old group, but the organization clearly needed money. Now, all Colette needed to do was to tail the women until they led her to Le Paon—and then approach the man to offer her services. Surely he'd understand her value as the daughter of Annabel Marceau.

She stepped out of line and slipped into the doorway beside the boulangerie, though she knew it would mean she'd be coming home with no rations. Twenty minutes later, the women emerged, each carrying a small loaf of bread, and Colette watched them from the shadows before stepping out to follow them at a distance.

When they parted ways at the corner, exchanging air kisses, Colette stayed behind the one in the red coat. The woman disappeared into an apartment building on the rue Oberkampf, and then an hour later, she reemerged, wearing the same coat. She had added a black scarf that almost entirely obscured her face.

Once again, Colette hung back, staying a half block behind her. Not once did the woman seem to sense that she had a tail; she never turned around and led Colette straight to a medical clinic on the Avenue de la République.

Colette hurried to catch up to the woman as she opened the door to the clinic, and when she reached out to enter behind her, the woman turned to her with wide eyes. "The clinic is closed, mademoiselle," she said, trying to shut the door on Colette.

"I'm here to see Le Paon," Colette said firmly, standing her ground. The woman looked her up and down.

"But you're a child," she said at last.

"Not anymore," Colette said.

The woman searched Colette's eyes for a moment. "How do you know Le Paon?"

"My mother knew him," Colette said, and the woman sighed in understanding before nodding and letting Colette in. She beckoned for Colette to follow her down a long hall.

In silence, they cut through a darkened examination room that appeared to have been stripped of all its medical supplies, and then the woman in the red coat stopped abruptly in front of a door leading to the back. "Wait here," she said. "I will tell Le Paon you are here. But you should know that half the people here are armed, so you'd better not be trying to pull a fast one, kid."

Colette nodded, and she waited in the darkness, her heart hammering. A moment later, the door to the back swung open, but instead of the woman in red, it was an older man in a green fedora, two blue feathers sticking out the left side. *Le Paon.*

"To what do I owe the pleasure?" the man asked, his gaze suspicious and his tone cold as he looked Colette up and down.

"I'm Annabel Marceau's daughter," Colette said quickly.

At the mention of her mother's name, his face softened, but he didn't speak for a long time. "Colette, then. I heard what happened to your mother," he said at last. "I'm terribly sorry. And your sister. A great tragedy. Are you here about the man who killed her?"

Colette's mouth went dry. "You know who he is?"

"No, I'm afraid not," Le Paon said right away. "I've made inquiries with all my sources, and the rumor is that a French police officer betrayed your mother to the Germans and then took your sister—with the goal of stealing your mother's jewels. But that's all I know."

Colette closed her eyes and could see the image of the man's back as he disappeared with Liliane. "I saw someone in uniform hurrying away from our apartment that night."

"Your mother was a friend, Colette, and I wish I could help you. But this is no time for personal vendettas."

"I know," she managed. There would be time for that later. "But I'm not here about that, sir. Not yet, anyhow."

He blinked and waited for her to go on.

"I'd—I'd like to help," she blurted out. "In the same way my mother helped you."

He studied her. "Theft, you mean."

"Yes, sir." She took a deep breath. "I know you're having trouble paying for false documents."

His eyebrows shot up. "And how would you know that?"

She wasn't going to betray the woman in the red coat, but Le Paon should know that there were members of his group with loose lips. "I overheard something to that effect."

"I see." He stared at her for a long moment. "How old are you?"

"Nearly fifteen, sir."

"Quite young."

"Does it matter, as long as I know how to steal?"

He smiled slightly. "And do you? Know how to steal?"

"I believe my mother was bringing you pieces I obtained before she died."

He frowned. "Yes. I was concerned about it then, and I'm concerned about it now. If you should be caught . . ."

"I won't be."

"I imagine your mother thought that, too." The words were delivered gently, but they still felt like a punch in the gut.

"I imagine she did," Colette answered evenly. "But I will learn from what happened to her. I won't let emotion get in the way."

"Why do you want to help?"

"Because when we find ourselves in darkness, we can't wait for the light to find us," Colette said slowly.

"Indeed. Well, in that case, I look forward to seeing what light you can bring, Colette. But don't take any unnecessary risks. I would never forgive myself."

"I won't, sir," Colette promised. "I won't let you down."

"We'll see," Le Paon said, already turning away. "We'll meet here again at this time next week. If you're here with a stolen piece in hand, I'll introduce you to the group." And then he was gone, leaving Colette alone in the exam room, wondering what she'd just gotten herself into.

# CHAPTER TWENTY-SEVEN

2018

Two days after the death of Hubert Verdier, Colette was sitting at her kitchen counter, staring off into space, when her doorbell rang. Finding her sister's likely murderer after all these years and then losing him before he could admit the truth made her feel as if she had failed Liliane anew, a sense that left her numb with grief. She had shared a table with the man seventy years ago. She'd had a chance for justice then, and she hadn't realized it. How could she live with herself?

The doorbell rang again, and she got up slowly, tightened the tie of her robe, and shuffled to the door.

She was surprised to find Daniel Rosman there, dressed in khakis and a button-down shirt and looking perfectly normal— not like death warmed over, which was how she was certain she must have appeared to him. It confused her for an instant to see him looking so well, but then she remembered that for him, there was no mystery to how his parents had been killed, no dangling threads that he had spent a lifetime trying in vain to weave back together.

"Colette," he said, his deep voice warm and his expression full of concern as he gazed at her. She noticed dully that he was holding a small cardboard box and a carrier with two cups of coffee, steam still rising from the holes in the lids.

"What are you doing here?" she asked, surprised by the raspiness of her own voice. She had barely spoken since leaving the hospital.

"Aviva told me what happened to Hubert Verdier." He held up the cardboard box. "I've brought croissants and coffee, and I have a proposal for you, if you have a moment."

"A proposal?"

He nodded. "But first, my friend, you'll have to let me in."

There was something about the way he referred to her as his friend that cracked the shell of her grief. She turned away before he could see her tears. How could she explain them? They hardly made sense to her. "Make yourself comfortable," she said over her shoulder. "I'll just get dressed."

Ten minutes later, when she walked into the kitchen, she was startled to see that he had taken the croissants out of the box and arranged them on a plate. "I hope you don't mind that I went searching for dishware," he said with a smile.

"Not at all." She felt a strange swirling in her belly, a sense that this must be what it was like to be taken care of by someone who wanted to make her happy. She couldn't remember the last time she had felt that way; she had always stayed away from anyone who was too solicitous, too kind, feeling that she didn't deserve it. But with a plate of croissants in front of her, and a man smiling expectantly at her in her kitchen, she couldn't quite recall why it had felt so repellant to be tended to. "This is very nice," she admitted.

"I didn't know how you took your coffee," he said, "so I took a guess and got it black, the same way I take mine."

"That was a good guess." Was it her imagination, or did he sound a bit nervous, too? Had he noticed that she had taken extra care with her makeup? Why *had* she bothered with it? She couldn't quite say—just that when he smiled at her, she was glad that she had. For goodness' sake, she was nearly ninety and acting like a teenager. She shook her head and took a long, bracing sip of the coffee. "This is very good," she said, because it was easier to talk about coffee than to think about the butterflies in her stomach.

"I found a little French bakery in Brookline. The hotel concierge assured me it was the best in Boston."

"You didn't have to go to so much effort." But she was glad he had. She took another sip. "I would have made you coffee myself."

"Perhaps you will next time," he said with a smile, and she found herself smiling back before she remembered that he didn't live here, that whatever was fluttering inside her right now— even if it was just the small joy of a new friendship—was bound to be temporary.

"I imagine you'll be returning to New York soon." Suddenly, she realized that his departure was probably imminent; he could hire an attorney there to stake his claim on the bracelet at the museum; there was no longer a reason for him to be in Boston. "Is that why you're here? Have you come to say goodbye?" The instant the words were out of her mouth, she realized that they had probably made her sound needy. "Of course you have," she amended quickly.

"Actually," he said, watching her closely, "I *am* headed home—but not to New York. I came to see you today because I have an invitation for you."

"An . . . invitation?" She picked up a croissant and took a bite, just to have something to do. The moment the flaky pastry hit her tongue, she closed her eyes for a moment and resisted the urge to moan in pleasure. This was the best croissant she'd had in years. "This *is* quite good," she said.

He chuckled. "I thought the same thing. Just like the ones I remember from Paris, before the war." His expression turned serious. "That brings me, Colette, to what I wanted to ask you." He hesitated, and she had the strangest sense he was nervous. "Would you like to go to Paris with me?"

She was so surprised, she started choking on the croissant, which meant that the next moment was spent with Daniel rushing to her cabinet to locate a glass and pouring her some water, while she struggled to regain her composure. It took her several seconds after she'd taken a drink to spit out, "Paris?"

"Yes. Tomorrow, in fact."

"I'm sorry." She barked out a laugh. "You're inviting me to go to Paris with you *tomorrow*?"

"I know it sounds quite mad. But Colette, I spoke by phone last night to the great-nephew of the jeweler who made the bracelet for my father. The jeweler died in Auschwitz, like my mother, but after the war, his brother took possession of his implements, receipts, and client roster, and tried to open his own jewelry shop in Paris. It was short-lived—but they kept the paperwork, even after the family relocated to Antwerp. I emailed the nephew a few days ago to ask him to search through his records for any proof that the bracelets were made for my parents, and just last night, he called to say he had found the original designs and the invoice his great-uncle had drawn up—and that he's on his way to Paris today and could bring the documents with him but that he will only be there for the next two days. He offered to scan the papers and then FedEx them to me, but a scan won't be enough for an attorney here, and I couldn't risk them getting lost in transit. Colette, I'd like to go get them in person, and I'd like you to go with me."

She stared at him. "To Paris," she repeated dully.

He smiled. "To Paris," he echoed. "I mean, that is, I'm not certain whether you've kept your passport up to date, or—"

"I have," she said, her mind spinning. "But Daniel, I haven't been back to France since I left in 1945." Years had turned into decades, and here she was, more than seventy years removed from the place where she had last seen her mother and sister. Then again, why had she continued to renew her passport for all these years if she didn't plan to return at some point?

He nodded. "I thought that might be the case. For me, my last trip there was decades ago, and it was very difficult. I felt the ghosts of my parents everywhere. But lately I've been thinking that I'd like to go back before I die. There's something to be said for facing ghosts rather than running from them. And now is as good a time as any. I can still get around pretty well, though I fear my marathon-running days are behind me."

She laughed. "As are mine."

"Besides, I've been accumulating airline miles for decades."

She blinked at him. "I can't let you pay for *my* ticket to Paris."

"Colette," he said, suddenly serious, "it is the very least I can do. In giving your half of the bracelet back to me, you've given me a piece of my parents, my past. I couldn't have imagined it after all this time."

She stared at him for a long moment, her heart thudding. He looked right back at her, his gaze steady. She took a deep breath. "What about Hubert Verdier's funeral? I know it's ridiculous, but I feel I should be there to see the man buried, if only to make sure he's dead and gone. It—it feels like one last thing I can do for my sister."

"It's not ridiculous at all. When is the funeral?"

She had seen the obituary in the paper just this morning. It had made her blood boil to read of his long life, his successful accounting firm, his membership in the local chapter of the Shriners, as if he had a decent bone in his body. "Friday. Three days from now."

"Then we'll make it a quick trip. In fact, I'll see if we can leave tonight."

"Are you certain about this, Daniel?" she asked. "And certain you'd like to take me with you?"

"Colette," he said, looking at her in a way that set her butterflies fluttering once more, "I've never been more certain of anything in my life."

She held his gaze. "Well, then," she said, hardly believing that she was agreeing to such a thing. "I suppose I'd better go pack."

Daniel left after booking their tickets with a promise to return in two hours to pick her up for their 5:15 flight. Colette packed an overnight bag and then called Aviva, who couldn't believe that Colette had said yes.

"Are you sure this is safe?" Aviva asked. "I mean, Daniel Rosman seems like a nice man, but—"

"Darling," Colette said, exasperated. "This isn't a stranger. This is someone with whom I have more in common than nearly anyone else on earth." She realized as she said the words how very true it was, on so many levels. Being around Daniel Rosman felt like returning to a home she'd thought she'd lost forever.

"It's just that it's so spontaneous," Aviva said. "You don't really do spontaneous."

"Well, maybe I should."

"I'm still going to worry about you the whole time you're gone."

"Well, that makes us even, then, because I'll be worrying about you and Lucas O'Mara," Colette said. She was annoyed that the two of them had looked very much like a couple at the hospital. She still wasn't ruling out the possibility that Lucas was involved in the cover-up about the bracelet, or that he knew more than he was letting on. Aviva's carelessness was further complicating an already tangled situation. "I know Lucas O'Mara is very handsome, Aviva, but you hardly know him. The situation he's a part of is very complicated, and—"

"Colette, he's a good man," Aviva said. "I promise, he understands what's at stake for you. He's doing his best to find out what his grandfather might know."

"Yes, well, I'll believe that when I see it." Besides, what did it matter if Lucas's grandfather knew a thing or two? The full story had died with Hubert Verdier.

"Do you promise you'll call me if anything goes wrong?" Aviva asked.

"What could go wrong in Paris?" Colette asked, but the words were absurd, weren't they? The worst moments of her life had happened in Paris.

"Just—I love you, okay?" Aviva said. "I know I don't say it often, but you're my family. You always will be."

"I love you, too, dear," Colette said, touched. They said their goodbyes, and then she sat holding her phone for a moment before calling Marty.

"Hey, kid," he said when he answered, sounding entirely like himself, which was a relief. She had been worried that after the awkward dinner they'd had together, culminating in their mad rush to the hospital, things would feel strange between them. "I'm glad you called; I have some news for you. You feel like coming over for lunch today?"

"I wish I could." Colette closed her eyes, bracing herself for his reaction. "But I'm going to Paris in a few hours."

"Paris?" He sounded confused. "You're joking, right?"

"No. Daniel Rosman has tracked down the documents proving his claim on the bracelets, and we're going to get them."

"You're going to Paris with Daniel Rosman," Marty said, his tone flat. "Whom you've known for less than a week."

"Technically, we first met in 1986 through a symposium at the center," she said, and Marty let out a guffaw of disbelief. "Marty, you have to understand. His mother and mine were friends. Being with him feels like reclaiming a piece of my past."

He was silent for a few seconds. "I see." His tone had suddenly turned stiff and formal. "Well, then, it might interest you to know that I've found another piece of your past, too."

She gripped the phone more tightly. "The ring? You've found it?"

"Turns out it never left the collection of the man we sold it to in 1972. His grandson recently inherited the jewels, and he says he's open to negotiating a price."

"Oh, Marty," Colette said, her eyes suddenly damp. "I don't know how to thank you."

"Yeah, well, you can thank me by coming home from France in one piece," Marty grumbled. "I'll let you know when I've reached a financial arrangement with the seller." He hung up before she could say another word, and she wiped a tear away. There would be time to reconcile with Marty later. For now, she had to do what she could to set the past right.

There was one more thing to do, though, before she departed. When Daniel arrived in a taxi at two o'clock, she asked him to come inside for a moment. After asking the driver to wait, he followed her in and sat opposite her on the sofa. "What is it?" he asked. "Are you having second thoughts about the trip?"

"No," she said. "But I want to give you the opportunity to back out if you want to."

He cocked his head to the side. "Why would I back out?"

"Because I need to be honest about something." She took a deep breath. "I've told you that my mother stole your mother's bracelets back from that Nazi officer. But what I haven't told you was that the theft wasn't an isolated incident. My mother was a jewel thief, as was her mother before her."

He nodded slowly, but he didn't look upset. "A jewel thief?"

"There's more." She took a deep breath. "I, too, steal jewelry. It is—it's a family tradition that has been passed down for centuries, and with no heirs, it will die with me. But you should know the truth about who I am, in case that changes your mind about traveling with me."

He was silent for a long time. Finally, she snuck a look at him, expecting his face to have darkened in disappointment. But instead, he merely looked curious. "You steal jewels?"

"For nearly my whole life."

"And yet you haven't taken the bracelet back from the museum."

She took a deep breath. "I'm descended from Robin Hood, you see."

Daniel's eyebrows went up. "But he's just a fairy tale, isn't he?"

"So the world believes, but he was very much a real man who raised his children to lead with their hearts in rebalancing the scales of justice. It is my family's code that we steal only from the cruel or unkind. And while it would have meant everything to me to have the bracelet back in my possession, and to be able to give it to you, it would violate all we stood for. A theft from the museum would have badly damaged the reputation of the museum director, who didn't deserve that. I couldn't do it."

"I see," Daniel said, staring at her as if he was trying to put the pieces together. "But what do you do with the jewels you steal?"

She looked at him. She knew what she was risking by being honest with him. But this felt like a time for honesty, wherever the chips fell. "I sell them, and then I use the funds on projects that I hope will make people's lives better." She took a deep breath. "For example, the Boston Center for Holocaust Education."

He blinked at her. "What about it?"

"Well . . . I founded it."

"*You* founded it?"

"Anonymously. In 1972. Mostly with jewels I'd spent years stealing from Nazis."

He stared at her. As she waited for his expression to change, her heart thudded. She had trusted him with her deepest secret. What would he do with it?

But what he did next was the one thing she hadn't expected at all. He laughed—a short bark of surprise at first, followed by hearty, merry laughter.

"Daniel?" she chanced when he still hadn't said anything.

"You're telling me that the Holocaust center was funded by jewels stolen from Nazis?"

"And for the most part, it still is," she said with a small smile. "I make it a habit to steal at least a few times a year from people who align with the Nazi party. If they're foolish enough to walk around with such beliefs, then I'm happy to relieve them of their valuables."

His laughter grew deeper. "Colette Marceau, you continue to astonish me."

"You haven't changed your mind about me, then?" she asked hesitantly.

"On the contrary," he said, his tone suddenly serious. "It only makes me want to know you better. At our age, there are few surprises left, but you, Colette, are full of them."

She took a deep breath. "There's one more thing."

He raised his eyebrows. "It couldn't possibly be more surprising than what you just told me."

She smiled slightly. "Well, as it turns out, your parents helped found the Boston Center for Holocaust Education, too, and by extension, the New York Center for Holocaust Education as well."

His brow creased in confusion. "Pardon?"

"You see, my mother, sister, and I went to the Vél' d'Hiv two days after you and your family were taken, to see if we could find you." She blinked to steady herself, as the boy she'd lost suddenly flashed through her mind. *Tristan.* She'd been looking for him that day, too, but it had been too late. "You and your sister were already gone, but we saw your mother, and as she was walking to the transport, she managed to slip her ring to my mother. It was such a unique piece; six emeralds . . ."

Daniel's mouth fell open. "And thirty-six diamonds. My father designed it for her. I was certain Möckel had taken it."

Colette shook her head. "She had sewn it into the lining of her dress, as my mother had suggested. And then my mother sewed it into the lining of mine. I kept it for years, but then in 1972, when I knew I wanted to found the center, I thought perhaps your mother would have liked being part of something that kept alive the memory of all those lost, so I sold it along with several stolen pieces and used the proceeds to fund the purchase of our building and staff salaries for the first year. I felt certain that it was the right way to honor your parents, to make sure that she lived on, if only anonymously."

He stared at her. "You're telling me that I've been volunteering for decades at a center funded in part by my own parents' jewels?"

"Yes, but had I known you lived, Daniel, I would have kept the ring for you. I'm very sorry."

"Sorry? Colette, it's perfect. It means that my parents have been a part of my life all along." His eyes were damp now. "It means that they were never really gone, not entirely."

Colette's eyes misted over, too. "That is just how I feel about the bracelets." She took a deep breath. "I want you to know that I'm working on getting the ring back for you."

"But . . . surely it's gone."

"Diamonds are forever, Daniel. You just need to know where to look for them." He raised his eyebrows again, and she smiled. "My friend Marty thinks he's found it," she added. "He's doing his best to negotiate a price."

"I don't know what to say, Colette." His voice was hoarse with emotion.

"Say that you understand why I steal jewels, and that while my choices haven't always been the right ones, you know that I've tried to do good in this world."

"I believe that with all my heart."

She looked down. "And you're certain you want me to go with you to Paris? Knowing what you know now? About every-thing?"

"Colette," he said, standing and offering her his hand, "I'm more certain than ever. Now let's go revisit the past."

 CHAPTER TWENTY-EIGHT

1943

U ntil the Germans were driven out of Paris in August 1944, Colette stole nearly every day—not just jewels from high-ranking Germans and their lovers, but money from the fat wallets of collaborators, too. Having nothing to lose and no one to disappoint made her feel invincible, and with each pocket watch or pearl necklace or wad of banknotes she slipped to Le Paon, she felt a bit more of herself return.

She was her mother's daughter. She was fighting against the occupiers. She was helping to fund safe passage for innocent refugees. Never had she felt prouder or more in tune with her purpose. Her father would hate what she was doing, but it no longer mattered. He was dead to her, and though his abandonment still cut her deeply, it had also taught her that in the end, she could rely only on herself.

But despite her pride, she still felt a hollowness she feared would never be filled. She could save a million people, but it wouldn't bring her mother or sister back. It wouldn't make her father love her. It wouldn't save Tristan, nor the Rosmans, nor the chemist on her block who'd been deported, nor the schoolteacher who had worked with Papa and had been executed for distributing an underground newspaper. It would never be enough.

And then there was the fact that she was keeping secrets from Uncle Frédéric and Aunt Marie. She was grateful for the affection they'd given her, the safety, the roof over her head. She respected them greatly and knew that, at best, they would disapprove of her activities. At worst, they might decide to throw her out for engaging in behavior that could endanger them all.

Colette's uncle Leo came for her on a Sunday in September 1945, several months after the war in Europe had drawn to a close, after one of Uncle Frédéric's letters finally made it through. Mum's younger brother was a stranger to her, but when he pulled her into a tight hug and began to sob, she understood how much her mother had meant to him, and that made her feel an instant kinship.

"I would like to bring you to England with me," he told her over dinner that night with Uncle Frédéric and Aunt Marie, who had given her a home for the last three years but had never really been her family. Le Paon's group had long since disbanded, and there was no one to steal for anymore, no call to justice to answer. The lack of purpose left her feeling unmoored.

"I'm seventeen now." She didn't want to be a burden on Uncle Leo. "You don't need to feel responsible for me. I'm old enough to stay here in Paris on my own."

"I'm certain you are, Colette. But in 1940, when it looked certain that France would fall to the Germans, my sister sent me a letter. She asked me to care for her daughters if ever they found themselves alone. I wrote back to swear that I would do so, and I am determined to keep my word. It would be my great honor to show you where your mother came from, and to make sure you grow up in the way your mother would have wanted."

Colette held his gaze. "As a jewel thief, you mean."

Uncle Leo glanced at Frédéric and Marie and then scratched the back of his head uneasily. "Colette, my dear, I'm not sure what—"

"It's all right, Uncle Leo," she said. "They knew who my mother was and what she stood for."

"And we loved her for it," Uncle Frédéric confirmed. "But it is also what got her killed. And to put Colette in any sort of danger—"

"Is something I would never do," Uncle Leo confirmed. "I give you my word. But the work I do, the work Annabel did, is Colette's birthright, you see. I will teach her to follow in her mother's footsteps, to carry on our traditions."

"Uncle Leo?" Colette said after a pause. "I already know how to steal."

"Ah, so your mother began to teach you before the war," Uncle Leo said.

"Yes, but also—" She darted a glance at Uncle Frédéric and Aunt Marie. "But also, I have spent the war stealing to fund the underground."

"Did you, now?" Uncle Leo said softly, nodding his approval. "Good girl, then."

Uncle Frédéric was staring at her, stunned. "All those afternoons you went out for a stroll . . ."

"I'm sorry," Colette said, bowing her head. "I was very careful. I did my best to make sure I was never putting you in danger. But I couldn't turn my back on who my mother raised me to be."

"I see." Uncle Frédéric sighed and looked at Uncle Leo, an unspoken conversation passing between them. Finally, Frédéric turned to Colette. "My dear, if you must go, I want you to remember two very important things. The first is that Marie and

I love you very much. I know you never felt like you were ours; you had a mother, and your father still exists in the world. But please know that for Marie and me, who were never able to have children of our own, having you as a part of our lives these last three years has meant more than you'll ever know."

Colette wiped a tear away. "I always feared I was a burden. And now that you know about the stealing . . ."

"Colette, you are a joy, and we will be proud of you for the rest of our lives, wherever you go, whatever you do. Which brings me to the second thing I must say. It is a beautiful thing to learn about one's past. It will make you feel closer to your mother and to those who came before her. I know that firsthand; I am a jewel broker because my father was one before me, and his father was one before him. It is my family tradition, just as your family has its tradition."

He glanced once more at Uncle Leo before going on. "But please always remember, my dear, that there is a difference between a life that honors the past and a life dictated by it. When you let your history shape your future, you relinquish the ability to choose a better way forward."

"The girl is old enough to make her own choices," Uncle Leo said. "I will not force her into anything."

"I believe you," Uncle Frédéric said, but he wasn't looking at Uncle Leo. He was looking at Colette. "But it is also important that she knows she needn't force *herself* to be someone simply to honor her mother. I think that most of all, your mother would have wanted you to be happy. Don't you agree, Leo?"

Leo shrugged. "I do. But oftentimes, happiness springs from fulfilling one's destiny."

Before she left Paris with her uncle, Colette returned once more to the rue Pasteur, in hopes of seeing her father one last time. Had he returned now that the war was over? Part of her hoped he had—and that when he saw her, his eyes would fill with tears and he would realize the error of his ways and take her back.

But when she knocked on the door to the apartment that had once been hers, there was no answer. Reluctantly, she knocked on the door to the old concierge's apartment.

The war had not been kind to Madame Nadaud, who had sprouted a forest of hair from her nose since Colette had last seen her, and whose wrinkles and waistline had both multiplied. Apparently while the rest of Paris starved, she had been packing on weight like a squirrel preparing for winter. Annoyance flickered in Colette, but she swallowed it down.

"Who are you?" Madame Nadaud demanded with narrowed eyes, and the words cut into Colette. Had she really been that easily and fully erased from her former life?

"It's me, Madame Nadaud. Colette Marceau."

Madame Nadaud snorted. "The Marceau girl? I've spent years telling people you were dead. I almost believed it myself."

"I'm very much alive, madame." Colette closed her eyes briefly to steady herself. "I'm about to leave Paris, and I thought . . . Well, I hoped to see my father."

"Yes, well, you and me both. He owes me a lot of money."

"He hasn't been back, then? Do you know if he's still alive?"

"He'd better be. He keeps sending letters saying that he'll return by the end of the year and will give me the money then. You can remind him, if you find him first, that I'll tell the authorities his apartment is abandoned if he's not here by Christmas."

With one last snort, she slammed the door in Colette's face.

Colette stood there on the threshold for a full moment before turning and leaving the building. Her father was apparently still alive and hadn't bothered to return for her, though it was now safe to do so. It meant that he still hadn't forgiven her and had no interest in reclaiming her as his daughter. As the building's big door shut behind her, leaving her outside on the street, Colette felt as if the past itself had closed with a thud. Her father was gone forever. She was an orphan.

She stood on the sidewalk for a long time, rooted in place, before letting her feet carry her across to number 17, the building with the dark green door and the courtyard, a place she hadn't returned to in three years, for she knew how much it would hurt her.

She let herself in—the front door still didn't lock—and moved quickly to the wall. She counted eleven up, five across, and jiggled the loose brick until it came out, revealing an empty space behind. Her heart sank.

The poem she had left for Tristan in the summer of 1942 was gone, which could only mean that someone else had discovered their hiding place. There was no note left in its place, and she felt sure that if, somehow, Tristan had survived, he would not have kept her poem without leaving one of his own. He had taken his beautiful words with him to the grave.

The full impact of all she had lost hit her at once, and she fell to her knees, sobbing. Tristan was gone. Her mother and sister were long dead. Her father had abandoned her. She had nothing, no one. When she finally climbed to her feet a few minutes later, wiped her tears, and slid the brick back into place, she knew in her heart that Paris was no longer her home, and it never would be again.

 # CHAPTER TWENTY-NINE

2018

Paris was not at all as Colette remembered it, but then again, she hadn't really expected it to be. It had, after all, been more than seventy years since she had been here. It was just that it had changed so very much. The drive in from the airport was astonishing, in fact; what had once been a patchwork of quiet villages and pastures had given way to bustling, graffitied urban sprawl.

"It's quite different, isn't it?" Daniel asked from his seat beside her in the back of a hired car.

"I wasn't quite prepared for it," she said. "I knew it had changed, of course. It is just that when one leaves a place, one imagines that the place will remain just as it does in one's own memories."

Daniel smiled at her. "If only that were true. But change is necessary, I think. It's the only way to pave the road for future generations."

"I suppose. But it means that the past really is dead, doesn't it?"

Daniel didn't have an answer for that, and as they continued toward the city where they'd lived so long ago, the city that had ultimately turned its back on them both, they fell quiet, the easy silence between them punctuated by honking horns, protesting brakes, and the rumble and whine of passing commuter trains.

But as the car entered Paris from the north through the eighteenth arrondissement, and the boxy new construction of the suburbs gave way to the more familiar Haussmann buildings of Colette's childhood memories, her shoulders sagged in relief. Though the storefronts were different, and there were exponentially more people crowding the streets than there had been decades ago, it was all familiar. By the time the car turned onto the rue du Faubourg Saint-Martin, and the Porte Saint-Martin came into view, Colette felt as if she was home.

"Paris is still Paris," she murmured, turning to Daniel in wonderment.

He smiled at her. "Paris is still Paris," he repeated. "I'll just text André to let him know that we're nearly there."

Their overnight flight had gotten them to Charles de Gaulle before 6:00 a.m., but by the time they'd made it through immigration, retrieved their luggage, connected with the driver Daniel had hired, and crept through suburban traffic, it was nearly ten o'clock. They had both slept lightly on the plane, enough so that combined with the jolt of adrenaline that came from being back in France and from the double espresso she had ordered at the airport, Colette was nearly vibrating with eagerness. André Besner, the great-nephew of the long-ago jewelry designer who had conceived the bracelets, was meeting them at ten thirty at his attorney's office, although he had texted twice already to tell Daniel that he understood if they needed to move the meeting to later in the day.

As Daniel typed away on his phone, Colette stared out the window. It felt impossible that she was really here after all this time. They were planning to spend only a single night in Paris before an early afternoon flight back to Boston the following day, but Colette already had a list of things she wanted to do. She wanted to see the Eiffel Tower sparkle. She wanted to walk along the Seine. And she wanted to visit her old neighborhood one last time. This would likely be the last chance she'd ever have to bid adieu once and for all to this chapter of her past.

The car pulled up a few minutes later to the attorney's office on the Boulevard de Sébastopol, and Daniel offered a hand to help Colette out of the car. Together, they walked into the building and took the elevator up to the second floor.

"Are you ready for this?" Colette asked, glancing up at Daniel, who looked suddenly troubled.

"I expect it might be difficult for me to see my father's handwriting after all this time," he said softly. "When my sister and I came back to Paris, there was nothing left of our family. Our apartment had been seized, and everything in it had been stolen or discarded. I don't even have a photograph of my parents. To think that something my father wrote with his own hand has survived . . ."

Colette reached for his hand and laced her fingers through his. She understood deeply that sense of foundational loss, of having not only your loved ones stolen from you, but also all evidence that they'd ever existed in the first place. Objects were just objects until they became the last things that remained of a person's life. "The memory of your parents is alive in you, and in that way, they're still here. They always have been." She paused and waited until he looked down at her, tears in his eyes. "And so am I, Daniel. I'm right here with you."

"That means a great deal," he said, holding her gaze. "Thank you, Colette."

In the attorney's office, they were ushered immediately into a conference room, and Colette was startled to realize how familiar it felt to speak French with the pleasant young receptionist. She hardly ever used her native tongue anymore, but it turned out to be a bit like riding a bike; once she was rolling, it all came back to her.

"Welcome, Monsieur Rosman and Madame Marceau," said the attorney in French as he entered, followed by a man who appeared to be in his late seventies. "I'm Guy Lécuyer, and this is my client, André Besner. Would you be more comfortable in English?"

"No," Daniel said, glancing at Colette for confirmation. At her nod, he added, "It is nice to speak the language we grew up with. It has been too long."

"Very well, then," the attorney said in French. "Please, have a seat."

Colette and Daniel both shook hands with Monsieur Besner and Monsieur Lécuyer, and the four of them settled around a small conference table with a manila folder between them.

"Monsieur Rosman," said Monsieur Besner, "I was thrilled when my attorney told me that you might have found the bracelets designed by my great-uncle for your family. Is it true?"

Daniel glanced at Colette with a smile. "It is."

"Very good news indeed. My grandfather was devastated to lose his brother in the Shoah, so his brother's papers, which he managed to salvage before the Germans got their hands on them, were very important to him. They were passed down to my father, and then to me, and I treasure them, too. They are all that remains of that branch of my family."

"No," Daniel said, "the jewelry created by your great-uncle remains, too, Monsieur Besner. My father always used to say that diamonds would outlive us all by many millennia. Think of all the lives the bracelets will be a part of long after we're gone. In that way, a piece of Max Besner will live on and on."

Monsieur Besner smiled. "Did you know him yourself?"

Daniel's gaze turned faraway. "Quite well. When I was a small boy, he used to keep a jar of candy on his desk for the days my father would bring my sister and me along on his visits to his shop."

Monsieur Besner sat back in his chair. "Then I am even more moved to be sitting here today with you, sir. It feels like an improbable miracle."

"All of this," Daniel replied with a glance at Colette, "feels like a miracle." Colette felt a shiver run down her spine.

"And that brings us to why we are here today," Monsieur Besner said, nodding at his attorney.

"Indeed it does. Monsieur Rosman, I believe these belong to you." Monsieur Lécuyer reached for the manila folder that sat on the table before him, spun it around so that it faced Daniel, and flipped it open, revealing several pieces of worn-looking paper.

Colette could hear Daniel's sharp intake of breath as he leaned forward to look at the loose slip on top of the small stack. It was a letter, handwritten in French, addressed to "*Mon cher ami Max*," and signed by Salomon Rosman.

"My father," Daniel breathed, reaching for the paper and leaning over so that Colette could read it along with him.

In neat, slanted script that reminded Colette of her own father's handwriting, Daniel's father had thanked Max Besner for creating a pair of bracelets so unique that they honored his children in a way that no children had been honored before.

As you know, he went on, *Hélène and I love Daniel and Ruth so very much. In wearing these bracelets, one to represent each child, Hélène*

will be able to keep them with her until the end of her days—and in the
future, long after Hélène and I are gone, I hope Daniel and Ruth will be
able to pass the bracelets on as they see fit.

Daniel put a hand over his mouth and made a sound of strangled grief. Colette put a hand on his back and kept it there, but said nothing. Sometimes, words only got in the way.

Daniel's father closed the letter by expressing his admiration for Max Besner's artistry and saying that he hoped their friendship—and their business together—would continue for many years to come. When Daniel finally set the letter down, Colette could see his hand trembling. "It is like hearing him whisper from the grave," he said, his voice barely audible.

Colette folded her left hand over his right, and he turned his palm up and grasped hers tightly. Monsieur Besner and his attorney exchanged looks.

"If this is too difficult—" Monsieur Besner said.

"No, no," Daniel said, wiping his eyes with his left hand without letting go of Colette. "These are tears of joy. I thank you for bringing a small piece of my father back to me."

Monsieur Besner smiled at him and then tapped the stack of papers. "In that case, you'll find more of what you came for here, too. The original contract for the bracelets. My great-uncle's original drawings, in which he focuses especially on the clasp, which is unique enough that your claim should stand up in any court. And a copy of the invoice he drew up for your father."

Daniel leafed through the rest of the papers, tearing up once more when he got to the final one, which included his father's signature, the *S* in Salomon and the *R* in Rosman looping large and bold. Finally, he looked up at André Besner. "I can't thank you enough," he said.

"I think my great-uncle would have been very happy that his meticulous record-keeping will help reunite you with your family's treasures. But I'm very sorry you felt you had to come all this way. A trip to Paris at your age, sir . . ." Monsieur Besner trailed off, seemingly embarrassed by what he'd been about to say.

"A trip to Paris at our age," Daniel said with a smile at Colette, "might be just what the doctor ordered. And I'm glad I came, because it gives me an opportunity to ask if you might do one more thing for me." He turned to the attorney with his eyebrows raised.

"Certainly," Monsieur Lécuyer said cautiously.

Daniel glanced once more at Colette, whose hand he was still holding. "I'd like to draw up paperwork passing possession of both bracelets to Colette Marceau once I reclaim the one from the museum."

Colette drew her hand back in surprise. "Daniel, no, of course not! The bracelets belong to you."

"And to you," he said firmly. "All I want is to see them again, together, united. I'm ninety-one years old, Colette, and I have no children. What is an old man like me going to do with two diamond bracelets? It was never about the money. It isn't for you either. It's about setting the past right."

"If I may be so bold," the attorney said, "what exactly is Madame Marceau's claim to the bracelets?"

Daniel turned to face him. "Her mother retrieved them from the German officer who stole them, with the hopes of returning them to my mother one day—but the theft resulted in her mother's arrest and death, and indirectly in the murder of Colette's sister."

The attorney looked at Colette in horror. "I'm terribly sorry, madame," he said, and Monsieur Besner murmured his condolences, too. "But," the attorney went on, drawing the word out, "am I correct in understanding that her mother was a *thief*?" He let the words hang there, uncomfortable and raw.

"Yes," Daniel said without hesitating. "And were there more people as brave as she, the war might well have ended sooner."

Monsieur Besner and his attorney exchanged looks. "Are you certain, sir, that your father would have wanted the bracelets to go to the daughter of a woman who *stole* the bracelets? Perhaps he would prefer that they stay within your family." They were looking at him now like he was a misguided old man. How easily people slipped into seeing only a person's age when things became complicated.

Colette wanted to stand up, to cry out that she hadn't come here for this, that she was as surprised as they were by his offer. But she was rendered mute by the way they were looking at her now, too, as if she was here to swindle a man out of his fortune. "I don't really—" she started to say when she finally found her words, but she was interrupted by Daniel, whose tone had turned steely.

"I believe, sir," he said coldly, a flush spreading up from the base of his neck, "that my father would understand, as do I, that these bracelets were always meant to find a home with someone who cared as deeply about them as my family did. To be again in their presence is enough for me, and perhaps that is because I have come to peace with the past. Colette has been denied that opportunity."

He reached for her hand again, and she was too shocked to pull away. "You don't need to do this," she said. "This was never my intention."

"I know," he replied, smiling at her. "And that is why it is exactly the right thing to do."

An hour later, after eliciting a promise from Monsieur Lécuyer that he would draw up the transfer paperwork and have it sent to Daniel's attorney in New York, they said their goodbyes, and Daniel hugged Monsieur Besner tightly and thanked him once again for his help. They left with Max Besner's paperwork tucked safely into a manila envelope in the inner pocket of Daniel's coat.

Their hired car was waiting, and after they'd gotten in and pulled away from the curb, headed for their hotel, Colette spoke. "Daniel, giving me the bracelets is too much."

"Colette, what good are they to me? I meant what I said. My mother would be very pleased for them to wind up with you."

She looked at her hands. "It isn't as if I have anyone to pass them on to either."

"You have Aviva," he said quietly.

She looked up. "I do love her as if she was my own, you know."

He smiled. "And that makes her your family."

"I have felt that way since the day she came home with me after her mother's death," Colette replied. "But sometimes I think that my mother would have been very disappointed that I didn't have children. For hundreds of years, the generations that came before me produced heirs to carry on the family tradition, and now, because of my own choices, that line dies with me."

"Colette," Daniel said gently, "I suspect that knowing you lived—a long and beautiful life—would have been everything your mother needed."

Colette didn't say anything.

"If it's not too personal to ask, why did you never marry?" he asked after a moment.

She looked up at him. The question should have stung, but the gentleness of his tone softened the words and made her want to be honest. "I would have liked to, I think. But I feared that marriage would come with an obligation to have children, and when I was young, I felt that if I couldn't protect my own sister, I shouldn't have a child of my own. I'd failed her, and I was terrified of failing again."

"Oh, Colette," Daniel said, reaching for her hand.

"And then later, when the moment for having a child had passed, it was simply that there was no one I felt strongly enough about to fall in love with." She glanced at him and then looked quickly away. "How about you? You married, didn't you?"

"Yes, just a few years after coming back from the camps. Paulette. We were married until her death. She was only forty-nine; it's been nearly forty years now since I lost her."

"I'm very sorry. And you didn't have children?"

"No." He seemed to search for a moment for words. "My parents were very much in love. I remember the way my mother looked at my father, the way he gazed at her like he couldn't believe his luck. They used to put records on the old gramophone and dance together in the kitchen. They were the best of friends, you see. When I was a boy, I dreamed of having that one day. But that was not what I had with Paulette. I loved her, and I know she loved me. But when we married, it was not about finding the kind of perfect match that my parents had. It was about desperately trying to find a home in the world after it had all fallen apart."

Colette looked out the window at Paris rolling by. She remembered so clearly what it felt like in the years after her mother's death when she was living with Uncle Frédéric and Aunt Marie and felt as if she belonged nowhere. "I understand that."

"We both wanted children, at first," he continued. "But when Paulette had difficulty conceiving, we both decided that perhaps bringing a child into a family soldered together by grief rather than love would be a mistake. We stopped trying, and it was likely a moot point anyhow. In any case, we were very happy living together as companions and dear friends for many years."

"I'm sorry you lost her at such a young age," Colette said.

"When one has lived as long as we have, the sea of loss is nearly too great to fathom."

Colette nodded. They rode in silence for a moment, and then she asked, "Do you regret not having children?"

"I do," he said. "It felt like the right decision at the time, but like you, I now feel my family tree dying with me. I worry that in allowing that to happen, I've let my parents down."

"Daniel, I suspect that knowing you lived—and a long and beautiful life at that—would have been everything your parents needed."

Daniel smiled at his own words being parroted back to him. "Indeed. I think that in the end, my parents, and yours, would have wanted most of all for us to be happy."

As the car slowed to a stop in front of their hotel, Les Jardins du Marais, Colette realized with a jolt of sadness that they were in the eleventh arrondissement, mere blocks from where she had once lived. Her heart thudded as she and Daniel climbed out of the back seat. She breathed in, Paris itself assaulting all her senses at once. Yeast, smoke, flowers, exhaust, eternal spring. How was it possible that the air itself felt like home, like a reunion long overdue?

While Daniel paid the driver and retrieved their luggage from the trunk, Colette turned in a slow circle, taking in her surroundings. Everything had changed, of course, but she knew this street, the narrow rue Amelot. Before the war, Colette, Liliane, and their parents had frequented a café on the corner that was no longer there, and she was certain there had been a bookstore in exactly the spot where they were standing now.

"Daniel," she said as the car pulled away and he came to her side holding the bags. "I know this place. My family used to live very close to here."

He smiled. "I thought that might be the case. Mine did, too. I believe that's how our mothers wound up involved with the same Resistance group; the man who led it was from the neighborhood, and I always assumed that most of the group's members were, too."

"Le Paon," Colette murmured. She hadn't thought of the man in years; he had survived the war, but she'd lost track of him after 1945.

"That was it!" Daniel exclaimed. "I'd forgotten his nickname. In any case, I hope you don't mind that I booked a hotel in our old neighborhood."

"Mind?" Colette felt dazed. "Daniel, I couldn't imagine anything better."

"Good," he said. "Perhaps we can go for a walk after we've had a rest, and you can show me where you used to live."

But once they had checked into their side-by-side rooms, Colette found that she was too wired to lie down. It felt urgent, suddenly, to visit her old street, and she didn't want to wait a moment longer.

She knocked lightly on Daniel's door, but there was no answer. He was likely napping, and she didn't want to wake him. Besides, as much as she enjoyed his company, this was something she needed to do by herself.

She asked for directions to the rue Pasteur at the front desk, but she found that as she exited the hotel, her feet knew the way.

Everything had changed—different pavement, different storefronts, buildings that hadn't been here seven decades earlier—but the layout of the blocks was the same. It felt as if Paris had simply shrugged off its old wardrobe and tried on something new, and though a part of Colette wished that everything had remained just as it once was, she was mostly glad that it hadn't. The past was dead and gone, and maybe that was just as well. *Change is necessary*, Daniel had said that morning. *It's the only way to pave the road for future generations.*

She turned the corner onto the rue Pasteur, and suddenly, there it was, her old apartment building, the number 10 etched above the door. She stopped in front of the building and stared for a long time, the memories washing over her. There were wrought-iron bars over the ground-floor windows now, and as she approached to touch the windowsill furthest from the door, a sob rose up in her throat. There had been no need for bars like this in 1942, or so they'd thought, but if they had existed then, Liliane would not have been taken. She touched the cool metal now as tears streamed down her face.

She stood that way for a long time, barely noticing the concerned looks of passersby. She was saying goodbye to the past, to her parents, to her sister, in her own way, which meant that the adieus were spoken only in the depths of her heart. She said goodbye to her father and told him she forgave him for what he had become after her mother's death. She said goodbye to her mother and told her that she hoped she was proud of how Colette had lived her life. And she said goodbye to Liliane and asked for her forgiveness. "I would give anything to turn back time and to save you," she murmured, the first words she'd spoken since arriving outside her old home. "I'm so sorry, my sweet sister, that I failed you."

And then, she was done. Wiping her tears away and drawing a shaky breath, she turned and faced the building across the way. Number 9, where she had first met Tristan, who'd lost his life at Auschwitz. She could still remember the last time she'd seen him, the smile lighting his face, the spark in his eye. "*Je pense à ce que ça ferait / Avoir ta main dans la mienne*," she whispered, a line from the poem she'd written him just before he was taken away to his death. "Adieu."

Finally, she turned to the right and let her feet lead her down to number 17, the building with the courtyard. The ground floor had been turned into a micro-creche, a preschool, and she thought with a smile how Tristan might have liked knowing that a brand-new generation was forming their earliest memories right here. Was the garden still beyond the front door? She pushed against it, but unsurprisingly, it was locked. She sighed and had just taken a step back to try to figure out what to do when a young woman bustled up with groceries, talking on a cell phone, entered a code into the keypad on the right, and pushed the door open without giving Colette a second glance. Colette hesitated for only a second before catching the door and slipping in behind her.

Inside, the long hall opened into a small green space, just as it had all those years before. In fact, without the intrusion of the world outside the doors—the traffic, the noises, the new storefronts, the modern cars—Colette could almost believe that she had slipped backward in time. She floated to the wall on the left and counted eleven bricks up, five bricks across. She took a deep breath, steeling herself for disappointment. There wasn't a chance that in seven decades, the wall hadn't been repaired, was there?

But to her utter astonishment, when she jiggled the brick that had once hidden her secret correspondence, *it moved*. It was wedged into the wall differently than it had been then—perhaps a settling of the building over the years, but with both hands, she found she could budge it, inch by inch, until finally, it slid free.

Carefully, Colette set the brick on the ground and then straightened to stare into the space. Even in the shadows, she could see a yellowed slip of paper there, pressed against the back. Had someone else found the space over the years and used it to pass messages as she and Tristan had once done so long ago? She felt a surge of violation, but it was replaced just as quickly with a rush of guilt. She had no claim on this hole in the wall. And in reading someone else's message, wasn't she, therefore, the one trespassing on territory that wasn't hers? Still, she couldn't help herself.

Hand trembling, she reached inside and pulled the paper out, careful not to tear it. As she unfolded it, she went through a rapid succession of emotions: elation because she immediately recognized the handwriting; disbelief because certainly that wasn't possible; and then confusion, because it was dated May of 1952—a decade after Tristan had died at Auschwitz.

"*What?*" she breathed to herself, sinking down to her knees as she grasped the paper with both hands and began to read.

To my Isolde,

I am due to leave Paris tomorrow for good, and I'm not sure why I'm writing you this note. I know you will never receive it. But I cannot leave without saying goodbye.

As you may have guessed, I spent the war years in a camp. When I finally returned to Paris in the summer of '45, I went to your building, hoping that you would still be there. Instead, when I described the beautiful girl with the green eyes, the concierge told me that you and your family had all lost your lives. It nearly broke me to find your poem in the wall after receiving the terrible news. I will keep it with me always and hold your words—and you, my dear Isolde—in my heart.

We barely knew each other, but I think that sometimes, two like souls are drawn to each other like honeysuckle to hazel, like the Tristan and Isolde of the poem. To know that your soul is no longer here leaves me forever with a hole in mine.

I will carry you with me for the rest of my days.

Forever,

Your Tristan

For a long time, Colette could not breathe. Tristan had *lived*? And he had come back for her? A sense of dread knotted in her belly, a feeling of her whole life having unfolded differently than it was supposed to because the concierge had informed him—as her father had requested during the war—that the whole Marceau family was dead. But why hadn't Madame Nadaud told Colette, in the fall of 1945, that someone had come looking for her? What might Colette's life have been like if she and Tristan had found each other after the war? She had spent the remainder of her youth feeling adrift and unmoored, but would he have been her anchor? Could she have had a life with him if things had turned out differently?

It was just as likely, of course, that they would not have been meant for each other after all. The war had changed Colette, and she could only imagine how much it must have changed him. Who knew if they'd been truly compatible to begin with anyhow? She'd hardly known him, and now, she had no way of finding out what had become of him after he left Paris.

But wait. She had found his name in the deportation records: Tristan Berousek, who lived on the rue Ternaux, just a short walk from Colette's apartment. It had to be him; Tristan was not a

common French name, and both the age and location fit. And
then later, she had found the record of his death at Auschwitz.
Quickly, she pulled out her phone and looked up the US Holocaust Memorial Museum's Database of Holocaust Survivor and
Victim Names, to which she had directed hundreds of people
over the years at the center. The database brought together all
available records from both the museum's collections and other
organizations into a comprehensive search tool, and now, with
her hands shaking, she entered Tristan's first and last name. Had
the original information about his death been wrong? Had he
survived after all? If he had, the records would almost certainly
indicate that now.

But when the results came up, they were the same as ever.
Tristan Berousek had lost his life at Auschwitz in the fall of 1942.
It was right there in black and white, the same definitive proof
of a life that had ended far too soon. So what did that mean? Was
there another Tristan out there, one with the same age and from
the same neighborhood, who'd been among those who survived?
But if there was, why hadn't his name appeared on any deportation documents? She searched again for the first name Tristan,
entering Paris as the search location, but there wasn't another person with that first name anywhere to be found on any of the
deportation lists. When she broadened the search to include all
of France, the answer was the same. Tristan Berousek from the
eleventh arrondissement had been the only person with that first
name to appear in any of the documents, and he'd died in 1942.

She pulled up Google and typed in Tristan Berousek's full
name, thinking that perhaps she would find some trace of him
after Auschwitz if he'd lived, but nothing came up that seemed
to match anyone who'd been a teen in the 1940s, even when she
tried variations of the spelling of his surname. Finally, she sighed

and slipped the phone back into her handbag, feeling bereft. Maybe back in the States, Aviva could help her comb through records, but if there was no trace of Tristan anywhere, how would they find him?

Colette read the letter over again and again, letting the words burn their way into her heart. The boy had lived. *He had lived.* And though she felt a sense of gratitude and elation to know that he hadn't perished in the camps, she also felt a deep despair. He would be a year or so older than her now—ninety or ninety-one. She was still in decent shape, both physically and cognitively, but she knew that most people her age were not. The odds that he was still alive after all these years were slim, especially after what he must have suffered. And even if he had somehow survived, what were the odds that his memory was still intact? No, she had found him and lost him all over again, in the space of just a few moments.

It was an hour later by the time she rose to her feet, folded the letter carefully into her pocket, and slid the brick back into place for what she knew would be the last time.

The sun was setting as she returned to the hotel, and she was surprised to find Daniel sitting in the lobby. He jumped to his feet the moment she walked through the door, relief written all over his face. "I've been so worried," he said, quickly hurrying over to put an arm around her. "Where have you been, Colette? What's happened?"

She knew just from the way he was looking at her that her devastation must have been written all over her face.

"I had somewhere I needed to go," she said, her voice cracking. "I needed to say goodbye to someone." She wanted to tell him, to unburden herself to someone who she knew would care, but she didn't know how to explain Tristan's significance to her, the way his disappearance had left a hole in her heart, and the fact that knowing he had lived after all wasn't the salve it should have been. She had known him for only six weeks before he was taken away, after all. If she tried to tell Daniel that a part of her heart had gone missing years ago with a boy she hardly knew, he would think her mad. She felt an overwhelming sense of loss that she didn't yet have words for, and she was exhausted by all of it.

"Are you all right?"

"I will be." She looked up at him. "I'm afraid, though, that I don't feel much like being a tourist tonight." They had planned to take a stroll by the Seine before having dinner near the Eiffel Tower, but despite the fact that this would perhaps be Colette's last night ever in Paris, all she wanted to do was sleep.

"Of course. Let me walk you to your room," Daniel said.

"I loved a boy once," she said, trying for the right words as he opened her door with the key she'd handed him. "And I've just learned that he survived the war after all. But I never knew, and now it's too late. How many losses can one person bear in a lifetime, Daniel? How many?"

"Oh, Colette." She could see in his eyes that he felt her pain in his own bones, and that meant more to her than anything. "I'm very sorry."

Moments later, curled on her side, she sobbed into her pillow until she drifted off into a dreamless slumber. Daniel stayed with her, rubbing her back, until she was asleep, and when she awoke the next morning, he was still there, lying atop the covers beside her, his own eyes closed.

Maybe, she thought, the resurfacing of the bracelet had brought her more than just a window to the past. Maybe it had also brought her a true friend, the kind who understood when her heart was broken and who stayed to help her pick up the pieces.

As she got out of bed, he stirred, opening his eyes and slowly focusing on her. "Are you all right?" he asked.

"I will be," she said. "Thank you, Daniel, for last night. For being a friend. I'm very glad you're here."

He smiled. "I'm glad I'm here, too, Colette."

Now, there was just one thing left to do. It was time to return to Boston to bury the man who may well have killed her sister.

CHAPTER THIRTY

1945

Before Colette left Paris with Uncle Leo, she went to see Le Paon one last time.

She had been startled to learn, a month earlier, that the Resistance leader, who had seemed to her to be a shadowy, invincible superhero, was, in reality, Docteur Robillard, a mild-mannered pediatrician who had come out of retirement after the war due to the enormous need for those equipped to deal with childhood trauma. He specialized now in treating children who had returned from the camps or had suffered malnutrition during the war, and when she walked into his waiting room on the Avenue Parmentier, she was startled to see it packed with gaunt toddlers and hollow-eyed schoolchildren. It seemed she wasn't the only one for whom the war was still ongoing.

She approached the receptionist and felt her jaw drop when the young woman looked up and blinked at her. It was Marie, the one she'd followed to Le Paon's meeting two years before, the one with the red coat. "Colette?" Marie asked now, staring as if she might be seeing a mirage. "Whatever are you doing here?"

"I need to see him," Colette said. "I need to see . . . Docteur Robillard." It was still strange to speak the man's real name. To her, he would always be Le Paon.

"The doctor is with patients now, Colette." There was sympathy in Marie's gaze.

"I'll wait."

"He's quite busy. And he doesn't like to be reminded of—"

"I said I'll wait."

Marie sighed in resignation. "Very well. I'll let him know you're here."

It took two more hours before the waiting room cleared out and Marie reluctantly waved Colette through a door to the back. Inside an exam room, she found the man she'd known as Le Paon wearing a white coat and glasses and looking much smaller and slimmer than she'd remembered. Had she built him up in her memory to be something he wasn't? Or had he actually wilted upon returning to a mundane life? She hadn't seen him in more than a year, since the celebration the group had held on the 26th of August, 1944, the day General de Gaulle led a victory parade down the Champs-Élysées.

"Colette," he said, his voice flat. He seemed to be considering something, and then, he closed the distance between them in two long steps and pulled her into a tight hug. "Colette," he said again, and this time, his tone was tender. "It is very good to see you well."

"And you," she said as he pulled away. "I didn't realize, during the war, that you were a doctor. The clinic where we had our meetings—"

"Belonged to an old medical school colleague of mine," Le Paon supplied with a weary smile. "He fled south and stayed there for the duration of the war. Giving us the space to meet was his contribution to the cause."

"That was kind," Colette said, feeling awkward and stiff with this man she'd once known so well. Now, in his lab coat and his spectacles, he looked like somebody's kindly grandfather. He looked like a stranger.

"So many of us," Le Paon said, "played an unsung role in bringing an end to the war."

Colette bowed her head. She wished she had been older, that she could have done more. She felt a sting of regret at not being braver.

"Colette," he said after a moment. "I hope you realize that I am including you in that statement."

When she looked up, there was warmth in his gaze. "But I didn't do enough."

He chuckled. "You funded our entire movement almost single-handedly. Do you know how many Jewish refugees we were able to save because of you?"

She shook her head. He hadn't been able to tell her much during the war; he'd been firm about keeping everyone's responsibilities separate, so that if one of them was arrested, he or she could not betray the others. "Perhaps five or six?" She felt a surge of pride to think that she had played a role in helping at least a few people to safety.

Le Paon laughed again. "One hundred fifty-eight," he said, holding her gaze.

She felt the breath go out of her. "One hundred fifty-eight?"

He nodded. "From the time you joined us in 1943 to the time the war ended, we were able to buy false papers and arrange safe passage and lodging for one hundred fifty-eight people, including sixty-four children, Colette. *Because of you.*"

Tears stung her eyes. "Oh." It was all she could manage, for there was suddenly a lump in her throat.

"Your mother would have been very proud," he said, putting a hand on her shoulder.

"My mother is the reason I have come. You see, I am leaving for England with my uncle in two days." She took a deep breath. "But I couldn't leave without . . ." She trailed off, for he was already nodding in understanding.

"Without trying to find out one last time what happened to your family."

She nodded. "Two years ago, you said that the man who betrayed my mother—and killed my sister—may have been a policeman. I want to find out who's responsible for their deaths. Will you help me?"

Le Paon studied her face for a long time. "What would you do if you found him?" he finally asked with a frown.

"I don't know," she said, looking at the floor, but when she finally raised her gaze to meet his, she could see in his expression that he had correctly read between the lines.

"Colette," he said gently. "You have a bright future ahead of you. Your mother would have wanted you to live it looking forward rather than looking back."

"I'm afraid I can't do that, sir. Not without knowing."

"And will you continue to steal, then? After you leave Paris?"

"I think so." She drew a deep breath. "I've been thinking—I'd like to start an organization one day to make sure that people never forget what happened. To make sure it never happens again."

He wiped his eyes, suddenly emotional. "Your mother would be very proud of that, too, I think. But this quest for revenge—"

"It's not revenge," she said quickly. "I don't plan to harm the man if I find him. That would go against everything my mother raised me to be. But I do want to bring him to justice. The last thing my mother asked of me was to bring my sister home, and I couldn't do that. I don't know if I'll ever be able to forgive myself, but at the very least, I can make sure the man pays for his crimes."

Le Paon sighed. "There's no guarantee of that, you realize. I can't begin to count the number of people across France who did terrible things during the war and will never see the inside of a courtroom."

"But if I can make sure that this man is held to account . . ."

"Then, what, Colette? Do you think it will bring you peace?" She could hear the doubt in his tone.

"I don't know," she admitted. "But please, I must try."

He studied her face for a long time, as if trying to discern whether she was hiding murderous intentions beneath a placid surface. Finally, he nodded slightly to himself. "I know a policeman who might be of some help. He tends to . . . know things about his colleagues, which he is sometimes happy to share for a price."

Her heartbeat accelerated. "A policeman? You think he knows something about what happened?"

"He might."

"And your friend would be willing to speak with me?"

"He's not my friend," Le Paon said sharply. "But he is a man whose cooperation is easily bought, and he has a particular affinity for jewels. Do you have anything to trade?"

Colette hesitated and nodded, pulling a diamond choker from her pocket. She had nicked it just that morning from the neck of a woman who had lived during the war in the opulent apartment of the German military governor of Paris. She had planned to pawn it later that day and to give the proceeds to a group working to resettle Jewish children whose parents had been murdered—but there were plenty more jewels where this piece had come from.

Le Paon shook his head and chuckled. "Good. Greed will get the best of him, and he'll tell you what he knows in exchange for those diamonds."

Colette stared at the piece of jewelry. Was it possible that it was the key to unlocking secrets that had haunted her for the last three years? "Where will I find him? Who is he?"

"I'll arrange a meeting," Le Paon said. "His name is Verdier."

Colette and the policeman met, as arranged by Le Paon, at a table outside a café on the rue Saint-Sébastien. Verdier was a slight man with a flat nose, pale skin, and mud-brown eyes that seemed to be arranged in a permanent squint. He was out of uniform, but Colette recognized the rigid posture of a policeman when he slid in across from her, and the way he nodded stiffly, almost obsequiously, to a trio of French military officers two tables away.

"You are the girl Le Paon sent?" he asked with no preamble after he ordered a coffee. "The Marceau girl?"

"I am. And you are?"

"Verdier, of course. I understand you have something for me?"

The choker felt like a lead weight in her pocket. "In exchange for information."

He frowned at her, as if disappointed that she wouldn't just hand over the jewels and let him be on his merry way. "Information about the arrest of your mother, I understand?" There was neither warmth nor sympathy in his tone.

"And the death of my sister. Her name was Liliane. I—I believe she was murdered by a policeman."

He snorted. "That's absurd."

"I saw a man in uniform hurrying away with her on the night she was taken."

"That's proof of nothing."

"Then give me proof," she said, leaning forward, "and the piece I have in my pocket is yours."

He seemed to be considering something. Finally, he spoke. "There was talk about your mother just before her arrest. Someone had knowledge that she had stolen something from a German. A pair of bracelets, very valuable. Hundreds of diamonds."

"Who?" Colette demanded. "Who knew she had stolen the bracelets from a German?"

Verdier leaned back in his chair. "What did she do with the bracelets?"

"That's hardly—"

"*What* did she *do* with the *bracelets*?"

Colette held his gaze. "One of them disappeared with my sister. I believe the man who murdered her must have it."

Something flickered in his eyes. "Is that so? And the other half?"

Colette resisted the urge to look away. "It's gone."

He narrowed his eyes and didn't say anything.

"Who was talking about her?" Colette asked after a moment. "You said someone was talking about my mother before her arrest."

"First, show me what you have for me."

Colette glanced at the couple at the next table and then at the trio of officers nearby. They were all fully absorbed in their own conversations.

"This is no time to be coy," Verdier hissed, leaning forward. "You want me to talk, you show me what I'm talking to you for."

Colette took a deep breath and pulled the choker from her pocket, clenched in her palm. She glanced once more at the couple beside them, and then she quickly opened her fist, revealing the diamonds, before closing her fingers around the piece again and slipping it back into her pocket. When she looked back at Verdier, his flat, uninteresting face had transformed; he looked suddenly like a wolf who'd just caught a whiff of his prey.

"The diamonds are real?" he asked.

"Of course."

He stared at her, considering. "Fine, I had a captain by the name of Seguy. He was there the night your mother stole the bracelets. He tried to follow her, but he lost her."

"It was this Seguy who betrayed her? Who took my sister?"

"No. But rumor has it that he was desperate to identify her, to curry favor with the Germans, and one of his officers recognized her from a sketch. I believe it was *that* man who betrayed her. Find him, and you'll find the man who took your sister, too. I'm certain of it."

"Who is he?" Colette asked, leaning forward and feeling a surge of desperation. "What is the policeman's name?"

Verdier gave a slow, dramatic shrug. "That's all I know."

She stared at him. "But that's nothing."

He shrugged again. "I gave you Seguy. And I've told you that it was indeed a policeman who betrayed your family, as far as I know. It's all I have." He paused and gestured to her pocket. "Pay up."

"No," she said, crossing her arms. "My father had a student who is a police officer. Perhaps I'll ask him what he knows about this Seguy." She searched her memory for the man's name. "Charpentier," she said a moment later. "Guillaume Charpentier."

Something flashed in his eyes, a spark of interest, of curiosity. "You know Charpentier?"

"Yes." Colette tried to sound confident. Perhaps Verdier didn't know that Monsieur Charpentier was long gone from Paris. "I know him well." That was an exaggeration, but it wasn't as if Verdier would realize that. "He'll tell me the truth. Perhaps I'll give these diamonds to him."

Verdier snorted. "That weasel? You clearly don't know him as well as you'd have me believe, mademoiselle. He left Paris years ago. You won't find him anywhere."

Colette's heart sank. So Verdier knew. "Perhaps he's back."

"He isn't. Something about his wife's poor health, needing the country air. He's not around to answer your questions. And I have told you what I know. I gave you Seguy. Now, my payment?"

Colette exhaled. "You're sure you know nothing more?"

"Have I not said that already?"

She hesitated. "And *you* had nothing to do with it?"

His nostrils flared. "If I had stolen one of the most beautiful pieces in Paris, you really think I'd still be here, talking to you? No, I would have gotten the hell out of this place long ago. I bet that's just what the man who took the bracelet did, too."

She could see the truth of it in his eyes, and as much as it disgusted her to pay the man, a deal was a deal. At least he had given her a name. *Seguy.* It was a place to start, and maybe Le Paon would be able to find out more. "Fine," she said, pulling the choker from her pocket and depositing it into his upturned palm.

He smiled for the first time since she'd met him, and the way his teeth glinted further enhanced his resemblance to a wolf. She shuddered, and before he could say another word, she rose from the table and walked quickly away.

He didn't even look up at her departure. She glanced back once before she turned the corner at the end of the street, and he was still sitting there, staring at the piece in his palm, his eyes alight with greed and desire.

Seguy turned out to be a dead end. Such a man existed, Le Paon was able to tell her, but he was in jail, and his wife was destitute. There was no way they secretly had possession of an exquisite diamond bracelet, or they would have used it by now to better their circumstances. Le Paon also sent someone to check the apartment of Guillaume Charpentier, in case Verdier had lied about the man's continued absence from Paris, but the news was confirmed; the only other police officer who might have been able to help her was long gone.

"It is time to move on, Colette," Le Paon said the day before she left Paris. "You have your whole future in front of you. Don't let the tragedy of the past consume all that lies ahead."

It was good advice, but how could she take it? She was the only one left to carry the torch forward for her murdered mother and sister. If she turned her back on that, she would be dishonoring their memory. "Very well," she told Le Paon, who looked relieved.

"I hope you find peace, Colette."

But she vowed then and there that she wouldn't rest until she had answers. Justice delayed was still justice, and she was determined to find out the truth, no matter how long it took.

A day later, Frédéric and Marie accompanied Colette and Uncle Leo north to board a boat across the English Channel to her new life. Colette had with her all her worldly belongings, which fit into a single suitcase.

"Your mother will always be with you, wherever you go," Uncle Frédéric said as he hugged her goodbye, holding her for an extra moment, as if he didn't want to let go. "She would want you to remember that."

"Thank you, Uncle Frédéric," Colette said into his shoulder, her voice muffled. "For everything."

"It is time," Uncle Leo said a few moments later as they stood on deck and waved to Frédéric and Marie, "for a new start."

"A new start," Colette repeated, but she knew, even as they pulled away, and as Frédéric and Marie and then all of France became tiny dots in the distance, that she didn't want to start over, not really. She wanted to find the man who had taken her sister, and she wanted her father to come to his senses and realize that although they'd been through a great tragedy, he still had a daughter who needed him.

In the meantime, she would settle for listening to what her uncle Leo was willing to impart. She had been stealing for years now, but she knew she still had much to learn—all the things her mother hadn't had the chance to teach her. She could feel in her bones the pull to the same shiny gemstones her mother had lost her life for, and she had no choice but to follow the call, to become the person she was always destined to be.

CHAPTER THIRTY-ONE

2018

"How are you holding up?" Daniel asked the day after their return from Paris, squeezing Colette's hand as he helped her into a pew in the back row of the church where Hubert Verdier's funeral was to be held.

"As you might expect," she said with a small smile as he settled in beside her. It had been two days since their evening together in Paris, when he'd relinquished his plans to see the sights in order to stay by her side. She would never forget it. And now, here he was again, though he could have chosen to return to New York right away. "Thank you for being here with me, Daniel," she added.

"It's important you know that you aren't facing this alone. I'm right here."

The words were enough to bring tears to her eyes. Just before the funeral mass began, Aviva slid in beside her and gave her a kiss on the cheek. "Sorry I'm late," she said, leaning over to give Daniel's arm a squeeze, too. "I can't wait to hear all about France. You've been holding out on me!"

Colette had called Aviva the moment they got home from Paris to tell her about Daniel's offer of the bracelets, but she'd been unable to say the rest. The story of Tristan had existed for so long in the silence of her own heart that she didn't know how to begin. But she would need Aviva's help to find out what had happened to him, and once the funeral was behind them, she would find the words to ask. "Thank you for being here today, dear," Colette said now.

Aviva smiled sadly at her. "I'm just sorry that Hubert Verdier died before you could find out the truth."

"Maybe it's enough to have found him after all these years," Colette said. "Maybe it's enough that I'm here to see him dead and buried." But as the funeral procession began then with Lucas and a few altar boys carrying in an ornate casket, Colette's heart was heavy with a sense of something vital left unfinished. It was devastating to come so close to some sort of closure, only to have it whisked away at the last second, like a mirage that had never really been there at all.

There weren't many mourners present; just Lucas, a pretty young woman Aviva pointed out as Lucas's daughter Millie, a handful of nurses from the assisted-living facility, and an old man in the front row who Aviva identified as Lucas's grandfather. "Lucas is going to talk to him again, I promise," Aviva whispered as a priest began the mass. "Hopefully this week. Lucas thinks he might know something about how the bracelet came into Hubert's possession."

And just like that, Colette felt a flicker of hope.

Lucas stepped up to give the eulogy after an opening prayer and some readings from the Bible. "Thank you all for being here today," he said, looking down at the small group. "I knew Hubert my whole life; we used to joke that he and his wife were my bonus grandfather and grandmother. 'You never asked for me, kid,' he said to me once, 'but here I am anyhow.'"

There were a few chuckles, and Lucas paused. "Despite knowing Hubert for all that time, though, I've realized recently that perhaps I never really knew him at all. And maybe that's true of all of us. We show people the sides of us we want them to see, and we hold the other pieces close. But perhaps it is those pieces—the ones we keep nearest to our vests—that define us."

He cleared his throat and looked out at the church, his gaze landing on Aviva and then Colette. "It's hard to make sense of a life when you don't know the whole story. We've all done things we're proud of. We've all done things we regret. Can a lifetime of good wash away a long-ago sin? Or are the choices we've made crosses that we must bear through eternity? I don't know the answers to that, but I do know that one of the gifts Hubert has left us with is a reminder to try. We must look inside. We must try to do what we can to right wrongs. And we must come clean about our pasts."

His eulogy was interrupted by a sudden coughing fit from his grandfather, who doubled over, hacking violently, until an altar boy rushed away and returned with a bottle of water. The old man took a sip and, with the woman beside him rubbing his back, gradually straightened back up in his seat and held up a hand. "I'm sorry, Lucas," he said, his words thick with a French accent. "Please continue."

Lucas looked concerned, but he went on. "In any case, there is no doubt that today we lay to rest a man who was very complicated. But without him, my mother and her family would not have been able to immigrate to the United States, so I owe him a great debt for that. He sponsored my grandparents' immigration application in 1948. Without him, I wouldn't have had the years I did with Vanessa, and we wouldn't have had Millie." He glanced down at his daughter and gave her a sad smile. "His legacy will live on, and Millie and I will make sure it's a good one."

He nodded at the priest and stepped down from the pulpit, rejoining his grandfather and his daughter in the front row. Colette watched from behind as his daughter tilted her head and laid it on her father's shoulder. There was something so familiar about the gesture, and it took Colette a few seconds to realize that it reminded her of the way Liliane used to lean her head on Colette's shoulder so long ago, when she was drowsy. Traveling to Paris, it seemed, had awakened long-dormant memories.

She held tight to Daniel's and Aviva's hands during the Prayers of the Faithful and the Liturgies of the Eucharist, and then, after communion, the priest closed the mass with a final prayer, followed by a song of farewell led by the church's organist. As the congregation sang the words printed on their programs, Colette was acutely aware that her mother and sister never had the dignity of being laid to rest like this, and her heart ached for the long-ago denial of such a basic right.

Lucas and the altar boys carried the casket back up the aisle and out the front door of the church. Colette had already decided that she wouldn't attend the graveside service; she didn't need to see Hubert Verdier lowered into the ground to know that he was well and truly dead. *He's gone, Liliane*, she thought. *He's finally gone, but it didn't bring you back.*

"Are you all right?" Daniel whispered in Colette's ear as they stood to leave.

"I think I am," she said as they made their way out of the pew with Aviva leading the way. "I have to be, don't I?"

"You don't *have* to be anything," Daniel reminded her, putting a hand on her lower back. "But I do think it's time for you to find some peace."

Outside the church, the handful of mourners milled around, chatting, before they dispersed. "I know Lucas wanted to say hello to you," Aviva said, gesturing across the parking lot to the museum director, who stood with his grandfather and daughter.

"I'd like to give him my condolences," Colette said. "But he looks busy with his family. We can speak another time."

"Okay. I'll go let him know." She gave Colette a quick peck on the cheek and stepped over to talk with Lucas, who had a hand on his daughter's back as he listened to something his grandfather was saying.

"There's something there, isn't there?" Daniel asked with a smile as they watched Lucas's eyes light up when he noticed Aviva approaching. "Does she have feelings for him, too?"

"I think she does." Colette shook her head in astonishment.

"How do you feel about that?" Daniel asked. "Given his connection to Verdier?"

She considered Lucas's words during the mass. *We must look inside*, he had said. *We must try to do what we can to right wrongs.* "We are not defined by where we've come from—or we shouldn't be, anyhow," she said. "Lucas is his own man, and as much as it pains me to admit it, he seems to be a very good one."

"Good," Daniel said with a nod. "His eulogy was perfect—a goodbye to someone he obviously cared about, but an acknowledgment that he might not have been the man he believed him to be."

"Aviva's fiercely independent, you see—so much so that I've worried about her at times. But perhaps she was only waiting for the right person to come along." She thought fleetingly of Tristan one more time, his letter from 1952 burning in her heart. But then, she pushed the thought away, because if there was one thing the last few weeks had shown her, it was that the past was gone.

She would ask Aviva to find out what she could, but she knew the odds were not in her favor. *Enough*, she told herself, closing her eyes for a moment. *Enough*.

"Ms. Marceau?" Colette opened her eyes and found Lucas approaching with Aviva.

"Lucas," she said. "That was a beautiful eulogy."

"That means a lot coming from you," he said. "I wanted to apologize for everything, Ms. Marceau. I still can't reconcile what I knew of Hubert with the idea that he could have done something so terrible—but I promise I'll continue to do what I can to find you some answers."

"I'm afraid it's very likely too late."

"Not necessarily. As soon as my grandfather is done over there, I'd like to introduce you. I think he knows more than he's saying about where Hubert's bracelet came from, and I'm hoping that he'll be willing to tell you." He turned to Daniel. "And Mr. Rosman, I understand from Aviva that you have obtained paperwork to set in motion a claim on the bracelet. I've spoken to my grandfather, and he has promised to lend a hand in helping us establish provenance, which should expedite the process."

"Your grandfather?" Colette asked. "What does he have to do with the bracelet's provenance?"

"He wouldn't say, but I assume it has something to do with the time he and Hubert spent together in France. Ah, here he comes. Perhaps you can ask him yourself." Lucas turned and raised his voice. "Granddad, I want you to meet two friends of mine."

Colette looked beyond Lucas to see his grandfather approaching slowly, with the help of his walker. Lucas's daughter was by his side, and when she looked up at her father and smiled, Colette had another strange flicker of recognition, though she was nearly certain she'd never seen the girl before.

But then Colette turned her attention to the old man, whose shoulders were stooped and whose ears stuck out from his head, and the world around her seemed to stop turning.

"I'd like to introduce you to my daughter and my grandfather," Lucas said, oblivious to the way every inch of Colette had turned to ice as his grandfather walked the final steps to close the distance between them. Suddenly, all the pieces were falling into place in rapid succession, and Colette realized that despite Hubert's ownership of the bracelet, he wasn't the man she'd been looking for after all. "Millie, Granddad, meet Colette Marceau and her friend, Daniel Rosman."

Colette could see the moment her name registered with Lucas's grandfather, because his eyes went wide and then darted to her in alarm. As they stared at each other, the years fell away, and she could see that he knew exactly who she was—and who she had been—just as she recognized a face from the past hidden amidst the wrinkled, faded skin of a very old man. It had been seventy-six years since she'd seen him last, but in an instant, it all came together. A policeman she and her sister had known and trusted. A policeman who must have been aware that there were jewels in the house. A policeman who would have known that in the chaos of that terrible night in 1942, a child with a bracelet in the hem of her dress would be all too easy to steal. It had never been Hubert Verdier at all; he was simply a weasel who liked nice jewels and who had known—after meeting with her in a café in 1945—exactly where to find one of the most beautiful pieces in Paris. She felt lightheaded, her vision blurring as her skin broke out in a cold, clammy sweat.

"It's you," she breathed.

He stared at her, and then his face crumpled. "Yes," he said, and the single word undid her.

"Guillaume Charpentier," she whispered as the two of them stared at each other, not moving. "What did you do to my sister?"

And then, before he could say a word, Colette fell to her knees as the world went black.

 CHAPTER THIRTY-TWO

1942

Guillaume Charpentier hadn't intended any of it. He had meant well, he really had. In his frazzled thoughts as he raced toward the Marceaus' apartment on the rue Pasteur that night, he had been thinking of only one thing: he needed to warn them, for it was his fault—no matter how indirectly—that the Germans were coming for them. He had seen Madame Marceau hurrying away from the Brasserie Roye that night a few weeks after the Vél' d'Hiv roundups, and he had known instinctively that whatever she'd done, there had to have been a reason. She was a good, kind woman, the wife of his former headmaster, and he'd made the snap decision to do all he could to protect her. The rest could be sorted out later.

So when his boss, Jean Seguy, came charging out of the brasserie after her, Guillaume had acted on instinct, stepping into Seguy's path and playing dumb while the blustering older man had tried to get by him. Guillaume had hoped to give Madame Marceau time to escape, and that night, he had, but a week later, Seguy had come to his door with a drawing prepared by a police artist.

"This is the woman who stole two valuable pieces of jewelry from a German commander," he'd said, stabbing his meaty finger at the picture. Madame Marceau's face was unmistakable, and Guillaume swallowed hard. "I know you saw her fleeing, too. Do you recognize her? Do you know who she is? Where she went?"

"No, sir," Guillaume said, heat creeping up his neck. "Never seen her before." Madame Marceau, a jewel thief? No, it was impossible. It was a misunderstanding, all of it, but it would not matter to the Germans whether Madame Marceau was guilty or innocent once she was in their custody. And if she had no information to give them—and surely she didn't—she would wind up dead. He had to protect her.

But then his wife, Francine, had come up behind him in the doorway and looked at the drawing. "Why, Guillaume," she'd said sweetly, "that's Madame Marceau, clear as day." When he turned to look at her in horror, her eyes were narrowed, and he could see in her expression exactly what had just happened. Francine, who was wildly jealous and possessive, had jumped to the conclusion that if Guillaume was trying to protect Madame Marceau, he must have amorous feelings for her.

"Is it?" he asked, trying to hedge, even as his face went red. "I'm not certain . . ."

"It's obviously her," Francine said, turning to a triumphant-looking Seguy. "Married to Guillaume's old schoolmaster, Monsieur Marceau. They live in the neighborhood, on the rue Pasteur. I've queued with her at the boulangerie a few times."

"I see," Seguy said, turning back to Guillaume. "Interesting that you didn't recognize her, while your wife knew her instantly."

"The sketch isn't clear," Guillaume mumbled.

"And yet you must have seen her face-to-face that night, when you stepped into my path and stopped me from following her," Seguy said, shooting a glance at Francine, who looked like she was about to blow her top. "Come see me first thing Monday, Charpentier," Seguy said, his voice sinking to a growl. "It seems we have things to talk about."

"Yes, sir," Guillaume managed, before shutting the door. Francine immediately began screaming at him, accusing him of stepping out on her, of carrying on a liaison with Madame Marceau while Francine was nursing the pain of yet another late-term miscarriage. As if Guillaume's heart wasn't broken each time they lost another child. He tried to protest, to insist that he had no feelings for Madame Marceau, who was at least a decade older than him.

"Then why would you risk yourself to protect her?" Francine shrieked. "You are lying to me!"

"I am trying to do the right thing!" Guillaume had shouted back, finally raising his own voice. "I am trying to be a good man!"

Francine had looked shocked by his outburst, and then her narrow lips had settled into a hard, thin line. "And yet," she said tightly, "you fail at that, too. Look around us. We are living nearly in poverty, thanks to you. No wonder we can't bring a child into the world, living in this hovel."

Guillaume felt the crushing weight of failure. It was his job to provide for his family, and now, with Seguy bearing down on him, he'd probably be fired on Monday morning. How would he support Francine without a job?

He felt powerless, deflated. But as Francine stalked past him, muttering about how she couldn't stand to look at him anymore and had to get out of the apartment, he realized there was still something he could do to redeem himself. He could warn Madame Marceau. He could tell her that the authorities were coming to question her, and that if she wanted to save her family, they should all flee immediately.

But what would happen if Francine found out? It would only make her more certain that Guillaume was having an affair, though for him, there had never been any other woman. Francine had always been temperamental and possessive, but in the past two years, during which they had lost three babies to miscarriage and another at just six days of age, she had come undone, her fury enveloping them both. One day, he was certain, the fog would lift, and they would find happiness again. And now, as Guillaume slumped beside the front door of their apartment, paralyzed by indecision, it occurred to him that if he could save Madame Marceau and those two beautiful girls she'd been blessed with, perhaps God would look favorably upon him. Perhaps he and Francine would finally be granted a child of their own.

He straightened, reenergized. This was the way out of the whole thing. Before he could second-guess himself, he raced out the front door and down the stairs, spilling onto the street below and continuing at a run toward the Marceaus' apartment a few blocks away. He would save their lives, and that would count for something.

It wasn't fair that he was denied the chance at redemption by the early arrival of the Germans, who were already pouring into the Marceaus' building when he turned, panting, onto their street. It wasn't his fault that he didn't have time to warn the older girl, whom he spotted opening her bedroom window as if to leap out. He went right away to the window, intending to call to her, to tell her that she had to warn her parents about what was coming, but it was already too late. When the German voices sounded from the other room, and when the older girl fled, he was left with no choice but to take the little girl. Otherwise, the Germans would haul her away with the rest of them, and he couldn't let his last chance at redemption slip right through his fingers.

He hadn't meant to do it, but she had looked at him with wide eyes, full of fear, and he'd thought to himself, *If I save this child, maybe God will give Francine the baby she so desperately wants.*

He had not intended what came next. He hadn't thought through any of it. Once he had the girl in his arms and was hurrying away from the Marceaus' apartment, his hand clamped firmly over her mouth to keep her from calling out, all that mattered at first was keeping her quiet. He didn't notice that she'd stopped struggling until her body went limp in his arms, and he realized that he'd been holding his hand over her mouth and nose too tightly, for too long. Horror flooded through him. What had he done? She was like a sack of flour, but he had no choice but to hurry on, tears stinging his eyes.

When Francine discovered the bracelet in the lining of the child's nightgown later that night, she couldn't believe their good fortune. "All our problems are solved!" she had crowed. But Guillaume saw the bracelet for just what it was: cursed.

"It isn't ours," he'd told her. "We will find a way to return it to the Marceaus."

Francine's eyes had blazed as she fastened the clasp of the bracelet, adorning her own wrist. "We will do no such thing," she said as she held her arm out, admiring the diamonds on her wrist. "It's the most beautiful thing I have ever seen."

"We cannot keep it," he'd said in a whisper. "Please, Francine."

"Can't I just enjoy it without you ruining everything?" she asked, tears suddenly glistening in her eyes. "Besides, Madame

Marceau will not survive, will she? Guilty or not, the Germans have her now. And good riddance." She was sobbing now, and it was so at odds with the sharp steeliness of her tone that he wondered for a moment if they were alligator tears.

But just like every time she cried, he backed off. If he didn't know better, he might think she did it on purpose, knowing that she could bend him to her will. But that wasn't Francine. Francine was troubled, certainly, but she was a woman he had sworn to cherish and protect, in sickness and health, in good times and in bad. Lately, the bad times had threatened to overcome them both, but he realized that he had been given a gift, an opportunity to change that.

Francine was right. Madame Marceau would not be coming home. He understood that with a bone-deep sorrow, and it was a guilt he would carry with him for the rest of his days. But the bracelet could make Francine happy. It could give them a better life. As her husband, he owed that to her, didn't he? What harm could there be in keeping the treasures of a dead woman?

"I'm sorry, Francine," he'd said, and she had nodded, satisfied.

"You'll see, Guillaume," she said. "Everything will be different for us now."

And she was right, in a way. She'd had the idea a day later that he should go back to the Marceaus' apartment to search the linings of the girls' other clothing, and though he had protested, he made it in undetected, simply by going in through the front door the police had left unlocked. The concierge hadn't given him a second look; his uniform had convinced her that he was there on official business. In the wardrobe in the children's room, he'd found six other pieces with hems heavy with treasure, and he had come home with enough jewels to start a new life anywhere they chose.

Their future changed in an instant, and they were able to move first to the countryside, and then, when the war was over, to America. The bracelet that had been sewn into the hem of the little girl's nightgown on the night he took her, the one that sparkled like a universe of stars, bought the Charpentiers entry into a new life across the sea. Guillaume had given it in 1948 to Hubert Verdier, a greedy former police colleague, who had called him in 1945 to say that he knew Charpentier had the bracelet that had disappeared the night Annabel Marceau was arrested. "I want it," said Verdier, who was in the process of immigrating to the United States, thanks to the fact that he had an American grandfather. He'd apparently come into some money recently and could finally afford the move. "If you let me have it, I will help you move to the States, too. Leave the past behind once and for all."

It had taken nearly three years to convince Francine, who loved that bracelet more than she loved anything. But she knew, as did Guillaume, that their future wasn't in France. It was across the ocean. It was the only way.

In return for the bracelet, Hubert had sponsored their citizenship application and furnished the necessary false papers. Verdier had always been a bastard, and in retrospect, it seemed he had remained one, betraying Guillaume for years by carrying on an affair with Francine, who had never forgiven Guillaume for trading the beautiful bracelet in for their chance at a better life.

CHAPTER THIRTY-THREE

2018

When Colette came to, there were two paramedics kneeling beside her, and another behind them with a stretcher at the ready. "Where is he?" she asked, struggling to sit up, looking around wildly. Had she dreamed it, or had she really just come face-to-face with her sister's killer, mere moments after the funeral of the man she'd thought was the culprit? Was he still here? Or had he taken advantage of her collapse to flee once and for all? As Daniel swam into her still-blurred field of vision from the right, she blinked and reached for his hand. "Daniel, where is he? Where's the man who killed my sister?"

"Whoa, whoa, easy does it, ma'am," said one of the paramedics.

"What happened?" she asked.

"You had a reaction to the stress of recognizing Lucas's grandfather," Daniel said. "And don't worry. He's still here. Lucas won't let him go until we clear this up."

"Clear this up?" Colette repeated blankly. What was there to clear up? She would have known the man anywhere, even after all these years. It was him; she was sure of it.

"I believe you've experienced what we call vasovagal syncope," the other paramedic explained as Daniel squeezed her hand. "A sudden drop in your heart rate and blood pressure, as a response to stress, leading to reduced blood flow in the brain. That sounds consistent with what happened here." She glanced at Daniel, who nodded, his expression full of concern. "But we still need to take you into the emergency room to get you looked at."

"No," Colette said, struggling once again to sit up. "Absolutely not. I need to see Guillaume Charpentier."

"Who is he, Colette?" Daniel asked. "How do you know him?"

"He's an old student of my father's, the policeman I saw disappearing with my sister the night she was taken."

"Are you certain it's him?" Daniel asked.

"More certain than I've been of anything else in my life." Colette looked up at Aviva, who was hovering uncertainly behind the paramedics. "Aviva, dear, what name did you say he was using?"

"Bill Carpenter," she said, stepping forward. "Are you all right?"

Colette closed her eyes. He'd been hiding in plain sight all along. William Carpenter was a direct anglicization of the name Guillaume Charpentier, probably picked out decades ago when he stepped off the boat from France. She opened her eyes and refocused them on Aviva. "So I was wrong about Hubert Verdier. I badgered an innocent man to death."

"Colette, he had the bracelet. And he had an affair with Lucas's grandfather's wife. He was obviously tied to this somehow."

"I need to talk with Charpentier," Colette said. "I need to talk with him now."

The paramedics exchanged looks. "Ma'am, without knowing for sure what caused your loss of consciousness, we need to take you in," said the fair-haired one. "You'll need an echocardiogram and some blood tests at the very least."

"No," Colette said. "I'm sorry, but no. I have been searching for seventy-six years for a monster, and now I have found him. I'm not about to let him walk away before he gives me some answers."

They looked to Daniel for help, obviously assuming he was a husband who would talk sense into her, but he put a hand on Colette's back. "This is something she needs to do," he said firmly. "She's staying."

The paramedics exchanged looks, and the darker-haired one sighed. "We'll make you a deal," said the fair-haired paramedic. "We'll give you five minutes, with us standing right here with you, and then you'll let us take you in. But the moment you start to get worked up, we'll need to end the conversation. All right?"

"Fine, fine," Colette said. "Now, where is he?"

Aviva beckoned to Lucas, who was standing several yards away with his grandfather, as Daniel and one of the paramedics helped Colette to her feet. She expected to feel woozy and unsteady, but as she watched the old man shuffle slowly toward her, a look of shame and resignation on his face, everything suddenly felt crystal clear. She straightened her spine, drawing herself up to her full height. Daniel's hand was on her back, and both paramedics were hovering uncertainly nearby, but she didn't need their support. She had been waiting for this moment for most of her life.

"Guillaume Charpentier," she said when he had finally reached her. "Why?"

His face was red as he leaned on his walker. "Please, you must let me explain," he rasped. "I thought until very recently that you were dead. I was told that your whole family had died. If I'd known, I would have—"

"You would have what?" she shot back. "As if there's some excuse for creeping to our window on the worst night of our lives and kidnapping my defenseless sister?"

There were tears rolling down his cheeks now. Lucas and Millie were standing beside him, listening to every word, and they looked horrified. "I was trying to save her, you see," he whimpered. "I was trying to save you both."

She stared at him, understanding suddenly settling over her. "You *knew* the Germans were coming for my mother."

"I—I fear it may have been my fault. You see, my wife told my boss that your mother was the one who stole the diamond bracelets from a high-ranking German officer." He drew a deep, shaky breath. "It all happened so fast. I was trying to warn you."

She choked out a laugh. "Oh, a monster with a conscience?"

He flinched. "Please, allow me to explain—"

"No!" She could feel rage rising within her. "What explanation could you possibly give me? The one thing my mother asked of my father and me before she died was to find Liliane. And instead, we returned home to the news that her body was found floating in the Seine."

"Granddad?" Lucas breathed, his expression horrified.

"No," Guillaume Charpentier rasped. "It isn't true. You must believe me, Ms. Marceau."

Colette glared at him. "Why on *earth* would *I* believe *you*? The man who took her? The man who murdered her?"

"Because I *didn't* murder her!" he said desperately. "I would never harm a child!" He was crying now, and his grief made her skin crawl. "I took her because I thought I was saving her life, you see. And then, later, when the concierge of your building told me that you had all died . . ."

"So what happened?" Colette spat, her fury at the long-dead

concierge fueling the fire of her anger now. "Liliane became a handful? She was upset that she'd been kidnapped by a monster like you? You had no choice but to end her life?"

"No!" He looked so upset now that the fair-haired paramedic had taken a step in his direction, reaching his hand out in concern.

"Sir," the paramedic said, "if you'll just calm down—"

"No," Colette snapped, glaring at the paramedic. "This bastard has spent the last seventy-six years running from what he did. If he feels a bit of emotion now, so be it."

No one spoke for a moment. Guillaume Charpentier stared at Colette, breathing hard, and she stared back, daring him to deny her the closure he had owed her for so long.

"What . . . did . . . you . . . do . . . to . . . my . . . sister?" she finally said, drawing each word out.

"I saved her, Ms. Marceau," he whispered. "I saved her life. We made her our daughter, and when we moved to the United States, she came with us."

Of all the things that might have come out of his mouth, that was the last thing Colette expected. She was vaguely aware of Lucas's sharp intake of breath, of Millie's gasp a second later, but she still wasn't grasping what he was saying. "No. Liliane is dead. She was found floating in the Seine wearing her nightgown . . ."

Guillaume Charpentier put a hand over his face. "We got rid of the nightgown that first night. It matched the one you were wearing, remember? My wife—my wife said it would have been a sure sign that she was the missing Marceau daughter if anyone came looking. We threw it away, Ms. Marceau, and perhaps someone took it from the trash. Those were desperate times. But the child found floating in the Seine was not your sister."

"But the bracelet . . ."

"We felt it in the hem of her gown when I was trying to revive her."

"Revive her?" Colette was beginning to feel hysterical.

"She lost consciousness in my arms as I ran from your apartment. I—I had my hand over her mouth, and it all happened so quickly . . ." He drew a shuddering breath. "I didn't want to keep the bracelet, but my wife insisted. She was obsessed with it— she thought I'd had an affair with your mother, and I think she felt triumphant having something that had been stolen from her. Later, we gave it to Hubert Verdier as a payment for helping us to immigrate to the United States."

Colette stared at him. "You're telling me that Liliane lived?"

"I swear it on the lives of my family." He looked her right in the eye. "I thought we were saving her life—and that she was the answer to our prayers. My wife and I had lost three babies to miscarriage, and a son in infancy, and it was destroying us. I was desperate to make things better for Francine, and I thought—after your family was taken—that I finally had the perfect solution. Your sister became our daughter. If I had known, though, that you and your father had lived . . ."

Colette still wasn't sure whether to believe him, but even if he was telling the truth, what he had done was abhorrent. "You certainly didn't look very hard for us, did you?"

"I went back. I swear it. Your building's concierge said you'd all been killed by the Germans. We left Paris the next day—my wife wanted to raise our new daughter in the countryside, in her family home."

"Well, while you were enjoying the countryside with your wife and my sister, my father went to his grave thinking that she was dead. And my guilt over her death has been at the very core of who am I. *You* did that to us. You took her, and then you took everything."

Tears were rolling down his cheeks now. "Ms. Marceau, I'm so terribly sorry. I truly thought I was doing what was right for her. I thought I was giving Anne a future."

Lucas stepped forward then. "Granddad, you're not saying . . . ?"

"Her name," Colette growled, "was *Liliane*."

"It was, yes. But Anne was a family name, and my wife had always hoped to name a daughter that." The old man turned to Lucas, who was gaping at him. "I'm sorry, son." He looked back at Colette and said weakly, "Lucas here is your nephew."

Colette put a hand over her mouth and stared at Lucas. She saw it now, in an instant—the resemblance she'd missed before because she hadn't been looking. He had his mother's green eyes, the slope of her nose, the dimples in his cheeks.

"But my mom never said . . ." Lucas said, glancing at Colette as his voice trailed off.

"She was only four years old," the old man said. "We didn't want her to remember her past, to know that she'd had any other parents before us. For a while, it seemed to be working—but when she was a teenager, she began to rebel. Just after she turned eighteen, she told your grandmother that she hated her. That she would never consider us her parents. It was the biggest fight they ever had—and it was the night your mother left home. She didn't come back until after she'd had you."

"My mother always talked about a terrible fight," Lucas said. "But she never explained."

"She reconciled with us, but I believe it was because she needed our help with you after your father died. There was always a distance there. You know that. Your grandmother was so insistent that the only way forward was to forget. She refused to talk to your mother about the past. She told her that she had imagined the life she had before she came to us. But there was a piece of her that remembered."

"And you never thought to be honest with her?" Lucas demanded. "Even after Grandma was gone?"

He looked down. "I was trying to respect your grandmother's wishes."

"Ms. Marceau." Lucas turned to Colette, looking dazed. "I can't tell you how sorry I am. About all of this. I couldn't have imagined . . ."

"It isn't your fault, Lucas," Colette said as she reached out to squeeze his hand. "And to know that after all this time, you are my family . . ." She turned to Lucas's daughter, who was looking on with wide eyes that were so obviously familiar. They were Liliane's eyes, her mother's eyes, Colette's own eyes. "You and Millie."

Colette couldn't stop the tears from rolling down her face now. So much had been lost. But so much had been found, now, too. If only her sister had lived long enough to witness it, but perhaps it would be enough to know that she had survived for a time, and that she had gone on to have a son, and then a granddaughter. Another generation after all.

"Now, please," she managed to say after a moment. "Will someone tell me what happened to my sister? How long ago did you lose her?"

Millie and Lucas exchanged looks. "Lose her?" Lucas asked.

"How long ago did she die?" Colette said, hardly believing that she was asking the question. She'd lost Liliane once so long ago, and now she was bracing herself to lose her all over again, just as she had found and lost Tristan in a blink a few days before. "Aviva mentioned that she was gone."

Lucas glanced quickly at Aviva, and then he stepped forward and grasped Colette's hands. "Ms. Marceau . . . my mother isn't dead."

Colette felt the air go out of her lungs. "What? But Aviva said . . ."

"What I told Aviva was that my mother was gone—as in gone to another state. She lives in Vermont."

"Vermont?"

"What do you say we pay her a visit?"

"Visit Liliane?" Colette whispered. "She's alive? You're telling me that in just a few hours, I can be face-to-face with my sister for the first time in seventy-six years?"

"Not so fast, ma'am," said the fair-haired paramedic. Colette had almost forgotten that they were still there. "We still need to get you checked out."

"But—" Colette started to protest.

"What do you say I drive?" Lucas said. "Mr. Rosman and Aviva can come, too. We'll make a quick stop at the hospital just to make sure you're all right—and then we'll head up to my mom's."

"Yes, please," Colette replied. She could hardly believe she was saying the words. "Let's go see my sister."

 # CHAPTER THIRTY-FOUR

2018

Liliane Marceau was four years old when she was told she was no longer Liliane Marceau. Her name was Anne, said the new lady, the one with the glassy eyes who insisted Liliane call her "Maman." Anne was close enough to her first name that the transition shouldn't be any trouble, the lady told her. Also, it was the name the lady and the policeman had picked out for their daughter, though the first three had died, along with a son.

Perhaps it was that knowledge that kept Liliane in line, even when she wanted to scream for her sister, or for her real mother and father. How on earth had the first three Annes and the nameless boy died? Was that what was in store for Liliane, too, if she didn't cooperate? The thought terrified her, and then there was the fact that her new mother repeated to her again and again, "Your old family is gone. We are your family now, Anne."

It was confusing, though, because sometimes Maman told her that her old family was dead, like the three little Annes who'd come before her. But then sometimes when she got angry, she would tell her that they had left her behind, that they didn't want her anymore because she was a bad, thoughtless child. Liliane wasn't sure which felt worse: thinking that her first family had died, or thinking that they were all out there having a gay time without her.

The policeman, whom she was to call Papa, was much kinder. He was the one who came to soothe her when she had nightmares, which was very often in that first year. Sometimes when she was crying, he would cry, too, but only when Maman wasn't around. "I tried to save them," he would say as he wept. "I tried, Anne, you must believe me."

And perhaps it was the fact that he, too, called her Anne that sealed the deal. He was, after all, a policeman, and Mummy and Colette had told her she should trust the police. It was easier, he told her once, to just do what Maman said. "She always gets her way in the end anyhow," he reported.

So she would be Anne, then, and over time, the memories of her family slipped away, bit by bit. Maman began to tell her that they had never existed in the first place, that they had been imaginary friends from Anne's early childhood, and when she looked to Papa for confirmation, he always nodded solemnly. Surely Papa would not lie to her.

Still, some of the memories stuck stubbornly around, like the memory of a long-ago sister bent over her desk, fervently writing poems, or the image of a mother who sang her songs and told her stories of Robin Hood and made sounds like the call of an eagle. At night sometimes, in the silence of her home in the French countryside, and later, in the quiet of Boston's South Shore, she could sometimes hear a distant *kyi-kyi-kyi*. And how was she supposed to believe that those dreams were just dreams when she knew with all her heart that the correct answer was *ko-ko-ko*? That wasn't the sort of thing a little girl made up on her own.

The winter after she turned eighteen, she was living with Maman and Papa in Weymouth, just south of Boston, when Madame and Monsieur Verdier came over for a small holiday party her parents were throwing. The Verdiers were her parents' closest friends, a couple whom they'd known vaguely in France because Mr. Verdier had been a policeman along with Papa. The Verdiers had come to the United States first, and then they had agreed to sponsor her family's immigration application. She knew that Papa felt indebted to them for that kindness.

But at that holiday party, she was on her way to the restroom when she heard voices coming from her parents' bedroom. The door was partially ajar, and she charged in, ready to scold whoever had barged their way into a private area of the house. She was surprised to find that it wasn't an ill-behaved party guest after all; rather, it was Maman, who was fluttering her eyelashes at Monsieur Verdier as he fastened a bracelet on her wrist.

"Maman?" Anne asked, uneasily aware that she had walked in on some sort of intimate moment. "What are you doing?"

"Oh, dear," Maman tittered, her face turning pink, "Hubert was just showing me a bracelet." She held out her arm to show Anne, whose breath caught in her throat as she stared at the diamonds sparkling on Maman's wrist.

Anne knew that bracelet. And she knew at once that her real mother, the one she'd been told was a figment of her imagination, had once possessed it. "That belonged to my mother," she said, unable to look away as the diamonds sparkled in the dim light.

Maman tittered again, but she sounded uneasy and her eyes had turned cold. "Why, yes, dear, this did belong to me. You see, your father and I gave it to Hubert as a payment for helping us to immigrate to the United States. Hubert knows that I miss it, and so he lets me try it on sometimes. That's all. Don't tell Papa."

It was very clear that Maman was having an affair with Monsieur Verdier, which disgusted Anne. But that didn't matter now. What mattered was that seeing the bracelet again was bringing up a torrent of memories that had all but washed away. "The bracelet belonged to my *first* mother," she said slowly. "She sewed it into the hem of my nightgown. I remember. She said it was to protect me."

Maman's face went from pink to beet red. Anne could see veins bulging out of her neck.

"Francine, what is she talking about?" asked Verdier, who had traces of Maman's lipstick smeared across his chin.

"I haven't any idea!" She glared at Anne. "The insolent child is making up stories!"

"It isn't a story, Maman. I'm certain it's true! I remember—" But she didn't complete her sentence before Maman crossed to her in two long strides and slapped her across the face so hard that she could taste blood. She put a hand to her smarting cheek and looked at Maman in horror. "Maman!"

"Don't you ever tell filthy lies like that again," her mother said, her hand still raised as Anne shrank from her. "You ungrateful little brat. We gave you everything, and we can take it all away."

Slowly, Anne backed out of the room, and then she ran to her own bedroom, where she slammed the door and, with her back pressed against it, slid down until she was sitting on the floor. Maman was probably already whispering in Papa's ear about what an ungracious good-for-nothing Anne was, and how she had caught her making up lies.

But it was all true. Anne knew it. Maman was having an affair, and the man she was having an affair with had possession of a bracelet that had once belonged to Anne's real mother. But what had happened to the woman? Anne couldn't see her face in her mind's eye anymore; it had been washed away by the years. She had existed, though. She hadn't been a figment of Anne's imagination. The bracelet was proof of that, wasn't it?

One thing was clear: she could not remain in this house anymore. She had graduated from high school in June, and she had spent the last six months living at home, taking a couple of classes at Suffolk while she tried to figure out what she wanted to do with her life. Maman's plan, she knew, was to marry her off to someone wealthy, who could help better their family's station in life. She knew it galled Maman that after a decade in America, Papa still hadn't made much of himself. He wasn't particularly successful, not like Monsieur Verdier. His job as a contractor paid the bills, but it wasn't prestigious. The idea now was that Anne would marry well and enhance the family fortune.

But Anne wanted nothing to do with that. She would figure out who she really was and what Maman was hiding, and one day, she would marry not for money but for love. She grabbed her school backpack and stuffed as many clothes as she could fit inside, and then she emptied her piggy bank, which contained hundreds of dollars saved over the years. Without a glance back, she left her room, and then walked, head held high, through the living room, where the holiday party was still going in full swing.

"Where are you going, Anne?" Papa called out, taking a step in her direction.

"Far away," she called back. "Ask Maman why."

And just as she had predicted, the mention of Maman stopped Papa in his tracks. He would let Anne go, assuming she'd be back, and he would rush to do damage control before Maman flew off the handle.

But Anne wasn't coming back. And whatever Maman had done couldn't be brushed under the carpet anymore.

Anne made it nineteen years before she ran out of options and had to come home. She had done just what she set out to do: She had worked at a diner in Vermont to support herself while she took two college classes at a time. She had completed her degree and gotten a job at a small bookstore, which she loved, because to give people books was to give them the world in their hands. She fell in love with a good, kind man named Ronan O'Mara, a hardworking Irish immigrant who Maman would have hated because he wasn't from a wealthy family, which Anne supposed was part of his charm. He proposed on a spring Tuesday in Crystal Lake State Park; they were married in the very same spot that fall; and a month later, she discovered that she was pregnant. Ronan was overjoyed, and after Lucas was born in spring of 1975, Anne was certain she had never been happier. Their little boy was healthy, and they made a perfect family of three.

But then one day, Anne kissed Ronan goodbye as he left for work. Four hours later, she had just put little Lucas down for a nap when there was a knock at the door. She opened it to find two police officers alongside Ronan's boss, who informed her that Ronan had been killed in an accident on the construction site where he'd been working. She hadn't believed it until she walked into the county morgue to identify his body. Then, and only then, seeing him cold and gray and lifeless on a slab, her world fell apart, and she fell to her knees, wailing in despair.

She survived for three more months on her own before it became clear that she could not support Lucas without help; she simply didn't make enough to pay for both her rent and her son's care while she worked.

"I knew you'd come home," Maman said smugly when Anne showed up at their door, her eyes not on her newfound grandson but on Anne, who squirmed under her gaze. "Well, you might as well come in. I suppose you're here because you couldn't make it on your own? And you got yourself knocked up, too, I see."

Never mind that nearly two decades had passed; Maman picked up just where she'd left off on the day of the holiday party. Papa fell in love with Lucas instantly, and over time, Anne watched as Maman was charmed by her infant grandson, too. They stayed for ten long years, and then they set out on their own, moving a few hours away to Marlboro, Vermont.

When Maman was diagnosed with colon cancer in 1998, Lucas, who had just graduated from college, returned home to help his grandfather tend to her. After Maman died, Anne tried to come home, too; she thought that it would feel easier to be in the old house again, to be around Papa. But even with Maman gone, he wouldn't speak honestly with her about the past; he was still defending his wife's honor long after she'd gone to her grave. And finally, Anne had had enough.

She didn't tell Lucas about all that had come before; she had always hoped that Papa might in some way fill the hole that had been left in Lucas's life after Ronan had died. A boy shouldn't grow up without a paternal influence.

But Anne couldn't be there anymore, so while Lucas stayed and built a life in Boston, Anne retreated to the home where she'd raised Lucas, some three hours away, in a town known for a small private college and an annual music festival, and perhaps more importantly, for its privacy and isolation.

Her son visited often, especially after he married and had Millie, and Anne rarely felt lonely. She wished sometimes that she could reconcile with Papa, but she didn't know how, and anyhow, he never tried to mend that bridge with honesty. She was seventy-nine years old now, and she had gotten used to being by herself, to delighting in the joy of spring blooms and autumn leaves, and the magic of each year's first snowfall. The little house in Marlboro was her haven, at last, the place where she could be herself, whoever that was.

That's where she was late one April afternoon, sipping her tea on the front porch of her home, when she saw Lucas's car turn into her long driveway. What on earth was he doing here? Wasn't today the funeral of her parents' old friend Hubert Verdier, the one she'd caught Maman with years before? Her son got out of the car first, and she recognized her sweet granddaughter Millie, of course, but there were three strangers with them. Had Lucas finally found a girlfriend? He hadn't dated much since Vanessa's death, and it would make Anne happy to think that he had found love again. But who were the other two?

"Lucas?" she said, rising from her chair as the old woman behind him stared at her. There was something familiar about her, but Anne couldn't quite place her.

"Mom," he said, starting up the front walk toward her, a broad smile on his face. "I've brought you a surprise."

"A surprise?" Her eyes went back to the old woman, who was perhaps a decade older than her. Again, she was struck with a sense of knowing her.

"Liliane?" the woman said, and Anne swallowed hard.

"My name is Anne," she said, but even as the words were leaving her mouth, she knew they weren't true. They never had been, had they?

And somehow, the old woman seemed to know this, too. "I knew you as Liliane," she said gently as she walked up the steps toward her. The woman looked deep into her eyes, and Anne was frozen to the spot, pinned by the familiarity of the penetrating gaze. "I'm Colette. Do you remember me?"

Liliane hadn't heard that name in seventy-six years, but the word itself was the key to unlocking a box of memories, and suddenly, Liliane could see flashes of a past she had been told again and again did not exist. A fourteen-year-old Colette holding her hand as they walked down the rue Pasteur. Colette reading her a picture book at bedtime. Colette beside her as their mother laughed and repeated her eagle's calls.

"*Kyi-kyi-kyi,*" Liliane said softly now, and she watched as the older woman's face broke into a smile.

"*Ko-ko-ko,*" Colette responded, and that was when Liliane knew for sure.

"You're my sister," Liliane whispered.

Colette smiled at her and reached for her hands. "I'm your sister," she repeated, and the two of them stared at each other in awe before they fell into each other's arms.

CHAPTER THIRTY-FIVE

2018

Colette couldn't believe how much Liliane still looked like Liliane after all this time. She had the same rosebud lips, the same piercing green eyes, the same milky skin, the same rosy cheeks, even the very same dimples, the ones that had looked so familiar on the face of Lucas's daughter, Millie.

Yes, Liliane had aged, but Colette could still recognize the girl who had once shared her room, had snuggled up against her to fall asleep, had held her hand as they hurried along the streets of Paris. "I thought I'd lost you," Colette said when they finally pulled back from their embrace. "All these years, Liliane, I thought you were dead."

"I've been here all along," Liliane said, staring into Colette's eyes. "They . . . they told me you didn't exist. That I had dreamed you. That you were an imaginary friend I should try to forget."

Colette wiped away a tear. "Who told you that?"

Liliane glanced at Lucas. "The man and the woman who raised me. But they were not my parents, were they?"

"No, they were not." Colette took her sister's hands again. "The man took you from our bedroom window on the night our mother and father and I were arrested."

"Arrested?" Liliane asked. "What for?"

"Our mother was a jewel thief," Colette said, and she watched as the light came on in Liliane's eyes. There was some corner of her that knew, that remembered. "She stole from Nazis and collaborators to give to the French Resistance."

"Like Robin Hood." Liliane nodded slowly. "Our mother used to tell us stories about him, didn't she? That's what the eagle's call was from."

"Yes, Liliane," Colette said, her heart overflowing.

"I thought I had dreamed it all."

"It was real. It was all real."

Liliane blinked at her, as if not quite sure she wasn't seeing a mirage, and then turned to Lucas. "How on earth did you find her?"

"She found me, actually," he said. "With a little help from the bracelet."

"The . . . bracelet?"

"The one that belonged to Hubert Verdier. It turns out Granddad took it from the hem of your nightgown the night he took you. He gave it to Hubert as payment for sponsoring his citizenship application."

"I've had the other half all these years," Colette said. Liliane's eyes widened.

"Hubert loaned me his half for display in the museum, which set everything in motion," Lucas said. "Colette spotted it, and then Daniel did, too, and, well, now we're here."

"Daniel?" Liliane said, looking perplexed as she glanced his way.

"Daniel Rosman," Colette said. "The son of Maman's friend Hélène Rosman, the one we saw that day we went to the Vél' d'Hiv."

"I remember," Liliane said. "But how . . . ?" Her voice trailed off, as if she couldn't imagine what to ask next.

"It's a long story, Mom," Lucas said. "And we'll tell you everything. Can we come in?"

"Yes, of course, of course. Where are my manners? Come in, everyone, please, come in."

After Liliane had served them all coffee, Lucas introduced Daniel and Aviva, and then Lucas and Colette dove into an explanation of how Colette had come across the bracelet, how Daniel had become involved, and how the road had eventually led back to Hubert Verdier—and to the man who had raised Liliane as his own.

"And where is your granddad, Lucas?" Liliane asked. "Does he know about all of this?"

"He does," Colette answered. "He said he thought our parents and I had died at the hands of the Germans and that he was saving you by keeping you."

Liliane nodded slowly. "But you all lived?"

"No." Colette's heart felt heavy. "Our mother was killed. But our father and I survived. Papa was broken, Liliane, and he left me with Uncle Frédéric and Aunt Marie, friends of our mother's who you knew when you were young. After the war, our mother's brother, Uncle Leo, came for me. He was a jewel thief, too, as am I."

Liliane raised her eyebrows. "You steal jewels?" She glanced at the others, who were listening intently. "And they all know?"

There was laughter around the room. "They do now," Colette said. "In truth, Aviva has known for only two weeks. I told Daniel just a few days ago. And now that Lucas and Millie are family, I figured they might as well know, too. I thought the secret would die with me, that there would be no one to carry on our family tradition. But now . . ."

Liliane's eyes widened. "You want to train Lucas and Millie to be thieves?"

"Only if they want to," Colette said. "But whatever they do, as long as they are doing good in the world, they're honoring our mother and their family. Our tradition will live on."

"Do you not have children of your own, Colette?" Liliane asked gently.

"No." Colette felt a lump of regret in her throat. How might she have lived her life differently if she hadn't blamed herself for Liliane's death? Would she have fallen in love? Had a family of her own? She had denied herself those pieces of happiness for so many years because she believed she didn't deserve them. "But Aviva has been like a daughter to me." Aviva reached over and squeezed her hand as Colette added, "My life has been filled with love, despite my best efforts to sabotage myself."

Liliane leaned back in her chair and stared at Colette. "I still can't believe this. After all these years."

"What do you remember, Mom?" Lucas asked, and as Liliane turned to him with a smile, Colette felt a surge of joy. Here she was with her sister—her *sister*—and two new family members that she hadn't even imagined. "Do you remember anything about your past with Colette?"

Liliane considered this for a moment. "I remember little things. The smell of a pipe—it must have been our father's."

"He used to smoke by the fire in the winter," Colette said.

"Our mother sitting in a chair in the living room, sewing."

"She used to sew her stolen jewels into the linings of our clothing, so that we would always have valuables with which to bargain our way out of a jam." Colette smiled sadly.

"She couldn't get herself out of trouble?"

Colette shook her head. "It was too late for her. She knew that Papa and I had been released, and I think she believed we would find you, and that we'd all be together. I think she must have found some peace as she met her end. I have spent decades feeling that I failed her."

"I'm so sorry," Liliane said.

"I am, too. Think how different both of our lives could have been."

Liliane reached for Colette's hands and held tight. "But we are here now, my dear sister. And we will never lose each other again."

Colette wiped away a tear. "Maman would be so proud."

Liliane smiled sadly. "I hardly remember her. Perhaps you could tell me stories."

Colette blinked to clear her eyes, then she squeezed her sister's hands and looked into her eyes. "It would be my honor." She took a deep breath. "Once upon a time, in the village of Wentbridge, just at the edge of the Barnsdale Forest, lived a man named Robin Hood . . ."

Something flickered in Liliane's eyes, a spark of familiarity, and as Colette recited the words her mother had said to her so very many times, she had the sense that at long last, an ocean away from where their story had begun, she and Liliane had finally found their way to where they belonged.

CHAPTER THIRTY-SIX

2018

Two days after Colette's reunion with Liliane, Lucas's grandfather turned himself into the Weymouth Police Department. "I destroyed a family," he told the officer on duty, who hadn't known what to make of the old man. "I deserve to be put away for the rest of my life."

But the evidence of his crime had long since disappeared, and Colette wondered if what he had done was really a crime at all, or merely a series of bad decisions by a weak man who had been trying to do the right thing. Yes, his choices had shaped the course of her life, but he had saved Liliane, who may well have perished if she'd been taken into German custody that night. Who was to say how things might have turned out if different decisions had been made?

The authorities in Paris had, unsurprisingly, declined to get involved in a seventy-six-year-old wartime kidnapping case, and with Colette's and Liliane's blessing, the Weymouth Police Department had released him without charge. He had never stopped apologizing, though, and when he died two weeks later after a series of small strokes, his last words were to Liliane.

"I never meant you harm, you know," he'd rasped as he reached for her, his hand trembling.

"I know," she'd replied through her tears.

He had breathed his last holding the hand of the child he'd raised, who had never been his at all.

Two weeks later, Liliane was still staying at Lucas's apartment in Boston, and she and Colette were seeing each other every day, slowly filling each other in on the yawning blanks in each other's lives over the course of hours-long conversations that stretched well into the evenings. To Colette's surprise, Daniel Rosman was still there, too. A week earlier, she had invited him to move out of his hotel into her guest room, a temporary arrangement that neither seemed to be in a hurry to upend.

"I don't want to impose," Daniel said after he brought her a cup of coffee on his seventh morning in her home. "Just send me packing whenever you get tired of me, Colette."

"Daniel, if you hadn't come into my life, I'm not certain I would have found my way back to Liliane," she assured him now. "You are welcome here as long as you'd like to stay." She hesitated, and feeling heat creep up her neck, she added, "Besides, Daniel, I can't imagine getting tired of you. Ever."

He held her gaze, and as they stared at each other, Colette felt her heart flutter with something warm and unfamiliar.

Perhaps it was this feeling of reuniting with a lost past—finding Liliane, slipping into a comfortable ease with Daniel, burying Guillaume Charpentier—that finally gave Colette the courage to tell Aviva about Tristan Berousek, in hopes of finding a definitive answer about what had become of him.

"I've spent all these years thinking he was dead, but he came back," Colette concluded, her voice cracking, after she'd relayed the whole story. "There was a note from him in 1952, and I just need to know how that's possible, and what happened to him after that. I can't imagine he's still alive, after what he must have undergone in Auschwitz."

"But Daniel survived Auschwitz," Aviva pointed out. "And he's still alive and well."

Colette sighed. "I know, but certainly he's the exception to the rule. Think of how many survivors we're losing all the time at the center."

"But think of all those who still remain, telling their stories and keeping the past alive," Aviva said softly. "Don't give up hope, Colette. Maybe he's still out there."

Colette glanced down at her hands. "I've looked at the USHMM's records, and the only thing I can find is an entry of his death. But I thought that maybe you have some search tools at your disposal that I don't have."

Aviva smiled. "I can have Marilyn look into it. If he's out there, we'll find him."

Colette felt a bit lighter as she straightened and said, "Really?"

"Really," Aviva confirmed. "What does Daniel say about all of it?"

Colette bit her lip. "I haven't told him."

Aviva looked like she was trying not to smile. "And why not?"

"Because . . ." Colette paused and exhaled. "Because perhaps it feels silly to be chasing a ghost when the perfect man is right here in front of me."

Aviva's expression cracked into a grin. "The perfect man, huh?"

Colette could feel her cheeks getting warm. "You know me, Aviva. I don't get sentimental. But there's something different about him. I don't know if it's the connection we have through our mothers, or perhaps the fact that he's part of the story of bringing me back to Liliane . . ."

"Or maybe he's just the person you've been waiting for all these years," Aviva said. "You've given me so many explanations over the years about why you never married. Guilt over your sister, not wanting to have a child, not believing that you deserved happiness . . . But what if it was just that you hadn't met the right person? Until now?"

"You know I don't believe in that one-person-for-everyone nonsense," Colette said, her cheeks fully flaming now. But what if Aviva was right? What if it wasn't that there had been something wrong with her? What if it was just as simple as the fact that, sometimes, the people who are meant to be in your life don't always arrive when you expect them to? What if she *had* been waiting for something like this, the feeling of finding a family again, for nearly eighty years?

"You don't have to believe in it for it to be true," Aviva said. "But what will you do if we find Tristan Berousek alive?"

Colette had thought about this. "I would write to him, I think. I would tell him how much he'd meant to me, and how much losing him shaped my life. I would tell him how sorry I am that so many years had passed, and I would explain that I hadn't known until recently that he had lived. But Aviva, we knew each other when we were just children. I think perhaps I've been carrying a flame all these years for someone I've idealized in my mind. And maybe knowing he survived, and letting him know that I did, too, should be enough. Maybe it's time to put the past to rest once and for all, and to think instead about the future."

"And would that future include Daniel Rosman?" Aviva asked, a twinkle in her eye.

"Maybe," Colette said, her eyes sliding away. When she looked back at Aviva, the expression on the younger woman's face was so warm and happy that it lit Colette from the inside out. "Let's just take it one day at a time, okay?"

"If you say so," Aviva said. "But life is short, Colette. You and I both know that. And if the future is standing right in front of you . . ."

"Then maybe I should have the courage to follow my heart," Colette said with a smile. "Fine, point taken. But let's cross one bridge at a time, shall we? Let's find out what became of Tristan, and then, maybe I can put the past to rest."

Two evenings later, Aviva arrived early for the dinner Colette had offered to host, wearing a grim expression.

"I'm sorry," she said, following Colette into the kitchen. "But the only Tristan Berousek from Paris that Marilyn could find in any public records is confirmed dead in 1942, along with the rest of his family."

Colette felt tears stinging the backs of her eyes, and she busied herself with whisking Dijon mustard into olive oil and champagne vinegar for the green salad she'd already tossed. "Then who wrote that note?" she asked softly. "Could I have been wrong about his surname, Aviva? Could there be another Tristan who was deported but who came home?"

"I thought of that. But there's no record of any other Tristan in the correct age group deported from France during the Holocaust. It wasn't a common name. Could it have been a nickname?"

Colette frowned. The thought had occurred to her, too, but the name Tristan wasn't short for anything. "And if it was? Where would I even begin to look for him?"

Aviva shook her head and was about to reply when Daniel strode into the kitchen, wearing one of Colette's old aprons.

"Coming through, ladies," he said cheerfully. "That beef bourguignon isn't going to take itself out of the oven."

Colette forced a smile and turned to open the oven for Daniel. It had been his idea to host a meal for Aviva, Lucas, Millie, and Liliane, and the others were due to arrive at any moment. As Daniel lifted the Dutch oven out, and the scents of wine-roasted beef and onions filled the kitchen, Colette shook off thoughts of the boy she'd lost long ago and vowed to spend the evening focusing on the man at her stove, and the family she'd just found. It was enough. Her life was beautiful. Mum would be proud.

Liliane, Lucas, and Millie arrived together, three generations of a family Colette still couldn't believe belonged to her. Liliane held Colette tightly for a long moment; Lucas kissed her on the cheek; Millie called her "Aunt Colette"; and a moment later, when everyone was seated and Daniel came bustling in from the kitchen carrying the beef bourguignon, Colette felt as if her heart might burst from joy.

Aviva chose a seat next to Lucas, and as Colette walked around filling wineglasses, she noticed that the two were holding hands beneath the table, clearly the start of something they weren't ready to talk about yet. When Aviva looked up and saw Colette watching her, she smiled sheepishly and shrugged, raising her eyebrows. Colette's eyes filled with tears as she nodded. Aviva had always been her family in all the ways that mattered, but what if she had a future with Lucas, who was Colette's own flesh and blood? Colette couldn't imagine anything more perfect.

Daniel brought out the salad Colette had dressed, Millie hopped up to bring in the bread basket, and then they all sat together, chattering happily as Daniel heaped piles of meat, onions, and carrots on the plates passed down to him.

"This reminds me of dinners in our parents' apartment in Paris," Liliane said after they had all begun eating.

"I thought you didn't remember much," Colette said, holding her sister's gaze.

Liliane smiled. "Being with you again has reawakened so many memories. They started as little flashes here and there, but they've become a flood. The parents who raised me tried so hard to erase who I'd been before, but it was all there, just beneath the surface, all along."

Colette nodded, a lump in her throat. "What else have you remembered?"

"The way Papa cursed at the newspapers, sometimes, like the bad news they contained was their fault. Or that terrible turnip soup Mum used to make once a week because the shops were out of everything else."

Colette shuddered. "It really was awful."

Liliane chuckled. "You know what else I was thinking of just this morning? You sitting at the desk in the bedroom we shared, writing poems for the boy you loved. What was his name? I can't remember."

Colette smiled sadly and exchanged looks with Aviva, whose eyes were filled with tears. In the medieval poem, Tristan and Isolde had found their way back to each other, becoming as intertwined as honeysuckle and hazel, so reliant on each other that they would die if separated. Real life, however, had not unfolded that way. "Tristan," she murmured. "His name was Tristan. He disappeared on the night of the Vél' d'Hiv roundup, and I never saw him again."

Suddenly, Daniel jumped to his feet, startling all of them. "Tristan?"

Colette looked up at him, hope fluttering in her chest. She hadn't known how to broach the subject of the boy with him, but it should have occurred to her that two boys of the same general age, living in the same neighborhood, might have been acquainted. Had the answer been in front of her all along? "Did you know him, Daniel?" she asked, her heart thudding.

"Where did you live, Colette?" Daniel asked without answering the question.

"In the eleventh, you know that. Just as you did."

"Yes, but on which street?"

It was an odd question, but he was obviously waiting for an answer, so she said, "On the rue Pasteur. I planned to take you there when we were in Paris, but when I went there myself, I found a note in the wall from a boy named Tristan Berousek, someone who was very special to me. I'd always believed he died in the camps, but it seems he came back, and I never knew. That night in Paris—the night you and I were supposed to see the Eiffel Tower—I was grieving him all over again. Do you— Was he someone you knew?"

He slowly sank back down into his chair, his eyes never leaving hers.

"What is it?" she asked.

"That wasn't his name," he said softly. "He wasn't Tristan Berousek."

"What?" Colette asked, puzzled.

"Tristan. It was a pen name. A romanticization. From the poem."

"'Chevrefoil,' yes," Colette agreed, impressed that Daniel knew it. "An old Breton lai. But what makes you think that Tristan wasn't his real name? I found his deportation record, and all the details fit—the age, the neighborhood, everything. It has to be him."

"It isn't, Colette." Daniel was looking at her, his eyes wide. "*Comme un port dans la tempête*," he whispered after a long pause. "*Elle est mon refuge dans le conflit.*"

"Daniel? How do you know those words?"

He held her gaze, his eyes brimming with tears. "What comes next, Isolde?"

"But how . . . ?" And then she understood, and the world fell away as she looked into his eyes. "*Elle scintille et brille,*" she whispered. "*Comme tous les diamants de Paris.*"

"She sparkles and shines," Daniel said in English. "Like all the diamonds in Paris. You remembered the poem, Colette."

"Daniel," she breathed. "But . . . the name Tristan—"

"—was just a silly nom de plume. I was fifteen. I was a schoolboy with a crush. I thought I was being romantic, referring to myself as Tristan, meant for you even if the world stood in our way." Without another word, he reached into his pocket, withdrew his wallet, and pulled out a yellowed piece of paper. "*Je pense à ce que ça ferait,*" he read aloud. "*Avoir ta main dans la mienne. Un jour nous traverserons ce qui nous divise. / Tu seras mon roi, et moi, ta reine.*" He drew a shaky breath. "I think of what it would feel like / To have your hand in mine. / One day we will cross that which divides us. / You will be my king, and I, your queen."

"But . . . you were gone already," she said. "I—I left that poem for you in the wall after you had been arrested. I imagined that if you ever returned, you would find it . . ."

"I found it after the war," he said. "I had seen the concierge of your building by then, Colette, and she'd told me you were dead. I thought—I thought they were the last words I would ever have from you. I thought of you for years, but over time, I convinced myself that it was just a youthful crush. But it wasn't. It was more. It was always more. And we never had the chance to discover what it could be."

Colette reached for his hands, and with her sister beside her, and a room filled with family, she looked into the eyes of the final piece of the puzzle of her past. "Maybe we have that chance now," she said.

"We do." His eyes never left hers as tears slid down his face. "God willing, we do."

"Perhaps the diamonds have done what they were always meant to do," Colette said, looking first at Daniel, then at Liliane, and then at Aviva, Lucas, and Millie, who were all looking on in astonishment. "The diamonds have brought us all home."

EPILOGUE

Two months later, Colette married Daniel in a small ceremony in her backyard in Quincy, in the shade of a row of hazel trees wrapped in honeysuckle, which Colette had planted many years before because they were the symbol of Tristan and Isolde and their love.

Liliane, Aviva, and Millie were her bridesmaids, and Marty and Lucas served as Daniel's groomsmen. They were family now, all of them, united by blood and so much more.

Colette wore her half of the butterfly bracelet, and Liliane wore hers. Daniel had, true to his word, returned the bracelets to the Marceau sisters, insisting that his mother would have wanted them to have the pieces of jewelry that had brought them back to each other. It was Liliane who walked Colette down the aisle, holding her hand until she had delivered her sister safely to Daniel.

The ring Daniel slipped onto Colette's finger after they'd said their vows was the emerald-and-diamond one that had once belonged to his mother, the one that had helped fund the Holocaust education center that had brought them all together. Marty had returned it to Colette a month earlier, grudgingly giving her his blessing along with it, and she, in turn, had given the ring to Daniel, who kept it a surprise until their wedding day that he'd always planned for her to wear it.

"My mother would be so happy," Daniel whispered after the officiant had pronounced them husband and wife. "I wish she and your mother could have been here."

Colette looked at the ring glittering on her finger, then at the bracelet sparkling on her wrist. "I think they are, Daniel. In fact, I'm certain of it."

After the wedding ceremony, there was a small dinner prepared by a private chef among the hazels in Colette's backyard, and before the meal was served, Colette took a moment to pull Aviva aside.

"You've been like a daughter to me, Aviva," she said, taking the girl's hands. "I know I could never take the place of your mother, nor would I try to, but it's important to me that you know how much I love you, and how for many years now, I've considered you my own."

Aviva's eyes filled. "I love you, too, Colette. And I feel the same. You're my family."

"Good." Colette smiled. "I'm glad you feel that way, because I've made a decision. When I die one day, my half of the bracelet will go to you."

"Colette, I couldn't possibly—" she began, but Colette held up a hand to cut her off.

"No arguments. I've already discussed it with Daniel, and with Liliane. We are all in agreement. Daniel's parents always hoped that the pieces would stay in the Rosman family, and now, in a way, they will. Liliane will give her half to Millie when the time comes, and the bracelets will connect the two of you forever, though I have a suspicion that there will be something bigger than jewelry bringing you together." She cast a pointed look at Lucas, who was nursing a glass of wine across the yard, his eyes on Aviva. It was clear as day that the two had fallen for each other.

Aviva looked as if she might try to protest, but after a few seconds, she shook her head and smiled. "Then I would be honored to keep the bracelet when the time comes. But let's hope that day is a very long time from now."

Colette smiled. "Indeed. I'd like at least a little time to experience life as Mrs. Daniel Rosman."

Later, as the chef was putting the meals on the long wooden table that had been set up to accommodate the whole group, Daniel put an arm around Colette's waist and drew her aside. "Did you tell Aviva about the bracelet?" he asked.

"Yes, and Liliane has told Millie," Colette said. "What was it your father always said?"

Daniel smiled. "Diamonds have witnessed the past, and they will witness a future we can't begin to imagine."

Colette tilted her chin up. "I never could have imagined this, my love."

He touched his lips gently to hers. "Au contraire, my love. Tristan was always meant to find his way back to Isolde."

"Against all the odds," she said softly.

"It was written in the stars."

She smiled and looked down at the constellation that sparkled on her wrist. The bracelet had bound them together all these years, a bit of magic from her mother and his, which had led them here, to this moment, in the shade of the hazel trees, the sweet scent of honeysuckle heavy in the air.

Long after she and Daniel were gone, long after Liliane and Aviva and Millie were gone, the bracelets would live on.

Diamonds always do.

AUTHOR'S NOTE

All the Diamonds in Paris is the most difficult book I've ever written—but that's not because the subject matter is necessarily more complicated or more emotional than that of my previous books. It's because this is the book I pitched to my publisher before being diagnosed with breast cancer in late 2022. I didn't begin writing it until the summer of 2023, after I'd been through surgery, chemotherapy, and radiation therapy.

I was terrified to find, during my cancer treatments, that I couldn't seem to summon the words for this story at all, although I tried. I think that, in retrospect, it had something to do with the effect of the chemotherapy drugs on my body, and something to do with the fear that overshadowed my every waking thought. Regardless of the cause, it was terrifying to feel that I'd lost my ability to write. I've been writing novels for twenty years, and being a writer is at the very core of my identity. For eight long months, as the novel-writing side of my brain consistently refused to cooperate, I faced a very real worry: *What if that's not who I am anymore?*

Fortunately, once my treatments concluded and my life slowly returned to normal, the old me resurfaced. I found my way back to this story, and back to the page. But my first draft was saturated with the trepidation and fear of someone who'd lost something profound and didn't yet know whether she'd find her way back.

I share this because I think that search for self goes to the very heart of this story, too. Colette has essentially spent her whole life clinging to the sense of identity that comes with being a thief. She is her mother's daughter, and she is a descendant of Robin Hood. These are the things that she feels define her, and part of her journey in this story is learning that she has value that goes beyond just the millions of dollars she has "redistributed" over the years. Once Colette is able to truly see that she's more than just a thief—she's a woman worthy of love, whose identity isn't determined by her vocation—her world opens up. I, too, went through a similar process of discovery, and I feel like I'm a better person for it. In that way, I think there's a little piece of me, and of my journey over the past couple of years, baked into this book.

Now, a few notes on the research:

I've written novels before about the many and varied ways civilians helped the war effort in Europe during the Second World War. In *The Book of Lost Names*, for example, I focused on document forgers and those who helped save children. In *The Room on Rue Amélie*, it was those who worked on Allied escape lines. In *The Winemaker's Wife*, it was champagne makers who used their wine caves to smuggle arms and refugees, and in *The Forest of Vanishing Stars*, it was Jewish refugees hiding in a forest who found a way to fight back and survive.

One of the things that fascinated me about the choices those brave civilians made was that, in many cases, they had to choose to do illicit things for the greater good. For example, certainly document forgery is illegal, but breaking the law was necessary to save lives. Smuggling arms is clearly a crime, but had the region of Champagne not engaged in this subterfuge, who knows how the tide of the war might have changed?

I wanted to tackle that a bit more directly here by conjuring up a family of dedicated, virtuous jewel thieves, who follow in the footsteps of Robin Hood. Certainly theft was one way in which Resistance movements were funded during the war, and it was really interesting to delve into that. But it was also intriguing to give Annabel and Colette an even broader scope. They didn't just steal out of wartime desperation; theirs was a lifelong duty to rebalance the scales.

But that calls into question the definitions of right and wrong—and of who, in fact, has the right to tinker with justice. For example, in the opening chapters, we see Colette steal a ring from a neo-Nazi. Surely we can all agree on the value of undermining someone with such atrocious beliefs—but is that justification for a crime? That's something Aviva has to wrestle with when she learns the truth about Colette. I think that so often in life, we live in the gray areas between right and wrong, and it was fascinating to explore how someone like Colette rationalizes her thefts—and to ask myself whether that reasoning is valid. For those of you reading this novel in a book club, I hope that's something you'll discuss with your group.

If you want to learn more about Paris under German Occupation, or about the role the French Resistance played in winning the war, the following books were helpful in my research: *When Paris Went Dark* by Ronald C. Rosbottom, *And The Show Went On* by Alan Riding, *Fighters in the Shadows* by Robert Gildea, and three titles by Maurice Rajsfus: *The Vél d'Hiv Raid*, *Operation Yellow Star*, and *Black Thursday*. Annabel's experience in the

Cherche-Midi prison was inspired in part by *Résistance,* a memoir by Agnes Humbert, herself a hero of the French Resistance.

I delved deep into the world of jewels and jewelry design with *Gemstone Settings* by Anastasia Young, *Gems & Crystals* by Anna S. Sofianides and George E. Harlow, *The Jeweler's Directory of Gemstones* by Judith Crowe, *Metalsmith Society's Guide to Jewelry Making* by Corkie Bolton, and *Jewel: A Celebration of Earth's Treasures,* published by the Smithsonian. To research jewel theft, I relied on numerous videos—many from sleight-of-hand magicians—and the wonderful memoir *Confessions of a Master Jewel Thief,* by Bill Mason with Lee Gruenfeld. *Robin Hood: The Shaping of the Legend,* by Jeffrey L. Singman, was also helpful as I delved into the fictional history of Colette's maternal family.

Speaking of Robin Hood, that was a fascinating avenue to explore. The history of the man known as the Prince of Thieves is murky; some believe that he's merely legend, but others are convinced he actually lived. Obviously, in making him a long-ago ancestor of Colette and her mother, I chose the latter opinion. My past novels have looked at how the trauma and choices of those who came before us are passed on to future generations, so it was very interesting for me to examine that in the context of a group of fictional descendants who feel strongly that they have not only the duty but the *right* to steal, as long as they live by a code of honor.

In most of our modern tales of Robin Hood, the benevolent thief is associated with Nottingham and the Sherwood Forest, but for the purposes of this story, based on my research, I decided to link his family's history to Wentbridge and the Barnsdale Forest in West Yorkshire, more than fifty miles north, which is where author Brian Lewis argues that Robin Hood originated, in his book *Robin Hood: A Yorkshire Man.* In fact, English Heritage

Trust has placed a blue plaque (a permanent historical marker used throughout the UK) in Wentbridge, calling the town "one of the only place names that can be located in 'A Lytell Geste of Robyn Hode' (circa 1492–1534)." Wentbridge is also mentioned in "Robin Hood and the Potter," a fifteenth-century ballad that is one of the oldest surviving pieces of Robin Hood lore.

The eleventh-century Church of St. Mary Magdalene in Campsall, just outside Wentbridge, is also mentioned in "A Lytell Geste of Robyn Hode," and in fact is thought to be the church where the thief was married. And Pontefract, a historic market town five miles north of Wentbridge, is thought to be the place where Robin Hood joined a failed rebellion led by Thomas, Earl of Lancaster, in 1322, thus kicking off his career as an outlaw.

In other words, the argument can certainly be made that Robin Hood was a real man who lived in the fourteenth century—near Wentbridge—and whose descendants might still be living today.

Though this is a work of fiction, the historical happenings are accurate. For example, the 1938 run of Wagner's *Tristan und Isolde* at the Opéra Garnier, with Norwegian soprano Kirsten Flagstad, was reviewed in detail in *The New York Times*. The mass exodus from Paris just before the Germans arrived is also well-documented, as were the Jewish roundups mentioned in the book. The Vélodrome d'Hiver, near the Eiffel Tower, notoriously played a horrific role in holding more than eight thousand Jewish citizens captive before they were deported, in what remains an appalling example of French complicity during the Occupation. And in the Cherche-Midi prison, real-life prisoners, many of whom were later murdered by the Germans, chanted "*Notre France vivra,*" or "Our France will live," every night at seven o'clock, their own quiet and continued resistance.

People often ask me why I've been so drawn to writing about World War II. I think it's largely that the civilian efforts during that war serve as a powerful reminder that we're all capable of doing extraordinary things to effect change.

When I was in high school, in the mid-1990s, I had pictures of John F. Kennedy Jr. and Martin Luther King Jr. taped to my walls as a reminder to myself to go out and try to change the world for the better. For a long time, I thought that I would need to go into politics, law, or nonprofit work to make a difference. But the more I learned, the more I understood a truth that I think shines through in every book about Resistance efforts during the Second World War: One doesn't need to have a specific title or a specific education to become an agent of change. Change happens one act of courage at a time, one act of kindness at a time, one act of faith at a time. And those are things that *all* of us are capable of.

In *All the Diamonds in Paris*, Colette and Annabel spend their lives trying to make a difference in their own corners of the world. They use what they have, and they keep their focus on the greater good. I think that Colette achieves her goal of bettering the world not *just* through her "redistribution of riches," but also through her volunteer work—and through the way she chose to show up for Aviva in her darkest hour.

Changing the world doesn't require money or power. It doesn't require influence or higher education. Most of the time, it doesn't even require big, bold acts of courage. It simply requires us to look inside our hearts, to ask how we can help others, and to do what we can to stand up for that which is right and just.

And while I certainly hope that this novel doesn't inspire you to take up jewel theft(!), I do hope it makes you look around and ask yourself each day, "What can I do—in the small moments of my life—to make the world a better place?"

Finally, if you love to read, I hope you'll join me—along with fellow *New York Times* bestselling authors Patti Callahan Henry, Kristy Woodson Harvey, and Mary Kay Andrews—over at FriendsandFiction.com, or on Facebook, where our Friends & Fiction group has more than 250,000 members. On our webshow and podcast, we interview other authors and bring you a unique look at the story behind the story of your favorite books. We hope to see you there.

Thanks for reading *All the Diamonds in Paris*. I wish you a life that sparkles just as brightly as all the diamonds in Paris.

ACKNOWLEDGMENTS

I've long said that I have the best publishing team in the world, but these past few years proved that to me beyond a shadow of a doubt. In late 2022, on the evening that my breast surgeon called to tell me that I had breast cancer, I told my husband and mom first, and then my next phone call was to my literary agent, Holly Root.

You see, I knew I couldn't focus on the fight ahead until I got the publishing side of things squared away. I had a book due in April, and it was clear to me that I would no longer be able to meet that deadline. But I hate to let people down, so I wanted to know what Holly thought I should do.

Because Holly is not only an incredible agent but also an amazing human being and a great friend, she immediately took over, telling me that this was something she would handle and that I shouldn't worry about it at all. I can't even begin to put into words what a relief that was to hear. The next morning, my longtime editor, Abby Zidle—also a dear friend—said the same thing. They would figure out the scheduling on their end, whatever it took, and they were fully behind me. In the coming weeks, as I shared my news with Gallery Books publisher Jen Bergstrom, my amazing publicists Jessica Roth (Gallery) and Kristin Dwyer (Leo PR), and the rest of my Gallery team—including Jen Long, Eliza Hanson, Aimée Bell, Mackenzie Hickey, and Sally Marvin—I received the same message again and again: *We've got you.*

Not only did they push my publication date a year to allow me to focus on my treatments, but each of them stepped up in incredible ways, including sending me handwritten cards of encouragement, calling or texting to check in on me, and offering to connect me to oncologists they knew. The incredible Jen Bergstrom even sent me a pair of Sleepy Jones pajamas—still my favorites—for the days I couldn't get out of bed. I was bowled over by their kindness and support, and even now, as I'm writing this, there are tears in my eyes. I truly am the luckiest—and my core team (which also includes foreign rights agent Heather Baror-Shapiro, another incredibly supportive friend who stepped up for me)—is honestly the best in the business, both personally and professionally.

Speaking of stepping up, you know who else made a huge difference? My film/TV manager, Jonathan Baruch (of Rain Management), whom I'd known for just under two years when I was diagnosed. When I called to tell him the news, not only did he offer his full support as my friend, but he immediately offered to connect me with a friend of his, Dr. Mauro Ferrari, a renowned nanoscientist and breast cancer researcher who also happened to be the former president of the European Research Council. Within forty-eight hours of learning that I needed chemotherapy—which was terrifying—I was on the phone with the illustrious Dr. Ferrari, who spent more than a half

hour of his valuable time talking to me about the science behind various chemo regimens. It was not only a huge help in my
decision-making process, but also a tremendous comfort. The
fact that Jonathan would so readily offer that connection—and
that Dr. Ferrari was so willing to hop on the phone with a
friend of a friend—moved me deeply. (As a sidenote, the de-
lightful Mauro Ferrari is also an accomplished musician; look
for his songs on Apple Music!)

But wait: I'm not done telling you about the incredibleness
that is Jonathan Baruch. Would you believe that with his support and encouragement, I continued developing and pitching a
television project that we were in the midst of before my cancer
diagnosis? I mentioned in my author's note that I found myself
unable to write my next novel during treatment—but working
on this TV project gave me a creative outlet that went a long way
toward restoring my sense of self in a dark time. My wonderful
cowriter, Stephen Tolkin, and I—along with our phenomenal
production team—developed an entire television show, pitched
it, *and* received an offer for it *while I was going through chemotherapy
treatments.* In fact, our last pitch coincided with the final day of my
final chemotherapy cycle. None of that would have been possible
without Jonathan's support and belief in me.

I also owe a great debt of gratitude to Davis DuBose-Marler,
Jonathan's assistant at the time, who is very smart and talented
(not to mention an amazing watercolor artist!). I can't wait to see
what she does with her career.

While I mentioned my medical team in this book's dedi-
cation, I would be remiss if I didn't mention them here, too.
First and foremost, Dr. Anu Saigal—the breast surgeon who
performed my biopsy, diagnosed my cancer, and then operated
to remove my tumor—is one of the warmest, kindest people

I've ever met, and her generosity of spirit has been an enormous comfort over the past few years. At Florida Cancer Specialists in Winter Park, my oncologist, Dr. Sonalee Shroff, and her PA, Rochelle Drayton, are such nice people that I actually look *forward* to my ongoing oncology appointments. Tara Thomas was the best chemotherapy nurse I could have asked for, and I love that we're still friends. The whole team at Florida Cancer Specialists is incredible. AdventHealth's Afshin Forouzannia was my radiation oncologist, and he, along with his team, were also warm, informative, and supportive through a difficult time. My primary care physician, Dr. Neha Doshi, was a lovely guide through the whole process, and I'm also tremendously grateful to the team at AdventHealth Imaging (where I had the mammogram and follow-up ultrasound that indicated the possibility of cancer), especially Dr. Clark Rogers, who generously took the time to explain his findings to me in the gentlest, clearest way possible as tears streamed down my face.

Kindness matters. All the people I mentioned above could have chosen to simply do their jobs and nothing more. Instead, they led with warmth, understanding, and compassion, and that made all the difference.

I also want to thank all the wonderful readers who heard about my diagnosis and took time to send me a note or an email, to write me a card, or—in some cases—to send me thoughtful gifts such as blankets and "cancer warrior" bracelets. Your support—and knowing that so very many of you were behind me—gave me strength through some of my most difficult treatment days, and I'm forever grateful.

I'm also tremendously thankful to my Friends & Fiction partners in crime: Mary Kay Andrews, Kristy Woodson Harvey, Patti Callahan Henry, and Meg Walker—along with Ron Block,

Lisa Harrison, Brenda Gardner, and Shaun Hettinger. The F&F family was a huge part of my support system during my cancer treatment, and I'm deeply grateful for the friendship—and partnership—I have with each of you.

A huge thanks to Paula Schneider, Trish Ellis, and the whole Susan G. Komen organization for all the incredible work you do and the groundbreaking research you continue to fund. I was deeply honored to speak at last year's Komen Impact Luncheon in New York, and I continue to support and advocate for this wonderful organization, which not only continues to fund breast cancer research, but also does a tremendous amount of work in advocacy, patient support services, education, and health equity. Thanks also to Lynn Rasys and the rest of the team at the Florida Cancer Specialists Foundation, who are doing great work to make sure that cancer patients throughout the state of Florida are able to pay their nonmedical bills such as rent and car payments while undergoing cancer treatments. And thanks to Susan McBeth of Adventures by the Book, who sprang into action after hearing of my diagnosis and pulled together a breast cancer fundraiser that featured more than seventy authors. (Thanks, too, to all the authors who donated their time to such a meaningful cause!)

Dana Spector of CAA remains an amazing film agent, and I've been so fortunate to add Andrew Hurwitz and Lauren Bishow, both of Frankfurt Kurnit Klein & Selz (FKKS), to my team, too. A special thank-you to Andrew and Lauren for going above and beyond on a particularly complicated issue last year.

Thanks, as always, to the rest of the amazing people I work with at Gallery Books/Simon & Schuster, including Jonathan Karp, Ali Chesnick, Heather Waters, Chelsea McGuckin, Nancy Tonik, Linda Sawicki, Wendy Sheanin, the Book Club

Favorites team, and the whole fabulous team at S&S, especially the incredible sales force, who have been so supportive. A special thanks to Gary Urda, who was always such a pleasure to work with; may he rest in peace. Special thanks to Molly Mitchell at Leo PR; Alyssa Maltese and Stacy Jenson at Root Literary; Christine Hinrichs, Jenn Hoffman, Jeni Shirley, and Amy Loomis at Authors|Unbound; and on the TV side: Bob Greenblatt, Jon Wu, Stephanie Germain, Matt Rosen, Michael Wright, Alec Strum, Rachel Horowitz, J. D. Williams, Luca Sosa, Hal Froelich, and especially my screenwriter partner, Stephen Tolkin. A special thank-you to Madeleine Maby, who always does such a beautiful job of narrating my books. And, of course, a big thanks to my team at Simon & Schuster Canada, Headline in the UK, Armchair Publishing House in Israel, and my publishers in more than thirty additional languages worldwide. It's such a tremendous honor to work with you all, and I'm so grateful to you for helping me to connect with readers around the globe.

Thanks to all the booksellers and librarians I've had the pleasure of meeting on tour—and all those who work with books and who spend their time and effort helping readers find just the right picks. To give someone the joy of a great read is a tremendous gift, and by opening up new avenues of thought and imagination to people, you're making the world a better place each day.

Thanks to my siblings, Karen and Dave; my dad, Rick; and to the rest of my family, including Janine, Barry, Johanna, James, William, Emma, Sophia, Donna, Steve, Anne, Fred, Janet, Courtney, Jarryd, Brittany, Chloe, and all the cousins. Thanks to my amazing in-laws, Wanda and Mark, to Grandma and Grandpa Trouba, and to all the Troubas, along with Bob and JoAnn, and the Rivers family. And a special thanks to my mom, Carol, who was with me every step of the way during my cancer journey, although I understand (as a mother myself) how difficult it must have been to watch one's child go through something like that. Mom, I couldn't have made it through that time in my life without you. I love you so much.

To my dear author friends, including Wendy Toliver, Allison van Diepen, Linda Gerber, Emily Wing Smith, Alyson Noel, Jay Asher, Kristina McMorris, Kate Quinn, Fiona Davis, Marie Benedict, Pam Jenoff, Lisa Scottoline, Alison Hammer, Stephen Kellogg, Jamie Brenner, Sadeqa Johnson, Madeline Martin, and many more. And to my many dear friends outside the author community, including (but not limited to) Kristen, Marcie, Melixa, Lisa, Amber, Megan, Albany, Aldo, Naila, Jouti, Dema, Melody, Mark, Weez, Rob, Christina, Lisa P., Jason C., Shari, Robbi, and many more!

To my husband, Jason, and my son, Noah: I love you both more than words can say. I know that last year was a tough one for us as we all went through my cancer treatments, and I can't thank you enough for standing by my side. Jason: You were there for me in every way I could have imagined, including surprising me with a sign in our garage bearing the phrase that I repeated to myself each day: *The only way through it is through it.* And, Noah, I am so tremendously proud of the young man you're turning out to be. You're such a great, talented, smart, and kind kid, and I can't wait to see what your future brings.

And finally, to you, the reader: Thank you so much for picking up *All the Diamonds in Paris.* I know you have a ton of options when it comes to what to read—and if you're anything like me, your TBR list perhaps feels overwhelming sometimes. I never take for granted how special it is to have you choose one of my books to spend your time with, and I'm so grateful for your support. I hope to see you on tour! Please visit me at KristinHarmel.com for tour dates, links to Friends & Fiction, and more information about mammograms and breast cancer awareness.

ABOUT THE AUTHOR

Kristin Harmel is the *New York Times* bestselling author of more than a dozen novels including *The Paris Daughter, The Forest of Vanishing Stars, The Book of Lost Names, The Winemaker's Wife, The Room on Rue Amélie,* and *The Sweetness of Forgetting.* She is published in more than thirty languages and is the cofounder and cohost of the popular web series Friends & Fiction. She lives in Orlando, Florida with her husband and son.